The Advocate's Ex Parte

Teresa Burrell

Silent Thunder Publishing

Dedication

To my family.

Every day I realize just how lucky I am to have the love and support of the best family in the world. So many people have no family they can count on. It almost seems unfair that I have all of you.

Acknowledgments

A special thanks to my editor, Marilee Wood, who is not only the best editor but a dear friend.

Thanks to a very special beta reader, Stephen Connell, who can spot an inconsistency better than anyone I know.

Thank you, Chris Broesel for your law enforcement expertise. And for always responding so quickly when I'm in need.

Thank you, Ron and Kim Vincent and David Servantes, for always being there to answer my quirky questions. I'm always amazed at your vast knowledge in so many areas and your constant willingness to share it.

THE ADVOCATE'S EX PARTE. Copyright 2013 by

Teresa Burrell.

Edited by Marilee Wood

Book Cover Design by Karen Phillips

ISBN: 978-1-938680-08-3

Silent Thunder Publishing

San Diego

Also by Teresa Burrell

THE ADVOCATE SERIES

THE ADVOCATE (Book 1)
THE ADVOCATE'S BETRAYAL (Book 2)
THE ADVOCATE'S CONVICTION (Book 3)
THE ADVOCATE'S DILEMMA (Book 4)
THE ADVOCATE'S EX PARTE (Book5)
THE ADVOCATE'S FELONY (Book 6)
THE ADVOCATE'S GEOCACHE (Book 7)
THE ADVOCATE'S HOMICIDES (Book 8)
THE ADVOCATE'S ILLUSION (Book 9)
THE ADVOCATE'S JUSTICE (Book 10)
THE ADVOCATE'S KILLER (Book 11)
THE ADVOCATE'S LABYRINTH (Book 12)
THE ADVOCATE'S MEMORY (Book 13)
THE ADVOCATE'S NIGHTMARE (Book 14)
THE ADVOCATE'S OATH (Book 15)
THE ADVOCATE'S PHANTOM (Book 16)

THE TUPER MYSTERY SERIES

THE ADVOCATE'S FELONY

(Book 6 of The Advocate Series)
MASON'S MISSING (Book 1)
FINDING FRANKIE (Book 2)
RECOVERING RITA (Book 3)
LIBERATING LANA (Book 4)

CO-AUTHORED STANDALONE

NO CONSENT
(Co-authored with L.J. Sellers)

Prologue

Attorney Sabre Orin Brown leaned against the wall outside of Judge Lawrence Mitchell's chambers as she waited for him. Although she was thirty-one years old, she always felt like a schoolgirl in trouble whenever a judge requested her presence. And this was "Scary Larry." Who knew what he might say or do? He was known to shout at attorneys when they did something he didn't like.

Sabre recalled a few times as a child when she had sat outside the principal's office with the same sick ache in her stomach. But then she usually knew what she had done wrong. It was always the same things: She just couldn't keep her mouth shut in class and she loved to argue. Once she told a teacher his statement about inner cities was not only stupid, but racist. She knew the second she said it, she shouldn't have. The teacher yanked her out of her seat and marched her past the other sixth grade students and down the hall to the principal's office.

Pulling her back to the present, Judge Mitchell said, "Thank you for coming, Sabre."

"Of course," she said.

Judge Mitchell opened the door to his chambers, removed his robe from his tall, lanky body, and hung it on a clothes tree in the corner of his office. "Have a seat," he said.

Sabre took a seat without responding. She watched the judge, in his early sixties, as he sat down behind his massive oak desk. He picked up a photograph of a younger self, three small children, and a woman whom Sabre knew to be his first wife, among many. Admiration covered his face, but as he set the photo down and turned to Sabre his brow wrinkled and his smile disappeared.

"I may as well get right to the point, Sabre, since there's no easy way to say this." He paused just briefly. "We have a problem on a case."

"You mean a conflict?"

"No. It has to do with a party on one of our cases. Something of which I've recently become aware."

"Your Honor, shouldn't we have the other attorneys here? County Counsel at least?"

"No one else can know this. I wouldn't be telling you except...."

"Your Honor," she interrupted him again, "I mean no disrespect, but I'm really not comfortable with this interchange without the other attorneys on the case present." She felt her hands quiver a little. No matter how many years she had lived or how many letters she had after her name, authority figures still made her nervous. But she had several cases right now that were very touchy and she didn't want to risk an appellate issue on any of them because of an ex parte hearing with a judge.

She expected him to rebuke her, but he didn't. He calmly said, "Sabre, I know this can jeopardize your case and it can get me thrown off the bench, but it has to be said." Voices filled the hallway from a courtroom that had emptied. "Please shut the door," the judge said.

His comments made her even more wary. Sabre stood up, took one step toward the door, and looked out. She spotted Tom Ahlers, a deputy County Counsel, walking with a bailiff. "Tom," she called. "Can you come here a second?"

She turned back to the judge. His face was red with anger and for a second Sabre thought she saw fear in his face.

"We need a County Counsel in here, Your Honor. I'm just not comfortable with this."

"There's no need for County Counsel," he said louder.

"So, should I get the DA? Is it a delinquency case?"

Scary Larry jumped up from his big leather chair and flung his arms out, making a dismissal gesture just as Tom stepped inside. "Get out! Both of you. Just get out. You're on your own," he bellowed.

Chapter 1

The Durham Case
  Child: Matt Durham, Defendant
  Type: Delinquency case
  Charges: Two counts of First Degree Murder
  Victims: Hannah Rawlins & Mason Usher
  Facts: Double homicide. Two teenagers bludgeoned to death with a baseball bat.

"Scary Larry is dead," her best friend, Bob Clark, told Sabre as he approached her in the parking lot of San Diego Juvenile Court. Sabre had just opened her trunk to remove her briefcase.

She turned abruptly, her shoulder-length brown hair dusting across her face as she swung around. "Oh my God! What happened?"

"Hit and run. Right here at the courthouse." He pointed south. "Back there where the judges park. He was hit walking to his car and left there to die."

"Did anyone see it?"

"I heard it was almost six o'clock before he left and nearly everyone was gone. It's kind of secluded back there. I guess a man found him when he went for a walk with his dog. He called 9-1-1, but the judge didn't make it."

Sabre removed her briefcase, closed the trunk, and started to walk with Bob toward the courthouse. The blood had drained from her face, leaving it void of color, and her petite body appeared unsteady as she took her first step. Bob took her briefcase, reached over, and put his arm around her.

"Are you okay?" he asked.

She stopped. "I'm not sure."

"I didn't expect you to be so upset over that crazy, old coot. He was a nice enough guy, but he was totally whacked. I'm sorry he's dead, but you seem overly affected. What is it?"

"He called me into his chambers yesterday afternoon."

"And?"

"And he wanted to tell me something about a case we're on." Sabre took a deep breath.

"So, what did he tell you?"

"Nothing, really. The other attorneys weren't there and I was uncomfortable having an ex parte hearing."

"Did he tell you what case it was?"

"No, we never got that far. I saw Tom Ahlers in the hallway and invited him in, but Judge Mitchell flipped out and bellowed at us to get out. And then he said I was on my own."

"What do you mean? What exactly did he say?"

"He said, 'You're on your own,'" Sabre said, pronouncing each word slowly and deliberately. "So Ahlers and I left. I don't know what he meant, but like you said, 'He's whacked.' It could've been anything."

"Or it could have been something that got him killed."

"Oh no! Do you think if I had listened to him he wouldn't be dead now?"

"No. What could you have possibly done?"

"Told the police, maybe."

"*He* could have done that."

"He seemed afraid of something, but he's such an odd duck, I didn't really give it that much thought."

They stopped talking when they stepped through the courthouse door. After dropping their files on the metal detector belt, they walked through.

"I wonder who's covering Judge Mitchell's cases today," Sabre said, as she picked up her files.

"They have a pro tem in the dependency court, and they've disbursed the few delinquency cases he had among the other judges."

"He shouldn't have too many of those since he was easing out of delinquency. He didn't seem too happy to be spending his time in dependency court."

"Naw, he pretty much hated it. I think the presiding judge wanted to get rid of him. Maybe he thought Scary Larry would leave if he was unhappy enough."

"I don't think he could afford to retire. He has too much alimony to pay. What was he on? Wife Number Six?"

"Five or Six, I've lost track, but who cares. He's dead now. I guess his ex-wives will all have to find another cash cow." Bob paused. "And did you know we have a new County Counsel in Mitchell's department?"

"No, I didn't hear anything about that. Who is it?"

"It's Marge Benson."

"Are you kidding me? She's back?" Sabre frowned. "But she stayed with the DA's office when they made the conversion. What's she doing with County Counsel?"

"I don't know. Maybe she missed us."

"Right," Sabre said sarcastically. "She liked us about as much as we liked her." Sabre wrinkled her nose. "It's been so nice around here and now it's going to be miserable."

"It'll be fine. We were newbies back then. Now we're the king and queen of juvenile court, remember?"

Sabre smiled. He was right. Benson was difficult to work with because she never compromised, but they could beat her on some of the legal issues. They both had a lot more experience now. She wouldn't be able to push them around like she did when they first came here. Even back then, they beat her on their first jurisdictional trial together. Benson hated losing to a couple of rookies and made their lives miserable the remainder of the time she was there.

But what bothered Sabre the most was that it would be more difficult for the clients. Benson was so bent on protecting children from physical abuse that she often didn't see the emotional damage that it caused. Sometimes providing services to keep a family together resulted in a better solution than ripping the families apart. But Benson was a bulldozer, tearing everything up and trying to build something new when a little refurbishing may have been a better way to go.

"Sobs?" Bob said. His nickname for her came from her initials, Sabre Orin Brown, his little S.O.B.

"Sorry, I was just thinking about life at juvenile court with Marge Benson," Sabre said. "What's up?"

"Sobs, I think you should call JP and tell him about your ex parte hearing with Scary Larry. Maybe have him look at the cases you two have — or had — in common. It could be the judge was trying to warn you."

"I could, but JP's on vacation." Sabre emphasized the word "vacation." "What's that about anyway? He never takes a vacation."

"That's right. I forgot." Bob looked away.

"What is it?"

"He has company...from Texas."

"Who?"

"His ex-wife."

"His what?" Sabre's eyes widened.

"I'm sorry, Sobs. I'm sure it's nothing. They're probably just friends."

"Who would be friends with an ex-wife?" Sabre flipped one hand up in a gesture of dismissal. "It doesn't matter. He can see whomever he wants."

Bob raised his eyebrow and tilted his head to one side. His full head of wavy hair was graying prematurely. "Honey, this is Bob you're talking to. I know you have feelings for him, no matter how hard you try to fight it. You two need to quit dancing around and sit down and talk this out."

Sabre shook her head and cleared her throat. "There's nothing to talk out. It could never work. Someone would end up getting hurt, and I would lose a perfectly good private investigator. I can't afford that now. I've got too many cases that really need some serious work, not the least of which is the Durham case this afternoon."

"Is JP working on that?"

"Yes, he started before he went on 'vacation.' He left me a message this morning and said he would bring me a report before the hearing this afternoon. He said he had something that might help me with the 707 hearing."

"Sorry, I don't speak 'delinquency.' Wait, I know, that's where the DA is trying to have him tried as an adult, right?"

"That's it. Sorry, I always forget that you don't handle delinquency cases. Stick with me and you'll have the language down in no time." Sabre pursed her lips as if she were thinking. "Here's the thing: Judge Mitchell presided over that case. Everyone believed he would rule against my client and send him downtown for the trial."

"Maybe Durham had him snuffed."

"Don't be silly. How could he do that? Besides, my client's just a kid."

"Yeah, a kid who's charged with a double homicide—a gruesome, bloody, double homicide."

Chapter 2

The Durham Case
  Child: Matt Durham, Defendant
  Type: Delinquency case
  Charges: Two counts of First Degree Murder
  Victims: Hannah Rawlins & Mason Usher
  Facts: Double homicide. Two teenagers bludgeoned to death
with a baseball bat.

The news reporters swarmed around juvenile court. Three vans from local television stations were parked in the concrete lot in front of the building. Men carrying huge cameras and reporters with microphones waited near the front door for anyone connected with the Durham case to enter or exit.

Sabre could see it all from the balcony, where she stood waiting for JP. She watched him as he walked through the crowd undetected by the news crews and into the courthouse. He passed through the metal detector and then walked directly to the door leading upstairs to the spot where they had agreed to meet. She lost sight of him until he turned the corner for the second set of steps. He wore jeans, a plain black T-shirt, and cowboy boots. His black Stetson must have remained behind in his car. JP seldom went anywhere without it—except to court, of course. Her heart fluttered a little and she thought about what Bob had said earlier. She pushed it aside. Right now she had to deal with Durham.

"Hi, kid," JP said, as he took the last step. He smiled his sexy half smile.

"Hi, JP. So what do you have for me?"

He handed her a report. "Not as much as I'd like, but this might help a little. The kid has a good school record, good grades, no previous delinquent history, and whenever he had problems in school he willingly did his punishment and seemed to change his behavior for the better. That, along with a good report from a psychologist, might help to show he can be rehabilitated before he reaches twenty-five-years old."

"That's assuming the psychologist I obtained provides us with a favorable report."

"You've always been able to find someone who has a more liberal view on these things. Why are you so concerned on this one?"

"I don't think he made a good impression on Dr. Heller. I spoke with her briefly on the phone and she didn't sound too positive about our client, but she'll be here with the report soon. Let's go meet with the kid. I just had him taken into an interview room. You can tell me what you think."

They walked down the steps in silence. Things had become a little awkward between them. Sabre didn't like it. She had always been so comfortable around JP. He made her feel safe and had saved her from more than one crisis. But after the last case ended, Sabre and JP went out for drinks and Sabre had a few margaritas. She didn't recall exactly how it all went down, but she knew she came on to him and he refused to engage because of her intoxicated state. She knew he had done the right thing and respected him for it. Or maybe he just wasn't interested. Either way, it was best. She just wanted things to return to normal.

At the landing at the bottom of the stairs, JP opened the heavy wooden door for Sabre. Though in the lobby, they were still about twenty feet from the front door. The news cameras were not allowed inside juvenile court, but they hovered close to the front entrance. As others entered the front door, Sabre could see that the crowd outside had grown bigger and the reporters more aggressive. They were trying to catch anyone who was remotely connected to the Durham case. She spotted a tall man whom she recognized from Channel 10, a local station. He caught her eye. Sabre quickly turned away.

"Did you have any problem getting past the reporters?" Sabre asked JP, as they walked through the lobby.

"No, apparently they don't know who I am," JP said.

"They will now. John Gavin from Channel 10 just saw us together. I expect you'll be attacked when you leave here."

JP looked toward the door and saw Gavin watching him. "I'm sure they'll be on me like stink on a polecat, but don't worry. I can handle 'em."

Sabre looked at JP and smiled. "I know you can." She knew what he would do. Nothing. Absolutely nothing. He wouldn't say a word; he'd just walk away, leaving them with their limp microphones dangling in their hands.

JP opened the door to the interview rooms. The area was a large rectangular shape, divided down the middle by a hallway. One side contained a couple of desks that the court interpreters used due to the lack of working space in the courthouse. The other half was divided into three separate rooms. Each had a door with a small glass window. So without opening the door, the attorneys could easily see if it was occupied or if their client had been brought in. Sabre glanced into the first one and observed an adult cuffed to the bench on the opposite side of a large glass partition. He was talking to his attorney. The second had a prisoner waiting either to be seen or to be returned to his cell. The third confined Sabre's client, Matt Durham.

Fourteen-year-old Matt was about five-feet-ten-inches tall, had a slightly rounded face, and was of average weight.

His light brown, wavy hair lay tightly against his head, not exposing the curls that were evident in earlier school photos. He looked innocent sitting there. Just a child, Sabre thought as she walked into the cubicle.

"Matt, this is my private investigator, JP Torn. He'll be helping us on this case. He may need to speak to you from time to time. If so, please cooperate with him."

"Howdy, Matt," JP said. The plexiglass between Matt and the two of them prevented JP from shaking his hand.

"Hi," Matt said.

Sabre and JP sat down in the worn, metal folding chairs. Matt was seated on a wooden bench, one hand cuffed to the bench by a two-foot-long chain that prevented him from moving very far in the tiny three-by-five area.

Sabre began. "As discussed earlier, we have our fitness hearing this afternoon. The DA will be arguing that you're not fit to be tried in juvenile court because of the specific crime you are charged with. We have to rebut that presumption. In other words, we have to prove that you are fit and that you can be rehabilitated before you reach the age of twenty-five. That's the longest they can keep you in custody as a minor."

"And if we lose?" Matt asked.

"Then you would be tried downtown in adult court, and if you're convicted your sentence would likely be much longer, perhaps life imprisonment."

"But I'm only fourteen," Matt said. His face and his voice both pleaded for help.

"I know, and if you were thirteen we wouldn't be having this hearing, but the law says when you are fourteen and have been charged with murder you are presumed unfit for juvenile court and we have to show otherwise. I'm hoping the psychological evaluation you did with Dr. Heller will help us."

"But will they have the hearing this afternoon since our judge is dead?"

"How did you know that?" Sabre asked, a little surprised that her client knew about Judge Mitchell.

"Everyone in the Hall is talking about it."

"Of course. It's been all over the news and the Internet." Sabre studied Matt's face for a few seconds. "It depends on whether there is a judge available to hear your case who feels ready to go forward. This case has received a lot of media attention so they will be careful with it. I could ask for a continuance to try to buy us a little more time, but it likely won't matter. If the new judge is ready, it'll be heard today."

"Judge Mitchell didn't seem to like me very much. Maybe we'll have a better chance with another judge."

Sabre wasn't exactly sure how to respond to that. It was true Scary Larry had made it pretty clear how he would rule and it wouldn't have been in Matt's favor. Matt apparently knew that as well.

Sabre explained, "Judge Mitchell was very outspoken and rather erratic, so even though he seemed to be leaning toward the prosecution he could still have gone our way. He actually may have been our best chance."

"Damn, I thought since he was dead maybe it would help us," Matt said with no regard for the judge's life. Sabre and JP exchanged glances. Matt looked from one to the other and then added, "It's not like I wished him dead or anything. I'm just sayin.'"

"I understand." Sabre deliberately changed the subject. "Matt, I have a couple of questions for you and I'll need you to look at some photos from the crime scene. They're pretty gruesome. Are you up to that?"

Matt nodded his head. "Whatever you need."

"As you know, we have an uphill battle here," Sabre said. "Your alibi is weak and the murder weapon—the baseball bat they found in the bushes in the park with blood from both victims—belonged to you."

"I know it's my bat, but it's been missing for a while. It was stolen at the baseball game. Someone walked off with it that night. I looked for it after the game, but I couldn't find it. The equipment had already been loaded in the van so I just figured someone put it in the bat bag and I'd get it at the next practice. You can ask my coach."

"I have an appointment to speak with him on Saturday," JP said. "And I'd like to verify your alibi, but I need to know the name of the friend you told Ms. Brown you were playing video games with."

Matt shrugged. "Just a friend. That's all I'm saying."

"We're going to need to know his name so we can corroborate your alibi."

"I don't want to get him involved."

Sabre cut in. "You understand you're on trial for murder, right? We need all the help we can muster."

"I didn't do it, so I don't need an alibi. You'll see."

JP and Sabre were silent for a few seconds and then Sabre proceeded with another line of questioning. "Can you tell me what happened earlier that day in the cafeteria between you and the victim, Hannah Rawlins?"

"What do you mean?"

"There are witnesses who say Hannah humiliated you last week in the school cafeteria."

"It wasn't that big a deal. She left when I sat down beside her. That's all."

"She left the cafeteria?"

"No, she went and sat somewhere else. Do they think I killed her because she wouldn't eat lunch with me? That's ridiculous. I didn't kill her. Someone must have set me up."

"Was anyone with you?"

"No, I was by myself, but there were lots of students there."

"I'll follow up," JP said.

Sabre removed a photo of the crime scene from her briefcase. She held it up to the glass and said, "I'm sorry you have to look at this, but I need you to focus on Hannah's arm. Do you recognize the blue wristband she's wearing?"

He glanced at the photo. "It looks like one I had, but I can't read it so I don't know for sure if that's mine."

"Did you give a wristband to her in the cafeteria?" Sabre asked.

"Yeah, she had given it to me a few months back when we were hooking up. I tried to give it back to her."

"You tried? What does that mean?"

"I offered it back to her, but she said, 'No thanks.' So I dropped it on her tray when she started to walk away."

"Please look very carefully. See if you can tell if it's the same one."

Matt looked at the photo, from top to bottom, covering every inch of it with his eyes. "I'm not sure," he said. He continued to stare at the dead body. At first, Sabre thought he was anxious or upset having to see Hannah's body, but then she saw what appeared to be admiration or even pride. His eyes almost twinkled and his lips parted, turning up ever so slightly on the edges. He closed his eyes for just a second and licked his lips. Sabre set the photo down and turned it over. She didn't show him the rest of the photos.

Chapter 3

The Durham Case
  Child: Matt Durham, Defendant
  Type: Delinquency case
  Charges: Two counts of First Degree Murder
  Victims: Hannah Rawlins & Mason Usher
  Facts: Double homicide. Two teenagers bludgeoned to death with a baseball bat.

"That was disturbing," Sabre said when she and JP had reached the balcony once again.

JP shook his head. "Very. He was getting excited just looking at the photo of the dead body."

"At least I know not to put him on the stand to testify."

"Are you going to continue to represent him?"

"As long as he stays in juvenile court, I will. He's a kid, he needs help, and he's obviously very sick."

"He's not sick. He's just plain mean. That boy would make a hornet look cuddly," JP raved on.

Sabre frowned. She knew this wasn't going to be easy and Matt frightened her, too, but he still deserved the best defense possible.

"I have to see this through...at least for the fitness hearing."

"And if you lose that?"

"I'm not sure. I've been thinking about letting it go if they send it downtown. My calendar is so full and it's difficult dealing with yet another courthouse."

"But not because you know he killed those two kids?"

"I still don't know that for sure."

"For God's sakes, Sabre. You saw how excited he got when he saw the photo. That boy is plain evil."

"Maybe, but even so, he still has a right to counsel."

"Well, I don't know if I can help you on this one," JP said.

"That's your choice," Sabre said coldly. "But I'm not going to dump him just because of the crime. I knew it was a gruesome double homicide when I took the case. You know how I feel about this sort of thing. I don't have to like what he did, but that won't stop me from defending his rights and that includes his right to a fair trial."

JP took about three steps away from Sabre, shaking his head in frustration. He stopped and without looking at her he said, "You heard his reaction to the judge's murder. He was pleased." JP turned abruptly. "Sabre, maybe he killed Mitchell."

"He couldn't have. He was locked up."

"He could have had it done. He may have a following."

"Do you really think he's that sophisticated? He's only fourteen years old."

"He's a fourteen-year-old rattlesnake. Do you think he cares who he bites?" JP said loudly. He sighed and walked towards Sabre, put his hand on her shoulder, and lowered his voice. "Perhaps you're right, but you still need to be careful. Someone had Mitchell killed right after an ex parte hearing with you. And Mitchell was trying to tell you something, maybe even warn you, about one of your cases."

Sabre wrinkled her brow. "How did you know that?"

"Bob told me. He's worried and so am I."

Damn him, Sabre thought. She didn't want Bob to involve JP. His girlfriend, or ex-wife, or whatever she is now, was in

town and staying at his house. Sabre certainly didn't want JP
to think she needed him right now, not if he was interested
in someone else. She looked at the time. "We need to go do
Matt's 707 hearing." Sabre grabbed her briefcase and they
started down the steps toward the lobby.

"Do you know who the judge is?" JP asked.

"No, but I know they brought in Jane Palmer to prosecute."

"Is that bad?"

"She's tough. She fights hard, which is fine, but I don't trust
her. She thinks all defendants are the scum of the earth, and
if she thinks she has any chance of winning at all, she won't
cut a deal. She treats even the slightest crime as if it were
a...a...."

"A double homicide? As if the perpetrator bludgeoned
them to death with a baseball bat?" JP smirked. "I guess she'd
be right with this one."

They walked into Department Three and took a seat in the
back.

"I still don't like her," Sabre said. Just then a woman in her
mid-fifties with short, blonde hair interspersed with wisps of
gray entered the courtroom. Sabre stood up. "Dr. Heller, thank
you for coming."

Dr. Carolina Heller spoke with a heavy South American
accent. "Here is your report, but can we speak for just a
minute?"

"Sure." She followed Dr. Heller outside the courtroom. "Is
there a problem?"

"If you notice in the report, I'm recommending that Math-
ew be tried in juvenile court. He has some serious problems,
but I believe he can be rehabilitated if he's kept in the system
for the maximum time allotted in juvenile court."

"You mean until he's twenty-five?"

"Yes. If they make a true finding on the facts, I couldn't
recommend a shorter sentence for him. He has some serious
problems. And although he vehemently denies his guilt, I

have my doubts. I know that's not my job and you know I wouldn't say that on the stand since it's just a gut feeling, but I'm telling you for what it's worth."

Sabre swallowed. "Thanks. I appreciate your candid assessment and I'll certainly keep it in mind as we go forward." Sabre didn't share her own concerns with the doctor. She wasn't sure what they meant anyway. Maybe she had it all wrong. She trusted Dr. Heller. Although she was a little more liberal on her assessments of children, Sabre knew the doctor wouldn't suggest Matt was fit to be heard in juvenile court if she believed otherwise. Sabre's job today was to keep this case in juvenile court and get this kid some help if it turned out that he committed these heinous crimes.

"I was very upset to hear about Judge Mitchell," Dr. Heller said. "Do they know who killed him?"

"Not that I've heard." Sabre wondered if the good doctor believed their client might have had a hand in the murder.

Sabre turned to see ADA Jane Palmer walk into Department Three. She was a tall woman with big bones. She wasn't overweight, but her large frame had never seen anything smaller than a size fourteen. Her light brown hair hung to her shoulders with just a bit of an upturn at the bottom, and her black-rimmed glasses perched permanently on her aquiline nose, suggesting a cool tactician with a business mind.

"There's the prosecutor now," Sabre said. "I'm not certain if the court plans to go forward with this hearing today or not. Let's go in and see what we can find out."

Dr. Heller took a seat in front of JP, and Sabre stepped into the well and approached Jane Palmer. "Good morning, Jane."

"Sabre," she said, without looking up from her files that she shuffled on the table.

"Are you going forward this afternoon on the Durham case?"

Again without looking at Sabre she said, "I'm ready."

"Okay," Sabre said.

When Sabre turned around she caught the bailiff's eye. Mike McCormick, an eye-catching sheriff in his mid-thirties, was her favorite bailiff. He moved his head in a slightly upward movement indicating she should come over to him. When she walked over to his desk, he said very softly, "Your case will be continued. No judge wants this one."

"Because of Mitchell?"

"Exactly. They're concerned that Mitchell's death is related to this case."

"Is there something else I should know?" Sabre asked.

Mike moved his head slowly from side to side. Then he stood up as Judge Charles Shafer walked into the courtroom and took his seat on the bench.

"We'll hear the Durham case first," the judge said.

Sabre walked over to the table and sat down.

"Would you like me to bring in the defendant, Your Honor?" Mike asked.

"Please," Judge Shafer said, looking directly at the bailiff. He turned back to face the attorneys. "Before we bring the defendant, in I want you to know this case will be continued for one week on my orders. Will there be any objection from counsel?"

"No, Your Honor," Sabre responded quickly.

The prosecutor hesitated for a few seconds, then said, "No, Your Honor."

Mike returned shortly with Matt Durham and seated him next to Sabre.

The court clerk said, "In the matter of the State versus Matthew Durham."

Mike remained standing behind Matt for the duration of the hearing, which took less than three minutes. After the case was continued, Sabre whispered to her client. "This is just as well for us. JP or I will see you in a day or so in the Hall."

A second bailiff came in the back door and escorted Matt Durham back to Juvenile Hall. Mike leaned down and whispered in Sabre's ear. "Watch your back. This kid is dangerous."

Chapter 4

Sabre made the mistake of telling JP about Mike's warning to "watch her back." Consequently, he insisted on following Sabre back to her office to go through her files and see if they could find any connection to her ex parte hearing with Judge Mitchell and his murder.

Sabre sat down at her desk and opened an Excel spreadsheet to view her open cases. She carried delinquency cases, which were criminal, and dependency cases, which included child abuse and neglect. Twenty-three of the open cases in her file cabinet were delinquency. The remaining 457 were open dependency cases. Many of those were in the review stage and had very little action on them. The spreadsheet had her cases listed alphabetically by the last name of the client, the date they were opened, the next hearing date, the department assigned to hear the case, and a few other bits of information. Although the list didn't include the judge's name, each judge was assigned to a particular department so an attorney could usually tell who the judge was on the case without checking the file. The only deviation from that would be when a judge was absent and someone else covered for them. On a rare occasion, files were sent to other departments because a judge was involved in another trial.

JP sat across the desk from Sabre as she prepared the list of cases where Judge Mitchell presided. He had a clear view of the computer screen because it sat on an arm that extended from the desk. Her desk was clean except for a wooden box that contained her keys; a black Montblanc Johannes Brahms ballpoint pen in a bronze penholder with her name engraved on the base; and a wooden Victorian hourglass.

"I see you got your brother's hourglass back," JP said.

Sabre smiled. "Yes, Detective Klakken brought it by himself yesterday."

"And how is Shane doing? Not that he'd even want me to know."

"Actually, he asked about you. I think he's trying to let go of the past. It would be good for both of you to make amends." There was a lot of history between JP and Detective Shane Klakken, some of which they had come to terms with.

"I'm just glad you have your hourglass. I know how much it means to you," JP said.

Sabre looked at the piece of art that sat straight and proud on her desk. The hourglass was one of the few things she had left of her brother's possessions. She missed him. And she missed her close relationship with JP. Everything was different now since JP had rejected her advances a few weeks ago. He said she had too much to drink and they would talk about it later, but they never did. Now their relationship was strained. They really needed to talk, but she couldn't bring herself to start the conversation, especially now that JP's ex was in town and staying at his house.

"Thanks again for saving my life. I owe you another one."

"No, you don't. But you really need to be more careful and we're starting with this case. We need to find out what Mitchell was talking about before something else happens."

"Okay." Sabre acquiesced. She printed two copies of the short list of her delinquency cases followed by a much longer list of dependency cases that were in Judge Mitchell's department. She handed one set to JP.

JP looked first at the delinquency list. "Only three cases with Mitchell?"

"Yes, the first two are both very petty. One was a shoplifting by a twelve-year-old which is on track to a voluntary probation under W&I 654. The other was a grand theft auto by a couple of teenagers that was essentially a joy ride. They stole the car from a parking lot, drove around for a couple of hours, and dropped it back in the same lot."

"In the same parking lot?"

"Almost in the same spot."

"That wasn't too bright."

"You're telling me." Sabre grinned. "They got picked up returning it."

"They should be charged with 'grand theft stupid' instead of grand theft auto."

She looked back at the list. "So, if it's a delinquency case, the most likely one is Durham, even though he was locked up. Just the nature of the case leaves it open to suspicion," Sabre said.

"I'll follow up on all three just to see if there is anything we're missing, but I'll concentrate on Durham. What about the dependency cases?"

"They're going to be a little tougher. The good news is that Mitchell had only recently crossed over into dependency or I would have a lot more cases with him than I do." Sabre glanced quickly down the list she held in her hand. "There are thirty-nine."

JP whistled. "Whoa, that's a lot of cases. That's gonna be harder than trying to put a g-string on an alligator."

Sabre chuckled.

"Can you prioritize them?" he asked.

Sabre perused the list again, marking off the review cases that had been inactive. She handed her list to JP. "Switch with me. I've marked off the cases that have had little action. If someone is angry enough to kill a judge over it, it's probably something current or at least active. I've also marked off the cases that were assigned to Mitchell's department that he never heard."

"Okay, they'll go to the bottom of my list. That leaves nine cases. Can we narrow it down any more?"

"Four of those are tox baby cases—numbers Three, Four, Seven, and Nine. The mother used drugs while she was pregnant; there's nothing unusual about those cases. If the mother does what she's supposed to do, she will likely have the child back within six months." Sabre marked them off her list. JP started to do the same. "Wait. Let's not dismiss number Nine yet. Both parents were pretty hostile on that case."

"Okay, so we're down to six dependency cases and one delinquency to start with. If we don't uncover anything in those, I'll investigate the remaining cases. Can you pull those files and I'll start reading through them?"

"Sure." Sabre stood up, walked to the file cabinet, and returned with an armload of files, one gray and five pink. She set them on the desk in front of JP. "The gray is the delin-quency case, the pink are dependency. And there's one more case: Wheeler." Sabre went over to the file cabinet again and returned with three pink folders and two thick manila folders. She dropped them on the desk. "This is the Wheeler case. The family has been here before. The pink folders contain detention reports, social studies, and anything that happened before the Permanent Planning Hearing, or PPH as we call it, was set. The manila folders have everything after the PPH. Bob represents the father, Willie Wheeler. He's crazy as a loon."

"Who? Bob or Willie?"

Sabre laughed. "Both, I guess." Bob Clark was Sabre's and JP's closest friend. It was Bob who introduced JP and Sabre. Bob and Sabre met at juvenile court over six years ago. They were thrown together on a difficult case when Sabre was first appointed to the panel. After weeks of constant contact, fighting for justice, and ultimately winning the trial, they discovered they really enjoyed each other's company. It wasn't long before they shared many of the same cases, lunched together daily, and occasionally socialized. Their relationship remained platonic with no romantic involvement. Bob was married to Marilee, whom Sabre came to know over time. She and Marilee were friends, but not like she and Bob were. He was her work spouse and helped Sabre fill a void created by her missing brother, Ron.

"Did you have a hearing on any of these cases yesterday prior to Mitchell's ex parte with you?"

Sabre ran the morning calendar through her mind. "Yeah. Durham. And I have two of them on tomorrow: Martinez and King. Fisher, that tox baby case with the wild parents, was on the day before. Oh, and the Tran case was on calendar yesterday morning as well for a special hearing. Judge Mitchell ordered a CASA—Court Appointed Special Advocate be appointed, and then continued the case for a week or so. The date's in the file."

JP stacked the files with Durham on top, followed by Fisher, Martinez, and King. "And the other two?"

"Howard and Wheeler were both on last week and they have hearings coming up again soon."

JP continued with his stack. Under King he placed Tran and Howard. He picked up the huge stack of Wheeler's files. "I'm leaving these until last," he said, as he placed them on the bottom of his pile. "That one is going to take a while. Why don't we go through each case and you can give me a quick synopsis."

"Okay."

JP walked over to Sabre's credenza and opened the door. "I need a legal pad."

"Sure."

He returned to his seat, took out his pen and wrote the date on the first sheet of yellow paper along with the name, *Durham*. He had beautiful handwriting, which had initially surprised Sabre because he was such a cowboy. But as time went on, she came to know his gentle, sensitive side that matched his script.

"Durham, as you know, is the delinquency case. A double homicide. Matt is accused of bludgeoning two teenagers as they walked home from a school play."

"And we know what he is capable of," JP said with a bit of an edge in his voice. "But he was in custody so he would have to have had an accomplice, maybe even more than one. Was there any evidence that a second person was involved in the murders?"

"No," Sabre said. "At least they don't have anything that puts anyone else at the scene of the crime, but to tell you the truth, I'm not sure they've ruled it out either."

"That boy is frightening."

"I know." Sabre didn't want to talk about Matt Durham right now. The last encounter with him had left her very uncomfortable. She picked up the Durham file and stood up. "I'll make you copies of this. You're going to need it anyway." She stepped toward the door on her way to the copy room but continued to talk. "Working our way through these files is going to take a while and I'm hungry. Do you mind if we get some food? We can get take-out. Maybe even have something delivered." She paused for just a second without giving JP time to respond. "Oh, I'm sorry. You probably have dinner plans. Never mind, I'll be...."

"Food sounds great. Let's order in."

Chapter 5

The Snow Pea Chinese BBQ had received their order for delivery. Sabre and JP continued through the files while they waited for their food to arrive. Sabre copied the Durham file, put the pages in a manila folder, and labeled it before she handed it to JP.

"Thanks," he said.

JP picked up the first thin, pink file folder and wrote *Fisher* on the second page of his legal pad. "And Fisher is the baby born on drugs with the volatile parents?"

"Right."

"So, how volatile? Any incidents or threats made?"

"The father threatened the social worker when the child was taken from the hospital and placed in foster care."

"So, the baby never went home?"

"No. And at the detention hearing the mother flipped out and started screaming, 'You'll all pay for taking my baby.' That time the father tried to calm *her* down."

"Did anyone take her seriously?"

"Not really. This stuff happens all the time. And I'm pretty certain she was high in court that day. Your typical meth freak behavior."

"So, both parents are suspect on Fisher."

"Pretty much."

JP picked up the next pink file. This one was a little thicker than the first, indicating it had been around a bit longer. He read the computer-generated label: "Martinez."

"Domestic violence," Sabre said. "They had one heck of a brawl one night in front of her house—three kids all screaming, neighbors coming out of their houses. One of the Martinez kids called the police and reported it."

"Did they arrest him?"

"Her."

"That's a switch."

"They took them both in, but she was the only one charged. It was about the fourth time the cops had been called this year."

"But this was the first arrest?"

Sabre nodded.

"Because it was the woman—not the man—doing the beating," he said in more of a statement than a question.

"Maybe. Anyway, by the time they arrived the guy had a broken nose. Blood had spurted everywhere. She'd beaten him with a Mickey Mouse lamp, of all things. The oldest child tried to stop her, but he got kicked in the face and ended up with a black eye."

"And none of the neighbors did anything?"

"Not at first. Even when they did finally intervene, they didn't stop the fight, but one of them picked up the two-year-old boy and held him so he couldn't see what was happening." Sabre stopped talking when she heard the front door open. She started to stand up. "That must be the food."

JP beat her out of her seat. "I'll get it," he said and walked out of her office.

Sabre wasn't sure if he was anxious to keep her from paying for the food or if he was concerned that it might not be the delivery. She heard an exchange of a few words between JP and another male voice, and a minute or two later JP returned carrying a white paper sack that smelled of shrimp, ginger, and garlic. He set the bag on Sabre's desk. She retrieved two paper plates, a couple of spoons, a fork, and two sets of cream-colored plastic chopsticks from a cupboard. She handed JP a plate. "Chopsticks?"

"No, thanks."

Sabre laid the other utensils on the desk. They dished up their food and for a moment ate in silence, JP with his fork and Sabre with the chopsticks.

"Why do you use those when you eat Asian food?"

"Actually, I use them for other food, too. At home, that is. It feels better than the taste of metal in my mouth. I learned to use them when I was a kid. My mother would get annoyed at me because I would eat so fast. She constantly told me to slow down because it wasn't healthy and it was bad manners. I think the manners thing bothered her the most. One day my father came home with a beautiful set of chopsticks with mother of pearl embedded on the handles. They were gorgeous. After a great deal of practice and my brother's harassment and teasing, I mastered using them. Now, they trigger pleasant memories for me."

JP smiled and for a second Sabre saw wonder in his eyes. She couldn't decide if it was out of fascination, admiration, or just curiosity.

"I could teach you how to use them."

JP shook his head. "There's no use trying to teach a pig to sing. It wastes your time and it annoys the pig."

She laughed. "Fair enough."

JP finished eating before Sabre. He threw his plate in the trash and picked up his file again. "So, back to Martinez. You were saying a neighbor helped with the youngest child."

"She finally tried to get the other two children away from the parents, but the oldest boy kept trying to stop the fight and the little girl just stood there screaming. The neighbor's contact information is in the report."

"How old are the other children?"

"The girl is five and the boy is seven."

"Same father for all three kids?"

"Yes. And according to the father's attorney, he puts up with the mother's behavior because of the children."

"Any drug or alcohol abuse on this case?"

"Of course. Mostly alcohol, I think. That's the common denominator on most of these cases, isn't it?" Sabre didn't wait for him to answer. "Both of them drink quite a bit, but the booze really sets the mother off. Apparently, she's pretty bad to start with and impossible with the help of her friend in the bottle."

JP made some more notes on his pad about Martinez, turned the page, and wrote *King.* "So, what is this one?"

"Physical abuse. Two boys, ages two and twelve. The dad beat the older boy, who is his stepson, with a belt. Left some pretty nasty bruises. He spent the last year in prison for a probation violation on an earlier assault charge."

"And the violation was for?"

"Drug possession with intent to sell."

"And *Tran*?" JP started a new page.

"Neglect. The mom left her eighteen-month-old baby girl locked in a room while she went to work. The apartment complex caught on fire. Apparently, someone heard the baby crying so a couple of young guys broke in and rescued her."

"Good for them." JP wrote his notes. "Do we know who the CASA worker is yet?"

"No, but I'll check on that."

"One more thing: Where does the mother on the Tran case work?"

"Initially, she named a dry cleaning establishment, but then she finally admitted to being a stripper."

"This case just got more interesting."

Sabre glanced at JP without turning her head toward him. "Oh, it did, did it?"

A hint of pink flushed over JP's face. "I'm sure she's a very nice girl." His face reddened more. He turned to the next page in his notepad. "Tell me about Howard."

"That's a shaken baby case. Someone shook the three-month-old and jarred his brain loose. The child died. There's a three-year-old sibling who was removed from the home."

"Anyone arrested?"

"Not yet. The parents are pointing the finger at the babysitter. The babysitter says the child was fine when she left."

JP turned to another blank page on his yellow pad. "That leaves Wheeler."

"Ah, where do I start with Willie Wheeler?"

"If this huge stack of files is any indication, this case has been going on for some time."

"It first came into the system about two years ago with a 'dirty home' petition. Bob was appointed for the father, Willie Wheeler, and Regina Collicott for the mother, Debbie Wheeler. I represented the twelve children."

"Twelve children?"

"Yep, and all the boys are named William and the girls are all named Debra. All of us involved with the case use the middle names of the children. Otherwise, it becomes way too confusing.

"Don't tell me the parents call them William and Debra?"

"No, that would be silly." Sabre couldn't keep a straight face. "They call them Willie and Debbie."

JP just shook his head and smiled. He looked back at the huge file. "This case has been going on for two years, you said?"

"Yes. We thought it would be a simple case. Get them to clean up the house and give them some services to teach them how to keep it clean, enroll them in a few parenting classes, and close the file."

"I take it that didn't work."

"We soon discovered the case was riddled with drug and alcohol abuse, an obsessive belief in ghosts, mental insta-bility, and some physical abuse—mostly 'spare the rod, spoil the child' type."

"Who's the mental case?"

"Both parents, really, but Willie is crazier than a loon. A few of the children have some mental problems, too. But now there are only eight children left in the system. Four of the twelve are no longer minors; the oldest Willie just turned twenty; the twin Debbies are nineteen; and another Willie is eighteen now. There are a sixteen-year-old and a fifteen-year-old who are in the delinquency system, so we're only dealing with five placements: two girls, eleven and thirteen; two boys, five and seven; and the nine-year old twins, Holly and Bradley. It's a lot easier to try to find placements for six children than twelve, especially if you're trying to keep some of them together."

JP and Sabre continued to search through the cases look-ing for clues to the judge's murder. Four hours later and after, a lot of reading, questions, and some bad Chinese take-out, JP said, "I'll hit the streets first thing in the morning."

Chapter 6

Tyson Doyle Cooper

The tall, lean Texan ravaged through each drawer that his wife, Robin, had in their home. Clothes were flung aside looking for clues. Drawers were emptied onto the bed, counters, and floors. He looked at every photograph and every piece of paper that she had once possessed in search of some clue as to where she might have gone. He loved his wife and he wasn't one to give up easily. He would get her back no matter what he had to do.

He attacked a file drawer filled with bills, insurance papers, and old tax forms. He threw the old bills and the insurance papers in the trash. The last file contained every tax form she filed. He thumbed through it until he found her ex-husband's name, John Phillip Torn, whose last address was in El Cajon, California. Ty knew from a previous discussion they once had that, unlike most women, she held her ex in high regard. In fact, she clearly stated that if she ever needed anyone, she knew she could count on JP.

Ty threw the papers down and pulled another file labeled, "Miscellaneous." Among other things it held a newspaper clipping, a little over a year old, about an attorney named Sabre Orin Brown and her PI, JP Torn, involved in a high-profile case in San Diego Juvenile Court that made national news. "JP Torn," he said aloud. He folded the article and tucked it in his pocket and then called his cousin Blake.

"I need you to rent a car for me, midsize, dark, something that won't stand out. I'm taking a little trip."

"Care to tell me where to?"

"It's better that you don't know."

"Do you know how long you'll be gone?"

"As long as it takes to get my wife back," Ty said. "I'll see you in about an hour. Oh, and make sure the car doesn't have a GPS. I don't want anyone tracking me. Besides, I have a portable one I can take with me if I need it."

Ty took a quick shower, threw some clothes in a small suitcase, and opened his safe. He removed a .357 Magnum and a wad of hundred dollar bills. He counted out twenty-five of them. He put four of the bills in his wallet, folded five in half and put them in his shirt pocket, and rolled the rest and stuck them in his front pants pocket. He strapped on a shoulder holster, placed the gun in it, and carried his suitcase and computer to his SUV. Then he drove to Blake's house.

~~~

Blake pulled into his yard just after Ty arrived and parked the dark blue Toyota rental car in front of the house. He stepped out of the car and walked up to Ty's window.

Ty nodded toward the car. "Good choice," Ty said. "Can I park my car in your back barn?"

"Sure. I'll drive the rental back there and open the barn door for you."

Blake reentered the Toyota and drove around the house. Ty followed him. They drove over a small hill and past some trees to an old building hidden from the home's view. It stood next to a pile of rubble that was once a house; now, only the house's foundation remained.

Blake jumped out of the car, leaving it running, unlocked the padlock, and pulled the barn door open. Ty drove inside.

"No one will ever know it's here," Blake said. "I'm assuming that's what you want."

"That's what I want. I don't even want Big Jim to know. You understand me? I need the element of surprise."

Blake slid the barn door closed and re-locked the padlock on it. "You can count on me, cousin. You just go get your woman and bring her back here where she belongs."

"She'll come to her senses once she sees me again. I know she loves me."

Ty took the seat behind the wheel on the rental. "I'll take you to pick up your car." He reached in his front pocket and pulled out the five hundred dollars he had put there earlier and handed the bills to Blake. "This should cover the car and a little for yourself. If I'm gone too long and it costs more, I'll get it to you."

"No problem, cousin." Blake was three years younger than Ty and as long as Ty could remember Blake had never called him anything but "cousin." He looked up to his older relative and often patterned himself after him. Blake resembled Ty with the same build and same height. From a distance they could easily be mixed up. But Ty was better looking, better at sports, and way better with the ladies. Ty knew it. Blake knew it. Heck, everyone in town knew it. Ty always took him along and tried to teach him a few things, although Ty made sure Blake always knew his place. When Blake became a policeman, he gained a little more confidence, but he still looked up to Ty. Ty not only still had the looks and the charm, but he also had money. Blake couldn't compete with that.

Ty dropped Blake at the car rental lot and drove away. He followed Hwy 20 until he reached Interstate 10 and headed west. It was nearly noon by the time he reached El Paso. He drove into the first Taco Bell he saw, ordered a burrito and a large Coke, made a pit stop, and took his food to go. He drove across the street to the Arco gas station and filled the tank. He shouldn't have to stop until he reached Tucson. Now that he had some direction, he didn't want to waste any time getting there.

The Toyota moved down the highway at eighty to eighty-five miles an hour, slowing down only when required. He passed through Las Cruces, Deming, and Lordsburg, all the while thinking about how he would approach his wife.

Most of the rage he felt at Robin had been replaced with a purpose. He knew where he had to go and he knew he had to find her. She'd be happy to see him. Maybe not at first, but he'd be able to reason with her once she saw how much he cared, when she realized he had left everything to find her.

Tucson was his second pit stop. He filled the gas tank, used the facilities, and grabbed some food, along with a Monster Energy drink and a bag of sunflower seeds. A truck driver friend of his had once told him that he never drove without his bag of seeds. "It's hard to fall asleep when yer popping sunflower seeds in yer mouth every few seconds."

Ty rolled on down the highway at a good pace until he hit Yuma. He was tired, but determined. If he made it to San Diego tonight he could start looking for Robin first thing tomorrow morning.

"No one messes with Tyson Doyle Cooper and lives to tell it," he said aloud.

Chapter 7

The Martinez Case

Children: Ray, age 2 (M), Falicia, age 5 (F), Jesse (Jesus), age 7 (M)

Parents: Father—Gilberto Martinez, Mother—Juanita Martinez

Issues: Abuse, Domestic Violence

Facts: Mother beat the father with a lamp in front of the children. Alcohol abuse by both parents.

"What the hell is taking so long?" Juanita Martinez bellowed as her attorney, Bob Clark, walked out of Department Three with Sabre. Bob sat down next to his client; Sabre remained standing in front of her.

Bob said, "We're waiting for your husband and his attorney."

"Why aren't they here?" She asked, throwing her hands out to the side, her palms up like she was the only one with a life.

"Mr. Wagner is in another hearing," Bob said. In an attempt to divert her attention from her husband, Bob said, "I want you to tell Ms. Brown what you told me about the program you're in."

Juanita stood up abruptly, jerking her head up and back as she stood, almost hitting Sabre in the chin with her head. Sabre jumped back, but she caught a whiff of alcohol as she moved away from her.

"I want my kids back. They can come live with me at my sister's house or I can go back home, but I need my kids."

"What about what your kids need?" Sabre said, immediately wishing she had been a little more tactful, but she was irritated at the smell of booze on the mother and the near clunk to the head. It wasn't even ten o'clock yet.

Juanita swung around and stepped into Sabre's space. Though Sabre wore high heels, Juanita stood a good three inches taller than her. Juanita's face was less than six inches from Sabre's, a position intended to intimidate, which she had probably used many times before on her husband. "My kids need me, not some stupid foster home or their wimpy excuse for a father."

Bob stood up, standing close to the two women. Sabre didn't back away. "Your children need to be safe and to feel safe," she said. She felt like she was standing up to the school bully. Bob placed a hand on each of their shoulders. Sabre turned and stepped away from Juanita.

Juanita jerked her shoulder away from Bob's hand, and took one step closer to Sabre. "My kids are safe with me," Juanita said louder. "I'd never hurt my kids."

Sabre looked back at Bob. "I know you have no sense of smell, but the rest of us do. Tell your client it's not a good idea to come to court reeking of alcohol." Sabre walked away.

She had gone halfway down the hallway before she realized she was shaking. She wasn't sure if it was out of fear or anger. Sabre didn't like confrontations, but she was more sensitive than usual this morning. She was frustrated at herself for pushing the mother's buttons. She knew how hard it was for these parents. Their lives were already a mess and just when it seemed like they had gone about as low as they could go, they came to juvenile court and lost their children. How can life sink any lower than that?

Sabre took a deep breath. She knew Juanita was in the wrong—drinking her breakfast and commenting about how *she* needs the kids rather than their needing her—but Sabre was the professional. She should have handled it better.

~~~

The Fisher Case
  Child: Baby Girl Fisher (Newborn)
  Parents: Father—Dale Fisher, Mother—Susan Fisher
  Issues: Substance Abuse, Neglect
  Facts: Baby born positive tox for methamphetamines

Sabre walked to the end of the hallway and on to Department Three. She spotted the parents on the Fisher case
with their attorneys, Roberto Arroyo and Erica Serlis. Good,
she thought, maybe they could complete this case. As she
approached she heard a heated discussion among the four
of them.

"I don't give a flying...," the father yelled.

His attorney, Erica Serlis, spoke over him as Sabre stopped
in front of them. "Good morning, Ms. Brown."

"Good morning. Are you ready on Fisher?" Sabre asked,
looking first at Erica and then Roberto, ignoring what the
father just said.

"Yes," Roberto said.

The father, an African-American man named Dale Fisher, stepped through the huddle. His six-foot-two, two-hun-
dred-and-thirty-pound sculpted body towered over Sabre.
He said, "I'm ready to have my damn kid home. Are you the
bitch keeping her from me?"

"Dale, we need to talk," Erica said, stepping in front of him.

Sabre turned and walked into the courtroom. The last
thing she heard before she closed the door was, "That bitch
better give me my kid back."

Anger filled the air at juvenile court today, she thought.
She wondered if there had been a full moon last night. Sabre

shook her head as she walked toward the counsel table only to encounter Deputy County Counsel, Marge Benson. And just when I thought things couldn't get any worse, Sabre thought.

"You okay?" Michael, the bailiff, asked.

Sabre set her files on the table and stepped toward Mike. "Sometimes this job just isn't worth it," Sabre said. "And this is one of those days."

"So you heard about Dr. Heller?"

Sabre's eyes widened. "What about her?"

"Another hit and run."

"Oh, no. Is she...?"

"No, she's alive but in critical condition."

"What happened?"

"All I know is that she went back to her office last night and just as she was leaving, she was hit by a car. A woman who had been working late in a nearby office reported it."

"Was it intentional?"

"It looked like it, although the witness didn't actually see what happened. The witness was the only one left in the parking lot and she was on her way to her car. She heard the tires screeching and saw a car speeding away. She just thought it was someone showing off until she saw the doctor lying on the ground. She called 9-1-1 and they rushed Dr. Heller to the hospital. If she hadn't been there, the doctor may not have been found for hours."

Chapter 8

By 5:30 a.m. JP had already taken Louie, his one-year-old beagle pup, for a walk, started on his second cup of coffee, and was sorting through Sabre's files. His concern for Sabre's safety had escalated even more now that Dr. Heller had been attacked. The modus operandi was the same as the judge and that worried him. Although the police had no evidence to connect the two attacks, JP couldn't shake the idea that Sabre was in jeopardy. And since Dr. Heller remained unconscious, he couldn't obtain any information from her.

JP knew Dr. Heller had completed a psychological exam on Matt Durham. He wondered how many other times Sabre had used her services. He would go through the files to see which ones were tied to both Judge Mitchell and Dr. Heller. He read through his list: *Durham, Fisher, Martinez, King, Tran, Howard,* and *Wheeler.* After the name *Durham,* he wrote *Dr. H.* He picked up the Fisher file which contained only a petition, a two-page detention report, and a skimpy social study. No psychological reports had been written on either parent. Since the only child was an infant, there was nothing on her either. He set the Fisher file aside.

He picked up the Martinez file. Domestic violence always called for an evaluation. JP turned to the heading *Psychological Assessments* in the social study. Dr. Murphy was scheduled to evaluate the father next week. There was a report from Dr. Heller on the mother dated three days prior, and nothing was ordered for the children. He set the file aside. He would read the psych eval as soon as he finished his list.

The next file was King, which involved physical abuse by the stepfather, Isaiah Banks. An evaluation had been ordered on the mother, but there was no indication it had been completed or who was performing it. An evaluation had been scheduled for yesterday by Dr. Heller on Isaiah Banks. He called Sabre.

"Do you know that Isaiah Banks was scheduled for a psych eval with Dr. Heller yesterday?"

"No, I didn't realize that. Do you know if he went?"

"No, but I'll see what I can find out."

JP made a note to follow up. Then he went back to his stack of files. Howard, the shaken baby case, had reports for both parents, but neither was written by Dr. Heller. JP put a line through *Howard*. He went back and did the same for *Fisher*. He would concentrate on the cases that had a connection to both Judge Mitchell and Dr. Heller.

JP picked up the Tran file. Louie growled. JP laid it back down and walked to the sliding glass door. Louie yipped as he paced back and forth in front of the window. "What's the matter, boy?" JP asked. "Do you want out?"

Louie barked, louder this time.

JP opened the door and Louie bounced across the yard as several small birds took flight. JP closed the door and left Louie to play. He refilled his coffee cup and then returned to the table to look at the Tran file.

Dr. Heller was scheduled two days ago to evaluate the mother, Kim-Ly Tran, but a written assessment was not available yet. JP made another note to follow up to see if the report had been written.

The last file was Wheeler. After sifting through several files, JP found reports on both parents. Dr. Heller had evaluated the father a little over a year ago. JP placed the folder on top of the Martinez file to read the complete report later.

JP looked at his list. He still had five strong suspects. He had eliminated Fisher, the case with the volatile parents, and Howard, the shaken baby case. It was just as well, he thought. If he had to come too close to the perpetrator on the Howard case, he wasn't sure he could prevent his new leather Tony Lamas from stomping on someone's head. JP hated child abusers, and a tiny baby, no less. As far as he was concerned there wasn't a lower form of life on this earth. They were right up there with men who beat women.

A tall, striking woman walked into JP's dining room wearing his faded, black George Strait T-shirt. Her long, shapely legs protruded from the bottom of the shirt. "Got any more of that coffee?"

Concentrating so hard on his work, JP had almost forgotten about his houseguest. "You bet," he said. He stood up and walked to the kitchen, retrieved a mug from the cupboard, and filled it up. He picked up the sugar bowl and a spoon and set all three on the table. "Have a seat," he said, motioning to the chair situated directly across from where he had been seated.

"Thank you."

"I hope Louie didn't wake you with his barking at the birds."

"No, I was already awake."

JP watched as she placed three heaping teaspoons of sugar into her coffee. He cringed, wondering how someone could ruin a perfectly good cup of joe.

As if she could read his thoughts, she said, "I know it's not good for me, but I can't seem to break the habit. I love the taste of sweet coffee. At least I don't load it up with milk and chocolate and whatever else is the fashion these days."

"Whatever puts stars in your sky," JP said.

Robin smiled. Her long, dark hair lay softly on her shoulders. At forty-five she was still as beautiful as she had been at twenty when she won the Reeves County Beauty Pageant—in spite of her swollen lip and the yellow and purple marks that now surrounded her left eye. JP looked again at her shirt. Why had he given her that shirt to wear? That was the second time a woman in distress had worn his George Strait tee. He thought of Sabre for a moment.

JP had been shocked to see Robin when she appeared at his front door two nights ago. Her hair was disheveled, her lip swollen, she had several bandages, and her eye was black and blue. She was such a mess he almost didn't recognize her until she opened her mouth and said, "I had nowhere else to go."

He took her in and learned she had driven from Texas, stopping only to fuel her tank with gas and her brain with caffeine. She was exhausted, yet wired, and didn't want to talk about what happened so he didn't push her. After a few hours of catching up on family and friends, Robin cleaned up and went to bed. JP moved her car into his garage in case someone came looking for her.

Robin ran her finger along the rim of her coffee mug. She looked up at JP. "I'm glad we kept in touch all these years. I never realized when you told me that you would always be there if I needed you just how much I would. It's time I explained a few things." She stood up, picked up her mug, and walked to the sofa. "Come sit with me." JP followed, noticing the scars on her left leg as she glided across the floor.

Chapter 9

The Wheeler Case

Children: Holly (F) and Bradley (M), age 9 years (twins), four other children

Parents: Father—Willie Wheeler, Mother—Debra Wheeler

Issues: Physical Abuse, NeglectFacts: Dirty Home, drugs, alcohol, physical abuse, mental problems

"How's 'Whacky Willie' Wheeler this morning?" Sabre asked Bob, as they checked into Department Three.

"I think he's making my hair turn gray," Bob said.

"Your hair is already gray."

"See, I told you. It's from spending the past two years on this case with Willie that's done it."

Sabre laughed. "You know you love working with him."

"He does add color to my otherwise drab existence. You gotta love a guy who calls you SpongeBob SquarePants."

"Yeah, I saw that in the report. Maybe he really thinks you are. I wouldn't wear anything yellow around him if I were you."

"He was just yanking the social worker's chain, but she bought into it. Oh, and it's not just SpongeBob SquarePants. It's Attorney SpongeBob SquarePants. The guy is actually pretty lucid. He's just 'off the wall' strange. And he cries all the time. Whenever he starts talking about anything serious like his kids, he starts to cry. I don't know what to do with that. I like it better when he acts nuts."

THE ADVOCATE'S EX PARTE

They walked out of the courtroom into the hall where Willie waited for Bob. Willie approached and unintentionally blocked the door so no one could get inside. Bob put his left hand on his shoulder and maneuvered him across the floor as they spoke. Sabre stayed to Bob's right, as far from Willie's body odor as she could without being rude.

"Attorney Sabre Orin Brown, you need to get my kids home to me. They need me. Holly was so upset when I saw her yesterday. Yep. She keeps asking to come home."

Sabre looked at this tall, gangly man in his forties, whom she surmised hadn't bathed in weeks, her expression soft and caring. "Willie, I know it's hard for you, but you need to try not to cry when you go see your kids. It makes it harder for them. It especially upsets Holly. Your attorney is doing all he can for you, and you know I'm trying to do what's best for your children."

"I know you are, Attorney Sabre Orin Brown. Yep, I know you are."

"You can just call me Sabre if you'd like," she told him for the umpteenth time.

"I think that would be disrespectful." He turned to Bob. "Are they gonna send the kids back after the house is cleaned up?"

"Not this time, Willie. There are a few more problems we have to deal with. Is someone helping clean the house?"

"Yep. The social worker, Miss Heather What's-Her-Name, said...."

"Heather Staples."

"Yep. That's it. Do you suppose she's related to the Staples store?"

"I doubt it, Willie. Focus. What did she say?"

"She said she'd send someone after we got the car engine out of the living room and the trash bags out of the kitchen."

Sabre was tempted to ask why there was a car engine in his living room, but decided it wouldn't serve any purpose. Instead she asked about his wife. "Did Debra go into rehab?"

"Yep. She went there yesterday and I think she maybe took the poltergeist with her 'cause I haven't seen him since she left."

"How is the resident ghost doing, Willie?"

"I was hopin' he'd help me rebuild my engine, but I don't think he knows nothin' 'bout cars."

Bob encouraged his delusion. "Maybe he lived when there weren't any cars."

Willie nodded his head a couple of times, taking his time to respond as if in deep thought. "Yep. That would explain why he dresses so funny."

"And how's that, Willie?" Bob asked.

"He most always has a white shirt with a high collar and one of them scarves around his neck. I think they call them ascots or something. It's bright blue with some kind of red pattern on it. Yep. And a black cape that comes to his waist. Not like a superman cape or nothin'. It's like a coat but with no armholes." Bob started to say something, but Willie continued. "Oh, and leather shoes with buckles. Yep, yep. And a round hat."

Willie paused. Bob waited a second and then with a straight face he said, "Does he wear the same thing all the time?"

"Sometimes he don't wear no cape."

"No cape."

"Yep. When it's hot, he don't wear no cape."

"That makes sense," Bob said.

Sabre turned away so Willie couldn't see her smile. She wondered just how much of this he believed and how much he made up. Bob was convinced that he did a lot of it to make people think he was crazy. Sabre wasn't sure. And there were so many things he did that were harmless, but the environment he provided for his children was not healthy and often not safe. And yet, the children seemed to function so much better when they were together and with their parents.

All of the children were presently at Polinsky Receiving Home, where they would stay until the paternal aunt returned from her father-in-law's funeral in Arkansas. They usually did okay at Polinsky as long as they had plenty of family contact. Sabre thought it was because they knew it was temporary. When they went to foster care they became very despondent. Holly, in particular, would suffer. She became very depressed, her grades dropped, and she would stop talking to anyone except her brother, Bradley, who reacted similarly but not to the same extreme.

The Wheeler case came into the system two years ago when a teacher made a home visit and discovered the dirty home. The children were placed with the mother's sister while services were provided to get the house cleaned and to train the parents on how to keep it clean and safe. The mental instability of the parents, which was exacerbated by the drugs and alcohol, soon came to light. The placement with the maternal aunt fell apart and the children went to foster care where they did not manage well, partly because they were all split up. After some time the paternal aunt came forward and took the children until they were returned to the parents approximately six months ago.

Unfortunately, the parents couldn't keep it together. The mother started using drugs again, the condition of the house deteriorated, and the father became more delusional. Sabre hated this case because she wasn't sure what to do. She had tried so hard to keep this family together because that's what appeared to be best for the children. Six months ago the therapists all agreed that the children were better off with their parents than without them, but now they were back in court again. Something had to change. The system was failing.

"Can anyone join this party?" Debra Wheeler's attorney, Regina Collicott, said as she approached.

"Sure," Bob said. "We were just discussing the Wheeler ghost."

"Oh, is Parnhart back?"

"His name is Parnhart?" Sabre asked.

"Parnhart. Yep. That's his name," Willie said.

"And how do you know that?" Sabre asked.

Bob put his hand on Willie's shoulder. "Willie, before you answer that, let's you and I have a little chat."

"Whatever you say, Attorney SpongeBob SquarePants."

"Before you leave, what are you doing with this case?" Sabre asked. "Will there be a trial set?"

Bob lowered his head and peered at Sabre over his glasses. "Well of course, Ms. Brown. My client wants his day in court." Bob led Willie down the hallway to a more secluded spot. The last thing Sabre heard him say was, "And maybe you should stop calling me that. At least while we're at court."

Chapter 10

Tyson Doyle Cooper

Tyson rose early, in spite of the previous day's long drive from Texas to San Diego and his restless sleep. Yesterday he had consumed too many Monster Energy drinks while driving and drank a six-pack of beer before he crashed last night. The bed wasn't all that comfortable, either. He wondered if he should've stayed at a nicer hotel, but he didn't know how long this journey would take and he didn't want the cash to run out. Besides, he could keep a lower profile here. No one paid any attention to him.

He made a pot of coffee and then spent about an hour on the computer Googling "John Phillip Torn" and "Sabre Orin Brown." He found little about JP but quite a bit about the attorney, most of which centered around the case that was the subject of the newspaper clipping he found in Robin's things.

He also found some addresses, but he couldn't be sure they were current so he decided to call Blake. "Can you verify a couple of addresses for me?"

"Sure, cuz."

Tyson gave him the names and information he had obtained. Ten minutes later Blake called back confirming JP's address, Sabre's office address, and a home address for Sabre Brown. He jotted them down and stuck the paper in his pocket. He picked up his holster and gun, put the holster on his belt, and covered it with a light windbreaker.

Tyson drove first to the address for JP Torn. It led him to a small strip mall. He pulled into a parking spot and double checked the address he had written down. The address he'd put in his GPS was the same as the one he had found online and Blake had confirmed. He drove his car past several businesses until he came to the exact address. Sitting between an Asian supermarket and a Home Town Buffet was a strip of buildings which included a Postal Annex. This time he parked a couple doors down and exited his car.

"Damn!" Tyson said on the phone to Blake. "Torn's address is a mailbox place. Make a few calls and find out if the attorney's office address is correct. Anything else you can find out about either of them would be helpful, too. There's a coffee shop here. I'm going to wait for your call before I start running around again."

Tyson took his laptop and walked into the coffee shop. He ordered a cup of coffee and took a seat inside where he could take advantage of the WiFi. He couldn't find a website for Torn or for Sabre Brown. With a little digging around, however, he found Sabre's photo in *martindale.com*. She looked to be around thirty, assuming the photo wasn't twenty years old, was quite attractive, and had a 4.9 peer rating, whatever that meant. JP proved to be another matter. He couldn't find anything of any consequence on him, no social media connections, nothing.

After about fifteen minutes, Blake called back. "Sabre's office address is correct. She's not there, though; she's at juvenile court. The address for the courthouse is 2851 Meadow Lark Drive in San Diego. The receptionist said she'd be back this afternoon after four if we wanted an appointment."

"Good work. And text me the picture on JP's driver's license. I can't find anything with his photo on it."

"Do you think Robin's with that JP fella?"

"He's her ex, and she told me once that he was always 'there for her,' whatever the hell that means. I'm sure that's where she is."

"What are you going to do when you find him?"

"I'm going to show him he can't mess with Tyson Doyle Cooper."

"Do you think Robin will come home with you?" Blake said, lowering his voice on the last few words as if he wished he hadn't asked.

"Of course. She's my wife." Tyson's nefarious tone made Blake pause. Tyson quickly added, "She'll come home—one way or the other."

Within a few minutes Tyson received the text with a photo of JP. He packed up his laptop and drove to juvenile court. He parked where he could see the front door and waited.

Tyson watched as people came and went from the court-house—men and women in suits, teenagers who looked like they should be locked up, and families with too many kids and not enough money. Many would come out for a cigarette break or just to smell the air. Occasionally an attorney came out with a disgruntled client and Tyson could hear them yelling at one another. Others would stand around near the door until a bailiff stepped out and called them for their hearing.

Well over an hour had passed before he saw Sabre exit the building with a man dressed in a suit, whom he assumed was another attorney. The man looked a little older than her and had started to gray. He looked at the photo of JP on his phone. That was definitely not him. They walked across the parking lot and got into a black Mercedes parked just a few cars away from his, Sabre on the passenger side and the man behind the wheel. Tyson waited until they left their parking spot and then followed them.

They made a left out of the parking lot, then a right, another right, and up over the freeway. He stayed back far enough so he wouldn't be spotted. He followed the car when it turned into a little strip mall. They parked, and Tyson drove past them and circled around the lot. He watched them enter a restaurant with a sign that read Pho Pasteur.

Tyson didn't wait there. He drove to a fast food place, picked up some food, and went back to his room to rest. He had a few hours before Sabre would return to her office.

Chapter 11

JP and Robin sat on JP's sofa in silence for several minutes before she finally spoke, still gazing at the floor and avoiding JP's eyes. "I met Tyson Doyle Cooper, that's how he introduced himself, at a church picnic about four years ago. He went there with my cousin Sandy and some other friends. He kept flirting with me and when I called him on it he told me he wasn't really with Sandy, that they were just friends. I found out later that was not entirely true. They had been friends, but this was their first—and what turned out to be their last—date. He started calling me, sending me flowers, and leaving me little notes on my car until he wore me down. I talked to Sandy before I ever accepted a date with him. She was over him by then and gave me her blessing."

JP reached for his coffee cup on the table, took a drink, and waited for her to continue. She sat next to him, her leg less than an inch from his.

"Ty was very good to me and he was incredibly charming. After about two months of a whirlwind romance, he pro-posed."

"And you accepted." JP said, glancing at the ring on her left hand.

Robin held her coffee mug tightly in her hand. She looked down at the mug as if she were talking to it. "I thought I was in love. I *was* in love." She looked back up at JP. "He wanted babies and my biological clock was ticking. Three weeks later

I became Mrs. Tyson Cooper. The first month everything was great. We spent all of our spare time together. He insisted I quit my job, which I was happy to do. We tried to get pregnant, but it didn't take. Then I started receiving phone calls from other women asking for him and lots of hang-ups. I figured it was just old girlfriends since I'd known him less than six months, but when I mentioned it to him, he became very angry. Somehow he turned the argument back on me and the fact that I hadn't gotten pregnant yet. And soon we were having 'angry' sex. It was like he was a different man. I'd try to talk to him afterwards, but he'd just turn over and fall asleep."

JP looked at this woman he had once loved. She had been so young and so beautiful. She was still striking, but her innocence was gone. As JP listened, anger at Tyson Cooper welled up inside him, but he forced himself to not let it show.

"One night he started drinking before he came home, but he wasn't drunk yet when he arrived. I could tell he was upset. When I tried to talk to him he just ignored me. He went to the refrigerator, took out a six-pack of Shiner Bock—that's what he always drank when he drank beer—and went into his study. I fixed dinner and then went to tell him it was ready. When I opened the door he flung a nearly full bottle of beer at me. It hit my shoulder, splattered beer all over me, and then smashed when it hit the tile floor. I stood there for a second in shock. He stood up and walked toward me. I think I expected him to apologize. I figured he was angry about something else and didn't realize I had entered the room."

"But he didn't apologize, did he?"

"No. He said, 'I've had a rough day. Clean it up.' Then he walked out the door and left the house. He stayed out all night. He had flowers delivered to me the next day with a note that read, *I love you more than all the stars over Texas.* When he came home he acted like nothing had happened. I tried to talk to him. He apologized for throwing the bottle, but he didn't want any further discussion. After that he reverted to his usual charming self."

"How long did that last?" JP asked.

"Not long. A couple of weeks later he came home very late and very drunk. He smelled of cheap perfume. He wanted to make love to me and when I told him no, he got belligerent. He said I was his wife and we would do it when *he* 'damn well pleased.' I tried to fight him off but he held me down. The more I fought, the more sexually excited he seemed to get." Robin paused and her face tightened. She swallowed and tried to compose herself. She looked directly at JP, holding his gaze. "I'm sure you don't need to hear all this."

JP placed his hand on her knee. "Robin, if I'm going to help you, I need to know exactly what happened."

She took a deep breath and with her eyes turned down toward the floor she continued, speaking rapidly as if she had to get it all out before she changed her mind. "I struggled to break loose from him until he backhanded me across the face. The blow stunned me and I just collapsed and decided to let him have me. But then he totally deflated and he became angrier. I think it was because I stopped fighting him. I was so frightened. My head pounded. I didn't know what to do, so finally I struggled just enough so he could keep his erection, the whole time praying that I wasn't getting pregnant. I just wanted it all over with." She took another deep breath and sighed.

"And did you get pregnant?"

"No. I guess God heard my prayers."

JP tried to contain his anger for this despicable man. Robin didn't deserve that. No woman deserved that. "What did you do then?"

"After he fell asleep I wanted to sneak out, but I was afraid he would wake up and stop me. The next morning when he got up, he acted like nothing had happened."

"No apology or anything?"

"No, and I was afraid to bring it up. When he left for work I packed a few things and I went to my mother's. Ty showed up before the sun went down. He brought me chocolates, apologized, blamed it on the booze, and promised he would never do it again. I told him I needed a few days to think things over."

"And he let you?"

"Reluctantly. He started courting me all over again. Every day I received flowers and phone calls from him. He professed his undying love to me and promised he wouldn't ever drink again. I went to the doctor and got on birth control. I hadn't decided if I was going back or not, but one thing I knew for sure....I didn't want to get pregnant."

"And then you went back?"

"Not until about two weeks later. He had been so sweet and my mother kept encouraging me to save my marriage. So, I went home. All was good for nearly another month. I still received some strange phone calls occasionally, but he always explained them and he totally abstained from alcohol. Then one Saturday I went shopping and when I returned he was sitting at the table with a bottle of whiskey and my birth control pills. He grabbed my arm before I could set the bag of groceries down. The groceries hit the floor and a jar of pickles broke and splattered across the floor. I tried to pull away, but I slipped in the pickle juice and fell. I landed on a piece of broken glass and my leg started bleeding." She gulped.

JP could see how Robin struggled to tell her story and he felt his face redden with anger. He placed a reassuring hand on hers, both of which were still holding the coffee mug tightly. She let go of her mug with her right hand and placed it in his other hand.

She continued. "He grabbed my arm and pulled me across the floor over the broken jar; the chunks of glass ripped my leg in several places. Then he yanked me to my feet, carried me to the bedroom, and threw me on the bed. He forced himself on me, all the time yelling at me, calling me a whore and screaming about how God meant for us to have babies. I was scared and angry and my leg hurt. I could feel pieces of glass push deeper in my leg. Somehow I managed to get out of the blood-soaked bed and away from him. I ran out of the room, but he caught up with me, spun me around, and hit me in the face with his fist."

JP felt her grip on his hand tighten. Her other hand on the coffee mug trembled. He took the cup from her hand, set in on the coffee table, and then took her other hand in his. "Go on," he said.

"When I woke up my clothes were soaked in pickle juice and blood. Ty was gone and so were my keys and my cell phone. We lived too far from civilization to walk for help and I was still bleeding. There was also a lot of dried blood on my body and when I moved my leg a couple of cuts broke open. I was scared and confused and tried to find something to bandage my leg. All I could find were some small Band-Aids and there were some pretty big gashes on my thigh. I decided to clean up so I took a shower and washed my hair so I wouldn't smell like pickle juice. When I stepped out of the shower, Ty was back. He stood there in the bathroom with some medical supplies in his hand. His head hung low as if in shame and his voice was soft. He told me...no, he asked me... to please sit down and he would take care of me. He gently dabbed the blood away with a towel, put peroxide on the wounds, and applied some butterfly bandages holding the gaps together. Then he wrapped gauze around the two larger cuts and applied smaller bandages to the others."

Robin finally looked directly at JP for just a second and then she turned her face away. JP wondered if she saw the contempt for Tyson in his eyes. She continued. "He kept my cell phone and my keys and pretty much locked the rest of the world out. I started to realize then and there that he had already been isolating me from my family and friends for some time. My mother called on his phone when she couldn't reach me on mine. He told her my phone was acting up and we were waiting on the phone company to fix it. After that, most of the time when she called he would tell her I wasn't home. On a rare occasion he'd give me the phone to talk to her, but he always stayed near me. I didn't want to scare my mother, so I was very careful what I said. A couple of times I told her I was sick, but then I was afraid that she was worrying about my health. I was more worried for her than me."

"So how long did that go on?" JP asked.

"For several months. Then one day he took me to see my mother. I think he was worried that she might start getting suspicious. We didn't stay long and I tried to act as normal as possible. There hadn't been any more physical confrontations, mostly because I did whatever he wanted and he hadn't been drinking. By then I hated having sex with him because I felt like a prisoner and I was so afraid I would get pregnant. Don't get me wrong. I really wanted to have a baby, just not *his* baby."

JP saw a flash of pain cross Robin's face. Her eyebrows furrowed and her forehead wrinkled. Then she took a deep breath. He waited.

"One night he came home about midnight. He was so drunk I don't know how he drove. He was angry because I didn't wait up for him and he just started slapping me. I didn't fight back. I never knew what to do because sometimes it made him angrier if I fought and other times it seemed to be worse if I didn't. This time he slapped me harder each time and then he took off his belt and hit me with the buckle. He threw me down on the kitchen table and tore my clothes off. I tried to escape, but I couldn't. He forced himself on top of me, raped me, and then passed out. I had to struggle to get out from under him, and he fell off the table when I did. The fall didn't even wake him up. That's when I decided it was my chance to escape. I dug his keys out of his pants. The key to my car wasn't on his keychain. So I snatched his cell phone off the counter where he had laid it, threw on some clothes, and jumped in his car and took off."

"Is that his car in the garage?"

"No, I went to my cousin Sandy's house. You remember her, right? She lived on Machado near the park."

"Of course. I remember how much she loved guns. Was a darn good shot, too, if I remember correctly. She always wanted to be a cop. Did she ever do it?"

"No. She became a nurse, worked at it for a while, and then married a cattle rancher," Robin said. "I stayed at Sandy's for one night. I knew Ty would want his SUV back and I wanted my car, so Sandy got a friend of hers to make an exchange. When they were kids, Little Joe was pretty small and he and Tyson would get into fights. Tyson always won. But then Little Joe grew up and one day he nearly killed Ty." Robin paused. "Besides, I think Ty was trying to get me back and thought he better act the nice guy. Anyway, as soon as I had my own car I left there and went to a shelter. I knew he'd find me if I stayed with her."

"Is that when you came here?"

"No, he found me at the shelter about a week later. I was taking the trash out back and he grabbed me. He covered my mouth, dragged me to his truck, and pushed me in on the driver's side. I screamed and he punched me in the face with his fist. I reached for the passenger door handle, but he had a large duffle bag shoved against the door. I don't know what was in it, but it was heavy. I tried to push it off the seat, but I couldn't. I tried reaching around it, but I couldn't get to the door handle. Then I saw a rope running from the grab handle above the window down to the door. He must have tied the door shut. He drove off with me, but my car stayed behind. The shelter called Sandy because that's who I had for an emergency contact. She came and picked up the car and took it to her house.

"That night the beating Ty gave me was the worst yet. He was livid because he missed the first day of hunting season and he blamed me for it. Early the next morning he packed up his gear and told me I had better be there when he returned. Sandy sent her friend to check on me. He waited until Ty left and then he drove up to the house. The door was locked so he rang the bell. I looked out the window and saw him. I tried to get the window up, but it wouldn't budge. I was in pretty bad shape so it took me a while to stumble downstairs and I feared he'd leave before I got there, but he didn't. He walked around the house trying to find a window to climb in. I expect he would've broken one if I hadn't arrived when I did."

"Where did you go?"

"We went to Sandy's."

"Did you call the police?"

A slight sarcastic laugh came from Robin's throat. "It's a small town and the local law enforcement consists of three people: Ty's cousin, Blake Cooper, who had gone hunting with him; his best friend, Jimmy Porter; and his father, Big Jim Porter."

"So, did you tell them?"

"No, when we found out Blake had gone hunting with Ty, we decided they would just alert him and I'd have less time to escape. Sandy cleaned me up and bandaged my wounds. I waited until dark and then left and came here."

"Do you think he'll keep looking for you?"

"He told me there was nowhere I could hide from him." She looked up at JP, her wet eyes filled with fear. "He knows my last name used to be Torn and I know I've mentioned you to him before. For that matter he could easily find out everything about you. He has lots of resources. He could get your address and come here."

"First of all, he has no reason to believe you would come to me. Second, he wouldn't be able to track me to this house because I've never used this address on anything. I use a postal box address on everything, even my driver's license."

"Is that legal?"

"No, but it's a lot safer in my line of work." JP put his arm around her shoulder and pulled her close. "You're safe here."

Chapter 12

The Tran Case
  Child: Emma, age 18 mos. (F)
  Parents: Father—unknown, Mother—Kim-Ly Tran
  Issues: Neglect
  Facts: Mother left eighteen-month-old girl in locked room and went to work. Apartment complex caught on fire.

Sabre had already gone for an early morning run, showered, and left the house for her usual Saturday "home visits" with her minor clients. Since her route took her near Scripps Hospital, she decided to stop and check on Dr. Heller. They were not friends, but they had a good professional relationship, one based on mutual respect. Dr. Heller was always the first on Sabre's list when she needed a psychological evaluation because she trusted her tolerant, yet honest assessment. She could not be bought, but she was certainly more open-minded in her views than many of the doctors used by the prosecutors.

Sabre stood in the hospital room looking at the unconscious Dr. Heller. What kind of animal would do this? She wondered if JP was right, that there might be a connection between Judge Mitchell's death and the attack on the doctor. She held her hand and spoke softly. "It's going to be alright, Carolina. You hang in there." She didn't know what else to say or if it mattered. She touched her lightly on the shoulder and left.

Just outside the door she encountered a tall doctor with disheveled hair and bags under his eyes who was just about to enter Heller's room. "Good morning, Doctor." She put out her hand to shake his. "I'm Sabre Brown, a friend of Dr. Heller's."

He shook her hand. "Dr. Brister," he said.

"You look tired. Are you just starting your shift?"

"It's been a long night," he said. "Were you here to see Dr. Heller?"

"Yes, I was just in there. Has there been any change in her condition?"

"Her vitals are a little better this morning. That's about all I can tell you at this point."

"Thank you," Sabre said and continued down the hallway and out to her car.

~~~

After stopping at Polinsky Receiving Home to see a newly appointed six-year-old boy, Sabre continued on to a group home in Mira Mesa to see a teenage girl who had just arrived there. She visited with the girl, and then continued on her way to see a maternal aunt home where a tox baby had been placed. Finally, she arrived at the foster home of Mr. and Mrs. Nguyen. Emma Tran, the eighteen-month-old girl on the Tran case was recently detained in this home. Sabre introduced herself to both foster parents and was invited in and offered tea, which she politely refused.

"Emma should be waking up from her nap any time now," Mrs. Nguyen said.

"That's fine because I have a few questions for you." Sabre sat down on the chair that Mrs. Nguyen offered her. Mr.

Nguyen left the room. "Have you met the Court Appointed Special Advocate on this case yet?"

"No, the social worker told me about her. Apparently, her name is Mae Chu. I've been waiting for her call, but so far I haven't heard from her."

"What about the mother, Kim-Ly, have you met her yet?"

"Yes, she had a visit yesterday. She's so young. She's still a child herself and trying to raise a baby."

"I know. And we haven't been able to find any family here. Has she said anything to you about them?"

"No. She didn't talk about her life much."

"How was she with Emma?"

"She held her and played with her appropriately. She seems to really love her daughter, but...." Mrs. Nguyen paused.

"But?"

"She asked me what happens when children are adopted, if the parents ever get to see them again."

"Did you get the impression she was considering giving her up?"

"I couldn't tell for sure. She looked very sad when she asked. She may have just thought she didn't have a chance of getting her back."

"What did you tell her?"

"I told her to talk to the social worker. She could answer her questions better than I could. And I told her to be sure to stay in her programs. She was real concerned about the baby being safe, which seemed a little odd considering she left the baby home alone. Maybe it's that she's so young."

"That's the second time you mentioned how young Kim-Ly is. She says she's twenty-one and she has a birth certificate that verifies it." Sabre noticed the foster mother shaking her head in disagreement. "But you don't think so, do you?"

"That girl is no more than sixteen at best."

Mr. Nguyen stepped into the living room carrying a beautiful, dark-haired, dainty little girl with hazel-colored, almond-shaped eyes. Sabre stood up and stepped closer to her. "Hello, Emma," she said. Emma didn't respond. She rubbed her eye with a tiny fist.

"She's still sleepy," Mr. Nguyen said. He continued to hold her for a few minutes and then he set her down on the floor. The child appeared very steady on her feet, but she didn't take any steps. He retrieved a book about baby animals and handed it to her. She took the book, plopped down where she had been standing, and slowly flipped the pages, spending close to a minute on each page and carefully studying the pictures before she went to the next one.

"Does she talk at all?" Sabre asked.

"She has a decent size vocabulary, mostly Vietnamese, but she's a very shy little girl," Mrs. Nguyen said, "so she doesn't express herself often. We speak to her frequently in English."

"I've only seen her once before at Polinsky and she seemed to be developmentally appropriate for her age. What do you think?"

"She seems quite normal. She walks quite well. In fact, she's very quick, but quiet. She covers a lot of ground so I sometimes need to be careful. I'll turn around and there she is, right under foot."

Emma stood up while holding her book and toddled over to Mrs. Nguyen. She handed her the book and said softly, but very distinctly, "Kit-ty."

Mrs. Nguyen opened the book to the page with a kitten. "Yes, kitty. Very good, Emma." Mrs. Nguyen looked up at Sabre. "The kitten is her favorite. Do you know if they had a cat?"

"Not that I'm aware of, but she may have."

"And there is no father in the picture?" the foster mother asked.

Sabre shook her head.

"That's a shame. Emma deserves two parents. I asked Kim-Ly about the father. She told me she didn't know his name, that she'd had a one-night stand, but she wasn't very convincing. I think she does know and doesn't want to tell for some reason."

"Perhaps," Sabre said. Even if she knew something more, which she didn't, it wasn't her place to share it with the foster mother. Kim-Ly told that same story to the social worker when questioned. It was not unusual to see young girls in the system with babies and no knowledge of who had fathered them. She had hoped that Kim-Ly had opened up to Dr. Heller in her psychological evaluation, but since Heller hadn't submitted the report, she wasn't certain it had even been written. Neither the report nor the usual tape recording of the session had been found in Dr. Heller's office. There was no way to tell what, if anything, might be missing without the doctor to verify it. Sabre decided to wait a few more days and then ask the court to order another evaluation on Kim-Ly Tran if there was no change in the doctor's condition.

Sabre spent a little more time with Emma and then went to four more home visits. Afterwards, she stopped at the hospital to check on Dr. Carolina Heller, but there had been no change.

Chapter 13

The Durham Case
  Child: Matt Durham, Defendant
  Type: Delinquency case
  Charges: Two counts of First Degree Murder
  Victims: Hannah Rawlins & Mason Usher
  Facts: Double homicide. Two teenagers bludgeoned to death
with a baseball bat.

JP left Robin at home with her car secure within the garage. She assured him she wouldn't go outside the house. Normally, Louie would go with JP on Saturday morning when he went out. They'd stop at Bob's house and Louie would play with Bob's dog, Alfie, while Bob and JP drank coffee and visited. But today JP had a full schedule and a late start so he skipped his visit with Bob and left Louie behind to keep Robin company.

JP walked onto the high school campus and headed toward the gym where the coaches had their offices. The school was quiet except for a few boys with baseball gloves showing up for practice. JP wound his way past the track and across the outdoor basketball courts and into the gym. He encountered a tall, African-American student, with a closely clipped mustache and beard walking out of the building. JP remembered trying to grow anything that resembled facial hair in high school, but to no avail.

"Could you direct me to Coach Arviso's office?" JP asked.

He pointed to his right. "Straight ahead to the end of the hallway, turn left, and it's the second door on the right."

"Thanks," JP said and walked to the office. The door was open. A short, muscular man in his early fifties sat behind the desk in the tiny office. Files and papers were stacked on the file cabinet, the bookcase, the desk, and one stuffed chair.

The man looked up when JP approached. "Come on in. You must be the PI."

JP held out his hand. "That's right. JP Torn."

"Gilbert Arviso. Have a seat," the coach said, pointing to the only empty chair in the room. "What can I do for you?"

"As you know, I'm here about Matt Durham. What can you tell me about him?"

"He's a good ball player. Not a star, but consistent. Never missed practice. Always on time. His grades were never an issue. He wasn't one of the 'popular' guys, especially with the girls, but he seemed to get along with everyone for the most part."

"Did Matt ever fight or argue with anyone?"

The coach shook his head. "I've thought about that a lot since his arrest. He usually got along well with his teammates. There was one incident when he got in a shoving match with another student, a kid named Darren Flynn, but to tell you the truth I don't think Matt started it. It didn't really amount to much, more of a squabble than a fight. It was during a game and the other players stopped it before it was out of hand. Matt came up to bat shortly after that and he took all his aggression out on the ball. It was bottom of the ninth, one out with a runner on second. We could usually count on Matt for a base hit and we expected him to move the runner to third and then Darren would come in as a designated hitter and hit the winning run. But instead, Matt hit a home run and won the game for us."

"I suppose that didn't make Darren too happy."

"I expect he was glad they won, but yeah, it meant he didn't get to hit and be the hero. Darren is a hot head and he demonstrated it that night. He slammed his bat against the fence and he didn't go out when the teams shook hands after the game."

JP turned and glanced toward the open door, distracted by the chatter of teenage boys.

"Sorry about that. The boys are here for practice."

JP stood up and started to close the door. "Do you mind?" he asked.

"Not at all."

JP sat down again. "When did the incident at the game take place?" JP asked.

"About a month ago."

"So, just a few weeks before the murder?"

"Yeah, a week or two, maybe."

JP glanced at his notes. "Matt says his bat disappeared at one of the games. Do you know anything about that?"

"Not that I recall. Why?" The coach wrinkled his brow. "Does Matt claim the bat used in the murders was stolen?"

"Yes," JP said, nodding his head. "He said to ask you, that he came to you and told you it was missing."

"I don't recall him coming to me, but that doesn't mean he didn't. But if he did, I'm sure I had him fill out a 'Missing Equipment' form." Coach Arviso reached down and opened a file drawer on his desk. He pulled out a folder, opened it up, and shuffled through the papers. About three forms down, he stopped and removed a completed form with Matt Durham's name on it. "Here it is." He handed the form to JP. "We always have the players fill these out. It saves a lot of hassle if something shows up a few months later."

JP looked the form over and noted the date. It was approximately one month ago. He pointed out the date to the coach. "Do you happen to know if that was the same game that Matt and Darren had the misunderstanding?"

"I don't know." The coach frowned as if he were thinking. He picked up a schedule off his desk. "Let me see....The game Matt hit the home run in was against Poway. That would've been on...yes, that was the same game. He must have filed it the next day. That's the day after the Poway game. That's right," the coach said, as if he were remembering the event. "It was Matt's last game."

"Where can I find this Darren, ah..." JP looked at his notes. "...Flynn?"

"He should be out there in the hallway."

"Do you mind if I take a few minutes of his practice time to talk to him?"

"No, not at all." Arviso picked up his clipboard as he stood. "I'll introduce you."

They walked out of the office and the coach raised his voice above the chattering crowd of the twenty or so boys standing around. Most of them leaned against the wall with their bags beside them. Some had just a glove in their hand; others carried bats. The coach looked up and down the hallway. "Where's Flynn?" he asked.

A tall, young African-American man came around the corner at the end of the hallway. "Yo, Coach," he said, as he walked toward them. He was big and muscular. JP thought his build would be better put to use on the football field than on a baseball diamond.

"Darren," the coach said, as he approached, "this investigator has a few questions for you." Coach Arviso made a gesture with his head toward his door. "You can use my office."

JP reached out his hand and shook the coach's. "Thank you," JP said.

"No problem. Let me know if you need anything else." The coach left and the players did the same, except for Darren.

JP entered the office and Darren followed. After closing the door, JP sat down behind the desk. "Have a seat," JP said, gesturing to the chair he had sat in earlier.

"You a cop?" Darren spit the word out.

"No, I'm a private investigator," JP said.

"So, I don't need to talk to you if I don't want to." This time he sounded cocky.

"No, you don't. But if you don't, I'll have to take what I know to the cops and then *they* will talk to you." JP watched as Darren's eyes closed slightly and his face tightened. JP hadn't meant to anger him and was frustrated at himself for the way the conversation was going. "Look, man, all I want is a few answers. You're not the one in trouble here."

Darren took a breath and said, "What do you want to know?"

"About a month ago you had an altercation with Matt Durham at a game. Do you remember that?"

"That murdering fool. I guess I'm not the one in trouble here," he said, emphasizing the word "guess." "That boy is crazy, beating those two to death."

"So, what happened at the Poway game?"

"We were in the dugout. Alex was up to bat, Adam was on deck, and Matt was in the hole. He would get all anxious before he came up to bat. I told him to calm down. I told him all he had to do was to get on base. I would do the rest. He looked at me and raised his eyebrow. Then he stepped in front of me and hit me with his shoulder as he went to leave the dugout. I shoved him back. He raised his bat and shook it at me. I dared him to bring it on, but a couple guys stepped between us. Matt went on deck and I stayed in the dugout until he went to bat."

"Then what happened?"

"Nothing. We won the game and that was it."

"You didn't have any further encounters with Matt after that?"

"No."

"Did you see him or talk to him after that?"

Darren thought for a moment. "I don't think so. I don't have any classes with him and we don't hang with the same people at school. We had one practice after that, but Matt wasn't there. Not long after that he was arrested." He shook his head. "That boy's crazy!"

"What has he done?"

Darren looked at him and scowled. "He beat two people to death with a baseball bat. That's just crazy, man."

"I thought maybe there was something else. Did you ever see any other behavior that was 'crazy,' as you say?"

"Isn't that enough?"

Chapter 14

The Durham Case
  Child: Matt Durham, Defendant
  Type: Delinquency case
  Charges: Two counts of First Degree Murder
  Victims: Hannah Rawlins & Mason Usher
  Facts: Double homicide. Two teenagers bludgeoned to death
with a baseball bat.

JP checked his watch. He had just about enough time to walk to the area in front of the school cafeteria where he was scheduled to meet with some students who had witnessed the confrontation between Matt and the victim, Hannah Rawlins. JP had spoken earlier to eight different students who were there that day. He'd determined that three of them hadn't seen enough to waste any more time questioning them. Of the remaining five students, two were unavailable today, so he had scheduled the others fifteen minutes apart.

When JP reached the area for the meeting, he checked his watch. He was two minutes late for the first appointment, but no one had shown up yet. He sat down on a picnic table and opened his file. He wondered about Darren Flynn. Could he have taken Matt's bat that day at the game? It was a stretch to think he stole the bat, killed two people with it, and set Matt up for the fall, all because of a little shoving and a home run that kept him out of the game. But then the whole thing was hard to believe, including Matt's possible motive for killing them. But maybe Darren's confrontational behavior was enough for Sabre to use to cast reasonable doubt.

JP hated to see criminals walk, especially for violent crimes. He enjoyed investigating and he was good at it, but it had been much easier when he was a cop. Back then he seldom came to know the perpetrators as people. They were just criminals, scumbags. He would investigate, arrests would be made, and offenders were prosecuted. But this job didn't allow that. He not only had to gather the facts, but also uncover a more humane side of the clients so their attorneys could try to present them in a more favorable light. He decided he had grown from the experience. It made him more sensitive to other people's circumstances. They often made mistakes that they regretted and sometimes they deserved a second chance. Heck, he had made plenty himself. But JP was convinced Durham hadn't made a "mistake." He was evil. JP cringed when he thought about the look in Durham's eyes when he viewed the photograph of the dead Hannah. Then JP shook it off. As Sabre would say, his job was to find out what happened, good or bad, and provide her with the facts. He was to be a "truth-seeker," as she called it, and that meant both the good and the bad. It was her job to represent the client. She often told him, "I don't have to like them; I just have to represent them." Unlike Sabre, JP had trouble separating the two.

"Mr. Torn?" a young female voice said.

JP looked up from his file. "Yes, you must be Lisa."

The thin girl in the green Victoria Secret sweat pants and two layered T-shirts nodded. Her hair was also layered, blonde on top and brown underneath.

"Have a seat."

She sat down and placed a large, leather Juicy Couture purse on the bench next to her, keeping her hand on her purse as if she had something valuable in it.

"Lisa, you seem a bit uncomfortable, but you don't have to be afraid. I just want to ask you a few questions."

She nodded.

"You know Matt Durham, correct?"

"Yes."

"And you knew Hannah Rawlins and Mason Usher?"

"Yes. Hannah was one of my best friends."

"I'm sorry for your loss," JP said. He hated this part. He never knew what to say. It was much easier questioning the scumbags, JP thought. "Is that how you know Matt? Because of Hannah?"

"The other way around. Hannah knew Matt because of me. I wish I had never met him." She looked down.

"You introduced them?"

"Not really. He was in my Spanish class. It was just before lunch period and Hannah would meet me there and we'd go to lunch together. Matt tried to become friends with me so he could hang around Hannah. They went out a few times, but she said he, like, made her uncomfortable." She ran her hand across her purse, almost petting it.

"Uncomfortable?" JP asked.

She nodded. "Yeah."

"How so?"

"I don't know. He just...like, wanted to be with her all the time. And he, like, told her he loved her on their second date. Stuff like that."

"Was she afraid of him?"

Lisa shook her head. "No, not really afraid. She just didn't like him that much, but he kept calling her anyway. She only went out with him because she wasn't into anyone else right then."

"Do you know anything about a wristband that either of them may have had?"

"Yeah. It was Hannah's. It was blue and it said, 'Love and Stuff' on it."

"And Hannah gave it to Matt?"

"She did, but only because he kept asking her for it. She finally just gave it to him to get him to stop asking."

"When was that?"

"I don't know, like the first time they hooked up, I think. I'm not sure, but they didn't go out that long." She paused, "Like, maybe a month."

"And then Hannah called it off?"

Lisa nodded her head. "She started, like, avoiding him at first. We started meeting for lunch in the cafeteria because she didn't want to come by my class. But he kept calling her and texting her. After a couple of days she came by my class and she told him she didn't want to hang with him anymore."

"Were you with her?"

"Uh huh."

"Do you remember what she said to him?"

"She said, 'You're a nice guy, but we're kinda over.' It was hard for her. She was nicer than I would've been."

"How did he take it?"

"He looked really sad at first and, like, confused. Then he asked to see her that night. She said no, and then his face turned really red and he looked angry. His free hand was in a fist and he was kind of shaking." Lisa stopped petting her purse and made a fist with her own hand demonstrating what he did. "But then he walked off really fast."

"Did his reaction scare Hannah?"

"No, not really. She felt bad for him. 'Nobody likes to get dumped,' she said."

"How long was it until the incident in the cafeteria?"

"Like, the next day."

"And you were there, right?"

"We were sitting across from each other when Matt walked up with his tray. He sat down next to Hannah before she even noticed he was there. I don't think he even saw me. He kept asking her to meet up with him that night, 'just to talk,' he said. She kept telling him no, but he, like, wouldn't let up. She finally told him she was with someone else. That's when he took the wristband off and he said, 'I suppose you want this back?' Hannah said, 'No, you can keep it.' She told me later that she didn't know what to say. She didn't really care that much about the wristband. She had others and she didn't want a fuss over it. Hannah looked at me and then she stood up. Matt tossed the wristband onto her tray."

"And then what happened?"

"He grabbed her arm and that scared her, but he let go pretty quickly and she walked away. I got up and followed her. We went and sat at another table about four or five tables away near some guys we knew. One of them was Mason—the other kid Matt killed."

JP thought about explaining to her that Matt may not have done it, but he decided he wouldn't be very convincing. In any case, he didn't think it would change her mind. "You said that Hannah told Matt she was 'with someone else.' Was that Mason?"

"No. She just told him that to get rid of him. She wasn't into anyone. Mason and her were just friends. They, like, lived only a few houses apart so they, like, hung out together a lot." Lisa reached down by her side and with the hem of her T-shirt she rubbed the buckle on her purse.

"New purse?" JP asked.

"Yeah," she said, picking it up and flashing it in front of JP. "Isn't it the coolest? I got it for my birthday."

"It's very nice," JP said. It looked heavy and glitzy to JP, but what did he know about purses. "Do you know any of Matt's friends?"

"Not really. I never saw him with anyone. I only knew him from my Spanish class and the few times I saw him with Hannah." She returned to polishing the buckle.

"And Hannah never mentioned anyone?"

Lisa looked up from her buckle-polishing task and said, "There was some friend of Matt's that Hannah said was real creepy. Once when we were driving on Convoy, she pointed to a garage and said that was where he worked."

"Matt or the creepy friend?"

"The creepy friend."

"Did she mention his name?"

"Hmm...it was a funny name. Like...oh yeah...Ralph."

"And the garage where he worked? Do you remember that?"

"I didn't pay any attention to the name of it, but it wasn't too far from Balboa."

JP thought there must be a dozen or so garages in that area. "Is there anything else you can remember about the garage or anything else Hannah may have said about Ralph?"

She shook her head. Then she said, "Only that he smoked and had lots of tattoos. But not, like, the cool kind...like, the creepy kind."

Chapter 15

The Martinez Case

   Children: Ray, age 2 (M), Falicia, age 5 (F), Jesse (Jesus), age 7 (M)

   Parents: Father—Gilberto Martinez, Mother—Juanita Martinez

   Issues: Abuse, Domestic Violence

   Facts: Mother beat the father with a lamp in front of the children. Alcohol abuse by both parents.

Sabre was driving to a home visit with the Martinez children when JP called. "Hey," he said.

Sabre wondered why he didn't add "kid" to his greeting. What was wrong? She felt a slightly uncomfortable feeling in her stomach. "Everything okay?" she asked.

"Everything's fine," he said. "Just wondering if you're going to see Matt Durham today?"

She chastised herself for being bothered for no reason. This is exactly why she didn't want to get involved with JP. She didn't want those feelings of insecurity. She didn't want to question his every behavior because she cared too much. She just wanted the comfort that came with the relationship they had shared for so long. "Yes, I'll see him this afternoon. Why?"

"I want you to follow up on a few things, or I can go see the little twerp myself, if you want."

"No, I think it might be better if I do it. I know you're not too happy working with this client and besides, you're supposed to be on vacation."

"I just needed a little break. I'm good. As for Durham, I can handle him."

Sabre wondered if his houseguest had left, but she didn't ask. "I know you can, but I need to go over some procedural points with him. Why don't we compare notes afterwards and if you need to do some follow-up, you can go another time, or we can go together."

"That's fine. Ask him about his stolen bat. The coach didn't remember Matt telling him that his bat was missing, but he had a form filled out to that effect from a game against Poway. He was in a scuffle in that same game with another player named Darren Flynn. Ask about him. And also ask about the wristband. Hannah's friend, Lisa, says Hannah gave it to him, but only because Matt insisted. See what he says about that."

"That's quite a laundry list. Maybe you should come with me."

"Actually, I expect he'll tell you more than he will me."

"Okay, anything else?"

"Just one more thing. Ask him about his creepy friend, Ralph."

"Creepy friend?" Sabre emphasized the word creepy.

"Lisa's words, not mine. He smokes, has tattoos, and works in a garage on Convoy near Balboa. I guess that makes him creepy in her eyes. And his first name is Ralph. That's about all I have on him. See if you can get a last name, phone number, home and work addresses, and any other information. It'll save a lot of time if you can get it directly from Matt."

"Will do. Anything else?"

"No. I interviewed two other students who witnessed the cafeteria incident that day. They all said about the same thing. Lisa was the only one who heard everything. The others only heard bits and pieces of what went down, but it all added up to the same story."

"Are you interviewing anyone else today?"

"I'm going to investigate Martinez and King. If I have time I'll follow up with Tran and Wheeler. Let me know when you get some information on Durham's friend, Ralph, and I'll call on him."

"Will do. I'm on my way right now to see the Martinez children. Thanks for your help today, JP. I'm sure you have other things to do." Again, Sabre wanted to ask if his guest was still here, but she refrained.

"I'm good," JP said. "You just be careful."

Sabre hung up, frustrated at herself for her anxiety about JP. She shook her head, took a deep breath, and concentrated on her task at hand. She ran through the facts in the Martinez case. Domestic violence was so traumatic on children. If the parents realized how much fear they instilled or what kind of scars they left when they fought in front of their children, she wondered if they would try harder. But Sabre knew it went much deeper. They couldn't control their tempers and their behavior was selfish.

~~~

The maternal aunt's large, yellow, ranch-style stucco home was situated on several acres surrounded by white fencing that seemed to go on for miles. A horse corral stood off to the right containing a paint horse and a palomino quarter horse. Sabre turned into the driveway and drove up to the house, passing the neatly groomed bushes that lined the drive. She heard a dog bark as she exited the car and walked to the front door, where she was greeted by a three-pound York-shire Terrier and an attractive Mexican-American woman.

"Fergie," the woman scolded, as she opened the door for Sabre. The little dog looked up and gave one last yip and then dashed across the floor. "She's harmless. Come on in."

"Thank you," Sabre said. "Nice to see you again." They had met at the detention hearing, and the children had been detained in her home immediately after the social worker did the home evaluation. Thirty-year-old Linda Rojas was an attractive woman with impeccable taste. Her large, blue eyes were accentuated with just the right amount of eye shadow and mascara. Her fair skin contrasted beautifully with her dark hair. She didn't resemble her sister, Juanita, at all. Linda was petite, whereas Juanita was big boned and her skin, eyes, and hair were all very dark. Linda could easily have passed for twenty-five while her younger sister Juanita looked closer to forty. Sabre gave credit to the cigarettes, drugs, and alcohol as the main culprits in Juanita's aging process. She already had two missing teeth, whereas Linda's were white and straight. The differences in the way children evolved from the same gene pool and the same households always fascinated Sabre.

"Come on in. Have a seat." Linda pointed to a sofa. "Can I get you something to drink?"

Sabre shook her head. "No, thanks. I'm good."

Linda sat down in a chair across from Sabre. "The children have been doing well. Falicia and Jesse have started school and they're mixing well."

"Have the parents been to see them?"

"I took the children to a park to meet with their mother yesterday. That's the first time they've seen her since they've been with me."

Fergie jumped up on the sofa next to Sabre and nuzzled her head up against Sabre's thigh. Sabre reached down and scratched behind her ear. "How did the visit go?"

"It went okay. I had to keep reminding Juanita to not talk about when they're coming home and to not whisper to the children. But they were happy to see her, especially Ray Ray. Falicia holds back a lot and stayed pretty close to my side. Jesse is very protective of Falicia. Juanita raised her voice a little once, but it wasn't in anger. She just spoke loudly, as she often does. But Jesse stepped in front of Falicia as if to block her from her mother. It was really sad to watch. He feels like he has to be her protector."

"What did Juanita do?" Sabre asked. Fergie rolled over and Sabre scratched her belly.

"She didn't even notice, but Falicia did. I was seated on a bench and Falicia practically crawled behind me. She seemed so afraid. I never realized just how bad it was before. I'm ashamed of myself for not noticing. I knew there were problems, but frankly, we didn't spend that much time around them as a family. On the holidays, there was always so much going on and the children were usually playing with their cousins, so it wasn't as evident. Sometimes I would take the children by themselves for an overnight, but Juanita didn't let me do that too often."

"And their father? Have you seen him?"

"Gilberto has been here four times already. And every night he calls and tells them goodnight. I've told him he's welcome any time as long as he hasn't been drinking. And so far, I haven't seen any indication of it."

"How are the children around him?"

"Falicia is totally comfortable."

"And Jesse?"

Linda hesitated. "I'm not sure what to say because it's just something I observed." She paused. Sabre waited for a second and Linda continued. "Jesse always gets right in his face when his father hugs him and I'm quite certain I actually saw him sniff. It was weird."

"Jesse or his father?"

"Jesse. I think he checks to see if he's been drinking."

"But Jesse doesn't say anything?"

"No, but you can see his body language change. He relaxes and smiles once he knows he hasn't been drinking. They both love being with their father. He plays with them, helps them with their homework, and he listens when they have concerns or they're excited about something. He's a great father," she sighed, "except for his alcohol abuse."

"Has Gilberto ever come here when he's been drinking?" Sabre asked. Then she added, "That you know of?"

"I don't think so. I haven't seen it and Jesse's alcohol barometer hasn't detected it...if that's what he's doing." Her sweet voice took on a more commanding tone. "But I told Gilberto when I took the kids that there wouldn't be any second chances. If he didn't follow the rules he'd have to have his visits elsewhere. His kids really need to see him, but they need a father, not someone else for them to take care of." She lowered her voice again. "So far he seems to be trying. I know he's not staying sober because he called once to say he couldn't make it and he sounded pretty wasted. But he had sense enough to not come by and to call and let us know. He wanted to tell the children goodnight and I let him, but I probably shouldn't have."

"Why? Did they notice?"

"I think they did. I'm sure Jesse did because he became sullen and his sleep was restless. That was one of the nights Falicia had a nightmare, but the call may or may not have triggered it. It's hard to tell with her."

"Has Falicia or Jesse talked to you about what was going on at home?"

"The social worker told me not to question them about it and I don't, but sometimes Falicia tells me things, usually after she's had a nightmare. Twice she woke up screaming. Then Jesse wakes up and comes running to check on her. The first time I couldn't get him to leave her room until she fell back to sleep. The second time he finally left, but only after I assured him I would stay with her. I just listened to what she had to say and tried to comfort her."

"Did she tell you what her dreams were about?"

"Both times her mother was beating her father. Juanita would knock Gilberto unconscious and the kids couldn't wake him up. I think Falicia's biggest fear is that her mother might kill her father. She's always relieved when she talks to him on the phone at night before she goes to sleep. I've tried to explain to her, without getting into detail, that they're not together, but I guess since she can't see that she doesn't quite get it."

"What an awful burden for her to carry."

"And Jesse, too. He checks with Falicia every morning when they leave for school to make sure she has her snack and her jacket, if it's cold. The teacher told me that he comes to the classroom on his recess and peeks in. He doesn't bother them. He looks around until he spots her and then he leaves."

"Has therapy been scheduled for the kids?"

"Yes, they start tomorrow."

"Good. May I see the children now?"

"Sure. I'll send Jesse in. I'll be in the back yard with Falicia and Ray Ray. You can have Jesse come out to me when you're finished."

Fergie jumped off the sofa and followed Linda. Within a few minutes a slender little seven-year-old boy with a fresh haircut walked into the room. He had fair skin and captivating blue eyes like those of his Aunt Linda.

"Hello, Jesse," Sabre said smiling at him. "How've you been?"

"Good," he said, without smiling back.

"Have a seat."

He sat down across from Sabre.

"This is a really nice house. Do you like staying here?"

He nodded his head. Sabre had seen Jesse on two previous occasions and both times he appeared cautious and defensive. She'd hoped being in a safer environment might loosen him up a little. She talked to him about school and the new friends he had made, and he seemed to relax somewhat. He told Sabre he liked his aunt and uncle and having his own room, and he enjoyed the visits with his father.

"I understand you saw your mother yesterday at the park."

Jesse nodded again.

"Can you tell me about the visit?"

He shrugged. "Mom came and saw us. She wants us to go home with her. She promised she wouldn't get mad anymore."

"And what do you think about that?"

"She always says that, but she can't help it. She gets mad and hits my dad with stuff."

"Does she ever hit you or the other children?"

"Just with her hand sometimes. She gets real mad at us, though, and she screams, and sometimes she comes at us with pans and stuff. And when she gets too mad at us, she hits dad more."

"You're saying, when your mom gets mad at one of you kids, she hits your dad?"

"Yeah. He tells her not to hit or yell at us like that and then she hits him."

Sabre continued her visit with Jesse, trying to reassure him things were going to get better and that he and his siblings were safe now. She knew she hadn't made much of a dent in the armor he wore; she only hoped time with his aunt and uncle would help to heal him. When they finished, Jesse left and Falicia appeared with Ray Ray in tow, followed by a playful Fergie nipping at Ray Ray's pants. The two younger siblings both had dark skin and brown eyes like their mother and father. Ray Ray, however, was built more like his mother. He had a bigger bone structure and was nearly as tall as his five-year-old sister. Falicia, short in stature and petite like her father and her aunt Linda, had large round eyes that were deep set with long, thick eyelashes. Sabre thought she was a beautiful child and that she would be a stunning woman someday.

Sabre re-introduced herself to the children. Falicia seemed to remember her. Ray Ray didn't care one way or the other. He romped around the room chasing Fergie. Falicia settled on the sofa next to Sabre and talked freely about herself and her family, much as a five-year-old is inclined to do. She smiled a lot and even laughed when Fergie got the upper hand on Ray Ray and started chasing him instead of the other way around.

Just as Sabre was about to complete their conversation Falicia said, "Did my mom kill someone?"

Sabre tried to conceal her surprise at her question, but she wasn't certain she did. "Why would you ask that, Falicia?"

Falicia shrugged her tiny shoulders. "I dunno."

Chapter 16

The King Case

   Children: Devon King, age 2 (M), Kordell King, age 12 (M)

   Parents: Father of Devon—Isaiah Banks, Father of Ko-rdell—Clay Walker, Mother—Brenda King

   Issues: Physical Abuse

   Facts: Isaiah Banks beat his stepson, Kordell, with a belt and his fist.

Sabre sat in her car for a few minutes as she set the GPS for directions to the home of the oldest boy on the King case. When completed she left, following the directions that Ursula, the voice on her GPS, issued.

Falicia's words resonated in her head. Why had she asked if her mother killed someone? Did she hear something that she wasn't supposed to have heard? Or was it because she saw her mother nearly beat her father to death on numerous occasions? She had tried to question Falicia further about it, but she had made no headway. Sabre chastised herself for her own reaction when Falicia asked the question. The poor little girl was frightened and she probably added to it. *I should have handled it better.*

Sabre pulled up to the address she had listed for Kordell King's paternal grandmother just off Euclid Avenue. It was a small house that was surrounded by a chain link fence and had a yard that consisted mostly of weeds. A car sat in the driveway with two flat tires. An old bike leaned against the side of the house. Before getting out of her car, Sabre looked at her file and read her notes.

Physical abuse. Two children, both boys: Devon, aged two, and Kordell, aged twelve. Kordell's stepfather, Isaiah Banks, beat him with a belt less than two months after his release from prison for probation violation on an earlier assault charge.

Sabre didn't like that the boys had to be separated, but Kordell was living with his paternal grandmother and she wasn't yet certified to take in a non-relative child. The social worker was working on that, but Isaiah, Devon's father, was fighting the placement. It appeared the only way these brothers would be together was if the mother were able to get them back. Unfortunately, the mother was so determined to have her man that she had lost sight of what it was doing to her children. This frustrated Sabre. She felt sorry for women in this position because she knew it wasn't easy, but she felt worse for the children. They were the ones who suffered the most.

The street was quiet and almost eerie, Sabre thought, as she exited her car and walked across the sidewalk to the fence. None of the neighbors were outside their houses and only one car had passed down the street since she had arrived. The gate, although unlocked, stuck and Sabre had to lift it and push hard with her body to open it. It squeaked as she pushed it forward, and she hesitated before stepping inside in case there was a watchdog around. When none came forward she closed the gate behind her and walked the eight or ten steps toward the house. A single stair lead to the front door. She stepped up on it and rang the doorbell.

A heavyset, African-American woman opened the door. After Sabre introduced herself, the woman smiled and said, "I'm Mrs. Walker, Kordell's grandmother. Please come in."

Sabre followed the woman inside.

"Have a seat," Mrs. Walker said and motioned toward the sofa in front of the window. "I'll get Kordell."

"I have a couple of questions for you first, if you don't mind." Sabre sat down next to an end table with several framed photos, her back to the window.

"Sure," the grandmother said and took a seat in a chair opposite Sabre.

"How has Kordell been doing since he came here?"

"He's doing just fine. He's a good boy, a lot like his father when he was that age. He even looks like him." She pointed to a photo on the end table. "That's my son when he was just a couple years older than Kordell."

Sabre picked it up and looked at it. She didn't really see any physical resemblance, but perhaps her reference was to his behavior.

"Tell me about Kordell's father," Sabre said. She set the photo back down.

"You already know he's serving time. And I'm not saying he shouldn't be there, but Clay's a good man, a kind-hearted man. He was a good kid, a real good kid. He never really got into trouble until after high school. He started running with the wrong crowd. Same old story. I'm sure you've heard it a million times. It's no excuse. He made bad choices. Got into drugs—more selling than using, I think, which I suppose is worse in a way."

Sabre listened as Mrs. Walker continued to try to reconcile her own words.

"He went to prison the first time for possession of drugs. He never had a history of violence. He wasn't like that. He was very sensitive and hated men who beat their women or children. He loves Kordell, I can tell you that, and he doesn't think much of Isaiah Banks."

"Do you know Isaiah?" Sabre asked.

Mrs. Walker nodded. "Yes, I know him. Not well, but he's from the neighborhood. He's a few years older than Clay and he hung out with a different crowd. Isaiah is a mean man, always beating people up. He even hit his own mama."

When Sabre and Mrs. Walker finished their conversation, Mrs. Walker rose. "I'll fetch Kordell for you."

Sabre looked around the room. The furniture was old but not yet worn out. No big flat screen TV appeared anywhere in this house. There was only a small television on top of a runner on a rosewood cabinet. The TV was surrounded by more framed photos, mostly of Clay growing up. The cabinet was simple but elegant. Sabre stood up and walked over to it. The grain of the wood was extraordinary and so distinct it drew Sabre to touch it. It felt smooth as glass.

"My father built that," Mrs. Walker said, as she walked into the room with Kordell. He was following her and tapping away on his Gameboy. "It's Brazilian Rosewood. Hard to find now. It's about seventy-five years old. When my father was young he worked for a man who built furniture. He learned from him. That was way before I was born. We didn't have much growing up, but we always had nice furniture. That's the only piece left that my father made."

"It's beautiful." Sabre turned to the boy. "Hi, Kordell."

He paused his Gameboy and stuck it in his pocket. "Hello, Ms. Brown."

"Come sit with me," Sabre said and took her seat on the sofa. He followed.

Mrs. Walker turned to leave the room. "I'll get us all some lemonade," she said on her way out.

"Are you doing okay here at your grandma's?" Sabre asked.

"I miss my mom, but Grandma's good to me. She tells me stories about my dad when he was little and I like that. She makes me do my homework before I can play and she even helps me with some of it. My mom never helped me. Mostly I miss my little brother." He looked at her with his soulful dark eyes and asked, "Why can't he live with us?"

"The social worker is trying to make that happen, but your Grandma has to be certified, which means there's a lot of paperwork before she can have Devon because she isn't *his* grandma. Do you understand?"

"Yeah, because we have different dads."

"Have you seen Devon since you came here?" Sabre asked.

Kordell shook his head from side to side.

"I'll see what I can do to set up a visit for you."

Mrs. Walker returned with two mismatched glasses and handed one to Sabre and one to Kordell. Just as Sabre took the glass, she heard a loud noise from down the street that sounded like a firecracker exploding. She instinctively turned her head toward the sound. A louder bang rang out, closer this time.

"Get down," Mrs. Walker yelled, pulling Kordell from the sofa and onto the floor with a thud. His lemonade flew through the air and landed cold and wet on Sabre's face and shoulder. The glass crashed as Sabre flung herself to the floor, her glass joining Kordell's in the pile of broken shards.

A third shot echoed through the air, followed by breaking glass outside and then the front window shattered. Each of them turned their face to the floor as the glass fell like hail in a storm. Sabre wrapped her arm around her head. She heard the thunderous roar of a high-powered engine as a car sped away. Then silence. Sabre lowered her arm and turned her head to her right. She could see Kordell a few feet across the floor, his thin body nearly covered by his grandmother's. He shifted his face upward and she could see the terror in his eyes. No one rose and no one spoke for what seemed like an eternity.

Sabre scooted slightly so she could see Kordell's grandmother's face. The woman's eyes were closed.

"Are you okay, Mrs. Walker?" Sabre asked, almost in a whisper.

The grandmother opened her eyes. "Just asking the Lord for a little help."

They continued to lie there for another minute or two. Sabre wondered how long one should stay down after hearing gunshots so close. When sirens broke the silence in the room, Sabre said aloud, "That's when."

"What?" Mrs. Walker asked.

"Nothing," Sabre said. The sirens were on their street. One after another they zipped by the house. Sabre stood up and extended a hand to Mrs. Walker, who had pushed herself up on one knee. Kordell started to get up, but his grandmother told him to stay there. Sabre peeked out through the broken window. Police cars were lining the street. More sirens. More black and whites.

Sabre stepped toward the door.

"I wouldn't open that if I were you," Mrs. Walker said in a calm voice that seemed out of place to Sabre. "You might get shot."

Sabre realized this wasn't the grandmother's first experience like this. "Does this happen all the time?"

She shook her head. "Lordy, no, but it's not the first time either." She looked out the window and then turned to Kordell, who was still lying on the floor. "Kordell, you can get up now." The little boy stood up and the grandmother wrapped her arms around him. "You okay?"

He nodded his head.

She loosened her hug and pushed him slightly away from her, examining his head and body for cuts. "It's all okay now. You go to your room. I'll bring you some more lemonade and your attorney will talk to you in a few minutes."

Kordell glanced out the window and then darted to his room.

"How many times has this happened here?" Sabre asked, concerned now about the safety of this placement.

"Not *this* exactly. We had a shooting a couple of years ago a few houses down. A drug deal gone bad. The cops are here a lot for different things. Usually it's some tough guy beating up his woman, or kids stealing cars or just breaking up stuff. But most of the time it's pretty quiet here. A lot of folks have been on this street for more than forty years. It's the newcomers and the renters that are bad." Mrs. Walker pointed to a chair. "Have a seat. I'll get us some more lemonade." She looked around the room at the glass. "I better leave the mess until the cops see it. I'm sure they'll be showing up shortly." She stepped toward the kitchen.

Sabre moved to where she could see out the window. The sirens had stopped except for a few in the distance. The house was situated far enough from the street that she could see people outside talking to the officers in blue. Three policemen walked toward the front door.

"Mrs. Walker, the police are here," Sabre called out.

They knocked and yelled, "Police," just as Mrs. Walker returned to the living room. She let them inside and they checked the house to see if anyone else was there. Then they questioned each of them about what they had seen. One of them examined the window and appeared to be following the path of the bullet that had broken it. Another officer remained outside the house near the window.

"So you didn't see anything? Make or color of the car?" Officer Jensen asked.

"No," Sabre said, "we fell to the floor as soon as we heard the shots."

"And you, ma'am?"

Mrs. Walker shook her head. "Sorry. All I could think about was protecting my grandson."

"It was green," Kordell said from the doorway. "And it had some white writing on the back window like when someone dies."

"Come here," the African-American police officer said. His name tag read *Jones*. Kordell came closer. "You saw the car?"

"I was waiting for Ms. Brown and I saw her drive up. She stayed in her car for a few minutes and a green car passed by."

"Did you see someone shooting from the car?"

"No, but the street ends down the block. They had to come back, didn't they?"

The other cop took out his radio and reported the information to his fellow officers.

"Did you see who was in the car?" Jones asked.

"Two guys."

"What did they look like?"

"I couldn't see the driver, but the other guy was black. His arm hung outside the window and he looked pretty big and real strong."

"You mean muscular?"

"Yeah, huge muscles."

"Did you see his face?"

"Not really."

"What else can you tell me about the car?" Jones asked.

"It wasn't that old. I don't know what kind it was or anything."

"Could you read the writing on the back window?"

Kordell shook his head. "There were some letters on top." He made a half circle with his finger forming an arch. "And it looked like a big rose to the side and some words and dates, like one of those stickers on a car about dead people."

After a few more questions that didn't glean any more knowledge of the events, the second officer said to Sabre, "You might want to check out your car. There's been some damage to it."

Sabre moved quickly toward the window and looked out. "My window is broken," she said.

"Both of the front windows. The bullet went straight through and probably hit this window as well." The officer turned to Mrs. Walker. "There'll be some detectives here shortly who will take a statement from you." Turning back to Sabre, he said, "You'll need to speak to them before you leave."

After the police left the house, Sabre called the social worker to report what happened. Then she sat down for a minute with Mrs. Walker.

"They won't take Kordell from me because of this, will they?"

"I can't be certain what the social worker will do. He'll be here shortly to assess things. We all just want Kordell safe."

Mrs. Walker looked frightened. Sabre surmised that her fear came not from the gunshots, but from the prospect of losing her grandson. "I just wanted Kordell to be safe from Isaiah. To keep him from getting beat up all the time."

"Do you think Isaiah could be the one who shot up the neighborhood today?"

"I doubt it. He's more of an 'in-your-face' guy. He has a terrible temper and he likes people to know how tough he is."

"It's going to be okay," Sabre said. She chastised herself for saying that. She didn't know that for sure, and she hated when people said things like that when they didn't really know. Sabre stood up. Her hands were shaking. She hadn't realized until that moment how the events had affected her. She wanted to leave, but she needed to talk with Kordell first. She took a deep breath and went to Kordell's room to see him.

"Are you okay?" Sabre asked.

"Yeah. It was pretty scary at first, but not as bad as when Isaiah would get mad at me or my mom."

"What would he do to you?"

"He'd just start whuppin' on me. He'd grab me by my arm and flip me around and whup me. He's so big."

"Did he do that often?"

"Only a few times, but I never knew when it was coming."

"Tell me about the last time."

"I got in trouble at school. This bigger kid kept picking on me and pushing me around. Then he started taking whatever he wanted from my lunch. That time, when I tried to stop him from taking my sandwich he pushed me right off the bench. It made me so mad that I choked up, and then he called me a baby and told everyone that I cried. I didn't. I was just mad."

"So, what did you get in trouble for at school?"

"I stole a bunch of Jell-O from the school cafeteria and I put it in that big kid's locker. Someone saw me, I guess, and squealed on me."

"And then you got in trouble at home for stealing the Jell-O?" Sabre asked.

"No. Isaiah got mad because he said I was a coward and there was nothing worse than a coward. He told me I should have fought like a man and then he started whuppin' on me."

Chapter 17

Sabre sat at the bar waiting for Bob to arrive, sipping her blended, Midori Margarita. It had been a rough day, and she wouldn't be driving since her car sat in the body shop around the corner awaiting new windows. She looked around the bar at the young crowd who frequented the place. It appeared to be mostly college students who were probably there for Happy Hour. The prices were good and it wasn't far from San Diego State College. More importantly, it seemed to be one of the last places around to still serve a good spread of appetizers for free. The bar jutted out from the wall with three barstools on the end. Then it curved around and extended for another fifteen stools before it turned back into the wall.

From where Sabre sat, on the end barstool closest to the curve, she had a good view of the front door. She watched people enter. Few left. A man about sixty or so came in, still wearing his construction work clothes. He sat at the opposite end of the bar, directly across from her. He must've been a regular because the bartender brought him his beer before he even ordered. Three more young patrons entered through the front door. They quickly found their way to their friends.

The next guest appeared to be more interesting and a little older than the barrage of students. Probably thirty-five, Sabre thought. He was tall, handsome, and sported an expensive-looking black cowboy hat. The cowboy looked around for just a second as if to acclimate himself, then walked toward the bar and took a seat next to Sabre. He didn't look at her. When the bartender arrived, he asked, "Got any Shiner Bock?"

"No, sorry," the bartender answered.

"A Bud then."

The bartender nodded and went to retrieve his beer. The man laid a twenty-dollar bill on the counter.

Sabre found herself staring at the man but thinking of JP. It must be the hat, she thought. He must have felt her looking at him because he turned slowly toward her and said in a strong Texas accent, "Good evening, ma'am."

"Hi," Sabre said. "Sorry...er...your hat reminded me of someone."

"Someone you like, I hope," he said.

Sabre smiled. "Yes, a good friend."

"You from these parts?"

"I live in San Diego, but not around here. I brought my car to the shop near here to get a broken window or, windows fixed. I have to leave it because there's not enough time to fix it today so I'm waiting for my ride." Sabre didn't usually explain so much to strangers, but she felt like she owed him for staring.

"You said windows? More than one?"

"Yes, it's a long story." She decided that was more than she needed to tell. "Do you live here in San Diego?"

"No, I just have some things to take care of here and won't be in town long." The bartender returned with his beer, took the twenty, and walked away. "Say, you don't know a good lawyer do you?"

"I know a few. What kind of lawyer?" Sabre thought about what he might need. Her first guess was a DUI.

"The good kind."

"I mean, what kind of trouble are you in?"

"Oh, it's not me. It's my sister. She has herself in a mess and I'm worried about her kids."

"What happened?"

"She hooked up with some guy who keeps beatin' her up. Told her over and over again to leave him, which she did, but she always goes back. Offered to give him a bit of his own medicine, but Sarajean begged me not to. Now he's hitting the kids, too."

"Is she still with him?"

"Not living with him now. Social Services came in and took the kids away. That's why she needs the lawyer." The bartender returned with the man's change and laid it on the edge of the bar. The man left it there. "So, do you know any good ones? Lawyers, that is."

Sabre reached into her pocket, took out a business card, and handed it to him.

He flipped the card over and read her name aloud. "Attorney Sabre Orin Brown." He looked surprised. "You're a lawyer?" he asked. Then he looked her over. "Knew you wasn't just some ordinary working girl. You're much too classy for that. Right pretty, too."

Sabre felt her face heat up. It must be the margarita, she thought. She couldn't decide if she appreciated the comment or if it annoyed her.

"Sorry, ma'am. I didn't mean to be fresh." He reached his hand out to shake hers. "Clint Buchanon."

Sabre shook his hand, smiled, and said, "No problem. Thank you for the compliment. Have your sister call me and I'll talk to her. If I can't represent her, I'll give her a referral."

"Really appreciate...."

Bob Clark walked up, put his arm around Sabre, and gave her a quick squeeze. "How's my snookums?"

"I'm fine." Sabre nodded toward the cowboy. "Bob, this is Clint Buchanon. He's looking for an attorney for his sister."

Bob reached out and shook his hand. "Bob Clark," he said.

"Bob's an attorney also," Sabre said. "He does this kind of work as well."

"Nice to meet you, sir."

Bob turned back to Sabre. "You ready?"

Sabre took one last drink of her margarita, stood up, and said, "Let's go."

"Aren't you going to finish your drink?" Bob asked.

"No, I'm good," Sabre said. She looked at Clint. "It was nice to meet you. Enjoy your stay here in San Diego...if you can."

"Thank you, ma'am," Clint said. "I'll be sure to give your card to Sarajean."

Sabre took a step toward the door. Bob picked up her margarita glass and finished it off.

"Picking up guys in bars now?" Bob asked, as they reached the door.

"He was just telling me about his sister. That's why he's in town."

"I bet she never calls you...but *he* will."

Sabre gave him a funny look. "You think? Well, if so, it was a pretty bad pickup line."

"It worked on you, didn't it?"

"No, it didn't work on me. I'm not going out with the guy or anything. And besides, that's not fair. I've had a rough day, dodging bullets and all."

Bob shook his head. "That's why I don't represent kids if I can help it. Too dangerous."

"Yeah, your clients are so much better. They just get *you* thrown in jail."

They stepped into Bob's car. "So, when can you get your car?"

"Monday. The repair shop couldn't get to it today. I just barely made it in there before they closed. I'm lucky I could get it back from the San Diego PD."

"They didn't want to keep it for evidence?"

"No. They just took a bunch of photos and gave it back. It's not like they needed prints or anything." Bob's car entered the freeway that would take them toward Sabre's home. "Can you pick me up on Monday morning and give me a ride to court?"

"Sure, but you'll be without a car the rest of the weekend. You don't want to get a rental?"

"No, I don't really need one. I'm not going anywhere. Besides, I have a bike if I need to go to the store for anything."

~~~

Shortly after the two attorneys left the bar, the bartender returned and bussed the area where Sabre had been sitting. Clint Buchanon, aka Tyson Doyle Cooper, asked, "What was my lady friend drinking?"

"A Midori Margarita—blended."

"Yeah, that's right," Ty said, as if he had forgotten.

He finished his beer, stood up, removed the card from his pocket and flipped it over so he could read it. "You'll hear from me soon, Attorney Sabre Orin Brown."

Chapter 18

The Martinez Case
Children: Ray, age 2 (M), Falicia, age 5 (F), Jesse (Jesus), age 7 (M)
Parents: Father—Gilberto Martinez, Mother—Juanita Martinez
Issues: Abuse, Domestic Violence
Facts: Mother beat the father with a lamp in front of the children. Alcohol abuse by both parents.

A medium-sized, mixed-breed dog strolled down the sidewalk as JP drove slowly toward the Martinez residence in National City. Three young Latino boys halted their soccer game so JP could pass. The neighborhood was old but generally well kept. Most of the lawns were manicured and contained beautiful flowering plants. Several of the houses were painted bright colors. A few had white picket fences, but more were surrounded by chain-link. JP counted three red doors in a two-block span. He looked for the number 422. The curbs weren't marked, nor were some of the houses. He noted the numbers were declining as he passed 424. When he saw a house with only the four and the two, he pulled his car up to the curb. Other than the lack of recent attention to the yard, the house looked much like the rest of the neighborhood.

JP exited his car and approached a Mexican-American woman next door who was watering her plants. The woman appeared to be in her seventies. He introduced himself, explaining he was there on behalf of the Martinez children.

"I feel so bad for *los niños*. They are all very sweet, especially Jesse. He comes every Monday evening to put my trashcan out on the street. And when he comes home from school on Tuesday afternoon, he brings it back in for me. I offered to pay him, but he said no, so a lot of times I will give him cookies for his lunch and he always shares them with his brother and sister."

"Do you know the parents?"

"Yes, they've lived here quite a while, maybe three years. Gilberto is a nice man. Juanita is another story. She's *muy loca*. I hear her yelling and screaming all the time. When they first moved in, my husband, may he rest in peace..." She made the sign of the cross. "...wanted to give Gilberto a bit of his own medicine, but it didn't take too long to see it was her, not him, creating the problems."

"When Juanita lived here, did you talk to her very often?"

"She hardly talked to anyone. One time she saw me in the yard and she screamed at me because my cat went in her yard. She was *muy boracha*...you know, drunk. She threatened to kill my cat if he went there again."

"Did anything happen to your cat?"

"No, but I try not to let him outside anymore."

"Were you here the night Juanita was arrested?"

"You mean the last time, a couple of weeks ago?"

"Yes."

"The cops come a lot to that house. Once this was a good, safe neighborhood. Now, you never know what is going to happen. I've lived here for almost fifty years and never saw a cop for the first forty. But it's different now. A lot of the people are gone who raised their children here." She paused.

JP wondered if she forgot the question, so he prompted her. "And the night of the arrest?"

"Yes. Yes, I was here. I didn't go outside, though. I could see and hear it all from my window. I heard a lot of yelling inside the house and then Gilberto ran outside. Juanita followed right behind him, beating him with a lamp. He tripped and fell down and she jumped on him and just kept hitting him. The kids were all screaming and Jesse tried to pull his mom off of his dad. I wanted to help, but I knew I couldn't really do anything. Several other neighbors came out of their houses, but no one really did anything except Patricia, who lives across the street. She took the two younger children away from the fight. She tried to get Jesse, too, but she had her hands full. I think she's the one who called the cops."

"Have you seen either of the parents since that night?"

"Gilberto has been there. I see him come in after work most days. Juanita came by late one afternoon with some tall woman. She took some things with her when she left."

"Did you talk to her?"

"No. I haven't spoken to either of them since they left. But she also came here earlier in the week, one evening, with that same woman."

"Do you remember what day that was?"

The neighbor woman rubbed her brow. "Tuesday, I think. Yes, it was Tuesday because it was trash pickup day. I was on my way outside to get the trashcan. With Jesse gone I have to do it myself, you see." She pointed her index finger at JP and shook it. "I miss that young man. I hope he's getting cookies in his lunch. What do you think?"

"About what?"

"Do you think he's getting a good lunch?"

"Yes, he's in a good placement and I'm sure he's getting plenty of cookies." He placated her. He didn't know whether the children were getting cookies or not, but according to Sabre the aunt was taking good care of them. "You say you saw Juanita on Tuesday. About what time?"

"Maybe five or six. It wasn't quite dark."

"Tell me what you saw."

"Juanita was just coming up to the driveway when I saw her. I had just started out my door to get the trash, but I stopped when I saw her." She pointed toward the driveway, moving her hand toward the house. "She walked right up there to the house and went inside. Gilberto came home right after that. And she must've been drunk because she started yelling right away."

"Did you see or hear anything after that?"

"It was quiet for about fifteen minutes or so and then she got really loud again. Then Gilberto came out carrying his shirt, jumped in his car, and left. She ran out in her underwear, screaming at him as he drove off. Then she went back inside, got dressed, and left, too."

"Did she get in a car?"

"No, she walked down the street."

"Did you see when she came up if she was walking or in a car?"

"She walked part way up the walk with that tall woman, but then the woman turned around and walked down the street. I think she drove off."

"Did you see what kind of car she drove? Or the color, perhaps?"

"No, not really."

JP thanked her for her time and walked across the street to speak to Patricia and several other neighbors. The stories were all about the same. Everyone loved Gilberto and hated or feared Juanita. Every neighbor had had some incident with her. Most of them were afraid of what she might do. CPS had been called several times. The police had been there on numerous occasions, but this was the first time anyone knew of an arrest. Patricia was the only other neighbor who knew anything about the Tuesday visit and she hadn't seen Juanita or Gilberto arrive. She only saw them leave.

As JP opened his car door and was about to step out, his phone rang. It was Bob.

Chapter 19

As Sabre showered, she wondered why the water seemed to wash away some of the load she carried from a rough day. The feeling didn't last long, but it helped for a little while. She made herself a cup of herbal tea and sat on the sofa in her pajamas. No matter how hard she tried to clear her mind and relax, the thoughts just wouldn't go away. She wondered how Dr. Heller was faring and why she had been attacked. She wondered who killed Judge Mitchell. She thought about her cases: Kordell King and what he had to endure with his step-father; the Martinez children and the fear they dealt with every day; and Emma Tran and how she could have died in the fire if those boys hadn't saved her. And she thought about how she had dodged a bullet today—literally.

She jumped, almost spilling her tea when the doorbell rang. She set her cup on the end table, stood up, and went to the door. She peeked through the peephole, saw a familiar face, and opened the door.

"Bob called you, didn't he?" she asked.

"Yep," JP said. He stood there in the doorway. For a few seconds there was silence. "Can I come in?"

Sabre stepped back, opening the door wide. "Of course. I'm sorry." Her emotions spread from anger at Bob for squealing on her to pleasure at JP's concern for her. However, this isn't the way she wanted his attention. She hated playing the role of victim.

"I just wanted to make sure you're okay."

"I'm fine, really."

"Getting shot at is not all in a day's work," JP said.

"I wasn't shot *at* exactly."

"And you know that for certain?"

"I just happened to be where someone was shooting. It was a drive-by. The guy shot up the whole neighborhood."

"That makes me feel better," JP said sarcastically.

"Would you like some tea?" Sabre asked. "Or something else to drink?" She moved toward the kitchen. JP followed.

"No thanks."

Sabre turned back, almost bumping into JP. His hand went up automatically and caught her before she crashed into him. He stood there for a second with his hand just below her shoulder. A second passed when their eyes caught. Then Sabre stepped away, walked around JP, and sat down on one end of the sofa. "Have a seat," she said, gesturing with her hand to a spot near her. JP sat down, leaving about a foot between them. "Tell me what you found out today on the Martinez case."

"I found out that everyone loves Gilberto and hates or fears Juanita, which is no surprise. I also discovered that Juanita went back to her house on Tuesday evening in violation of the restraining order. According to the neighbor, she was intoxicated. Gilberto came home shortly thereafter. There was a loud scene when he came in, followed by a half hour of quiet. Gilberto came out carrying his shirt and drove away with Juanita yelling obscenities at him while he was leaving. She left shortly thereafter."

"So, the same night that Scary Larry was killed Juanita stopped to see her husband, probably had a conjugal visit, and then left drunk and angry," Sabre said. "Did anyone see how she left?" Sabre picked up her teacup from the end table and wrapped her hands around it.

"A tall woman had dropped her off before Gilberto arrived home and then she left, I think. The neighbor was unclear about that. She saw that woman walk part way up the walkway with Juanita, but then the woman turned around and left. The neighbor saw a car leaving, but she didn't actually see Juanita get in or out of the car. And she couldn't tell me anything about the car, not even the color."

"Would she have had time to go kill the judge?"

"Possibly. I told Bob what I knew about his client and asked him to see if she had an alibi. If she does, it's in her best interest to tell us. If not, then I'll investigate further to see if I can find out where she was."

Sabre took a sip of her tea.

JP started to reach out and touch Sabre, but then pulled his hand back. "Are you sure you're okay?"

She nodded. "Yes, I'm fine. Really."

"I don't like your going in those neighborhoods and getting shot at."

Sabre started to protest again. "Those bullets weren't meant for me. It was...."

"Just a random drive-by," he finished her sentence. "You don't know that for sure."

"It could've happened in any neighborhood. Children are being shot in schools, and there are innocent victims in malls and on street corners. It's not safe anywhere, and I have to see the children if I'm going to represent them. I have to see their living environments. And I'm not going to stop doing my job because of some crazy, random drive-by shooting."

JP stood up. "You're about as stubborn as a mule halfway home from plowin' all day."

Sabre smiled. "You're a bit of a mule yourself, you know." She set her teacup down and stood up. "You do need to check out Isaiah Banks, the stepfather on the King case. I think he's a pretty bad actor."

"I'll do that tomorrow, along with Tran."

"Speaking of Tran. I saw Emma today. She's a beautiful little girl. The foster mother swears that Kim-Ly, the mother, is not as old as she claims to be. She thinks she's no more than sixteen. Maybe you can see what you can find out because if she's a minor herself, it'll change how we proceed."

"I will. By the way, did you get a chance to see Durham?" JP asked.

"No, I planned to go today but I ran out of time. I'll go see him tomorrow morning."

"But you don't have a car. Do you want a ride?"

"I have my bike and it's only a few miles to the Hall."

JP walked to the door. "Well, be careful."

Sabre touched him briefly on his arm as he opened the door. He stepped out. "Lock your door," he said.

She heard him walk away, but not until after the dead bolt was secured.

Chapter 20

"I made you grits with your eggs," Robin said to JP. "Aren't you going to eat?"

JP looked at her sternly with an edge in his voice. "Where did you get the grits?"

Robin scrunched her face and bowed her head slightly, like a child caught in the act. "I walked to the market yesterday. It was only a couple of blocks and it was such a beautiful day."

"You can't do that," JP said a little louder than he intended. He reached across the table and touched her hand. His voice softened. "Robin, please don't go out until we know for sure it's safe. I can't be here every minute to watch you. I really need you to be careful."

"You're right. I'm sorry. I won't do it again." She looked at him with her big doe-like eyes. "Your eggs are getting cold."

JP took a bite of his grits. "It tastes like home."

After a moment or two of silence Robin said, "I talked to my cousin, Sandy, last night. They've been watching Ty's house and his work. He's been gone since Thursday. He left his house in the morning. Sandy's brother-in-law works at Wedgewood where Ty works. He's been keeping tabs on Ty, and he said Ty didn't show up on Thursday morning and he hasn't been there since."

"What kind of company is Wedgewood?"

"It's Ty's father's business. He's a big developer, owns half the town and a good part of the county. Ty has worked there since he returned from college. He expects to take it over some day, although I don't really think he wants to. He wants the power it wields, but other than that he couldn't care less about it."

"Maybe he's just on a hunting trip or something."

"Maybe," Robin said. But JP knew she didn't really think so, nor did he.

~~~

The Tran Case
  Child: Emma, age 18 mos. (F)
  Parents: Father—unknown, Mother—Kim-Ly Tran
  Issues: Neglect
  Facts: Mother left eighteen-month-old girl in locked room and went to work. Apartment complex caught on fire.

The neighborhood where Kim-Ly Tran had lived with her daughter looked worse than normal since the fire. A good part of the small apartment complex was burned down and remained uninhabited. The apartment building adjacent to Kim-Ly's appeared to be undamaged except for the tapestry of black soot marks on the outside wall.

JP knocked on the door of the apartment that appeared to face Kim-Ly's window. A teenager of Asian descent, who looked to be about fourteen years of age, answered the door. JP introduced himself.

"I'm Quang Pham," the boy said, as he politely extended his hand to shake.

JP was impressed. Most of the teenagers he came into contact with, especially through Sabre's cases, were not so schooled in their manners.

"Nice to meet you. Do you mind answering a few questions?"

Quang moved his head toward the dining room table. It held several books, some papers, and a laptop computer and a small jade statue of what appeared to be an Asian monk. "I was just working on a project for my Advanced Physics class, and I really need to get it done."

"I'm sure you're very busy, but this will only take a minute. I work for the attorney who represents Emma Tran."

"Emma is just a baby. Why would she need an attorney?"

"You know about the fire, right?"

"Yes."

"It's our job to make sure Emma is safe and nothing like that ever happens again." Quang nodded but didn't speak. JP looked at the table where Quang's school project awaited him. The window above the table gave the young student a perfect view of Kim-Ly's apartment. "Were you here the day of the fire?"

"Yes."

"What were you doing when the fire started?"

"I was here studying with my friend."

"Was anyone else here?"

"No. My mother was working. She came home just after...." Quang stopped.

"Just after you and your friend saved Emma?" JP asked. He remembered two young men had rescued Emma from the burning building, but their names weren't listed in the reports. Either the social worker didn't know who they were or they were intentionally kept confidential.

Quang's lack of response answered JP's question.

"I'm not sure why you don't want anyone to know about the rescue, but you two boys are heroes. You saved that little girl's life."

"My mom was upset. She was afraid we'd get in trouble for breaking into the apartment. And when people started calling us heroes, my mom said, 'A hero who boasts about it is soon just a braggart.' She said it was saving the child that was important, not getting recognition for doing it."

"Your mother sounds very wise."

"She's a very private person. She didn't want news reporters hanging around here."

JP walked over and looked out the window into Kim-Ly's apartment. "So, tell me what happened the day of the fire."

"My friend, Kevin, and I were working on a report for our American Government class when we smelled smoke. At first we didn't think too much of it, but it kept getting stronger. We looked out the window and saw where the smoke was coming from. We ran outside and then I saw the flames. That's when we, uh, went inside and got Emma."

"How did you get in?"

"Through the front door."

"And her mother wasn't home?"

"No. I saw her leave for work earlier."

"And she left her front door unlocked and her child without anyone watching her?"

Quang popped his knuckles in what appeared to be a nervous gesture. "Not exactly."

JP asked, "What do you mean?"

"I used a key."

JP was a little surprised at his response. "Where did you get the key?"

"From Kim-Ly. Look, she's not a bad mother. I know she shouldn't have left Emma alone, but she has to work and she can't afford a babysitter. She had someone staying with her for a while. The girl babysat for her, but she left about a month ago."

"So, you know Kim-Ly?"

"I don't know her well, but she's always very nice to me. We'd talk sometimes through the window. When it's warm we'd both have our windows open. She always asks me about my schoolwork. I knew she left Emma alone and she knew I knew. One day she told me she couldn't afford a babysitter and asked if I'd keep an eye on her. That's when she gave me the key."

"Did you ever use the key before?"

"Just once when Emma was sick and she wouldn't stop crying. I went to check on her, but I didn't really know what to do. I held her for a little while and she finally fell asleep, but she woke up again and started crying soon after I came home. My mom came home right after that so I couldn't go back there."

"Did you tell Kim-Ly?"

"Yes. She didn't have to work the next day and she bought her some medicine."

"What else can you tell me about Kim-Ly?" JP asked.

Quang shrugged his shoulders.

"Do you know where she works?" Quang's face turned red, but he didn't respond. "Quang?"

"I heard a rumor that she was a stripper. So one day Kevin and I followed her to work. We couldn't go inside or anything, but we saw the club. It's called 'Muffs.' It's only about a mile from here."

"Thank you for the information." JP reached out to shake the young man's hand. "And for saving that little girl's life."

"Is she okay?"

"Emma is fine. She's in a good home."

"I mean Kim-Ly. Will she be able to keep her daughter?"

JP wondered if Quang was smitten with Kim-Ly. "That depends on her. If she does what she's supposed to do, she'll be able to raise her daughter. The court has to be sure she won't put her in danger again." JP started for the front door. "One more thing: Do you know the name of the girl who lived with her?"

"She said her name was Jade, but I heard Kim-Ly call her Bich, which means Jade in Vietnamese. Jade got angry when she called her that and said it was no longer her name. I don't know her last name. I thought they were sisters because they looked a lot alike, but Kim-Ly said they weren't."

"How old is Jade?"

"She claimed to be eighteen, but she acted about twelve. She thought she was a princess or something."

"Do you know why she left? Or where she went?"

"She never went anywhere. It was almost like she was hiding there. One day a man drove up in a real expensive black car and took her away. She didn't scream or anything, but you could tell she didn't want to go with him. I thought maybe it was her father or brother or something."

"What did the man look like?"

"He was Asian—Vietnamese, I think. He had short dark hair. He was pretty buff, and he wore a black suit."

"How old would you say he was?"

"Thirty, maybe. I'm not sure."

"Had you ever seen him before?"

Quang shook his head. "No, that was the first time."

"Did you see him after that?"

"I think he came here a couple of nights ago. I came home just as a woman walked away from Kim-Ly's apartment. The man seemed to catch her by surprise, but they walked together down the sidewalk right past me. Neither of them spoke. Just as I got to my door I heard the man say something in Vietnamese. I turned around, but it was getting dark and I couldn't see them that well from where I was standing. It looked like the same man who took Jade. They walked to the car together, but this woman didn't seem to want to go with him either."

"What exactly was she doing?"

"He had his arm around her, but she seemed to be pulling away. She didn't scream or anything so I didn't think that much of it. Do you think there was something wrong?"

"I don't know. It may be nothing," JP said. "Did you hear anything they said?"

"The man opened the back door of the car and it sounded like he said, 'Get in,' but I can't be sure."

"What did the woman look like?"

"She was Asian, thin, pretty. She wore nice clothes."

"How old do you think she was?"

"Twenty or thirty, maybe. I don't know. I'm not very good with ages. I thought Kim-Ly and Jade were a lot younger than they said."

Chapter 21

The Durham Case
  Child: Matt Durham, Defendant
  Type: Delinquency case
  Charges: Two counts of First Degree Murder
  Victims: Hannah Rawlins & Mason Usher
  Facts: Double homicide. Two teenagers bludgeoned to death with a baseball bat.

Sabre parked her bike in front of San Diego Juvenile Hall, fastened the lock to the bike rack, and went inside. She filled out the form and took a seat. Sabre went there early because family visiting hours were in the afternoon and the place would be packed. For now, she was the only one in the waiting room. Within five minutes an African-American woman in her thirties appeared. She was dressed in khaki pants and a white shirt. She didn't smile, but her words and tone were pleasant. Sabre noticed how aware she was of her surroundings as she escorted her through the hallways with stark walls painted institutional tan. They walked through one locked door after another, each time waiting for the door to close before the next one could be opened. The cells they passed contained delinquents who were charged with minor offenses. The violent felons were housed in a different unit towards the back. They stopped to let a group pass that had just left the cafeteria.

The officer who escorted Sabre instructed her to wait in the cubicle provided for interviews until they brought out Matt Durham. It took another five minutes or so for the officer to return with him. Durham took a seat across the table from Sabre.

"Hi, Matt," Sabre said.

Before he could answer, the officer asked, "Would you like me to remain in here with you?"

Sabre had never had the question asked of her before. She wondered if the officer was new or if it was something Matt had done that prompted him to ask. "No, thank you."

The officer nodded. "I'll be right outside," he said just before the door closed behind him.

Sabre and Matt exchanged greetings and then Sabre asked, "Do you remember JP, my private investigator?"

"Yeah."

"He's been interviewing some people to help with your defense. He talked to your coach about the baseball bat."

"So, you can prove it was stolen then?"

"Unfortunately, the coach didn't remember your saying anything about it being missing."

"I told him the next day at practice. I didn't even realize myself that it was gone until I went to use it. But you can check. I even filled out the stupid form."

"Yes, he did have the form."

"So there. Now all you have to do is find out who stole my bat."

"And who do you think took it?"

"I've been thinking about that," Matt said. "The only one I can think of is Darren Flynn."

Sabre wanted her client to be innocent, but there was something in his voice that didn't set well with her. "Your teammate? The one you had a fight with at the Poway game?"

He looked up in genuine surprise. "How'd you know about him?"

"I've made it my business to know what's gone on in your life. That's what JP is doing. He's trying to find the truth so we can mount the best defense for you, but I need a little help from you, Matt. Tell me about the fight with Darren."

"That guy has an awful temper. He's always going off. Ask anyone on the team."

"Okay. So, what happened that day at the game?"

"He had my bat and I was coming up, so I asked him for it real nice. He got a little huffy with me, but he handed it over. Then as I started to leave the dugout he stepped in front of me and I accidentally bumped him. He freaked out and started shoving me."

"Did you try to hit him with your bat?"

"No. Did he tell you that?"

"I didn't say that," Sabre said. "I'm just asking."

"Well, I didn't. It might have come up with my hand when he shoved me back or maybe I raised it without thinking." He shook his head and his eyes seemed to gloss over. "The fool. You don't shove a guy who has a bat in his hand."

Sabre wondered if that was his feeble attempt at being humorous, but it seemed more threatening than funny. She had a difficult time reading this young man. He seemed to go from an innocent little boy to someone menacing with the shake of his head.

"Let's talk about your alibi again. I need more information than what you gave me the last time we spoke about it." Sabre watched Matt's face, but saw no change of expression. "So, where were you?"

"I was playing video games with a friend."

"Who?"

"I can't get him involved."

"Matt, now is not the time to be a 'good friend.' You're facing a murder rap. If you have an alibi, we may be able to make this all go away."

"Just find out who took the bat. Then you'll have the guy who killed Hannah."

"Were you with your friend, Ralph, who works at the garage on Convoy?"

Matt's eyes widened and his mouth opened slightly. "How do you know about him?" This time Sabre thought his surprised look was exaggerated, maybe even faked. She was either losing her touch or convinced he committed this horrible crime and therefore was having trouble believing him. She shook it off.

"Just a little investigating, and if *we* can find him so can the police. So, you need to tell me so we can question him first."

"Okay," Matt said, but he didn't answer for a few seconds. "His name is Ralph Fletcher. He works at Jim's Oil and Lube."

"Where does he live?"

"I don't know his address, but it's in Clairemont right off of Mt. Alifan Drive. You know, where the terrorists lived."

"The terrorists?"

"Yeah, from Nine-Eleven. You know, the guys who blew up those buildings in New York City."

Sabre felt a chill run through her body. She hadn't thought about them in a while or how close they had lived to her. She was living with a friend who attended Mesa College and had a condo only a block or two away. It was a temporary arrangement for Sabre and she had used the Mailboxes, Etc. across the street to get her mail for that semester—the same place the terrorists used to send and receive their packages from Saudi Arabia. For weeks following Nine-Eleven, Sabre couldn't go in there without seeing an FBI agent.

"I know the apartments," she said.

~~~

Sabre pedaled her way along Meadowlark and onto Genesee Avenue. She crossed over Linda Vista Road and started down the long hill toward Balboa Avenue. The wind from the speed of the bike blew her hair in her face. She flipped her head around to throw it back. The sun was shining, the sky blue, and the air felt good. Traffic was minimal. Only one car had passed her since she crossed over Linda Vista. She picked up speed. She let everything that had been on her mind just blow away. For a few minutes it was just her and the air. She stayed in the bike lane as it curved around and continued to descend. She approached a green traffic light, slowing down just slightly, but still moving at a good pace. A late model Honda approached the red light at the cross street on her right. Sabre was less than fifty feet away when she realized the Honda was not going to stop; it continued rolling into the intersection.

The car was too far out in the intersection for Sabre to swerve left and go around it. If it kept coming, they would surely collide. She saw the young man in the driver's seat looking down at his phone and tapping it with his finger, never looking up or at her. She slowed as much as she could and swerved around to the right, hoping the Honda would keep going and she could zip around it.

Without warning, the car jerked and made a sudden hard turn to the right. Sabre reacted instinctively. She squeezed the hand brakes just hard enough to slow the bike down and then wheeled the bike around behind the Honda, just missing the rear of it by a few inches. She quickly steadied her bike and for a few seconds she was even with the car.

The driver still did not look at her and she suspected he never knew she was there. He sped away without a backward glance.

Angry at the texting driver and shaken up by the near accident, Sabre finished her trek home. By the time she reached her condo she had calmed down. She called JP. He updated her on the Tran case and she in turn gave him the information she had obtained from Durham. She didn't mention her bicycle incident for fear he would think someone was after her.

Chapter 22

The Durham Case

   Child: Matt Durham, Defendant

   Type: Delinquency case

   Charges: Two counts of First Degree Murder

   Victims: Hannah Rawlins & Mason Usher

   Facts: Double homicide. Two teenagers bludgeoned to death with a baseball bat.

"Are you Ralph Fletcher?" JP asked the man in the white shirt with *Ralph* embroidered on the patch just above his heart. The tall, thin man looked older than his twenty-four years. He struck JP as someone whose drug use had left its mark on his body as well as his yellow teeth. An incisor on the left side was missing.

"Yeah, why?"

"I'm a private investigator for Matt Durham. I understand you're a friend of his."

He raised his right hand, palm up to JP. "Look, man, I don't need any trouble."

"I just need to verify his whereabouts on the night Hannah Rawlins and her friend, Mason Usher, were killed. He says he was with you. Is that true?"

"Yeah, we were together all evening."

"What were you doing?"

"What did he say we were doing?"

"I'm not asking you to cover for him. I just want the truth."

Ralph walked back into the empty lobby of Jim's Oil and Lube and purchased a can of Pepsi from the vending machine. He turned around to face JP. "I thought you said you were working for Matt."

"I *am* working for Matt, but I need to know what really happened so his attorney can present the case. I don't want something the DA can use against him." Ralph took a drink of his soda, looked at JP suspiciously, and still didn't answer the question. "Were you playing video games?" JP continued.

Ralph nodded, bobbing his whole upper body. "Yeah, video games. That's it."

JP wanted to smack the cocky look off his face. "Where?"

"At my pad."

"Where is that?"

"Over on Mt. Alifan Drive."

"Was anyone else there?"

"Nope. Just the two of us."

"Is there anything else you can tell me about Matt that might be important to his case."

Ralph raised his eyebrows and scrunched up his face as if he was actually thinking, which JP had already decided he was incapable of doing. Then Ralph bobbed his head and upper body again. "I don't think he did it," he said, as if he was suddenly an authority on Matt's behavior.

JP didn't say anything to Ralph, but he thought that was an odd thing to say since Matt couldn't have done it if he was actually with him playing video games. So far, JP wasn't sure anything Ralph had said yet held any truth. And who knows? Maybe he didn't even get his name right.

Ralph walked out of the lobby. JP followed. "I gotta get back to work," Ralph said.

"Matt is only fourteen years old. What's the connection between you two?"

Ralph spun around and moved close to JP's face, their noses just a few inches apart. "What are you saying, man?"

JP raised both hands, palms up. "Calm down. I'm not insinuating anything. I'm just asking. He's just a kid. What do you two have in common?"

Ralph's face turned red, but he backed off a little. "Look, man, I'm not some pervert or something. We met at a video arcade. He likes to play video games. So do I. He doesn't seem to have a lot of friends, so I'm nice to him."

"How long have you known him?"

"A few months. And I didn't know he was only fourteen until all this stuff came out about the murder and all. He told me he was sixteen."

"That makes sense then," JP said sarcastically, but it went over Ralph's head.

Ralph nodded. "Yeah, that's what I mean."

"Sure," JP said. "Do you mind answering a couple of more questions?"

Ralph stopped and looked at JP without responding. JP took that as a yes.

"Did you work on Tuesday?"

"No, it was my day off. I went to see Matt."

"What time was that?"

"Around four."

"And then where did you go?"

"Why?"

"I'm just trying to put some pieces of the puzzle together."

"I went home. I wasn't feeling well."

"Were you alone?"

"Yeah. What's this all about, man?" He scowled at JP. "Are you trying to pin that judge's murder on me?"

"So, you heard about the judge getting killed?"

"Yeah, Matt told me."

"When you went to see him on Tuesday?"

"Yeah." Ralph nodded his head, then shook it from side to side, "No. He told me on Wednesday."

"So you saw him both days?"

"That's right."

"I thought you were sick."

"I *was* sick, but he's lonely, man. No one goes to see him."

JP thanked him and went back to his car. He needed an oil change but decided he didn't trust Ralph enough to have it done at Jim's Oil and Lube. His criminal record check had told him that much, but talking to him confirmed it. His record contained no violence, mostly misdemeanor drug busts, shoplifting, and one DUI. None of it was in the last year and a half. Perhaps he had reformed. JP thought it more likely he was getting a little better at not getting caught. And what was he really doing hanging out with a fourteen-year-old kid?

Chapter 23

The Wheeler Case
    Children: Holly (F) and Bradley (M), age 9 years (twins), four other children
    Parents: Father—Willie Wheeler, Mother—Debra Wheeler
    Issues: Physical Abuse, NeglectFacts: Dirty Home, drugs, alcohol, physical abuse, mental problems

"Thanks for letting me tag along," JP said to Bob as they drove up to Renette Park in El Cajon.

"I don't know how helpful it'll be. It's hard to get much out of Willie, but I appreciate the company. Spending an hour and a half with 'Whacky Willie' Wheeler isn't my idea of a good time, but he usually manages to provide some kind of crazy entertainment."

JP knew Bob would rather be doing something else, but the truth was, in spite of the way he talked about his clients, he had a soft spot for them. "It's nice of you to supervise the visit."

"Willie wanted to see his twins on their birthday and no one else could do it today. Besides, if I was home, Marilee would just be nagging at me to finish painting the guest room."

"You haven't finished the painting yet?"

"Not quite."

"I don't blame her. You started that six months ago."

"What can I say? I'm a busy guy."

They left the car and walked toward the picnic bench where Willie and Debbie Wheeler were waiting.

"They're prompt. I have to give them that," JP said.

"They're a mess, but they do love their children...in their own perverted way," Bob said.

What a sight, JP thought. Both Willie and Debbie had cigarettes dangling from their mouths. Willie was tall and lanky, his face beginning to take on the look of tanned leather that comes from too much sun and smoke exposure. Debbie's thirty-eight years had taken a toll on her thin body. Her tangled, blonde hair peeked out below a poufy red hat wrapped in orange and green feathers, several of which had broken loose and extended outward. Their clothes bore a few stains, but were otherwise clean. Two buttons appeared to be missing from Willie's shirt, and a seam had broken apart about an inch long on the shoulder of Debbie's yellow, cotton dress.

"Nice hat," Bob said to Debbie as they approached.

She beamed an appreciative smile.

"Attorney SpongeBob SquarePants," Willie said.

Bob extended his hand to Willie. "Hi, Willie." He turned toward JP. "This is JP. He works with Sabre, your children's attorney."

"Yep, nice to meet you, sir," Willie said to JP. He turned quickly toward Bob. "Where are the kids?"

Bob looked at his watch. "It's still early. Don't worry. They'll be here."

Willie leaned in toward Bob's ear and asked, "Did you bring it?"

"Yes, I did, Willie. It's in my trunk. I'll get it a little later. And my wife made the twins a cake."

Willie slapped Bob lightly on the shoulder. "Thanks, Attorney SpongeBob." He pointed to a couple of gift bags sitting on the table as he bounced around. Willie didn't stand still very well. He paced or bobbed constantly. "And we got the kids each a little somethin'. Yep, the wife insisted. After all, you only turn ten once, right?"

"Yeah, and they had these bags at the dollar store," Debbie added proudly, blowing smoke out as she spoke. "It ain't much, but it's a little something." She took a drag from her cigarette. "I wish we could tell them they're coming home for their birthday." Again her hand brought her cigarette to her mouth. "Any chance of that?" She took another drag.

"No, Debbie, you know that can't happen just yet."

JP spoke up. "Perhaps we can talk a bit before the children get here."

"Good idea," Bob said. "Would you like to sit down?"

"Yep," Willie said, but remained standing and fidgeting. "You sure you brought it, Attorney SpongeBob?"

"Yes, I'm sure."

"It'll be a special surprise for them, don't you think?" Tears started to well up in Willie's eyes. "Debbie doesn't know, either. It's a surprise for her, too."

"Yes, it will be special. They're going to be real happy, but you have to keep it together now. No crying."

Willie sniffed. "Okay, but you got it, right?"

"Yes, Willie, now please just focus for a minute and answer a few questions for JP. Then I'll go get it. Okay?"

Willie nodded. Ashes fell from the cigarette in his mouth. He seldom removed it from his lips. Occasionally he would reach up and hold it with his index finger and thumb as he puffed. But mostly he just used his mouth to control it.

JP thought he had never seen anyone smoke quite like that before, but then Willie was a little different on a lot of levels. JP noticed that Debbie, on the other hand, had almost the opposite habit. Her cigarette flew in and out of her mouth at a record pace.

JP finally asked, "Willie, do you know where you were last Tuesday evening?"

"Hmm," Willie said. "Let me think. Did I see Parnhard that night?"

"Who's Par...?" JP started to ask.

"Don't ask," Bob said to JP. He turned to Willie. "Think, Willie, it's important. Where were you on Tuesday night?"

Willie still appeared to be searching his brain for an answer when Debbie spoke up. "We were at the church bingo."

"You were playing bingo?" JP asked.

"No, we weren't playin' bingo, but we were there," Willie said. "We don't play, but most Tuesdays we help set up the chairs and then break them down. The *padre* feeds us sandwiches for dinner, and then whatever is left of the sandwiches we get to take home. It was especially good when we had the kids living with us. Yep, they really looked forward to bingo night."

Before JP could ask another question, Willie swung around and made a little hop like a two-year-old kid seeing a new puppy. His face lit up and he pointed toward the street. "There they are."

Willie and Debbie started toward the children. Bob followed. JP remained behind. The children ran toward them and Holly jumped in her dad's arms. He swung her around and carried her back to the picnic table. Bradley walked with his mother, holding her hand. Bob spoke with the man who had transported the children and then went to his car and retrieved something from his trunk.

Willie set Holly down and gave Bradley a hug. "Daddy has a surprise for you. Wait here."

Willie went to help Bob and they soon returned with a birthday cake and Bob's Les Paul acoustic guitar. Bob set the cake on the table and opened the bag his wife, Marilee, had sent with paper plates, forks, a knife, and candles.

Holly's eyes widened. "Are you going to sing for us, Daddy?"

"Yep, you bet, Pumpkin," Willie said. "First, we'll have some birthday cake and then we'll have some music."

Debbie put the candles on the cake and lit them. The family all sang "Happy Birthday" together. Bob joined them; JP mumbled a few of the words. Then the twins blew out the candles simultaneously.

"Can we have some cake now?" Bradley asked.

"First, your gift." Debbie handed each of them a gift bag. "It's not much, you know. But we wanted to get you a little something. And you know you can't have too many things at Polinsky or they'll just get stolen."

"Yep, that's right. We'll get you somethin' real nice for your birthday when you come home. Maybe dirt bikes or somethin'. Would you like that?"

Bob and JP both knew there wouldn't ever be a dirt bike. JP wondered if the kids knew, too, or if they just hoped each time would be different. But JP suspected everything about their life was a series of empty promises. Were the children used to it? Perhaps Willie's childhood was like that as well.

"That would be cool, Dad." Bradley said.

"Yeah, Dad. I'd like that too. Then when I race Bradley and I beat him, I bet he won't call me a girl."

Willie gently grabbed Holly's chin and pulled her face upward. "And a beautiful girl you are," he said.

Bob whispered to JP. "Just when I want to reprimand him for the dirt bike thing he goes and says something appropriate. A voice of reason in a wilderness of pain."

Both children sat holding their gift bags without opening them until Debbie said, "Go ahead. Open them up."

Bradley reached in his bag and pulled out a blue Hot Wheels car. It looked like a vintage Pontiac. He smiled. "This is nice. Thanks."

When Holly retrieved her diary from her bag she smiled broadly and said, "Wow, I really wanted one of these."

"I know," Debbie said. "And you can write in it every day if you want."

JP was impressed. They were simple little gifts, but the children seemed genuinely appreciative. He wondered how many children from well-to-do homes would be pleased with such modest gifts.

Debbie served them all cake. They chattered about Polinsky and about their siblings. Both parents started many sentences with, "When you come home...." JP counted at least seven of them. Each time Bob would shake his head at Willie or Debbie, but it didn't seem to register that it might be hard on the children since they weren't coming home any time soon. On the other hand, Debbie and Willie seemed sincerely happy to be with their children. They obviously loved them, even if they hadn't been able to provide a safe environment for them.

"Okay, now for your best birthday present." Willie reached down and picked up Bob's guitar. For the first time since they had arrived, Willie sat down on the bench of the picnic table. Debbie stood next to him. The twins scampered around in front of him and sat on the grass. He started to play. His fingers moved with precision along the strings like he had been playing all his life. The children looked up at him in awe.

Bob nodded his head in a gesture of pleasant surprise. "You're very good, Willie."

Willie said, "Yep." And then he sang and it was beautiful, a real Susan Boyle moment. He was truly gifted.

When it came time to leave, Willie cried. Holly hung on to him so tightly it appeared they would have to be pried apart. Tears rolled down her little face as she sobbed. Finally, Bob coaxed her to let go and after the children left Bob reminded Willie again that he needed to make parting a little easier or the social worker might try to curtail his visits.

As JP and Bob walked to the car, Bob said, "I hope their alibi checks out. Regina, Debbie's attorney, said Debbie had told her earlier that they were at the church on bingo night."

"I hope so, too." JP paused. "Willie sure doesn't have the voice of a killer."

~~~

The church steeple stood tall against the blue sky. The cross at the top extended up another fifteen feet. Stained glass windows displayed splashes of color along the side of each wall. JP pulled into the parking lot and walked toward the rectory. A man wearing a light, solid blue shirt, jeans, and tennis shoes greeted him.

"May I help you?" the man asked.

"I'm looking for Father Maher."

"You found him," the priest said.

"I'm JP Torn." They shook hands. "I'm the investigator for Attorney Sabre Brown and we're representing some children in a juvenile dependency case. I was hoping you could answer a few questions for me."

"Are they parishioners?"

"I'm not certain." JP looked pensive. He hadn't asked Willie if they were. It didn't seem relevant at the time, but still, that's a question that he should've asked. He felt a little uncomfortable that he wasn't paying close enough attention to details. He gave the priest the names.

"Ahh...Mr. and Mrs. Wheeler. Quite a flock they have. The good Lord certainly made that woman fertile. Interesting family. Good about attending church, but always late. They were lucky if they made it to mass before Communion some Sundays. But I guess when you have to get that many ready and moving it can't be easy."

"That would be them, Father."

"I heard the children had been removed again."

"That's correct. What I'm here about today is your Bingo Night last Tuesday. Willie and Debbie claim to have been here helping with the event."

"Yes, they don't miss many Bingo Nights. They are quite helpful, actually. They take a few too many cigarette breaks for my liking, but since they're volunteering their time, I can't really complain. When they first started helping they brought the whole brood with them, but we had to stop that since they weren't getting much done. They spent the whole time chasing after the kids. I limited their helpers to two of the children and they had to be at least nine years old. They rotated the kids and most of them seemed to like to help. The younger twins were exceptionally good. I would give the Wheelers the leftover sandwiches to take home to the rest of the children. They all seemed to appreciate it."

"So, you remember seeing them last Tuesday?"

Father Maher nodded. "Yes, they were here."

"What time did they arrive?"

"About five. I fed them before we started. They always seem to be hungry, but as I said before, they are very grateful for whatever I give them."

"And they stayed here the whole evening?"

"Yes." He thought for a moment. "They set up the tables and chairs before we started. They helped throughout the evening with markers and bingo sheets, and they cleaned up after we were done. They left here about ten o'clock."

"And they remained here the whole time. Neither of them could have left and come back for, say, an hour?"

"No, they took their cigarette breaks, but never for more than ten minutes," Father Maher said. "It sounds like I may be their alibi."

"Yes, you are. Something pretty awful went down and although I didn't think they were involved, we had to make sure."

"Well, if it happened during that time frame, it couldn't have been one of them. Of that, I'm certain."

Chapter 24

The bell Bob had installed on Sabre's office door jingled as it opened. Sabre wasn't expecting anyone so she assumed it was someone looking for David or Jack, the other attorneys who had office space in the old Victorian house. Elaine, the receptionist, would take care of it.

Sabre continued to prepare her cases for the morning calendar, filling out the appropriate colored form for each hearing. She reached for a pink form just as Elaine walked into her office.

"There's a gentleman here to see you. A very charming man with a Texas accent," Elaine said.

Sabre glanced up and then continued putting the form in the file, her eyes back on what she was doing. "Is it JP? Just send him in."

"No, it's not JP. He says his name is Clint Buchanon."

Sabre looked up again. "Hmm...." This time her face showed surprise.

"Would you like me to send him in?"

"Sure," Sabre said. She stood up. "No. Tell him I'll be with him shortly."

Sabre took about five minutes to finish preparing her files, set them aside, and left her desk. She walked out to the reception area where Clint sat in a comfortable, dark brown, leather chair. He stood up immediately when she walked in.

"Howdy, ma'am," he said, tipping his expensive-looking, dark, olive-colored cowboy hat.

"Hi, Clint. Nice to see you again. Are you here about your sister?"

"Yes, ma'am."

Sabre wondered if any woman in Texas was ever called anything but ma'am. "Let's go to my office." Sabre stepped into the hallway but not before she saw Elaine shake her hand back and forth in a gesture indicating she was captivated and mouth the word, "Wow."

Sabre smiled at Elaine. She was impressed with his looks as well. She hadn't noticed just how attractive he was in the dim light of the bar where they met. Her state of mind after the bullets had blown past her that day had likely added to her lack of attention to his good looks.

Once inside her office, Sabre seated herself behind her desk. "Please, have a seat," she said, pointing to the chair across from her.

"Thank you, ma'am," Clint said.

"So, what can I do for you?" Sabre asked.

He removed his hat, revealing a full head of dark, wavy hair. He was even more handsome without the hat, Sabre thought. He set the hat on the chair next to him.

"Couldn't get my sister to call you or any other attorney. I don't think she wants anyone telling her not to see that loser boyfriend of hers."

Sabre waited a few seconds. When she had met Clint in the bar, he had told her that his sister was being abused by her boyfriend, but she still didn't know exactly what he wanted from her. When he didn't speak, she said, "It's difficult for a woman, or a man, in an abusive relationship to break loose. Even when they are no longer physically connected, a psychological connection remains. They begin to second-guess their actions, constantly wondering if they're doing the right thing. It's a process. It'll take time for her to disentangle herself and establish boundaries. Hopefully, she'll get the help she needs from social services."

"You sure know a lot about it. I hope it's not from personal experience?"

Sabre shook her head. "No," she said rather bluntly. Then added, "But I've dealt with a lot of women who have been in an abusive relationship." She thought of the Martinez case. "And even a few men."

"Sorry, ma'am. I guess that wasn't an appropriate question. Guess I need to learn the boundaries myself."

"It's okay. Just support her and keep an eye out for her safety. And you needn't worry for the children. Now that DSS is involved, they'll see to it that the children are protected." Sabre paused. "If she went to court for the hearing, she should have a court-appointed attorney. Does she have one?"

"She doesn't like him very much."

"So, what is it exactly that I can do for you?"

"The truth is ma'am...."

"Sabre," she corrected him.

"Sabre, that's a beautiful name. Sabre, I came here because I just don't know what to do for my sister." He paused. "But also to see you again." He raised his hands up and out to each side, palms facing out. "Hope you won't be offended, but I'm going to be here a while and I just don't know another soul in this town." He smiled and his eyes twinkled.

Sabre hesitated and then shook her head slightly. She was caught off guard. When a man came into her office for legal help, she automatically shut down any personal interest in him. She seldom even noticed his looks or his charm once they were engaged in a legal matter. On occasion she caught them flirting with her, but she just failed to acknowledge it and dealt with them professionally.

"Before you say no, please hear me out. I'd like to take you out to a nice dinner and dance the night away with you, but I could understand that you might be reluctant to do that. So, all I'm askin' is that you join me for a cup of coffee and some conversation."

"I don't mix business with pleasure."

"In all fairness ma'am...Sabre," he corrected himself, "we haven't really done any business. And since you aren't wearing a ring and you didn't respond that you are otherwise involved, I'm assuming you're single. Am I correct?"

Sabre looked at Clint. He was quite attractive and charming. She had mixed emotions about whether or not she wanted to get to know him a little better. She didn't know if she wanted to be involved with anyone again. "Yes, you're correct. I'm single," she said, "but I really don't need any distractions in my life right now."

"I'm flattered that you see me as a distraction."

Sabre smiled. "I...I just don't want to start something." She said the words but she wasn't emphatic enough. She could hear the reservation in her own voice and she knew he did too.

"Come on. I'm not askin' you to marry me. Just want to break a few breadsticks." Sabre laughed and Clint continued, "Come on, what do ya' say? I'm sure you need a break. Let's go."

Sabre looked at the time on her phone. "Okay, a cup of coffee, but not today. I have an appointment in about fifteen minutes. How about tomorrow afternoon, four o'clock?"

"That'll work."

"There's a place in Seaport Village called Upstart Crow. It's a coffee shop and small bookstore, only a few miles from here and easy to find. Do you know where Seaport Village is?"

"No, but I'll find it." He picked up his hat, stood up, and ran his fingers through his hair front to back before he placed the hat on his head. He winked at her and nodded his head just slightly. It reminded Sabre of JP. She wondered if it was a Texas thing.

"See you tomorrow," Clint said and walked out of her office.

Chapter 25

JP arrived at Sabre's office right on time, report in hand. Sabre had just hung up the phone when he walked in.

"Thanks," she said, as he handed her the report. "Have a seat." Sabre hated that her stomach giggled whenever she saw him. "Do you think any one of my clients killed Judge Mitchell?"

"I've eliminated Wheeler. Both of the parents have an alibi—a Catholic priest, no less. They were helping the good padre with his Bingo Night. Besides, as crazy as those two are, I really don't think they're capable of murder."

"So, who does that leave?"

"Durham, Martinez, King, and Tran. If Durham wasn't locked up, he'd be my first pick. That kid is scary."

"What about his friend, Ralph?"

"Maybe. I'm still working on that. Ralph's not too bright. In fact, he's proof you don't have to have a long neck to be a goose. But that doesn't mean Durham wasn't pulling his strings. Ralph likes to brag and act like he's doing Durham a favor by hanging out with him. But, to tell you the truth, I think he gets more from the relationship than Durham does. Durham is a user and I think Ralph enjoys being his friend and more importantly, the alibi for an alleged killer."

"Do you believe Ralph was really with Durham when Hannah was killed?"

"It's hard to say, but I think his mouth writes a lot of checks that his butt can't cash."

Sabre smiled at his comment. "But even if Ralph is providing Matt with an alibi, it doesn't necessarily follow that Matt killed Hannah and Mason."

JP looked at her with an expression of complete incredulity. "Really? You still think he may be innocent?"

"I'm just saying that we really don't know. It all hinges on the bat. If he really didn't have the bat, then maybe he didn't do it. And according to the form Matt filed with the coach, his bat went missing the night of the Poway game."

"And you think Darren Flynn did it?"

"You said that Darren appears to have a real temper. If I can show that Matt didn't have the bat in his possession and point the finger at Darren Flynn, it may be enough for reasonable doubt."

"It's not like you to point at an innocent person."

"I'm not convinced he's innocent. If I were, I wouldn't do it. But juries need someone to pin it on and I think he's a real suspect."

"A jury? So you think he'll be tried as an adult, and you'll be there to represent him. Is that what I'm hearing?"

"I guess I'm getting ahead of myself, but it's not looking real good for keeping him in juvenile court. We haven't come up with much that supports that argument. And as for whether or not I'll follow him downtown, I haven't made that decision yet."

JP shook his head. "I don't like this."

"I don't either, but it's what we have to work with." Sabre glanced at JP's report. "What about the other cases? Anything that connects them to the judge's hit-and-run?"

"Juanita Martinez has some time unaccounted for. I had Bob ask her where she was that evening and she told him she went from her house back to her program."

Sabre saw the concern on JP's face. "But you weren't able to verify it?"

"She went back there alright, but she still could've had time for a hit-and-run. I can determine what time she returned to the house because that's logged in, but I'm not sure it's accurate since it appears she had been drinking, and Bob said she might not have signed in when she first arrived. I also can't pinpoint the exact time she left her house."

"Did she have a car?"

"She rode with someone. I haven't been able to track who she was with yet."

"And what about King and Tran?"

"The father on the King case, Isaiah Banks, is a bad dude. I'm going to Donovan tomorrow morning to talk to some of his cellmates. I'm not convinced it wasn't his doing when you were shot at the other day." He paused and looked at her, his expression somewhere between concern and frustration. "I wish you'd buy yourself a gun. I'm sure you'd qualify to carry a concealed weapon. I've offered before to teach you how to use it. That still stands."

Sabre drew a deep breath. "I know. A couple of the sheriff deputies at court have made the same offer."

"If you'd be more comfortable with one of them...."

"No, I didn't mean that. I'm just not comfortable with the idea of carrying a gun at all. I'd probably shoot some innocent person, or even a kid. I'm around kids too much. I could never live with myself if I did that."

"You could at least get one for your home."

Sabre shook her head. Guns scared her. She had never been around them. For a second she considered that maybe if she were more familiar with them she wouldn't be so hesitant, but she didn't want to talk about it. "What about Tran?" Sabre asked.

JP cocked his head, lowered his chin, and looked at Sabre with his eyes rolled up. Then he said, "I don't think she murdered anyone, but I need to do further investigation on her case for the custody issues. There's something strange going on there and I can't quite put my finger on it."

"Her behavior has been a bit odd. She seems to really love her daughter, Emma, yet she's been questioning the foster mother about adoption. It might be she's just afraid that her rights may be terminated, but the foster mother thought it was more than that. Ask around and see if she has talked to anyone else about giving up the baby."

"Will do. Anything else?"

"Not that I can think of. I left a message for the CASA worker, Mae Chu, but I haven't heard back from her. I'll let you know if I come up with something."

JP stood up, and on his way out the door without looking back said, "A nice little Sig Sauer would be good. I bet you can even find one with a pink pearl handle."

Chapter 26

The King Case
   Children: Devon King, age 2 (M), Kordell King, age 12 (M)
   Parents: Father of Devon—Isaiah Banks, Father of Kordell—Clay Walker, Mother—Brenda King
   Issues: Physical Abuse
   Facts: Isaiah Banks beat his stepson, Kordell, with a belt and his fist.

"Thanks for seeing me," JP said to the inmate who sat across from him, a huge African-American man with a large scar on his chin. The man's size alone would frighten a bear.

"I like visitors. Breaks up the day. But that don't mean I'm gonna tell you nothin'," he said gruffly.

"Fair enough. Tell me what you will. But let me tell you why I'm here."

"Why's that?"

"I'm working with an attorney who represents Isaiah Banks' son. She's trying to keep him and his older brother safe."

"From Isaiah?" the man's voice seemed to soften just a little.

"Not necessarily. We're trying to find the best placement for him. And we need to know if he is safe with Isaiah."

"How would I know that?" he snarled.

"You spent the last year in here with him. During that time, did he ever talk about his son?"

"Bragged about him all the time."

"Did his son ever come to visit?"

"Only once. Isaiah's old lady brought him, but I guess the boy's grandma was pretty upset. Said he had 'no bizness bringing that boy to see his selfish self.' I heard her givin' it to him one day after the boy had been here. The mother never brought the kid back after that. I don't know what the big deal was. He was just a baby. It's not like he'd remember it."

"Did the grandmother continue to come see him?"

"Every week."

"What about the boy's mother, Isaiah's girlfriend?"

"She came about once a month. That's pretty good. Most the time, the bitches don't keep coming. They find some other fool to keep them happy."

"Do you know who Isaiah hangs out with on the outside?"

"Nope. I met him in here." The big man's lip turned up just a little on the corner. "You know I wouldn't tell you even if I did, right?"

JP knew he wasn't going to obtain any real information from this man. He thanked him, spoke with a couple of guards he knew, and then went for his second scheduled interview with another inmate, Brandon Bennett, who knew Isaiah before he went to prison. Brandon and Isaiah had grown up on the same block. JP took a long look at Brandon as he walked into the interview room. He stood about five-foot-eight, was solidly built, and sported an angry woodpecker on his forearm. He apparently spent a lot of time in the gym, as he was buff and walked like he was proud of it.

After Brandon sat down, JP introduced himself. "I understand you know Isaiah Banks." The man didn't answer. "Is that correct?" JP asked.

"Yes, sir."

"How well do you know him?"

"We were friends when we were kids. We lived on the same block, only one house between us. We went to the same school, played on the same baseball and football teams. We were like brothers."

"And now?"

"Now it's different."

"How's that?"

"We grew up, man. Lives went on different paths. It's hard for two brothers of different color to stay friends in the hood."

"Because of the gangs?" JP asked, but it was more of a statement than a question. He knew both Isaiah and Brandon were affiliated with one.

"Yeah. We were only fourteen when Isaiah became a Skyline Piru. We foolishly thought I could be one, too. It nearly got me and Isaiah both killed."

"So when did you become a Peckerwood?"

Brandon glanced at the tattoo on his arm and then back at JP. "A few years after Isaiah hooked up with the Skyline Pirus, I joined a local group that called themselves Peckerwoods. They weren't affiliated with the motorcycle club out of Santee. I realize now they were mostly young 'wanabees.' The street gangs suck you in, but the prisons make it real. It's hard to survive either of them without a family. They become your family. The first time I went to the joint, the tattoo helped me fit in. The Skinheads seemed happy to increase their numbers." He lowered his voice. "You have to belong somewhere if you're going to survive in here."

"Do you have any contact with Isaiah?"

"Never inside. But outside on the streets, if we meet up, we speak."

"Do you know if Isaiah is involved with the Pirus now?"

"He used to lay pretty low on the outside—in prison too, for that matter. If called on, he'd do what he had to do, but he was no leader or anything. The word is things are different now."

"Different how?"

"They say he's done something that moved him up."

"Like killed a judge, maybe?" JP asked.

Brandon shrugged but made no response, leaving JP wondering if he didn't know or just wouldn't say.

Chapter 27

Sabre pulled into the Seaport Village parking lot and found a spot in the second row almost directly in front of Upstart Crow. She hesitated, wondering why she was doing this. She hated the discomfort of new relationships, but this wasn't going anywhere anyway. He would be here for a few days and then he'd be gone. After all, it was just a cup of coffee. Like Clint said, "I'm not askin' you to marry me. Just want to break a few breadsticks." She smiled at the thought of his comment. At least he had a sense of humor.

She stepped out of the car and walked into Upstart Crow. She looked around and didn't see Clint. Then she glanced at the time on her phone. It read 3:59. She should've been a few minutes late. She looked too eager. She considered turning around and leaving before he got there. If he called her again she'd tell him something came up and she couldn't call because she didn't have his number. Just as she turned to go, Clint stepped inside the front door.

"Nice place. Got here about fifteen minutes ago. Just been looking around. Hope I didn't keep you waiting."

"No, I just arrived."

He placed his hand lightly on her shoulder and guided her toward the coffee counter, then removed his hand and lowered his arm. He ordered a large, black, house-blend coffee. Sabre got her usual decaf mocha with non-fat milk. He paid for both, as well as for a little bag labeled "Duck

Food" that sat in a basket on the counter. They walked out back where a few tables and chairs gathered on the patio.

"We can sit here and watch the ducks," Clint said. "What do you think?"

"Perfect," Sabre said, as she looked toward the ducks. The temperature was seventy-two degrees, the air was still, and the sun was reflecting off the small pond. A wooden walkway formed a bridge over the water.

Clint set his coffee mug down on a table, pulled a chair out for Sabre to use, and then laid the bag of "Duck Food" on the table next to his cup. "San Diego is a beautiful city. Is your weather always this nice?"

"Most of the time. What's it like in Texas?" Before he could answer, she added, "What part of Texas are you from, anyway?"

"Dallas. I'm afraid I'm a big-city cowboy, but a Texan just the same," he said. "Have you lived here all your life?"

"Yes, I was born and raised here. Not in the city, though. We lived in the Poway area and there wasn't much there when I was growing up. The town itself only incorporated a few years before I was born."

"Any siblings?"

"Just one brother. How about you?"

"Two sisters. I was the youngest and the only boy, and I was quite spoiled according to my sisters. But now it seems I'm the one they call whenever there's trouble. I don't mind. I'd do anything for either one of them. Love 'em both more than all of Texas." He sipped his coffee. "Does your brother live here in San Diego?"

"No. He has moved on." Sabre couldn't explain where he really was and she didn't want to talk about it. Their conversation felt like a game of ping-pong, both giving short answers. She decided to ask a more open-ended question. "So, what was life like growing up in Texas?"

"Texas is hot and muggy much of the time. Don't get me wrong. I love Texas. But your weather and the ocean almost make me want to move here. My sister's been bragging about it for years."

"How is your sister, by the way?"

"'Bout the same, I guess. Sarajean was told by the social worker not to see her boyfriend, but she is anyhow. I think I may be making the situation worse, though."

"How's that?"

"I don't think her boyfriend would dare to do anything while I'm here and so my sister is thinking he's changed. I'm afraid once I leave, all hell will break loose."

"You're probably right. And her children won't be returned to her if she doesn't do what the court orders."

"Wish she would call you. Or maybe we should give her the number for that other feller, the one who was with you in the bar. That way, we wouldn't be mixing business with pleasure." He grinned at Sabre and gave her a quick wink. "I noticed that lawyer wore a wedding ring. You two just friends, right?"

"Yes, we're very good friends."

"Is he your law partner or something?"

"No, I'm a sole practitioner."

"You work all alone? No investigator or anything?"

"I hire an independent private investigator for a lot of my work."

"Always thought that would be an exciting job. Considered doin' it myself for a while. Was never quite sure how to go about getting started, though. What does he do for you? I mean, how does it work exactly?"

"When I have a case I need more information on, I give it to JP and tell him what I'm concerned about, and then he interviews witnesses, does a lot of research online, and writes a report for me. He was a detective with the San Diego Sheriff's Department for many years so he has a lot of experience." Sabre set her near empty cup down. "So, what is it you do for work back in Texas, Clint?"

"Construction mostly. I like working with my hands and I enjoy the outdoors. Not much for being cooped up. Figured an investigator doesn't spend much time inside, but the way you describe it, I might just be wrong. Guess I'll stick to what I know."

Sabre finished her coffee and pushed the cup forward on the table. "I should be going."

Clint picked up the bag on the table. "Not before we feed the ducks."

"Of course. We have to feed the ducks."

They walked onto the little bridge. Three ducks floated around as if they didn't have a care in the world. Clint opened the bag and then handed it to Sabre. "Go ahead," he said.

Sabre tossed a few pellets from the package into the water. One duck swam immediately to the food. The other two followed when they saw what he was after, quacking as they approached. Before the next pellet hit the water, four more ducks had appeared. Before the food was gone, Sabre had created quite a frenzy in the water. One of the smaller ducks couldn't seem to get his share. Sabre tried tossing it closer to him, but a larger, quicker duck snatched it up. She continued to throw the pellets at him, but she ran out before she was successful.

"Want me to get some more for the little guy?" Clint asked.

Sabre smiled. "No, I'm sure he isn't going to starve." She looked up and saw the sun starting to set on the water. "And I really need to be on my way." She took a step forward.

"I'll walk you to your car."

"Thank you."

His bright smile flashed across his face. "It's a selfish mo-tive. Just my way of spending a few more minutes with you."

When they reached Sabre's car he opened her door for her. "I'll call you soon, if that's alright with you."

Sabre was pleased that he made no attempt to kiss her. She nodded. "That would be fine."

Chapter 28

The Tran Case
  Child: Emma, age 18 mos. (F)
  Parents: Father—unknown, Mother—Kim-Ly Tran
  Issues: Neglect
  Facts: Mother left eighteen-month-old girl in locked room and went to work. Apartment complex caught on fire.

"Thanks for coming with me," JP said to Bob, as they sat down at a table in the dim light of Muffs.

"We're at a strip bar and you're buying the beer and the lap dance. It doesn't get much better than this."

"I just hope your wife doesn't kill me for it."

"Marilee's a good sport. She's not upset at you."

"So, you told her?"

"Are you crazy? Of course not. That's how I know she won't be upset. Of course, if she does find out, I'll blame it all on you."

"Of course you will."

The waitress came to the table wearing denim short shorts, a low-cut blouse with more than ample cleavage, and four-inch heels. Bob ordered a tap beer and JP ordered a Corona.

"You know you can't question Kim-Ly, right?" Bob said.

"I know. That's why I made sure we came when she wasn't here. At least she's not scheduled to be here. I called earlier acting as if I wanted to see her dance and they told me she was off today. I thought we'd ask around and see what we can find out about her."

"What's this 'we,' Kemo Sabe?"

"If you're going to have a lap dance, you may as well ask some questions."

"And ruin the moment? Not a chance."

JP looked around. "It seems pretty slow in here. I wonder if it's an unusual night or if it's always like this."

"I wouldn't know. I don't generally frequent strip bars. They tend to overcharge for beers, especially imported ones, and I don't see any point in looking at something you can't touch."

"Am I getting old or do these girls all look really young?" JP asked.

"They *are* young and yes, you are getting old."

"I'm going to go snoop around." JP stood up and walked to another area of the bar where three working girls, two blondes and a redhead, were standing around. He approached the bleached blonde with a purple streak in her hair.

"Got a minute?" he asked.

"Sorry, Sweetie, but I'm on stage in about thirty seconds. Come see me after my dance."

JP waited for a few minutes to see if either of the other two girls was leaving. Then he approached the redhead, whom he guessed to be about thirty years old, considerably older than the rest.

"Can I talk to you for a few minutes?"

"Are you a cop?"

"No, I'm not."

"If you want to pay for a lap dance, we can talk then."

JP pulled out two twenty-dollar bills from his wallet and held them out in front of him. The redhead snatched it from his fingers and stuffed it into her skirt pocket. "This way," she said and led him to an area somewhat secluded from the main bar where she pointed to a chair. A moment after he sat down, the redhead planted her stiletto heel on the corner of the chair.

"What's your name?" JP asked.

"Ginger." She started to lower her body toward JP's lap.

"You don't need to dance. I just want to ask a few questions."

She sighed. "What?"

"How well do you know, Kim-Ly?"

"You mean, Lotus. Why do you want to know?" she asked, and continued to descend toward his lap. She moved her hips around in a circular motion.

JP reached out his hands to halt the motion, but stopped before he reached her waist, remembering that the rules didn't allow any physical contact. "You really don't need to dance. I'm paying you to chat. I'm an investigator and we're trying to help Kim-Ly, er, Lotus." JP didn't want to mention the daughter in case it wasn't public knowledge in the bar.

"Is she in trouble with the law?"

"No, nothing like that."

"With the custody case, then?"

JP was a little surprised, but he didn't show it. "What do you know about that?"

She stopped gyrating, brought her leg down from the chair, and said, "I just know that CPS has taken her kid. They think because you dance for a living in a strip joint, you can't be a good mother." She sounded bitter as if she had some personal experience in the matter. JP didn't pry.

"How long have you known her?"

"She came to work here about a year and a half ago, shortly after her baby was born. But I don't really know her very well. She's very quiet. She comes to work, does what she has to do, and leaves."

"Have you ever seen her with her daughter?"

"No." Ginger scowled. "She'd never bring her baby here." Then she added, "You may want to talk with Star. She knows her better than I do."

"Which one is Star?"

"The blonde I was talking to when you walked up. Stay here. I'll send her to you."

"Thanks."

Ginger left and Star, a voluptuous blonde, appeared within a couple of minutes. The hair appeared to be natural, her breasts not so much. JP removed the cash from his wallet for the dance.

"Ginger said you were paying to talk."

"That's correct. I want to know what you can tell me about Lotus."

Star reached out her hand for the money before she answered. "She's young, she minds her own business, and she goes home to her kid. Or at least she did until the social worker snatched her away. Personally, I'd be glad. I wouldn't want to try to raise a kid if I was that young."

"That's the second time you said how young she is. Do you know her age?"

"No, but she sure ain't no twenty-one as she claims."

"Why do you say that?"

"Have you seen her? All those Asian girls look young, but she even acts young. She used to bring her teddy-bear backpack with her until Snake, that's the boss, made her leave it at home. She tried to claim it was her daughter's, but it was old and worn like she'd had it for a while and the baby was just a newborn."

"Do you know anything about her family or friends outside of work?"

"No, we're not, like, friends or anything. You should talk to Blossom. She spends more time with her than anyone."

JP started to think he was being duped. Each girl passed him on to another, probably just to get the money. Either none of them really knew anything, or they were dividing the information up between them so he had to pay more. His hands were tied either way. He waited for Star to send Blossom.

She appeared within a minute or two. Each dancer seemed younger than the one before. Convinced Blossom was jail-bait, JP made certain she didn't get too close. He didn't want to accidentally touch her.

He handed her forty dollars and asked, "How well do you know Lotus?"

"We're good friends," she said. She spoke so softly that JP had to strain to hear her. "And I wouldn't talk to you at all except I don't want her hurt."

"Do you think she's in danger?"

She wrinkled her brow. "What do you want?"

"I want to know anything about Lotus that might help her reunite with her daughter."

"And if she doesn't want to?"

"Has she told you that?"

Blossom raised her voice. "I thought you were here to help her." She walked away before JP could ask her anything else.

JP rejoined Bob at the table.

"How'd it go?" Bob asked.

JP took a drink of his warm beer. "I have more questions than answers." He set his bottle down. "You want a lap dance?"

"You're not my type."

JP shook his head.

Bob finished his nearly empty glass of beer in one swig and stood up. He took a quick look at the girl on stage. "Not really," he said, and they left.

Chapter 29

The Durham Case
   Child: Matt Durham, Defendant
   Type: Delinquency case
   Charges: Two counts of First Degree Murder
   Victims: Hannah Rawlins & Mason Usher
   Facts: Double homicide. Two teenagers bludgeoned to death
with a baseball bat.

Sabre read through the Durham file again. She tried to think of this young man as an innocent child, but the look on his face when he saw the photo of Hannah's body haunted her. She couldn't come up with any way to spin that even in her own mind. Dr. Heller's assessment only reinforced what Sabre had witnessed herself. She had to concentrate on protecting his rights. No matter what he had done, Matt still deserved the best defense. It wasn't her place to judge him. She would present the best case she could for him. That's all she could do. She shivered.

Sabre took a deep breath. Things weren't always what they seemed. Even if the kid did get some kind of perverse pleasure out of seeing the photo didn't mean he was the one to kill Hannah and Mason. Maybe it was the shock from seeing dead people that made him react so strangely. She knew she had to go forward in that mindset or she wouldn't be able to think clearly. After all, Matt claimed his bat was stolen and if it was, then how could he have committed the murders?

She read through JP's report again. She looked at the time. Baseball practice would start soon. Then she picked up her file, stood up, and walked to her car. If she hurried she could make it to the school before practice started. Maybe she could discover something that JP had missed.

Sabre watched the boys walk onto the baseball field. She took a seat in the bleachers. A young man hobbled up on crutches and sat down on the same bench, leaving space between them.

"What happened?" Sabre asked, glancing at the foot he had been favoring as he approached.

"I slid into second base, the base dislodged, and I jammed my foot against the metal pole that holds it in the ground."

"Sorry," Sabre said. "Is it broken?"

"No, just sprained, but I can't practice until it heals."

Sabre looked out onto the field. "Which one is Coach Arviso?"

"He's not there. Not sure where he is. It must be important, though, because he doesn't miss many practices."

After several minutes of small talk, Sabre asked, "Who do you think is the best hitter on the team?"

"That's a no-brainer. The catcher, Darren Flynn. He can hit the long ball like no one else on the team. He's the best this school has had since Tram."

"Tram?"

"Alan Trammell. Shortstop for the Detroit Tigers for nearly twenty years. He went to school here." The young man yelled out to the field as the shortstop dived for a line drive. "Good catch."

"That was impressive," Sabre said. "What's Darren Flynn like? Is he a good defensive player?"

"Yeah, he's real good. Catcher is a tough position. I've played it some, but I don't really like it. I'd much rather play third base."

"What's he like? Does he get along with his teammates?"

The young man looked up at Sabre curiously. "Are you some kind of scout or something?"

Sabre smiled. "No, I'm not a scout."

He sighed. "Good, because I sure would be bummed if you were scouting and I was sitting here on the bench with my crutches."

"That wouldn't be good, but I assure you I'm no scout."

"Darren's an okay guy. He's had a rough life. Grew up in the hood, so he's got a chip on his shoulder sometimes. He's got a quick temper, but most of the time he's okay. Since he doesn't do that well in his classes, a couple of us guys try to help him. He's in my history class and so we study together or work on projects sometimes. It's not easy for him and though he tries, he gets pretty frustrated."

"That's nice of you guys to do that."

"It's for the team." The young man seemed almost embarrassed by his good deed. "If he doesn't keep his grades up he won't be able to play. And we need him."

"Wasn't that kid that's charged with murder on this team?"

"Matt Durham. Yes."

"That must be kind of strange. Did you know him well?"

"I didn't hang out with him or anything, but I saw him at practice and games. And we had a couple of classes together. He didn't really have that many friends. I kind of felt sorry for him. Now I think he was just crazy. I mean, you'd have to be pretty crazy to beat someone to death, right?"

~~~

Sabre walked over to the gym to see Coach Arviso, not sure
what she had to gain by talking to him. She just wanted
answers. She had to prove that Matt didn't have his bat. That
was the key. What if Matt didn't do it? What if Darren stole his
bat like Matt said, beat those kids to death, and was trying
to pin it on her client? She had to find out.

When Sabre entered the gym area, she saw two male
students walking toward her.

"Could you point me to Coach Arviso's office?" Sabre asked.

"Right around the corner there. Turn left and it's the second
door on the right," one of them responded.

"Thanks."

Sabre walked to the office. The door was open. She stuck
her head inside, but there was no one there. She took a
few more steps down the hallway. Across from the coach's
office was an area with a large glass window looking into
the hallway. She could see three small desks inside. Only one
was occupied.

When she went inside the room, a slightly overweight,
young Hispanic girl who looked like a student was sitting
at the desk. She said, "May I help you?"

"I'm looking for Coach Arviso."

"He had a doctor's appointment today. He'll be back tomorrow. Anything I can help you with?"

Sabre was impressed with her professionalism. "I'm not
sure. I'm Sabre Brown, by the way. Do you work here?"

"Tracie Rodrigues. I'm a student worker."

Sabre looked around. "This looks like an interesting job.
How long have you had it?"

"I started working in this office at the beginning of last
semester. I like it, although it smells a little ripe in here
sometimes when all the guys come in from the fields. Before
they shower, I mean."

"I'll bet. Do you know most of the players?"

"Sure. I see most of them every day when their sport is on the roster. Some of them play several sports. I know those players the best."

The phone rang and Sabre waited until Tracie took the call. Then Sabre asked, "Do you know Darren Flynn?"

She frowned. "Yes, I know him," she said with a note of aversion in her voice.

"I take it you don't like him much?"

"He's a jerk. Always fighting with somebody. He never smiles. I tried a few times to smile at him and say hello, but he just grumbles. I don't know what his problem is."

"Did you ever see him fight with anyone?"

"He's a big guy and not too many people mess with him when he's mad. But several times I saw him arguing with someone...well, maybe not arguing exactly...Darren would just be swearing at them. Except at the Poway game with Matt."

"You were there?"

"Yes, I keep the unofficial stats for the games. Coach Arviso taught me. He looks for special things in the numbers. And I make sure the players stay in batting order."

"What happened between Matt and Darren?"

"Matt was going on deck and Darren had his bat. Matt asked for it and Darren got all smart with him, but then he gave it to him. Matt walked up the steps and Darren crashed into him."

"Then what happened?"

Tracie nonchalantly twisted her hair around her finger. "Matt just went up to bat and hit a home run and won the game. It was beautiful." She looked starry-eyed.

"Are you and Matt friends?"

"Not exactly." She shrugged. "Maybe, sort of."

Sabre found it curious that this young woman would talk so much without finding out with whom she was talking. But she was young and she knew many adults who may have done the same. "Look, Tracie, as I said, my name is Sabre Brown. I'm Matt's attorney and I'm trying to help him, so anything you can tell me may help us figure out what really happened."

A look of concern appeared on her face. "You don't think he really killed those other students, do you?"

"Matt says he didn't do it, but the DA doesn't see it that way. My job is to find out everything I can to prove his innocence. I can tell by the look on your face that you want to help him if you can."

"Yeah, I do...if he didn't do it. I can't believe he did it. He was always nice to me."

"Did you know him very well?"

"Not really, but he would come in all the time for practice. He'd smile sometimes." She turned her red face down toward her desk.

Sabre recognized the signs of a young girl with a crush. How hard it must be for her to think the guy she cared about may be a murderer. "Tracie, how do the players go about filing the forms for missing equipment?"

"They come in here and get one of these forms." She reached in her desk and took out a blank form titled *Missing Equipment*, and handed it to Sabre. "They fill it out and put it in this box on my desk, and then I file it in Coach Arviso's office."

"Do you remember Matt filling out the form the day after the Poway game?"

She shook her head. "No, but he might have done it when I wasn't here."

"Do you remember filing it?"

"Not really, but I might have. I file a lot of stuff. I really couldn't say."

"Does anyone else file the paperwork?"

"No, just me."

Sabre reached in her briefcase and pulled out a business card and handed it to the young woman. "Please call me if you think of anything else that might be helpful, especially anything that pertains to Matt or Darren. Even if you don't think it's important, it might mean something to our case."

Chapter 30

The King Case

   Children: Devon King, age 2 (M), Kordell King, age 12 (M)

   Parents: Father of Devon—Isaiah Banks, Father of Ko-rdell—Clay Walker, Mother—Brenda King

   Issues: Physical Abuse

   Facts: Isaiah Banks beat his stepson, Kordell, with a belt and his fist.

JP phoned his friend, Deputy Sheriff Gregory Nelson, to see if he could provide any information on Isaiah Banks. It bothered JP because if Banks killed Judge Mitchell, he likely did the drive-by shooting as well and Sabre may have been the target. He shared his suspicion with Greg, as well as his conversation with Brandon Bennett.

"I know he's become more heavily involved with the Piru gang," Greg said. "We're pretty certain that he's taken a leadership role with them, but why would he shoot at his girlfriend's son? The best I can tell, he's still pretty tight with Ms. King. He would have to have a damn good reason to go after her son." He paused for a second. "It doesn't quite compute for me."

"Unless the bullet wasn't intended for the kid. Or he may have ordered it but didn't do the actual shooting. Whoever did it may have messed up."

"In which case, the shooter is probably dead," Greg said. "I'll pass that on to The Gang Unit and to Homicide. They may not be aware of all the events in the juvenile case. I'm sure they'll appreciate the information."

"Thanks, Greg. If anything else comes up, I'll let you know."

~~~

JP hung up the phone trying to determine what his next step would be. He'd never forgive himself if Sabre was hurt because of this case. He wanted her to move in with him until everything settled down. She had done it once before when she was in trouble, but his house was a little full right now. Robin needed his shelter and protection. From the little information he had been able to gather, JP was convinced her husband was looking for her and that he'd kill her if he found her. His thoughts were interrupted when Louie bounded across the floor toward him, nearly crashing when he tried to stop.

"Hi, Buddy," JP said, as he reached down and scratched behind his ears. Louie ran toward the back door. JP followed him, opened the door, and Louie darted out with JP closely behind. Louie ran across the yard to his designated spot, lifted his leg, and then ran back to JP with all the enthusiasm of a beagle pup. Although well over a year old, he hadn't lost any of his "puppy" energy. JP picked up a Frisbee and tossed it across the yard. Louie zipped across the yard, jumped nearly three feet off the ground, and came down with the toy in his mouth. He proudly carried it back to JP and sat down and looked up at him with his big brown eyes until JP said, "Drop it." The Frisbee hit the ground and Louie bounced around, wagging his tail, until JP threw it again.

JP turned as Robin approached carrying two coffee cups. She handed one to JP.

"Thanks, and good morning," JP said.

"Is it? I'm not awake yet."

JP entertained Louie for a couple more throws and then said, "Enough." Louie nudged him with the Frisbee in his mouth, but after the second "Enough" command he dropped it and ran around the corner. JP accompanied Robin to the teak table and chairs where they sat down.

Robin circled the rim of her cup with her finger.

"Is everything okay?" JP asked.

"I'm just wondering how long I can stay here."

"As long as you need to. And that's until we know you're safe."

"I mean...I'm starting to get antsy. I need to go to work and start taking care of myself. I need some exercise. I need to do something before I start to like soap operas."

JP appreciated the humor, but he didn't smile. "I'm sorry. I've been so busy with the cases I'm working on that I haven't had a chance to do much investigating for you. I've made a few calls, but I haven't had the time to give it the attention your situation needs. I guess I just figure you're safe as long as you're here."

"But I can't stay here forever." Her voice held a hint of frustration. "Please, I don't mean to sound ungrateful. I'm not. I appreciate everything you've done. The truth is, I'd like to just hide away forever here. I feel safe and I'm sleeping better, but I can't ask you to give up your life. You haven't had one visitor since I've been here."

"I'm not exactly a social butterfly." He reached over and put his hand on hers. "As soon as I resolve this dead judge case we'll figure out what to do. In the meantime, I'd rather not be worrying about you, too."

"You're right."

"Look, I'm sure you feel like you're being hidden in a basement like a crazy aunt, but it won't be forever. I *have* done some investigating on this. I've alerted my friends in law enforcement. I've given them Cooper's license plate number and the make and model of his car, and if he's spotted in the area, I'll be alerted."

"Thanks. One minute I think I just need to face up to him and then the next I'm terrified." She swallowed. "I talked to Sandy yesterday. Ty's still not at home, which probably means he's out looking for me."

"But he's not here and he has no way of knowing you're here. So here's where you'll stay. He'll have to surface eventually and then we'll nab him."

JP's phone rang. It was Greg Nelson.

"I just spoke with Dave Lopez in Homicide. They found a body last night, a Piru gang member in a dumpster in the Valencia Park area. And get this: They think he was the shooter and they favor Isaiah Banks for ordering the drive-by."

"Have they found any evidence connecting Isaiah?"

"Nothing solid yet, but he's their number one suspect. I'd keep a closer eye on Sabre if I were you. We're doing what we can from here."

Chapter 31

The Wheeler Case
   Children: Holly (F) and Bradley (M), age 9 years (twins), four other children
   Parents: Father—Willie Wheeler, Mother—Debra Wheeler
   Issues: Physical Abuse, Neglect Facts: Dirty Home, drugs, alcohol, physical abuse, mental problems

It was nearly seven a.m. when Sabre arrived at the hospital to check on Dr. Heller. She went directly to her room and showed her ID to the policeman guarding the door. He checked his list and opened the door for her to enter.

Sabre sat down in the chair next to Heller's bed. It appeared very little had changed since her last visit. The doctor looked paler than before and she lay just as still. A nurse came into the room.

"Has there been any improvement?" Sabre asked.

The nurse shook her head. "Not really. Her vitals are good and she has brain activity, but she just won't wake up."

"Is this unusual? For her kind of injury, I mean."

"It's hard to say. A blow to the head can affect the body in many ways. I've seen patients become conscious right away and others who never do."

"I haven't talked with her doctor recently. Do you have any idea what he expects?"

The nurse changed a bottle on her IV stand. "They won't know any more until she wakes up."

"Has the doctor been in yet this morning?"

"No. He usually comes in before now, so he must be hung up somewhere."

After waiting for another half an hour by Dr. Heller's side without Dr. Brister appearing, Sabre left.

~~~

Bob met Sabre at the front door of the courthouse. "How is Dr. Heller?"

"No change," Sabre said as they walked inside.

"Sorry to hear that. She's a good psychologist."

"Mr. Clark, I do declare, you just said something good about a therapist. You must be feeling especially well this morning."

"Maybe I should qualify that. I like Dr. Heller. She's better than most and she tries to do the right thing. But I still think the whole therapy thing is a bunch of hooey."

"And...he's back." Sabre laughed. "So, are you ready for the Wheeler trial?"

"Always."

They walked together through the lobby. "Any chance we can settle this?"

"If you can talk some sense into that nubile little vixen."

"The social worker, Heather Staples?"

"I'm going to tear her a new one when she takes the stand."

Sabre smiled. She knew he could do it, too. Bob was quite adept at cross-examination and it was the social worker's first trial. "What are you contesting?"

"This petition is moot now. The car engine has been removed from the living room. The house is clean. I went there myself and took pictures. The mother is attending drug programs regularly and dad is back in therapy."

Sabre listened and then said, "And as for placement, I'm sure the parents want the children returned, but are they willing to leave them with the paternal aunt for a while longer? She's back now and there's no reason why these kids have to stay in Polinsky any longer, or go to a foster home, for that matter."

"Maybe," Bob said. "But I'm not sure you can convince that little twerp. How old is she, anyway? About twelve?"

Sabre smiled. "I'll be back."

Sabre walked toward Department Four. When she reached the courtroom she went inside. The court was not in session, so she approached the bailiff. "Have you seen Ahlers?"

"He just went upstairs with that cute little social worker that Bob loves to hate."

Sabre went up the steps and found the County Counsel sitting at a small table with Heather Staples, the social worker on the Wheeler case. "Just the people I'm looking for."

"Hi, Sabre," Ahlers said. "What can I do for you?"

"Can we settle this case?"

"No," the social worker responded quickly. At the same time Ahlers said, "Maybe."

Heather's face turned red and she puffed up. Ahlers raised his hand just slightly motioning her to stop. He turned to Sabre. "What's your position on this?"

"I've been told they've cleaned up the house and the mother is in treatment. Is that correct?" She looked directly at Heather.

"Yes, but...."

"So, the real issue is disposition, am I right?"

Ahlers turned to the social worker as she answered, "These kids are in danger. This family has so many problems. The parents are not fixable."

"They're not fixable?" Sabre said adamantly. "So, you don't think there is any hope for this family? Are you proposing we go right to a .26 hearing?"

"She's not saying that, Sabre," Ahlers said.

"Maybe I am. This family has already had too many chances. These kids need a better life," the social worker said.

Sabre shook her head. "It would be wonderful if we could give these children a perfect family, but first of all we aren't going to find one of those. Furthermore, the psychologists have all said these children need their parents and they need each other. All we can hope to do is keep them safe and provide for them the best we can. The court already has jurisdiction over this family. The 387 petition is really a dispositional issue."

"But...," Heather started to object.

Ahlers interrupted, "So, you want us to withdraw the 387 petition?"

"I don't care one way or the other. Like I said, we already have jurisdiction so the real issue is the placement. So, if we can agree to place these children with the paternal relatives, and I will fight for that because I truly believe that's the best place for them, then perhaps we can settle this without a trial."

Heather shook her head.

"Sabre, if you'll give us a few minutes. I'd like to talk to my client," Ahlers said.

"Certainly," Sabre said and walked downstairs.

~~~

About ten minutes later Ahlers came downstairs and met with Sabre. Bob and Regina, the attorneys for the Wheelers, joined them. After some discussion, the attorneys and an obviously disgruntled social worker agreed to settle the case. The petition was withdrawn with a new permanent plan placing the children with the paternal aunt. It was understood that after six months the parents could look again at placement. More importantly, to all the attorneys' satisfaction, they'd be dealing with a more experienced social worker.

Chapter 32

The Tran Case
Child: Emma, age 18 mos. (F)
Parents: Father—unknown, Mother—Kim-Ly Tran
Issues: Neglect
Facts: Mother left eighteen-month-old girl in locked room
and went to work. Apartment complex caught on fire.

"Hi, Marla," Sabre said to the social worker on the Tran case as she walked into her office. "It's nice to have you on a case again." Marla Miller was Sabre's and Bob's favorite social worker. She worked hard and guarded the children with everything she had, but she understood this wasn't a perfect world.

"Thanks. You, too. I don't think we've had a case since Alexis Murdock. At least nothing nearly that crazy." Marla pointed to a chair. "Take a load off."

Sabre pulled the chair to the side so she could see Marla. Her desk was piled too high to see over the stacks. "That was a pretty awful case. Do you ever hear anything from them?" Sabre knew Marla tried to keep track of her old cases, especially the ones that were the most worrisome or the ones that involved children with whom she had become attached.

Marla smiled. "You know me all too well. I spoke with Alexis' mother just last week. They're doing very well. You know the other children, Jamie and Haley, were placed with a maternal great-aunt in Decatur, which is only about seven or eight miles from Atlanta. The siblings have regular contact." Marla scooted her chair back from her cluttered desk. "So, enough of this trip down memory lane. I understand you have some concerns about the Tran case. So do I, especially in light of the CASA worker."

"What about the CASA worker?"

"I thought you knew. I'm sorry. A woman named Mae Chu was assigned to work on the case last week."

"Yeah, I knew that much. I've left her several messages, but she hasn't returned my calls."

"She seems to have disappeared."

"What do you mean, disappeared?" Sabre tilted her head to one side, looking a little confused.

"She received her assignment, but she never reported in and now no one can reach her."

"The court ordered the CASA appointment about nine or ten days ago. How long has she been missing?"

"We're not sure exactly. The judge made the order a week ago Tuesday. Wednesday, Mae Chu was assigned the Tran case. She picked up the packet on Thursday and no one at CASA has heard from her since."

"Was it reported to the police?"

"Yes, but not until a couple of days ago because initially the CASA supervisor figured Mae just got cold feet and didn't want the case."

"I know the volunteers often change their minds. They become overwhelmed or afraid they can't do the job."

"It happens. But then, after the supervisor called a few times and received no response, she tried Mae's emergency contact, a friend of Mae's, and the friend hadn't spoken to her for over a week. She claimed that wasn't unusual, though. They often went weeks without talking."

"And no one else reported her missing?"

"Mae doesn't work and she lives alone so there's no one to really miss her. The police are looking into it now, but I don't know if they have officially listed her as a missing person."

"Hopefully the cops will find she's just on vacation or something. Although, my investigator said there's something about this case that bothers him...but I don't have anything specific to give you." Sabre thought for a moment. "There is one thing. Has Kim-Ly ever said anything to you about giving her daughter up for adoption?"

"No. Do you know something I don't?"

"It's what she said to the foster mother, but it was more in the form of questions. It may be that she's concerned she's going to lose her child permanently."

Marla leaned back in her chair. "I haven't heard anything like that. Kim-Ly seems to take good care of the child for the most part. And she obviously loves Emma. I know she works as a stripper, but I don't care about that as long as what she's doing is legal. I know a lot of those girls are hooking and that could put the child in danger, but I don't have any evidence to support that Kim-Ly is involved in that activity."

"Have they assigned another advocate to replace Mae Chu?" Sabre asked.

"Yes." Marla shuffled through one of the six stacks of files on her desk. Then she reached for a second stack. "Here it is." Marla retrieved a file marked *Tran*, opened it up, and flipped through a couple of pages. "Her name is Nora Gonzalez. I'll copy this for you so you'll have all her information." Marla swung her chair around, placed the page on the printer behind her desk, made a copy for Sabre, and handed it to her.

"Thanks, I'll call her as soon as I return to the office. Do you know if she has started an investigation yet?"

"I don't know."

"Anything else I need to know on this case?"

"I don't think so. I'll let you know if I hear anything new on Mae Chu."

~~~

Sabre returned to her office, called Nora Gonzalez, left her a message explaining who she was, and asked for a return call. Then she called JP and told him about the missing Mae Chu. "Perhaps you can add it to the things you're looking for when you continue your investigation on this case. It probably doesn't have anything to do with Kim-Ly or our dependency case, but you never know."

"I'll do that. And Sabre, don't make any more visits on the King case without me, okay?"

"Have you found out something new?"

"Just a gut feeling. Isaiah Banks is a real badass and until I have more answers I'd feel better if you didn't make those visits alone."

"Okay. I didn't plan on going any time soon anyway. If I decide to go this weekend, I'll let you know."

Just as Sabre hung up the phone, Elaine walked in. "Your cowboy's here."

Sabre looked puzzled. She had just hung up with JP. Then she realized it must be Clint. She took a deep breath and reprimanded herself for the tingly feeling in her stomach. "Send him in."

Sabre smiled when he walked in. "Good afternoon."

"Let me apologize for barging in, but I wanted to ask you to dinner. How about tomorrow?"

"You could have called."

"I know," he smiled at her sheepishly, "but I figured you'd have a harder time saying 'no' if I came in person."

She laughed. "You're right about that." She looked at him for several seconds before she continued. She liked this guy, but she had mixed emotions about the fact that he wouldn't be here long. She could have a good time and then he'd be gone so she wouldn't have to be concerned about getting involved. But if she really liked him, then he'd be gone and she may be heartbroken again. "Okay. Saturday."

"Seven o'clock okay?"

"Yes, I'll meet you at the restaurant. Did you have a place in mind?"

"It's your city. You pick."

"World Famous. It's in Pacific Beach. Would you like directions?"

"Nope. I'll find it. See you Saturday at seven." He winked at her and turned toward the door. "I'm leaving now before you have a chance to change your mind."

Chapter 33

The King Case
  Children: Devon King, age 2 (M), Kordell King, age 12 (M)
  Parents: Father of Devon—Isaiah Banks, Father of Ko-
rdell—Clay Walker, Mother—Brenda King
  Issues: Physical Abuse
  Facts: Isaiah Banks beat his stepson, Kordell, with a belt and
his fist.

"Thanks for meeting me for lunch," JP said to Greg Nelson. Although they were friends, they didn't get together socially that often. Recently, however, they had found themselves on several cases together. Even though they were working them from totally different angles, it felt like old times.

"No problem, as long as you know you're buying."

"You're the one who makes the big bucks, Detective. I'm just a lowly PI, scraping to keep the dogs alive."

"Yeah, right." He smirked. "So, you're concerned about Isaiah Banks?"

"After our conversation yesterday, I got more worried about Sabre Brown. You remember meeting her, right?"

"Of course. Nice woman, even if she is a defense attorney. Are you still smitten with her?"

JP put his fork down. "What are you talking about?"

"Oh, come on, anyone who has seen you two together knows there's something going on there."

"Dang, I guess I better not play poker with you."

"There's nothing wrong with your poker face. At the tables no one can tell what you're holding, but when it comes to love, you're like a puppy with his master."

JP waved his hand in a gesture that indicated "enough." "Here's what I know. Isaiah Banks has a son who was removed from his home by DSS. The judge wasn't ruling in his favor and was killed by a hit-and-run. Dr. Heller was scheduled to perform a psychological evaluation on Banks the same day as she was hospitalized, also the result of a hit-and-run. Sabre went on a home visit to see Isaiah's stepson and she almost took a bullet from a drive-by shooter."

"And you think Banks is responsible for all of that?"

"I find him to be a very likely suspect. He's also a long-time member of the Piru gang and seems to have recently gained some stature in the organization."

"And if it is him, you think Sabre is in danger?"

"Definitely. The problem is I don't know what I can do about it. I can't exactly infiltrate the Pirus. No one in his neighborhood is going to talk to me. And if I go snooping around I'm liable to put Sabre in even more danger. I'm stuck. Can you help me out?"

"We're already on it, JP. Ever since you called me, Banks has been our primary suspect. We've got a couple of guys tailing him right now. When he makes a wrong move, and he will, we'll nail him. We're still waiting on the coroner's report on the dead guy who we think was the drive-by shooter, the one who almost hit Sabre. Maybe when that's in, we'll have what we need to arrest Banks. But more importantly, we're keeping our eyes on Sabre in case any unusual activity comes her way."

"Thanks, Greg. But you could've told me all this on the phone."

Greg pushed his empty plate away from him. "And miss a free lunch? Don't be silly."

"There's one other thing I need to ask." The waitress approached and they both ordered coffee.

"What's that?" Greg asked.

"Do you have any news on Robin's husband, Tyson Doyle Cooper?" Before Greg could answer, JP said, "What kind of ego uses all three names, anyway? A guy like that must think the sun comes up just to hear him crow."

"That's a mouthful to say every time you have to give your name. I'm sure it would be especially tough for you since you seem to have trouble just getting out two initials: 'J' and 'P.'"

The waitress approached with the coffee. JP took his black. Greg poured some cream in his cup and stirred it. They both thanked her.

"To answer your question," Greg said, "We haven't found a trace of him. Maybe if we were in Texas we might be able to find someone who could lead us to him. No one has spotted his vehicle. We can't find where he has used a credit card, so if he's in this area he must be using cash. Frankly, I don't think he's here. And since I can't talk to law enforcement in his home town—Robin says they're his friends—for all I know he's still there."

"I'm having the same trouble, which worries me more than ever. He doesn't appear to be back in his hometown so he's doing a good job of hiding, wherever he is."

"Robin is a sweet girl. I'm sorry you two couldn't make it together. How's she doing, by the way?"

"She's getting antsy, but she's also very frightened. She's not the same person I once knew. She was so full of life, bubbly, and happy. I'm sure you remember how she wouldn't stop talking."

"I remember. She's quite a character."

"Not now. She still talks to me. Told me all about what happened in great detail, like she normally would have, but her voice is different. She was beaten up pretty bad and her spirit nearly broken by that creep. The joy is gone from her voice. Tyson Doyle Cooper," JP stretched the name out, making it sound even longer, "is meaner than a skillet full of rattlesnakes. He's a coward who beats up on women. And worst of all, he has the money to cover his tracks."

"He's bound to surface, and when he does we'll grab him," Greg said.

"I just don't know how long I can keep Robin cooped up where she's safe."

Chapter 34

The Tran Case

Frustrated at his lack of ability to find anything leading him to Judge Mitchell's murder and not being able to find anything else on Tyson Doyle Cooper, JP decided to concentrate on finding out what was going on in the Tran case. It was coming up for a hearing soon and Sabre needed to make a recommendation about this little girl's life. After several hours of computer research, JP drove to the condo complex in Mira Mesa where Mae Chu lived. He knocked on the door of the condo next to hers, explained that he was a private investigator, and asked if anyone had seen her recently.

A woman in her forties lived there with her husband and two dogs. She said, "I haven't seen her for a couple of weeks, but that's not unusual. She drives into her garage in the back, closes the garage door, and goes in the house. Lots of the neighbors do that."

"How long have you lived here?"

"About a year. She was here when we moved in."

"Have you ever met her?"

"No. I wouldn't even know her name except that we get her mail once in a while."

JP thanked her and walked around the building to see where she would enter through the garage. Two rows of condos formed a line with the garages facing one another. Between the rows of condos was a driveway that formed an alleyway. Mae's condo was the fourth one in a row of six. The garage door next to Mae Chu was open and a man was cleaning his car. He looked to be in his late sixties, stood about six-foot-three, and was wearing shorts and a T-shirt.

JP introduced himself. "Do you know Mae Chu, your neighbor?"

"I wouldn't say I know her. I've seen her enough that I would probably recognize her in another setting, but we've never really had a conversation. She moved in here about two years ago."

"Two years ago? And you've never talked to her?" JP thought this quite odd. He was a private person himself, but he knew his neighbors. City folks are strange.

"I spend a lot of time in my garage with the door open and I see people coming and going, so I probably mix with more people than a lot of the other neighbors. You have to understand, there's no real meeting place, like in a house with a front yard, so unless you have a dog you walk, or you hang out with your garage door open, you're not going to see much."

"When did you last see her?"

"I saw her leave here in her car last Saturday around six or six-thirty."

"Was she alone?"

"Yes."

"And you didn't see her return?"

"No. I was in my garage working on a project until nearly midnight. It was a warm night so I left my door open. If she came back, it was after that." He pointed to the driveway that came off the street. It was directly in front of his garage. "As you can see, that's the only way in here in a car, so I would see anyone who comes in."

"Did Mae Chu have many visitors? A boyfriend, maybe?"

He shook his head. "Naw, not that I ever saw. I can't remember any visitors."

JP was hitting nothing but dead ends with the CASA worker. And for all he knew, she had simply decided that being a child advocate was too much for her and she split. She apparently had no one to answer to and she had the means to live without working. She could be basking in the sun or climbing a mountain somewhere. It was time to move on to something else.

~~~

Quang Pham, Kim-Ly's teenage neighbor, opened the door and let JP inside.

"Thanks for seeing me again. I just have a few more questions," JP said.

"Sure." Quang sat down at the table that looked out at Kim-Ly's old apartment. His laptop computer set in front of him with three books to his left and several sheets of paper on his right. The only other thing on the table was a jade statue. JP took a seat next to him.

"Have you seen anyone coming or going from Kim-Ly's apartment since we last spoke?'

"Nobody, except the landlord was there once."

"How do you know it was the landlord?"

"Because he owns this building, too."

JP picked up the jade statue from the table and admired it. "This is beautiful. Who is it?"

"King-Monk Tran Nhan Tong," Quang said. He reached for the statue. "It's...it's my mother's. She would be very upset if anything happened to it." He stood up, took the statue over to a shelf, and placed it there.

"Who is King-Monk what's-his-name?"

"Tran Nhan Tong," Quang finished the name for him. "He was the third king of the Tran dynasty. He became king when he was only twenty-one years old. He gave up the throne fifteen years later and became a Buddhist monk. He's best known for being the founder of Vietnamese Zen Buddhism."

"That's interesting. Are you Buddhist?"

"No, we're Christians, but I like learning about our culture."

"That's a good thing," JP said. "So, have you seen the man with the big, black car?"

Quang shook his head. "No. He hasn't been back, at least not that I've seen."

"What about Kim-ly or Jade? Have you seen either of them?"

The teenager looked down at the floor when he answered. "No...no, I haven't." He looked back up at JP and said, "I need to get back to my homework. I have a project due tomorrow."

JP thought he had hit a nerve. He already suspected that Quang had a crush on his attractive neighbor. He wondered if Quang had snuck back into Muffs to get a glimpse of Kim-Ly.

Chapter 35

The Martinez Case

Children: Ray, age 2 (M), Falicia, age 5 (F), Jesse (Jesus), age 7 (M)

Parents: Father—Gilberto Martinez, Mother—Juanita Martinez

Issues: Abuse, Domestic Violence

Facts: Mother beat the father with a lamp in front of the children. Alcohol abuse by both parents.

"Yes, I'm sure it's okay to give you the name of the person Juanita was with," Bob said. "She assures me that she had no part of the hit-and-run on the judge. In fact, she said she would be pleased if you could clear her name."

"Yeah, I'm sure she said that," JP said, as he responded on his cell phone.

"Okay, she said something more like, 'Tell that private dick to get his head out of his ass and figure this out so they'll leave me alone.'"

"That sounds more like the lovely Juanita. So, who was her chauffeur?"

"Her name is Reyna Garcia. I even have an address for you, but I'd like to go along if I could."

"You would?"

"Yeah. You know, to protect my client's interest and all."

"Right. Sure, you can come. I'd like the company. If you're ready, I'll swing by and pick you up in a few."

"See you shortly."

JP hung up the phone and wondered just how bored Bob was that he wanted to accompany him. Or was he up to something?

~~~

Bob and JP pulled up to the address Juanita Martinez had provided them. A blue, 1998 Mazda Millenia sat in the driveway in front of the light, coral-colored adobe cottage. Geraniums created a sea of red across the entire front of the house, stopping only for the three steps leading to the doorway. The lawn was green but it needed mowing.

Reyna Garcia opened the door before the two men reached it. "Well, to what do I owe this pleasure?" she said in a raspy voice. She stood about five-feet-ten without shoes. Her body was solid but not fat, nor did it appear shapely, a fact well-disguised by her choice of long tunic and black pants. Her attractive, almost regal, face was covered with tastefully applied make-up.

"Reyna Garcia?" Bob asked.

"Yes, that's me."

"That means queen, right?"

"That's correct."

"I'm sure you well deserve your name." He winked at her and reached out to shake her hand. "I'm Bob Clark, Juanita Martinez' attorney, and this is the private investigator for her children. He'd like to ask you a few questions."

JP frowned at Bob, wondering why he was acting so strangely. Bob always charmed the ladies, but today he seemed almost flirtatious.

"Come on in, boys." Reyna stepped back and let them pass. Then she took JP by the arm and led him into the living room and to the sofa. "Please, have a seat. Would you like some ice tea?"

"No, thank you," Bob said. He sat down in an overstuffed arm chair.

"Lemonade, perhaps?" When no one responded immediately, she said, "I could make a pot of coffee, if either of you would like coffee?"

"No, thank you. We're just fine," JP said. "We just have a few questions. A week ago Tuesday, Juanita told us you gave her a ride to her home. Is that correct?"

Reyna seated herself in the middle of the sofa right next to JP, brushing her leg slightly against his as she sat down. He scooted his leg over and crossed his feet.

"Oh yes, honey. She needed to pick up some clothes and to have a little 'you-know' visit with her man."

"Did you go inside?"

"No, I ran a couple of errands while she had her visit. I went to Walgreens and bought some Tylenol. I had a terrible headache that day." She cupped her hand over her chin, her head tipped downward, and rolled her eyes up as if she were thinking. "Then I put gas in my car. Afterwards, I stopped at one of those drive-by coffee buildings and picked up a cup of coffee. I drove back to Juanita's and sat in the car and drank my coffee while I waited for Juanita to finish her business. I think the caffeine in the coffee did me the most good."

JP looked at Reyna. "The most good?"

She looked directly into JP's eyes, holding his gaze. "Yeah, more than the Tylenol for my headache. Anyway, it went away."

JP felt uncomfortable, and he looked back at his notepad. "Do you know what time you left the house after you picked Juanita up?"

"Around six, I think."

"What were you driving?"

"My Mazda. It's the only car I have. Juanita told me that she may be a suspect for the hit-and-run of that judge. She couldn't have done it. I know that because she was with me, and I know I didn't do it. You're more than welcome to look at my car. It has a few dings, but nothing recent. I mean, you couldn't kill someone with your car and not get a few dents, right?"

"Would you mind?" JP was ready to stand up and put a little distance between Reyna and himself. She was attractive enough, and seemed nice enough, but something about her made him uncomfortable. He didn't like people in his space and she was just too close.

"Not at all," Reyna said. They all stood up and once again she took JP's arm and led him through the dining area and toward a door. "We'll go through the garage."

JP thought Bob must have noticed how uncomfortable she made him because JP heard him snicker. Leave it to Bob to enjoy someone else's discomfort.

She opened the door and stepped inside the garage. "See. No car in the garage." She pushed the button to open the garage door and they walked outside to examine her Mazda.

Bob stood back while JP examined the entire car. He looked carefully at the bumper, the fenders, and the front end of the car. It appeared to still have the original paint job and no indication of a recent accident or crash of any kind. JP bent down and looked under the car. When he started to stand up, Reyna leaned over to see what he was doing. He almost hit her chin with the top of his head, but she pulled back. That's when JP saw it.

He tried to sound unconcerned when he spoke. "Thank you, Reyna. You've been most helpful."

JP moved quickly toward his pickup. As soon as he was inside and Bob was seated, JP turned to Bob and with a red face said, "You son-of-a...."

Bob burst out with laughter before JP could finish his sentence and continued to laugh throughout the long rant of profane words JP spouted to describe his friend.

"What...haha...gave it...haha...away?" Bob's words were barely understandable for the laughter.

"I saw her...no, *his* Adam's apple, you jerk! Now I know why you were so eager to go with me. I should've known."

"She's quite...haha...attractive, don't you think?" Bob removed his glasses and wiped the tears of laughter from his eyes.

"You ass! I'm going to get even, you know. And when I do, you better watch out."

Bob doubled up with laughter.

"You're so ornery a snake couldn't bite you without dying," JP muttered as he drove away.

Chapter 36

The Durham Case
  Child: Matt Durham, Defendant
  Type: Delinquency case
  Charges: Two counts of First Degree Murder
  Victims: Hannah Rawlins & Mason Usher
  *Facts: Double homicide. Two teenagers bludgeoned to death
with a baseball bat.*

Bob and Sabre were just finishing their lunch at Pho's. She took some money out of her pocket and laid it on the bill just as her phone rang. It was a local number, but it was unfamiliar to her.

Bob stood up. "Go ahead, take it. I'll take care of the check."

She answered it. "Hello."

"This is Tracie Rodrigues. I work at the high school in the coach's office. You know, with Coach Arviso and the other coaches. I'm a student worker." She sounded nervous and Sabre tried to tell her she knew who she was as soon as she said her name, but Tracie kept talking. "I talked to you the other day when you were here...about Matt and other stuff. Remember me?"

"Yes, I remember you."

"I gotta go," she said suddenly and hung up.

Bob returned from the cashier. "That was quick."

"And strange." Sabre's forehead wrinkled. "That was a student worker whom I spoke to the other day on the Durham case."

"What did she want?"

"I don't know. She gave me her name, and then said she had to go and hung up. But she must have wanted to tell me something or she wouldn't have called."

They walked out of the restaurant and to Bob's car.

"She probably just got busy. Maybe another phone call came in. These kids can't do more than one thing at a time," Bob said. Sabre still looked concerned and confused. "We're right here by the school. Let's go over there."

"Do you have time?"

"Yeah, it's early."

Bob drove out of the lot, made a right, went through the intersection, and pulled into the school parking lot. "Nam-yam-yam-ya-nam," Bob chanted, as he pulled into a parking spot.

"What is that you're chanting?"

"It's the parking lot chant to Brodenia, goddess of love, lust, and parking spots. It works every time."

"But you didn't even say it until you were already pulling into the spot."

"It's all about timing."

"You're strange," Sabre said.

They stepped out of the car and walked onto the campus. The lunch hour had ended and most of the students were back in class. A few stragglers walked across the quad. Sabre didn't bother to stop at the office and check in. She just moved forward as if she belonged.

When they reached the gym, Bob said, "Do you want me to wait out here?"

"That would be best. She may be more comfortable talking to me alone."

"You don't suppose I can smoke out here?"

"No," Sabre said emphatically. "And you don't smoke any-more, remember?"

"I know, but it was always so much fun smoking on campus. It just feels like I should."

Sabre shook her head and walked inside. The smell of sweaty bodies hit her the minute she entered. Even though the locker rooms and the gym were down the hallway, the odor lingered. Two boys in shorts and T-shirts and a coach, dressed the same way and carrying a clipboard in his hand, walked past her. Sabre tried the first door to the office, but it was locked just as it had been the last time she was there. She then went around the corner and down the hallway a few steps to another door, passing a large window where she could see Tracie sitting at her desk and talking to a man. The door was open. She entered the small office.

Sabre waited for a moment. The man said, "Thanks," to Tracie and he left.

"What are you doing here?" Tracie asked abruptly. She waved her hands in a dismissal gesture. "I'm sorry, I didn't mean to sound rude. I'm just surprised."

"You called me and then you hung up. I was concerned."

"Everything's good. I shouldn't have called."

Sabre stepped closer to the desk where Tracie sat. "Tracie," Sabre said softly. "What is it? What do you know that you need to tell me?"

"It's probably nothing."

"Why don't you tell me and let me decide."

Tracie fiddled with her hair, twisting it around and around her finger, letting it go, and then doing it again.

"What is it, Tracie?"

"I'm afraid."

"Afraid of who?"

"I'm not afraid of someone. I'm afraid that if I'm wrong, it could hurt someone."

Sabre put her hands on the edge of the desk and leaned in a little toward Tracie. "Do you think you're wrong about what you saw or heard?"

"No, I know what I saw. But what if I'm wrong about what it all means?" Tracie stumbled over each word.

"Just tell me what you saw. I don't need to know what you think it means. Just breathe...and talk to me."

Tracie took a deep breath. "You know how Matt said he filed that form about the missing bat the day after the game?"

"Yes," Sabre said gently.

"He didn't."

"And how do you know that? I thought you said you didn't remember filing it?"

"I didn't file it. That's just it. Friday, the day of the Poway game, I went through the file in Coach Arviso's desk and removed all the old forms. Only one recent form remained in the file and it was for a missing basketball. On Tuesday afternoon just before I left for the day, I filed all the new forms that had been filled out. There were three of them and none of those was from Matt. Matt's form for the bat didn't show up until later. We discovered it when your PI was here talking to Coach Arviso."

"Why didn't you tell me this before?"

"Because I didn't really think it mattered until I remembered something else."

"What was that?"

"On Wednesday morning, the day after Hannah and Mason were killed, I was alone in the office and I went outside for my break, but I forgot my soda and I came back in through that door over there." She pointed to the door behind her desk. "We always keep that door closed and locked, but I have a key."

Sabre leaned in and listened.

"When I came back in I was behind this file cabinet." Tracie stood up and positioned herself behind the cabinet. "I could see right through that big glass window, but no one could see me." She stopped.

"Tracie, what did you see?"

"I saw Matt Durham. He was leaving this office and he had a paper in his hand. He went across the hall to Coach Arviso's office. He looked around and then he went inside. He stayed in there for about a minute or two. He peeked out of the door before he came out, and then he hurried away."

"Did he have the paper in his hand when he came out?"

"No." She twisted her hair again.

At first Sabre wondered why Tracie stood so long behind the file cabinet watching Matt, but then she remembered what it was like to be a teenage girl and have a crush on a guy. And at that point in time Tracie had no reason to believe Matt was a cold-blooded killer.

~~~

Bob was on the opposite side of the basketball courts when Sabre walked out of the gym area. He walked across and met her.

"He killed those kids," Sabre said quietly.

"Who?"

"Matt. He killed Hannah and Mason. He beat them to death with a bat," she said disgustingly.

"So? You already knew he did it. What's the big deal?"

Sabre took a deep breath and blew it out. "I guess I knew it, but now I *know* I know it." She threw her hands up. "And I didn't want to know it. I think what bothers me most is Matt's reaction to the photo of Hannah. I can't get that out of my mind. You should've seen the look on his face when he saw her bloody, battered body. How did he become such a monster?"

As they started walking across the campus toward the parking lot Bob broke the disquieting silence. "Some people are just monsters," he said. "This isn't anything new. The history books are filled with them: Jack the Ripper, Ted Bundy, Jeffrey Dahmer, Hannibal Lector."

Sabre chuckled in spite of her anger. "Hannibal Lector isn't a real guy."

"No, but he's like the real guys. They're just evil. I think it's in their DNA."

"It just seems like there's more now than there used to be."

"There's more people now. Hence, more monsters."

"Yeah, but this is *my* monster. I'm representing him."

Bob looked directly at her. "You know the drill. You take your clients as they come to you. You represent them, protect their constitutional rights, and let the chips fall. You do the best job you can. Chances are he'll be convicted and justice will be served." He paused. "Or, better yet, you let someone else represent him when he goes downtown to be tried as an adult."

"That's just the thing. I considered letting someone else take over if we lost the 702 hearing, but that's before I was convinced he did it. Now that I know, I don't feel right about it. I've never let someone go just because I knew they were guilty. That's not why I represent these kids. And now I don't know which would be worse: to represent him and maybe win, only to have him kill somebody else, or drop him as my client, knowing that it goes against everything I believe in."

Bob put his arm around her. "I'm sorry, snookums."

Chapter 37

The Martinez Case

Children: Ray, age 2 (M), Falicia, age 5 (F), Jesse (Jesus), age 7 (M)

Parents: Father—Gilberto Martinez, Mother—Juanita Martinez

Issues: Abuse, Domestic Violence

Facts: Mother beat the father with a lamp in front of the children. Alcohol abuse by both parents.

JP only had a few hours before the Martinez trial and Sabre needed answers. She needed to be convinced that Juanita was not involved in the death of Judge Mitchell or she couldn't comfortably encourage the reunification of her with her children. JP had already established that Reyna Garcia had no other vehicles registered in his or her name, whatever she was. He had spoken to some of Reyna's neighbors and determined that Reyna wanted to have a sex change, but couldn't afford the surgery, and that she always dressed in women's clothes.

With a photograph of Reyna and her car, JP went back to Juanita's next-door neighbor, the old Mexican-American woman with whom he had spoken before. He knocked and she recognized him the moment she opened it.

"How is Jesse doing?" she asked. "And the other children?"

"Very well. They seem real happy with their aunt."

"Good. I wish I would've known you were coming a little sooner; I would've baked them some cookies for you to take to them."

"I apologize. I had to do this at the last minute." JP handed her the photo of Reyna. Do you recognize this wom...person?"

"Yes, that's the woman I told you about who came here with Juanita."

"Was anyone else with Juanita?"

"No, this woman came twice. Once she went in; the other time she started up the walk and then turned around. Those are the only times Juanita has been here since they took the kids."

JP showed the woman a picture of Reyna's car. "Is this the car she was driving?"

The woman shook her head. "I don't know. It could be, but I'm not sure. I didn't see it that well."

JP thanked her and went across the street to see Patricia, whom he had talked to before as well.

"Have you seen Juanita since we last spoke?" JP asked.

"No. I just saw her that Tuesday evening that I told you about."

"What time was that again?"

"It was around six o'clock when I saw her leave, a little before, maybe. I don't know exactly."

"And she left in a car, right?"

"Right."

JP handed her both photos with the car on top. "Is this the car?"

"Yes," she said without any hesitation. "That's the car." She shuffled the photos. "And that's the woman who was driving the car."

From there, JP drove over to the drug facility where Juanita had gone when she finished her conjugal visit with Gilberto at their home that Tuesday afternoon. After questioning several people, he discovered a clerk in the thrift store next door who had just arrived for work that Tuesday evening when Juanita was returning. He looked to be about forty, his eyes were somewhat droopy, and his forehead was a little large. His speech patterns were slow, but he seemed to understand everything that JP asked and he answered coherently.

JP gave him the date again and asked him if he was certain he was there that night.

"Oh, yes," the man said. "It was my first night working."

JP took out the two photos: the one of Reyna and the one of the car. Then he opened his file and turned to a photo of Juanita. "Did you see this car or either of these two people that night?"

"Oh, yes. They were here."

"Do you know what time it was?"

"Six o'clock."

"You're sure about that?"

"Oh, yes. I started work at six." He pointed at the photo. "Before I went inside, this car drove up. Right in front of the store."

"Did you talk to them?"

The man pointed to the photo of Juanita. "That woman went inside...there." He pointed to the building next door.

"And the other woman? Did she get out?"

"Oh, no. But I could see she was real pretty. She said 'hello.' And then I said 'hello.' And then she left."

~~~

Sabre and JP walked upstairs in the juvenile courthouse and took a seat in the hallway on a bench near the wall. There were few places that afforded any privacy for the attorneys to talk with their clients or witnesses, especially if they chose to sit down. The choices consisted of a bench in a corner of the hallway across from one of the courtrooms, outside along the side of the building on a vacant planter, or upstairs in the massive hallway before it filled with other attorneys trying to do the same thing.

"You look upset. Is something wrong?" JP asked.

Sabre sighed and took a deep breath. "I just came from the high school Matt Durham attended, more specifically, from the Coach Arviso's office. The girl that works there, Tracie Rodrigues, told me that Matt was in her office and then in the coach's office the day *after* Hannah and Mason were killed." Her face reddened as she spoke.

"So?"

"So, the form for his missing baseball bat wasn't in the file *before* the murders. Matt didn't file it after the Poway game like he said he did."

JP nodded his head one time. "Uh...huh."

Sabre stood up and her voice rose. "That's all you have, 'uh...huh.' JP, he killed those kids and then filed the form for his missing bat to pin it on Darren."

"I already knew he killed those kids. *You* already knew he killed those kids. Why is this bothering you so much now?"

Sabre snapped at him. "Dammit, JP, you sound just like Bob." She sat back down. After a few seconds, she sighed. "I'm sorry. Please tell me you found out something definitive on Martinez. I need to know if Juanita was involved in the death of Judge Mitchell. It makes a big difference on how I proceed on the trial this afternoon."

"I don't think she had anything to do with it. I'm pretty certain she was with her friend Reyna. And the car they were in did not have any recent damage."

"*Pretty* certain?"

"As much as I can be. Some of the witnesses are a little shaky, but there are enough of them to corroborate the facts.

I'm convinced she didn't have anything to do with the judge's death."

"Alright, I'm trusting your judgment. Let's do this."

They walked downstairs to Department One. There was still not a permanent judge in Department Three, Judge Mitchell's courtroom, so Judge Hekman agreed to hear the trial. Juanita, Gilberto, and the maternal aunt, Linda, were all outside the courtroom. The children were upstairs with the social worker awaiting their time to testify. Sabre had talked to them earlier and tried to alleviate some of their fears of appearing in court. She didn't feel all that successful.

JP waited with the other witnesses and Sabre went inside the courtroom. County Counsel Elsa Norbeck sat at the table with Bob, the mother's attorney. Sabre was glad to see Elsa on the case. Elsa was no pushover, she was always reasonable, and Sabre liked her. Elsa and Sabre had started practicing at juvenile court about the same time. They were both members of a panel of attorneys who were qualified to accept cases appointed by the court. All of the attorneys on the panel were in private practice and worked independently, so they often found themselves working together on one case and fighting each other on the next. After a few years, Elsa applied for a job with County Counsel. Sabre remained on the panel. But Elsa never forgot what it was like to represent the parents or the children, even though she now sat on the other side of the table.

"I think we're all here," Elsa said.

"No, Wags just left," Bob said. Wags was the affectionate term Bob used for Richard A. Wagner, the attorney for Mr. Martinez. "We need him, unless you just want to give these kids back to this lovely couple and we can all go home?"

"Yeah, like that's gonna happen," Elsa said.

Mike McCormick, the bailiff, stood up from his post. "I'll get him."

Elsa turned to face Bob. "Seriously, Bob, can this be set-tled?"

"Let me see. You want to take jurisdiction, place the kids with the maternal aunt, and have limited supervised visi-tation with the parents. The parents want no jurisdiction, the kids returned, and DSS out of their hair. Nope, we don't sound very close." Bob smiled. "But with you two reasonable attorneys on the case," he glanced from Elsa to Sabre, "yeah, maybe, but we also need Wags here."

Sabre walked over and sat down next to Elsa who said, "The social worker says the mom has checked into a resi-dential drug treatment program. They offer all the programs she needs, including anger management and therapy."

"What about the dad and his drinking problem?" Sabre asked.

"He's attending AA meetings, but he just started."

"So, what do you think the social worker will settle for?"

"Well, we have to take jurisdiction."

"Absolutely, but what about disposition?"

The courtroom door opened and the social worker en-tered. Just as she approached them, the door opened again and Mike walked in with Richard Wagner, who mumbled something about having other cases to do elsewhere.

The next half hour was spent going back and forth, try-ing to work out a compromise that would settle the case. Sabre particularly wanted to come to some agreement so the children wouldn't have to testify. All the attorneys felt the same way, although Wagner acted indifferently to it, as he always did, to bolster his case. No one bought it though, except maybe the social worker who was fairly new to the process.

After a great deal of posturing, with the attorneys con-vincing their clients that it would be worse if it was left to Judge Hekman, they finally agreed on a settlement. The court would take jurisdiction and place the children with the maternal aunt, Linda. The children were already living there. The parents would be allowed to have supervised visitation. The social worker would have the discretion to lift the supervision upon completion of their programs and recommendations of the therapists. And in the meantime, the visitation would be very liberal at the home of the aunt as long as the parents remained in their programs and tested clean.

When it was all over, JP, Bob, and Sabre walked out of the courthouse together. "Want to go get a drink?" Bob asked.

JP looked at Sabre, then back at Bob. "I'd like to, but I better get home."

Chapter 38

JP's frustration at not being able to figure out who had killed Judge Mitchell was rising. He had eliminated every case connected with Sabre except Durham and King. He knew Matt hadn't done it because he was in custody, but he hadn't ruled out his buddy, Ralph, yet. The most likely suspect was Isaiah Banks. His unbridled anger at the judge provided the motive and he certainly had the ability to do the job himself or have it done for him. The thing that bothered JP the most was that it could be someone on a case they had missed. *Perhaps the case was inactive right now, which could explain why there hadn't been any attempts on Sabre's life. But what happens if she does something they don't like? And what about the drive-by? Maybe it was meant for her. How can I protect her?*

"Damn it!" JP threw his pen across the desk.

"Anything I can do to help?" Robin asked from across the room.

JP turned around, startled. "No. I'm just a little frustrated."

Robin walked toward JP. Her bruises were almost gone, the swelling had disappeared, and she looked beautiful. "Do you want to talk about it?" she asked.

At least Robin is safe, JP thought. But that bothered him, too. He had not been able to obtain much information about her husband. Other than a couple of gas purchases, his cards hadn't been used and only once was he purported to have been seen in Texas. JP hoped he was holed up somewhere, drinking himself into a stupor. It bothered him, though, that he didn't know where he was for certain.

"It's just some cases I'm working on. I keep hitting dead ends."

"I don't know anything about investigating, but I'm pretty handy on the computer. If you want me to do something, I really would be glad to help." She put her hand on his shoulder. "You've done so much for me. Taking me in and all. I want you to know how much I appreciate it." She hesitated.

"What are you thinking?"

"Maybe it's time to start living again. I can't just hide forever."

JP stood up. "Damn it, Robin. It's not safe," he said loudly. "We don't know where Tyson is."

"But you said he used his credit card at The Four Corners just the other day."

"*Someone* used his credit card. We don't know for certain it was him. Why hasn't anyone else seen him? It's a small town and he likes attention. I'll bet he makes an impression everywhere he goes. Am I right?"

"Yes, but if he's sulking...."

"Does he sulk?"

She sighed. "No, you're right. He's looking for me." She sat down on the arm of the sofa.

JP stepped toward her, put his arm around her shoulder, and gave her a little squeeze. Her face tightened and her eyes widened. "I'm sorry. I don't mean to scare you. I'm just concerned and I'm frustrated. I think he's up to something, and I don't have the time to go there myself and try to find out what it is." He looked into her eyes and saw the fear. "We don't have any reason to believe he's in San Diego or that he would even come here, but until we know, you just have to stay inside. That's the best way you can help me."

She forced a smile. "You're right. I'm being selfish. You don't need one more thing to worry about." She reached up and touched his cheek. "Thanks," she said and walked back to her bedroom.

JP sat back down at his desk and checked his online calendar. The Tran case was coming up for trial in a few days. Since he had eliminated Kim-Ly Tran as a suspect in the murder of Judge Mitchell, he had neglected giving it any attention. He needed to get more information on Kim-Ly's background, but he was at a loss as to where to start. He opened the file and re-read the social study ordered by the court and his own reports. This time more carefully than he had previously.

"Why didn't I see that before?" JP mumbled to himself. He picked up the file and walked out.

~~~

The Tran Case
  Child: Emma, age 18 mos. (F)
  Parents: Father—unknown, Mother—Kim-Ly Tran
  Issues: Neglect
  Facts: Mother left eighteen-month-old girl in locked room and went to work. Apartment complex caught on fire.

"Okay, Quang, level with me," JP said to the teenage hero.

"What are you talking about?"

"About Jade. She's Kim-Ly's sister, isn't she?"

"I don't know."

"I think you do know." JP looked down at the table where Quang had his computer. The small jade statue of the Asian monk sat next to it. JP picked it up. "You got this from Jade, didn't you?"

Quang reached for it. "So, what if I did?" JP waited for a moment then handed it back to the young boy.

"Here's what I think. I did a little research on the history of Viet Nam and this jade statue turns out be one of King-Monk Tran Nhan Tong, the third emperor of the Tran Dynasty of ancient Viet Nam. Jade is, or at least thinks she is, a descendant of his, hence the 'princess' title she likes to use. She looks a lot like Kim-Ly Tran because they're sisters. Kim-Ly is trying to protect Jade from whatever it is they're both mixed up in. How am I doing so far?"

Quang just stood there with his mouth agape, holding the statue.

JP continued. "You knew what was going on at Kim-Ly's because you were spending time with Jade. You like her, don't you?"

Quang looked at JP with an inquisitive expression. "She's nice enough."

"I think she gave you this statue. And now that she's gone you always keep it close to you."

"That's ridiculous. It belongs to my mother. She gave it to me."

"Should I ask her about it?"

"No," he said too quickly.

"Where is Jade?"

"I don't know."

"Oh, come on. You've been talking to her, maybe even seeing her since that Vietnamese guy took her away."

"No," Quang protested. Then he lowered his head and murmured, "No, I haven't seen her."

"Is she in trouble?" JP asked.

"I think so."

"Tell me what you do know. Maybe I can help her."

"I don't know that much."

"Have you had contact with her since she left?"

"No. I have a phone number, but she asked me not to call. It's not actually her number. It's a phone the girls all share so their boss can reach them if he needs to. She said she would call me if she could."

"She said her *boss*?"

"Yes, that's what she calls him. They're supposed to call him 'Uncle Dave,' but she says she only does that to his face."

"Do you know where she is?"

"Not for sure." Quang reached in his pocket and took out a piece of wrinkled, folded paper. It looked like it had been there for some time. He handed it to JP. "This is where she lived before she came to stay with her sister."

So they are sisters, just as JP had suspected. "Do you know how old Jade and Kim-Ly are?"

"Jade is only thirteen. I'm not exactly sure about Kim-Ly, but I don't think she's quite eighteen yet."

"One more thing," JP said, "do you have a photo of Jade?"

Quang hesitated, and glanced down at his cell phone next to the computer.

"You took pictures of her, didn't you?"

Quang nodded. He pulled up his photos on his cell phone while JP watched. There were at least twenty of them showing Jade in various candid poses. He started to flip through them.

"Text me the best two. Make sure I have a close-up," JP said. "And Quang, I need Jade's phone number."

Quang shook his head from side to side. "No, I can't. I won't give you that." After a moment he added, "I promised Jade. She could get in a lot of trouble if someone called her."

JP didn't push him as it seemed futile. He gave the boy his card and waited for the photos to download before he left. "Call me when you feel like talking," he said as he walked out the door.

Chapter 39

The Tran Case
  Child: Emma, age 18 mos. (F)
  Parents: Father—unknown, Mother—Kim-Ly Tran
  Issues: Neglect
  Facts: Mother left eighteen-month-old girl in locked room and went to work. Apartment complex caught on fire.

The address JP had received from Quang took him to a large, vacant house in Linda Vista. Quang had said it was Jade's last address, indicating that she moved a lot, but JP was still disappointed. He started knocking on neighboring doors but with little success.

An Asian woman came to the door of the adjacent house on the right.

"Hello, I'm JP Torn. I'm a private investigator and we're looking for a missing girl." He didn't know if telling her who he was would help or hurt. This was almost the truth and he hoped to appeal to her sensitive side. Most people seemed willing to help when a child was in danger. Besides, he couldn't come up with anything better. Selling something wasn't going to cut it. He needed to be able to ask the right questions.

"No," she said and started to shut the door.

"Excuse me," JP said quickly.

"No, no English," she said and closed it.

JP tried the house next to it with a similar experience. The third house brought him face to face with a couple of teenage girls, both of Asian descent. One had long, dark hair. The other was about five inches shorter than the first. He gave them the same opening as he did the others and added, "We need your help."

"Who is it?" the shorter girl asked.

Finally, someone with whom he could communicate. Someone who spoke English. He surmised their English was probably better than his. "Her name is Jade Tran. She's about your age. She lived in that house two doors down." He pointed to his left. "Did you know her?"

"We didn't know any of them by name, but there were a bunch of young girls living there for a while."

JP took out his phone and showed them her photo.

"Yes, she lived there," the taller girl said. "But they called her Bich." When the shorter girl gave her friend a peculiar look, the taller one shrugged and said, "When I walk home, I go by that house. I talked to a couple of them one day."

"When was that?" JP asked.

"A couple of months ago. Maybe three or four. They've been gone for a while."

The short girl chimed in, "There were a lot of them, about seven or eight, and I don't think any of them went to school. They mostly went out at night and I never saw anyone outside until late afternoon. I think they slept all day."

"Did you ever see any adults? Their parents, maybe?"

The two girls looked at each other. The shorter girl shook her head. "I never saw any parents, but that doesn't mean they weren't there."

The other girl said, "The only adult I saw was a man in an expensive car. I saw him there several times in the evening when I was on my way home."

"Do you know what kind of car it was?"

"No, but it was black and big. That's all I know."

"What did the man look like?"

She shrugged again. "I don't know. He was Asian, not tall, but not real short, either. He had dark hair and was kind of...." She held her hands out to each side about two-and-a-half feet apart.

"Stocky?" JP asked.

"Yes. He was wide, but not fat or anything. More buff."

"The time you said you talked to Jade, or Bich, what did you talk about?"

"She was carrying some groceries and her bag broke just as I was passing. I stopped and helped her pick them up. She thanked me several times. I asked her if she lived there and she said she did. One of the other girls yelled from the door, 'Bich, Bich, come inside.' I asked her if that was her name and she said yes, but she yelled something back to the girls in another language. I think it was Vietnamese because it sounded like when my parents talk to each other and they don't want us to understand them. I don't know what she said, but she sounded upset."

"So, your parents speak the language but you don't?" JP asked.

"I was born here and I never learned Vietnamese. I understand a few words but my parents mostly speak English around us kids."

"How long did Bich live there?"

"Maybe three weeks," the shorter girl said. "It wasn't very long. After they left, there were a lot of people coming and going from there."

"What do you mean?"

"Like people fixing it up—painters and such. A couple of men in suits. Then the real estate agents came, put up a 'For Sale' sign, and they've been showing people the house."

JP got both of their names and contact information. He gave them each a card and thanked them for their help. Then he tried a few more houses in the same direction before he walked back to the house where Jade had lived. No one answered the door at the house situated to the left. The same thing happened when he knocked on the door of the next house over. He continued to a few more houses and then crossed the street, but when he gained no more helpful information he got in his car and left.

As JP drove away he called Muffs, the strip joint where Kim-Ly worked, and determined that Kim-Ly would not be in for two more hours. He had time to drive there, have a lap dance/talk with Blossom, and leave before Kim-Ly would arrive for work.

~~~

JP walked up to the bar at Muffs and ordered a Corona. When the bartender returned with it, he set the glass aside and took one swig from the bottle as he looked around the room for Blossom. He spotted her heading to the area partitioned off for the lap dances. He laid six dollars on the bar, took his bottle of beer, and followed Blossom. Before he reached the area inside, he was approached by a bouncer, who although not very tall, had bulging muscles that JP didn't want to test.

"Can I help you?" the bouncer asked.

"I'd like to buy a lap dance from Blossom."

"Wait here. I'll get her." The bouncer walked away.

The bar was just beginning to fill with the happy hour crowd. Pitchers of beer and well drinks were half price. JP jokingly wondered if lap dances were on special as well. He was glad Bob wasn't there because JP was certain Bob would have embarrassed him by asking for a "happy hour dance discount."

He looked around at the crowd in the dimly lit room. It consisted of approximately thirty men and three women. Two women sat with three guys at a bar that ran across the back of the room near the pool table. JP expected they were there for happy hour. He had no plausible explanation for the one lone woman at the bar.

"Hello," the young woman said, as she walked up to JP.

"Hello, Blossom. I'd like a lap dance."

She looked at him with a hint of recognition, but she didn't acknowledge it. "This way."

JP followed her as she led him to a chair. Three other chairs occupied the small room. Two of them were filled. JP paid Blossom and then he sat down. She started to move in when JP said, "Blossom, please. I just want to talk."

She stopped and looked at him, recognition now beaming on her face. "*That's* who you are." She sighed. "I don't have anything to say."

"If you want to help Lotus...."

"Lotus doesn't need any help," she interrupted.

"I think her sister does," JP said. Blossom's eyes opened widely and her face showed surprise before she could stop it. "Her sister Jade. Or Bich. That's her real name, right?" JP pushed a little harder.

"Shhh." She looked sternly at JP. "You're going to get Lotus in trouble."

JP spoke softly. "Jade's already in trouble, isn't she?"

"I don't know." Blossom looked around as if she were being watched.

"You know better. And I bet you know how old she is, too."

Even in the dimly lit room, JP could see the color fade from Blossom's face. Her voice shook when she said, "Please, don't ask me any more."

"I need to find Bich. Do you know where she is?"

Blossom looked around again. Then she whispered to JP, "I don't know. I have an address but it's probably no good anymore. They don't stay in one place too long. Give me your card and I'll text you the address in a few minutes."

"One more thing: Do you know the Asian man who drives the big black car?"

She shook her head. "You need to go. *Now.*"

Chapter 40

Tyson Doyle Cooper, aka Clint Buchanon

"Nam-yam-yam-ya-nam," Sabre repeated Bob's parking lot chant aloud as she circled the parking lot in front of "World Famous." *I guess you have to believe in the goddess, Brodenia, in order for it to work.* She circled one more time and then pulled up to the valet, handed him her keys, and walked through the crowd into the restaurant.

The lounge was filled with people waiting for a table. She spotted a familiar cowboy hat about ten feet ahead of her against the partition between the check-in desk and the dining area. She walked toward him and caught a huge smile as she approached.

"I put our name in for us," Clint said.

"Thanks, but follow me," Sabre said and walked directly to the bar area where she found an empty high-top table near the back of the room. "Will this work for you?"

"I'm short on patience so if this means we don't have to wait, I'm happy."

For a second Sabre thought of JP; he had little patience, too. Maybe that's the way they raise them in Texas, she thought. She shook it off and boosted herself up onto the barstool. "I actually prefer this over the dining area. The menu is limited, but they have great fish tacos among other things. And a great view."

"This is a beautiful city you have. I haven't spent much time by the ocean, but I'm beginning to see why people stay here. It's very different from my little town in Texas, but this is almost worth fighting the traffic."

Sabre agreed. She didn't like the traffic either, but she loved the ocean air. Then she remembered something he had told her earlier. "I thought you lived in Dallas. They must have a lot of traffic there."

"Yes, we do. I haven't lived there that long. Not sure I'll stay. I grew up in a small town outside of Dallas. I just moved there for work."

"What kind of work?"

Before Clint could answer, the waitress approached and laid two menus on the table. "What can I get you to drink?"

Clint turned to Sabre and asked, "Midori Margarita?"

She looked at him with a furrowed brow. "Why would you ask that?"

"I thought that's what you were drinking when we met." He looked at her sheepishly. "Am I wrong?"

"No, you're right. That's my favorite drink, but I'm driving tonight so I'll pass. Just water, no ice, no lemon, and a straw, please."

Clint turned to the waitress. "Shiner Bock if you have it, a Bud if you don't."

When the waitress left, Clint said, "I hope I didn't overstep with the drink thing. You looked uncomfortable."

"No, I was just surprised. Most men wouldn't have noticed."

"Everything about you impressed me that day. I could even tell you what you were wearing....I hope I'm not starting to sound creepy."

"No, not at all."

"I'm afraid I'm a bit of a romantic. I even remember birth-days and anniversaries."

Sabre smiled. It had been a while since she had been courted. It might be kind of fun, she thought.

The waitress returned with two glasses of water and a Budweiser. "Sorry," she said, "no Shiner Bock." She set the bottle and an empty glass in front of Clint. He moved the empty glass aside. Sabre thought of JP again. JP always drank from the bottle; he never used a glass for his beer. She looked at the handsome man sitting next to her and told herself to let it go. She wasn't with JP and she needed to be fair to her date. She wanted to be, as a matter of fact. He seemed like a really nice guy and he deserved her attention. She made a vow to herself to not bring JP on any more of her dates.

Sabre turned to him and smiled. "So, tell me, what was it like growing up in a small town in Texas?"

The evening passed quickly as they shared their lives. Sabre told him about her brother, Ron, her work, and growing up in Southern California. He told her about raising cattle, riding bulls, and some of the scrapes he got into as a kid. Sabre was impressed when he not only asked lots of questions, but actually listened to her answers. The way he catered to her needs at the table captivated her, too. He was charming, made her feel very comfortable in his presence, and they laughed a lot. When it came time to leave Clint discreetly paid the bill in cash, but Sabre noticed that he left a generous tip.

He walked her out to the valet. While they waited, Clint said, "I had a great time."

"Me, too," Sabre said. "Thank you."

When the attendant walked up to them, Clint gave him a tip and said, "I've got this." He walked Sabre around to the driver's side of the car and opened the door for her. Although he made no attempt to kiss her, he said, "I'm limited on time in your fair city, but I'd love to see you again. How about tomorrow night?"

Sabre hesitated only for a second. "I'd like that. I'll meet you at The Brigantine on Shelter Island Drive in Point Loma. If we're there by six, we can make Happy Hour."

"It's a date," Clint said and sauntered away, cowboy style.

Chapter 41

The Tran Case
  Child: Emma, age 18 mos. (F)
  Parents: Father—unknown, Mother—Kim-Ly Tran
  Issues: Neglect
  Facts: Mother left eighteen-month-old girl in locked room and went to work. Apartment complex caught on fire.

The address in City Heights that he had received from Blossom led JP to another vacant house with a "For Sale" sign on the lawn. He walked around the house and peeked in the windows. It looked like numerous renovations had recently taken place, including a newly painted exterior.

Once again JP canvassed the neighborhood in search of answers. He knocked on door after door on one side of the street, but found no one who knew or admitted to knowing Jade. At a house across the street, he was greeted by a marine in his early twenties on crutches. The man was just leaving the house in his uniform with a nameplate that read *Simard*.

JP introduced himself and told him he was looking for a missing teenage girl. When he showed him the photo, Simard tilted his head to one side, and said, "It's possible that she lived there, but I can't be certain. All I can tell you is that there was a group of Asian girls there for a couple of weeks. At least six of them, maybe as many as ten. I never saw any of them close enough to identify them."

"How long ago did they leave?"

"A week or so, maybe. Not long. It was very strange because they moved in one evening and then they hardly came out of the house for two days. I was home with an injured leg so I pretty much sat around."

"What happened to you?"

"It was stupid. I was drinking with a friend of mine and we started wrestling. I caught my toe on the rug. When we flipped over, my foot went one way and my body the other. I've done a lot of stupid things when I've been drinking. You'd think I'd be old enough to know better."

JP chuckled. "My granddaddy use to say, 'If you get into the ignorant oil, you're gonna come out ignorant.'"

"I'll try to keep that in mind next time. Anyway, for several days I spent a lot of time on the porch just watching people come and go. Those girls seemed to go out mostly at night. And some of them looked really young, but like I said, I never saw them up close."

JP thanked him and left. He tried a few more houses, but didn't obtain any more helpful information. This was the second place now where the girls had lived for only a few weeks. Both were now vacant and listed for sale. He had no more leads as to where they may be but he knew there was something strange occurring and his gut told him it wasn't good. He called Sabre and arranged to meet her at her office in an hour.

~~~

It had been five or six days since Sabre and JP had met and discussed the cases she had piled upon him. Several hearings were approaching and Sabre needed an update, so when JP called she headed straight to her office. She thought about having him come to her house, but decided against it. She was having enough trouble maintaining a professional relationship; the office would be a better setting.

"So, what do you have for me, JP?"

"First, let's talk about Judge Mitchell's murder. I'm hitting a lot of dead ends. I haven't ruled out Ralph, Durham's buddy. Nor have I eliminated Isaiah Banks on the King case. I wanted to know what the police were doing on the investigation so I spoke to Klakken...."

Sabre cut in. "You spoke to Klakken?"

"Yes, we had quite a civil conversation. Anyway, it seems Banks is their prime suspect, but they don't have enough for an arrest."

"I'm not sure we need to spend much more time on this anyway. You and Bob were so concerned that I might be in danger and nothing has happened. It could very well be someone totally unrelated who wanted revenge on Scary Larry. The judge was on the bench for a lot of years and he heard a lot of criminal cases. I'm sure he made some enemies, most of whom we wouldn't know. Klakken can sort that out better than we can."

"Maybe, but you haven't had much action on either King or Durham since the judge was killed. And since Dr. Heller is still in a coma, they may just be waiting to see what happens at the hearings. I plan to be with you at court when you appear on those cases."

"That won't be necessary."

"I already have them marked on my calendar."

Sabre knew there was no point in arguing with JP when he made up his mind. "So, what else do you have?"

"The Tran case is really giving me trouble. We have a stripper mom who appears to be a minor; a younger sister who, along with other young Asian girls, is moving from one vacant house to another; and a missing CASA worker."

"I'm really concerned about Jade. She's so young. And it sounds like there are others that may be just as young. What the heck is going on?"

"I don't know, but I aim to find out."

"And another thing that bothers me is that the mother, Kim-Ly, who seems to be really attached to her daughter, is now making noises about giving her up for adoption. It just doesn't add up right," Sabre added. "We're on the trial calendar for Tuesday. I hope we know what's going on before then because I have some tough decisions to make."

"We need to check the tax records and see who owns those houses."

"I have a good friend, Jennifer Ross, a real estate agent. I'm sure she could get us the information a lot more quickly than we can. Give me the addresses."

JP wrote them on a piece of paper and handed them to her while she dialed the phone.

"Hi, Jenn, how've you been?" Sabre put the phone on speaker.

"Good. Busy, but good. This market sucks. I work much harder than I used to and for far less money. But you didn't call to hear me bitch. What's up?"

"I have a case I'm working on that involves a couple of vacant houses. Can you check and see who owns them?"

"Sure. This sounds intriguing. Anything else you can tell me?"

"Some very young girls were living in one house, possibly without adult supervision, for a few weeks and then they moved to the second house. Again, they only stayed for a few weeks and then moved. I don't know where to this time."

"That's strange. Give me the addresses and I'll see what I can find out."

"Thanks." Sabre gave Jennifer the information.

"This won't take long. I'll call you back in a few minutes."

Sabre hung up and turned to JP who was sitting across the desk from her. "What are your thoughts on the CASA worker?"

"At first it seemed that she just flaked out, but with all the other strange things going on, I'm beginning to think there may be foul play."

"Me, too."

"After I spoke to you, I drove to Mae Chu's house and snooped around her neighborhood a bit. I didn't find much when I spoke to Mae's neighbors but I can do some follow-up. Do you want me to investigate Mae further?"

"I think that would be a good idea. The police don't seem to have much, either, but I don't think they're taking it that seriously."

"Can you get me a photo of her?" JP asked.

Sabre picked up her cell phone. "I already did. I had it sent over from Voices for Children. Mae Chu had to take a photo for them as part of the CASA process." She touched her phone to forward a text. "There, you should have it now, too."

JP's phone beeped. "It's amazing what you can do with these phones."

"I've been telling you that for a while, but it's nice to see you're catching up with technology. I sent you the name and contact information of the woman Mae listed as her emergency contact as well. Maybe she'll lead you somewhere. Don't spend too much time on it, but it would be nice to know if she just took off or if we're dealing with something bigger here."

JP started to say something when Sabre's phone rang. "It's Jennifer," she said and then answered her phone. "That was quick."

Sabre put the speaker on so JP could hear. "I got the names of the owners of each house prior to Hilltop Credit Union taking over. That's who owns them now. The houses have both been foreclosed."

"Was it the same owner of both houses?" Sabre asked.

"No, different owners and they both live out of state. It's strange, though. Based on the dates, there shouldn't have been anyone living in either of those houses the last few months."

~~~

JP went back to his house and ran the information he had obtained from Sabre's real estate friend through every source available to him. He found nothing that connected them to each other or to the Tran case in any way.

"Can you stop and eat? I made you lunch," Robin said, as she approached JP's desk.

"Sure. I'm not getting anywhere anyway." He picked up the plates and followed her out to the patio. "You know you don't have to cook for me. And you've been doing the laundry and cleaning. I really don't expect you to do all that."

"I know you don't, but it's the least I can do. I just really appreciate your letting me stay here and all. Besides, I'd go plumb crazy if I didn't have something to do."

JP sat down at the small, teak table that already contained two glasses of lemonade that Robin had brought out earlier. She set a large bowl with cabbage salad on the table and then sat down next to him.

JP placed his hand on hers. "Just a few more days of this and I'll be able to give more time to finding out what Tyson is up to."

"It's alright. I spoke with my cousin this morning. Someone saw him at the gas station again yesterday. And Sandy's friend drives near his house every once in a while. They can't get too close, but she said there have been lights on in the house the past few nights. Maybe he has given up."

Robin looked him directly in the eyes. He thought some of the fear had dissipated and he was glad for that, but he didn't trust her assailant. "I hope so, but don't drop your guard. Men like that don't usually give up. They just regroup." JP removed his hand and began to eat.

Throughout the rest of their lunch they talked about old times—people they had known as a couple and things they had done. All they had to share was a past. There was no future, at least not a foreseeable one at the moment, and there was no present that didn't include the threat of Tyson Doyle Cooper.

Chapter 42

The Tran Case
Child: Emma, age 18 mos. (F)
Parents: Father—unknown, Mother—Kim-Ly Tran
Issues: Neglect
Facts: Mother left eighteen-month-old girl in locked room and went to work. Apartment complex caught on fire.

Jennifer's house was located a few blocks from the bay. Sabre drove there often to meet her for their run. Sabre ran at least five times a week, and two or three of them were usually with her friend, Jenn. They were both training for a half-marathon. The farthest they had ever run before was a 10K so they needed the practice. Besides, Jennifer had called saying she had some information regarding the two homes Sabre had asked about earlier.

Sabre parked in front of the Tudor-style home. Jennifer and her handsome Latino husband had recently purchased the home and completely refurbished it. Sabre laughed when she saw the sticky note taped over the doorbell that said, "Doorbell doesn't work. Use door knocker." Sabre slammed the piece of iron against its base three times. About a minute later Jennifer answered the door.

"You spend a hundred grand to fix up the house and you couldn't repair the doorbell?" Sabre joked.

Jennifer smiled. "Yeah. We ran out of money. Come on in."

Sabre stepped inside. "You said you had some information on those two houses where the Vietnamese girls were living?"

"Yes, it's all kind of strange, but there is no way they should be living there. Both houses have been foreclosed on by Hilltop Credit Union. They appear to be rentals or maybe even second homes because the owners had different addresses than the houses. One owner lived in Tucson, the other in Spokane, Washington."

"JP ran everything he could on them, but he didn't find any connection whatsoever to each other or to our case."

"I'm not surprised. I checked to see if the real estate agents or brokers were the same, but they weren't. In fact, only one house has a realtor. The other one isn't even listed in the multiple listing service. I called the agent for Hilltop. They already had the first home listed and they expected to obtain the second one once the asset management company cleared it for safe entry. I tried to think how else they could be connected. I checked the financial backgrounds of both houses to see if and when they were refinanced before they went into foreclosure. But that didn't lead me anywhere either. However..." Jennifer couldn't contain her Cheshire cat smile.

Sabre's eyes widened. "You found *something*, didn't you?"

"Maybe. They both have the same asset management company, which isn't unusual since they have the same bank. So whoever you're looking for has to be either someone in the bank or in the asset management company. My guess would be the asset management company. It's a relatively small business with maybe five or six employees plus the owner who runs the business. His name is Lawrence Foster. He would know when the buildings are empty. He's also in charge of having the maintenance crews prepare the homes for safe entry before they go on the market for sale or as a rental."

"So, could he delay the time when the houses were given to the realtors?"

"Of course. He could tell his maintenance crew to take their time fixing up a house and then tell the bank that his guys have to replace the pipes, rewire the house, retrofit the foundation, stuff like that. And he's the one who has to have the utilities turned on."

"So, he would know when the house became vacant and when it was ready to show."

"That's correct."

"Okay, let me see if this makes sense. The asset management company manages the homes where people have defaulted on their loans and the bank has taken them back."

"Correct."

"Okay, so he picks a property, then he moves his girls in there, stalls as long as he can, and then he moves them out and into the next place."

"That would work. And he would have some control over when the place is ready. So if he was using a house for his 'girls,' he could fail to sign off on it and extend the time a little longer if that's what he wanted to do."

Sabre took her phone from her pocket and called JP. She left a message explaining what Jennifer had explained to her and gave him the name and address for the asset management company. She placed the phone back in her pocket. "Ready to run?"

"Let's go," Jennifer said.

They walked two blocks to the bay, down the steps, and onto the boardwalk. After stretching for seven or eight minutes, they started their jog. They hadn't gone more than a hundred yards when Sabre's phone whistled, the sound she had set for incoming text messages. Sabre looked at the text without stopping. It came from JP and read, "Ok. I'm on it."

They jogged until they reached The Catamaran Hotel, or about one mile, and then they walked for another mile then alternated between running and walking until they returned to the place where they started on the boardwalk — six miles total. Finally, they made their way back to Jennifer's house.

"Next week we do seven," Sabre said, as she walked to her car. "But now I have to go home and get ready for my date."

Jennifer followed her. "Wait. Who is it? Where did you meet him?"

Sabre smiled sheepishly.

"Is it JP?"

"No, it's not JP," Sabre replied sternly. She wished people would quit pushing them together. Then she smiled again.

"But you like this guy. I can tell."

"The jury's still out on that." Sabre opened her car door. "I'll tell you all about it next time we run."

~~~

After about thirty minutes of research on Lawrence Foster's Asset Management Company, JP had discovered Lawrence was a sole proprietorship, but he couldn't find anything on the employees. He called Jennifer. "How can I find out what other properties this company is working with? I just need the name of one."

"I can get you one. Just give me a minute."

JP hung up, poured himself a glass of lemonade, and sat back down at his computer. He opened his Microsoft Publisher program and pulled up a file that contained a business card with the name JP Nelson, his phone number, and an email address he used just for this purpose. He added Greenbriar Realty with an address in Fallbrook, CA. It was crude, but it would serve the purpose he needed. He printed it on card stock that was already perforated in the standard business card size.

Jennifer called back just as the printer stopped. "The secretary at Foster's, Jeanne Bullard, is a friend of mine. If you have to, use my name to find what you need, but if you don't have to provide it that would be even better."

~~~

JP drove to the Lawrence Foster Asset Management Company that was located on Hotel Circle South in a building that housed two small real estate offices and a law office. Lawrence took up the entire first floor with glass doors spanning the front. The other three offices were upstairs. An attractive, brown-haired woman wearing a black Ann Taylor suit sat at the front desk. She appeared to be about thirty years old. JP thought she had a classy look, almost regal. Her nameplate read "Jeanne Bullard."

"May I help you?" she asked in a friendly voice.

"I hope so. I'm JP Nelson with Greenbriar Realty." He smiled as he handed her his fake business card. "I was sent here to find out about a property on Lookout Street," JP said and he gave her the address obtained from Jennifer. "I've been told your company is handling that property from Hilltop Credit Union."

"Let me check."

While she typed on her keyboard, JP said, "Nice operation here. How many work in this office?"

"There are six of us. And Lawrence Foster, of course."

"I'm new at this business, so please forgive me if I ask a lot of questions. I'm just trying to learn how this all works.

THE ADVOCATE'S EX PARTE
235

To tell you the truth, I didn't even know asset management companies existed before I studied real estate."

"No problem. I'd never heard of them either until I got this job. That was eight years ago. I started out as a receptionist." She smiled at him. "There are asset management companies that handle all kinds of financial investments, but we just do real estate."

"If you don't mind my saying, ma'am, you have a lovely smile."

"Thank you."

"So six of you under the big boss? Are you the office manager?"

"No, I'm the secretary. I report directly to Mr. Foster, but this company is divided into two parts. Alex Velasquez handles the rental properties and Scott Le is head of the real estate going to sale."

"So, Mr. Le would be handling this property on Lookout Street?"

"Yes, but he's not in this afternoon." She looked at the computer. "I can't really give you any information on the property since it hasn't been assigned to me yet to enter and begin marketing."

"Do you know when Mr. Le will be in?"

She looked up at a chart on the wall that listed the names of the employees down the left side and time slots across the top. Magnetic buttons titled "IN" on one side and "OUT" on the other followed each employee's name. Three of the buttons were "OUT" side up, right after the names. Mr. Le's button was placed on the *4:00* time slot "IN" side up.

"It looks like he plans to be back today around four," she said. "But you can't always go by the chart. They often get hung up somewhere."

"Thank you very much." JP moved a few feet to his right where several business card holders were arranged in a row across the counter. He picked up the card for Scott Le, which displayed his photo. "I'll give him a call and see if he can answer any more questions. I have a client that I think would be perfect for this house so I want to get a jump on it before it goes into the MLS."

Chapter 43

The Tran Case
  Child: Emma, age 18 mos. (F)
  Parents: Father—unknown, Mother—Kim-Ly Tran
  Issues: Neglect
  Facts: Mother left eighteen-month-old girl in locked room and went to work. Apartment complex caught on fire.

No sooner had JP left the building than he called his friend at the San Diego County Sheriff's Department, Detective Greg Nelson.

"What do you need this time, Torn?"

"An address, a photo, and a criminal check."

"That's all? You don't want me to make an arrest or anything?"

"Not yet."

"So, who is it and why am I doing this?"

"His name is Scott Le. He works for Lawrence Foster Asset Management Company and I think he may be involved in some illegal activity with minors."

"You mean like pedophile stuff?"

"No...I mean yes, but bigger. I just have pieces and lots of questions. I think this guy might be the key."

Greg texted JP the latest address for Scott Le and the photo from his driver's license. It matched the photo from his business card. "I'll run the criminal check and get back to you. Be careful."

~~~

JP drove over to see Quang Pham at his apartment.

"I need you to look at a photo and tell me if you recognize this man."

"Okay," Quang said, shrugging his shoulders.

JP opened his phone to the photo of Scott Le that Greg had just sent him and handed it to Quang. "Have you ever seen this man?"

Quang shook his head from side to side. "No. I don't think so."

"That's not the man who came to see Kim-Ly?"

"No."

"You're sure?"

"Yes."

JP handed him Scott Le's business card. "Here's another picture of him. Does that help?"

"It's not him. He looks a little like him, but it's not him. The man I saw is much bigger and has broader shoulders."

JP was disappointed. He thought he had found his mystery man. JP took the phone back and touched the screen accidentally. Mae Chu's photo came up.

"I've seen that woman."

JP held up his phone. "This woman?"

"Yes. She was the one who came to the house that night. The man in the black car took her away."

"You're certain of that?"

"Yes. I saw her up close. Both of them. They walked right past me."

"And you said before that you didn't think she went willingly? Is that correct?"

"She wasn't fighting or screaming or anything, but she didn't look like she wanted to get in the car."

"Of course," JP said. Mae Chu had started to work on this case. All this time, JP thought that the woman Quang saw was just another one of the "girls." He should've realized it sooner. "Thanks, Quang. You've been a big help."

"Have you found out anything about Jade yet?"

"We're getting closer. Have you heard from her?"

"No, not a word," he said. His voice was softly tinged with concern.

"Don't worry. I'm going to find her." JP meant what he said, but he was apprehensive about what he would find.

Chapter 44

Tyson Dole Cooper, aka Clint Buchanon

Sabre reached the top of the steps that led directly into the bar of The Brigantine. Clint Buchanon had already arrived and was waiting at a small booth across the room until they could get a table for dinner. A bottle of Budweiser was in front of Clint and a glass of water across from him. He stood up as she approached and waited for her to sit before he sat back down.

"You look beautiful," he said.

"Thank you." She nodded at the beer. "No Shiner Bock?"

"Unfortunately, they don't carry it. I ordered you a water with no ice, no lemon, and a straw." He tipped his head to the side, "Right?"

"Right. Thanks, you're very attentive."

"I didn't want to make another drink faux pas. I figured the water was safe. Would you like anything else?"

"No, that's good. I don't drink at all when I'm driving. Besides, I'm a lightweight. It doesn't take much to make me tipsy."

"That's smart. I always limit myself to no more than two beers," he said. "So, how was your day?"

"Good. We're making some progress on a difficult case."

"We? You and your friend that I met at the bar?"

"No. That's Bob Clark. He and I are both sole practitioners, but I have a private investigator that works with me."

"That's right, you called him PJ or something like that, right? You mentioned him when we were at Upstart Crow."

"JP."

"Like I said before, that sounds like an exciting job to have. Is he good at it?"

"He's extremely good at it, but most of the time it's routine...like my job...like most jobs. It's just been a little stressful lately with this case. There's a lot we don't know and I'm afraid it's taking up a great deal of his time."

"Time he'd rather be spending with his family?"

"Not his family exactly."

"Ahh, a girlfriend?" Clint sounded as if he knew what that was like.

"I don't know. Maybe. Just an old friend, really, who needs his help."

"Is this friend sick?"

"No," Sabre said. She didn't want to be talking about JP. It was time to get to know Clint. "It's just a tough case. That's all."

Before Sabre could change the subject further, Clint asked, "Anything you can tell me about?"

"No, not really. Sorry." Sabre took a drink of her water. "How about you? What did you do today?"

"I took my sister to the zoo. I thought it would be good to get her out of the house for a while."

"That was sweet. You're a good brother."

"I don't know about that. Perhaps if I were a better brother she wouldn't be in this mess." He took a swig of his beer. "But enough about that. I want to get to know you better. Tell me, what makes Sabre happy?"

They visited for another fifteen minutes or so until their name was called for a dinner table. Throughout dinner they talked about their lives. Sabre told him more stories about her brother Ron, about falling out of the tree house and breaking her arm when she was ten, and her training for a half-marathon that was coming up in the early spring.

He told her about life on a ranch in Texas, raising pigs, his belief in monogamous relationships, his dream to have a family, and the girl who broke his heart. "She was a beauty queen, smart and independent, quite a combination. She's the one who got away." He smiled when he said it, making his statement not sound so serious. "But you learn from those mistakes and make the next relationship better, right?"

"Or make better choices in the beginning."

"It was a long time ago. I was young. I'd like to think I'm a better man now."

"I'm sure you are," Sabre said. She found Clint to be an easy man to talk with and realized she was really having a good time.

When dinner was over, Clint paid the bill. He put his arm lightly around her waist as they walked through the restaurant. At the bottom of the steps, he stepped forward and opened the door for her. When they moved out into the evening air, he took a deep breath. "Love the smell of the ocean air."

"Just another day in paradise," Sabre said.

When they reached the car Clint said, "I had a great time."

"Me too."

"So, does that mean you'll do the honor of going out with this Texas boy tomorrow evening?"

"I can't go tomorrow. I promised my mother I would have dinner with her."

"We could spend the day together."

"I'm sorry. I would really like to, but I have to prepare for court on Monday. I have some cases right now that are really demanding my time." Clint looked very disappointed and Sabre did want to see him again. She knew he had limited time here and she didn't want him to think she wasn't interested. "Will Monday evening work?"

He smiled. "It's a date." He leaned in and kissed her on the lips, a soft kiss with lips slightly parted, lingering for only a few seconds. Then he opened her car door for her. "I'm an excellent cook. If I were at home I'd invite you to my house and cook for you."

"That sounds wonderful," Sabre said.

"I could come to your house." When Sabre didn't respond right away, he said, "Maybe I'm stepping over the line here, but I make a mean salmon dinner." He tipped his head slightly to the right and smiled. "I'm not asking for anything except dinner, you know. I promise I'll be a good boy."

Sabre thought about how considerate and attentive he had been and decided it would be fun to be pampered. She nodded. "Okay, you can cook for me. What do you need?"

"Just provide me with the kitchen and I'll do the rest. I'll bring everything we need. All you have to do is sit back and watch me work my magic."

"It's a deal."

Chapter 45

The Tran Case
  Child: Emma, age 18 mos. (F)
  Parents: Father—unknown, Mother—Kim-Ly Tran
  Issues: Neglect
  Facts: Mother left eighteen-month-old girl in locked room and went to work. Apartment complex caught on fire.

The sun had just begun to rise as JP parked across the street from Scott Le's house in Golden Hills. A jacaranda tree with its purple flowers peeking out of the blossoms blocked JP's car just enough so it wasn't obvious and yet he could still see if someone came to the house or left it. A large cup of black coffee rested snugly in the cup holder. He leaned his seat back just a little to be more comfortable, picked up his coffee cup, and waited.

Nearly an hour and a half passed before Scott Le drove out of his garage in a Gun Metallic Nissan 370Z. JP followed him as he left the neighborhood and drove straight up 30th Street into North Park. He dropped back slightly, keeping several cars between them. Scott Le zigzagged through several residential streets. JP stayed behind him, concerned that Le made so many turns. He hoped he hadn't been spotted. JP dropped farther back until he saw Le pull into a driveway. Noting the address, JP drove past the house and down the street. Then he turned around and came back, parking before he reached the house. There were enough cars on the street to keep him from being conspicuous. He waited, not exactly sure what he was going to do next.

JP jotted down the address in his notebook while he sat there. He discreetly checked the house every thirty seconds with his binoculars. In less than ten minutes he saw the front door open and an Asian woman in her fifties stepped outside. JP picked up his binoculars and watched as Scott Le stood at the front door yelling at the woman in another language, but JP wasn't close enough to make out the words even if he could have understood them. Through his binoculars, JP caught a glimpse of the woman's face, but most of the time Le blocked his view. When Le stepped away, the woman flung the door open wide before she re-entered. Before she closed it, JP saw what looked like several sewing machines lined up in a row with women sitting behind them. He was momentarily puzzled; he had expected to see a room full of standard living room furniture.

Le got in his car and drove off the same way he came. Again JP followed. This time he stopped at Diamond Dry Cleaners on 30th Street. He wasn't carrying anything to be cleaned when he approached the door. The sign read *Closed*. He knocked and a few seconds later someone opened the door. JP couldn't be sure, but it appeared to be a man. Scott Le went inside and about fifteen minutes later he left without any newly-cleaned clothes.

JP followed him back to his home in Golden Hills. He waited for a while and when all the lights in the house went out, he left.

~~~

When JP returned home, he immediately researched the property tax records on the house where Scott Le lived in Golden Hills, the house he visited in North Park, and the cleaners. He discovered that Le had owned the Golden Hills home for a little over two years. The Diamond Dry Cleaners property had belonged to David Leland for the past six years, and less than a year ago, Leland had purchased the home in North Park. Further research uncovered two more homes owned by David Leland. He had owned one of them for four years. It was a rental property that was situated in Linda Vista. He had purchased the other property in La Jolla two months ago and it was owner-occupied. Even more interestingly, he had purchased six more dry cleaning businesses in the last twenty-two months as well as one hundred twenty acres of land in Julian, a small town a little over an hour northeast of San Diego.

JP drove to the home in La Jolla, which sat on the side of a hill overlooking the ocean. Like many homes in that area, it had a spectacular view. Meticulous landscaping surrounded a driveway of natural stone. The house appeared to have been recently painted. JP drove past the house a couple of times and then headed to the other home owned by David Leland.

The house in Linda Vista was located in a residential neighborhood not too far from Padre Gold, a well-known local bar. This house was the complete opposite of the La Jolla house. It had no view, the exterior needed paint, and the front yard had a small patch of grass full of weeds. The front windows were covered with dark curtains. A window on the side appeared to be boarded up.

JP parked in front of the house, took a large white envelope out of his trunk, and walked to the front door. A dark-haired Asian woman answered the door. She didn't open it very wide so JP could see very little inside, but he could hear the whir of sewing machines as they plugged away behind her.

"What you want?" she said in a heavy accent, her tone more friendly than the syntax of her words.

JP looked at the envelope as if he were reading it. "I'm looking for someone named Quang Pham," he said, thinking of one of the few names he knew to be Vietnamese.

"No one here by that name."

"Are you sure?" He looked at the number on the side of the house. "This is the address on the envelope. It's very important that I get this to him."

"Not here."

"Thank you," JP said and left as the machines buzzed away. He had satisfied at least one of his suspicions.

~~~

The Durham Case
  Child: Matt Durham, Defendant
  Type: Delinquency case
  Charges: Two counts of First Degree Murder
  Victims: Hannah Rawlins & Mason Usher
  Facts: Double homicide. Two teenagers bludgeoned to death with a baseball bat.

Since he was not far from where Matt Durham's friend Ralph worked, JP decided to stop in and have another chat with him. All three stalls at Jim's Oil and Lube were empty, but JP parked off to the side and walked to where Ralph was standing out back smoking a cigarette.

"Good, I caught you on a break. Remember me?"

"Yeah, you're the private dick for Matt."

"Yes. JP," he said, extending his hand to shake.

Ralph put his cigarette in his mouth so he could reciprocate. "Is that good-looking attorney going to get Matt off? Get...Matt...off." He chuckled at his own double entendre.

JP felt his face redden at Ralph's sick joke, but immediately wondered how Ralph knew Sabre was "good-looking." He didn't think he had ever seen her. "Have you met Ms. Brown?"

"No, but I seen her on TV. Matt's been in the news a lot, you know. Besides, Matt said she's pretty hot."

JP wanted to punch this guy and his psycho buddy. He didn't want either of them even thinking about Sabre, much less talking about her. He could only imagine the disgusting conversations they had about her.

"You weren't with Matt the night when Hannah and Mason were killed, were you?" JP's anger made him change his tactics.

"Of course I was."

JP decided to call Ralph's bluff. He looked around as if he were making sure no one was listening, and then he lowered his voice. "The cops think he had an accomplice. They're looking for the second guy." JP watched the color drain from Ralph's face. "Have they come to talk to you yet?"

"No, why would they? Matt said you and his attorney are the only ones who know about me."

"For now, maybe, but when we go to trial they'll have to know."

"Yeah, but then it'll be too late, right?"

"Too late to charge you? Absolutely not. Besides, you've been to visit him. They'll be checking on you soon. You can be sure of that."

Ralph finished his cigarette. He crushed the stub against the brick wall next to him and lit up another one. "You think?"

"Look, Ralph, we work for Matt. We want what's best for him and all we need now is the truth from you. If you were really with him, tell me, and we'll use it to help Matt. But if you weren't and we go to court with it, he'll look worse when the prosecutor pokes holes in your testimony—not to mention how guilty it's going to make you look." JP's voice escalated slightly. "So level with me. That's all we want."

Ralph took a long drag on his cigarette. "I just wanna help the kid. He said he didn't do it. He said he was getting set up by that Flynn kid who stole his bat."

"And maybe he is. We're looking into that," JP said. "So, were you with Matt that night?"

"No, I was at a bar."

"What bar?"

"The Handle Bar."

JP nodded his head. "Okay. Did Matt ask you to cover for him?"

"Yes, he said he was out alone but nobody believed him. He was really scared."

"Was that before or after his arrest?"

"After. It was the second time I visited him." Ralph took a long pull on his cigarette. The smoke floated out of his mouth as he spoke. "He swore he didn't kill nobody. Do you think he did it?"

"It doesn't matter what I think."

"I never even seen him get mad really. Never heard him threaten nobody or nothing, you know. All he ever did was play video games. He liked to kill people in the games."

"What do you mean?"

"Nothing really. He was just good at it. I mean, that's the whole point of the games, right?"

Chapter 46

Sabre looked across her desk at JP. She couldn't help but think how ruggedly handsome he was. She shrugged it off. "So, what have you discovered on the Tran case?" Sabre asked.

"I'm not sure, but there are a lot of strange things happening. First, both Kim-Ly and Jade are younger than they claim to be. Second, I found two houses where Jade, whom we are not supposed to know is Kim-Ly's sister, has lived for short periods of time with other young girls. Third, those houses led us to Scott Le, who is connected to two more houses with women working on sewing machines and to several dry cleaning businesses."

"So the women on the sewing machines are probably working for the dry cleaners, which in itself is not illegal."

"Not if they are paid proper wages and are here legally. But I would bet my last possum they aren't," JP said.

"And how many possums do you have?"

"Not enough." He smirked.

"Even so, what do the sewing machine houses have to do with Kim-Ly? How does that affect the custody of her daughter? I realize we have to figure out the whole age thing, but that's a different issue. And we don't know if Scott Le has done anything illegal as far as the houses where Jade has lived or if he's even connected to Kim-Ly."

"Oh, he's connected alright. We just don't know to what extent. We know that Jade is Kim-Ly's younger sister who has lived in at least two houses that have gone into foreclosure. We know Scott Le is the one who signs off on the foreclosed houses so other people can enter and ready them for sale or rent. He'd have to know if someone was living there unless he is a total bumbling idiot."

Sabre shrugged her shoulders. "Maybe he is. What if he's not doing his job? Maybe he's passing his authority to sign off on the houses to someone else and that person is the one using them. Perhaps the sewing machine houses and the dry cleaners have nothing to do with Kim-Ly."

"Maybe," JP said. "I need to find the guy in the black car. I'll bet that'll give us the answers we need."

"How do you propose to do that?"

"I don't know yet."

"We go to trial in two days and I can't recommend anything until we have some answers. How can we prove Kim-Ly's real age? She has documentation that says she's twenty-one, but if she's a minor we need to provide her with a whole different set of services. And then there's Jade, or Bich, or whatever her name is. I know she's not our responsibility, but something's going on in those houses, something's that's not kosher. The problem is we don't have evidence of anything illegal.

"No, not yet," JP said. He waited a moment to allow Sabre's impatience to dissipate. "I have some more information on the Durham case."

Sabre shook her head in frustration. "Do I want to hear it?"

"Probably not."

"Tell me anyway."

"Ralph lied about being with Matt the night Hannah and Mason were killed. Ralph was at The Handle Bar in Kearny Mesa. He only claimed to be with Matt because Matt asked him to give him an alibi."

"Why would he do that?"

"Because he's dumber than a bag of hammers."

"Or he's an accomplice," Sabre conjectured.

"I considered that and I haven't ruled it out yet. I just haven't had a chance to check with the bar where Ralph claimed to be."

Sabre slumped slightly in her chair. She had too many cases without answers, decisions that needed to be made, and not enough information to know how to deal with them. The Tran case was wrought with all kinds of problems. Matt's 702 hearing was quickly approaching and she had little to fight with to keep him in juvenile court. She had a psychological report but no doctor to support it since Dr. Heller remained in a coma. In a way, that could work in Matt's favor if she could get the DA to let the report in without testimony. She knew Dr. Heller had concerns about Matt, too.

And then there was the decision she had to make about whether or not to keep Matt's case if she lost the 702 hearing. Did she want to take the case downtown? It was always a struggle trying to balance her calendar when she had a case outside of juvenile court. But her biggest concern was that she believed Matt bludgeoned those two kids to death with his own baseball bat, especially now that Ralph recanted his alibi. Many of her past clients were guilty, but that never stopped her from defending them before. So, why was this one bothering her so much?

"Are you okay?" JP broke her chain of thought.

Sabre sat up straight. She was glad she had JP to investigate the facts in these cases and to figure out who killed Judge Mitchell. She could concentrate on the legal issues. "I'm fine. Just trying to sort this all out."

"What can I do to help?"

"Exactly what you're doing. Figure out which time Ralph was lying. Is he an alibi for Matt or not? And find the man in the black car or something that resolves the Tran case." Sabre picked up a file from her desk. "What do we know about the King case? Anything more on Isaiah Banks?"

"No. I've reached a dead end on that one, but the police are really watching him. They think he has gained some new status in the Piru gang. I'm sure I'll hear if anything breaks on him. Also, I spoke to Klakken again about the judge's murder. They don't seem to be any closer to an arrest. And they still don't know if Dr. Heller's hit-and-run is connected to the judge's murder."

"I'm working on something that might help us."

"What's that?" JP asked.

"I had lunch with Jeanette, who was Judge Mitchell's clerk, the other day and she said Scary Larry had her keep a record of every case he ever presided over. At the end of each day she had to enter the info into a spreadsheet."

"Why would he do that?"

"That's the funny thing. She asked him about it once and he told her that if anything suspicious ever happened to him, she should give the list to the police because the murderer was probably someone on the list. He said to make sure they eliminate his ex-wives first. At the time she thought he was kidding. Now she's not so sure."

"So do the police have it?"

"Yes, she sent it to them this morning. She emailed me a copy earlier today."

"Why did she wait so long? Have they ruled out the ex-wives?"

Sabre chuckled. "I don't know, but she'd forgotten all about it. About a year ago he stopped adding to the list. He gave no explanation; he just told her she didn't have to do it any longer."

JP stood to leave. "Let me know if you find something," he said. "I'm just a phone call away."

~~~

After JP left, Sabre opened her computer and googled "places to buy Shiner Bock in San Diego." When the list popped up she clicked on Keg N Bottle, but when she searched on the site it read "not in store." She called each one of the locations to make certain. She phoned Pat's Liquor in Ocean Beach, but they didn't carry it either. She hadn't intended on spending this much time on her search, but now it had become a challenge. Besides, she wanted to let Clint know that she was interested enough to make the effort.

She tried a couple other stores to no avail. Then she clicked on BevMo! She tried the Mission Valley store because it was closest, but they were out of stock. Then she tried the Point Loma and Carmel Mountain stores with the same result. Finally, she found it in the Mira Mesa store. The beer was available for pick-up in one hour so she ordered two six-packs. Even if Clint wasn't around long enough to drink all of the beer, it had been too much trouble to just buy one six-pack.

Sabre finished the preparation on the rest of her cases for court the next day. Then she perused the list Jeanette had provided of Judge Mitchell's cases, starting with the most recent date and working backwards through the list. It contained thousands of cases but the information on each was minimal. It included the date, the type of case, the defendant's name, the charges, the attorneys (both prose-cution and defense), the end result, and a brief note about disposition and/or sentencing.

Since the judge had stopped posting to the list last year, Sabre's dependency cases were not there. She did have several delinquency cases with him. None of those cases seemed to stand out except for one: the Juarez case. Renaldo Juarez was a sixteen-year-old gangbanger charged with armed robbery. Immediately following his sentencing, he pointed his finger at the DA, the judge, the bailiff, and Sabre in a sweeping motion around the courtroom. The bailiff grabbed his hands, pulled them behind his back, and handcuffed him. As the bailiff led him from the courtroom, Renaldo threatened the lives of everyone involved in his case. Sabre pulled his file from her file cabinet of completed cases. She made a few phone calls and found he was safely tucked away at a juvenile camp in Arizona. To her surprise, Renaldo Juarez was purported to be doing quite well.

She continued through the list in reverse chronological order for another fifteen minutes with no luck.

She glanced at the time. If she left now she could pick up the beer, drive home, put it in the refrigerator to cool, and have time to relax a bit before she showered and dressed for her date.

She decided to take one last look at the list before she left. This time she clicked on the defendants and shifted them into alphabetical order. She quickly glanced down the list. Bingo!

Date: April 3, 2002
Type of case: Juvenile Delinquency
Defendant: Isaiah Banks
Charges: PC 215, PC 12031
Attorneys: Prosecutor Jane Palmer, Defense Jerry Leahy
End result: Convicted
Sentence: Four years at CYA, one-year enhancement under PC 12022

Sabre saved the list in her Dropbox so she could look at it from any computer. She gathered up her things and headed out the door. She punched the address for BevMo! into her GPS and then called her friend, Jerry Leahy, using the Bluetooth technology between her phone and microphone clipped to the visor.

"Do you remember a case from a little over ten years ago with a kid named Isaiah Banks?"

"Sounds familiar, but I can't be certain. What court?"

"Delinquency."

"Let me pull the file. I'll be right back."

Sabre turned onto Interstate 15 and headed north toward Mira Mesa. She drove about five miles before Jerry came back on the line.

"Yeah...I remember this case: a carjacking with a firearm. We used the 'It-was-the-other-dude' defense because Isaiah claimed it wasn't him. He swore he was somewhere else, but we couldn't substantiate his alibi. He was only fourteen and had just joined the Piru gang. Unfortunately, he was a little too proud of his affiliation and a bit cocky. That hurt him. The two eyewitnesses in the car didn't help, either. They swore it was him. He swore it wasn't. I believed him. The judge believed the witnesses. I really liked the kid, though. If he hadn't hooked up with the Skyline Pirus, he might have made it. Why do you ask?"

"I have his son on a dependency case and the judge was Mitchell. I just discovered that Mitchell was also the judge on his juvenile case eleven years ago."

"Yes, it was Scary Larry alright. He was on a crusade to crack down on gang crime. It was the kid's first offense, but his grades had dropped, he was missing school, and because of his gang membership the judge gave him a pretty harsh sentence: California Youth Authority. Five years, I believe. Anyone else would've likely given him camp time, not CYA." Jerry paused. "Are they looking at him for Mitchell's murder?"

"Maybe."

"That's too bad. I really thought that kid had a chance."

"Thanks, Jerry." Sabre hung up the phone and called JP. She reached his voice mail. "The list of Judge Mitchell's cases has Isaiah Banks on it. He was the judge on Isaiah Banks' first offense. He found him guilty of carjacking with a firearm and gave him a pretty harsh sentence. You may want to pass this on to Klakken if they haven't discovered it already." She hung up just as she pulled into the BevMo! parking lot.

Chapter 47

Tyson Doyle Cooper aka Clint Buchanon

When the doorbell rang Sabre glanced at the clock and realized it was way too early for Clint. He surely wouldn't arrive forty-five minutes early. She was dressed but her hair was still wet from the shower. She dashed downstairs and peeked out her front door's peephole. It was Bob Clark.

"Hi. What are you doing here?" Sabre said, as she opened the door.

"I was in the neighborhood and my phone is dead," Bob said. "I need to use your computer for a second."

"Come on in." She stepped back and Bob followed her inside. "Would you like a Shiner Bock beer?"

"I've never heard of it. Is it good?"

"I don't know. I don't like beer." They stepped into the kitchen.

"So why do you have it?"

Sabre opened the refrigerator, removed a bottle of the beer, and handed it to Bob. "I have company coming and that's what he drinks."

"He? Who is he? Do you have a date?"

"Sort of."

"How do you have a 'sort of' date? Is he taking you out or not?" Bob pulled his glasses down on his nose and looked over the top of them to examine the label.

"He's coming here to fix dinner for me."

"Who is this guy?"

"None of your business."

Bob held the bottle out in front of him, then smiled and nodded his head. "It's that cowboy you met in the bar, isn't it?" he asked smugly.

"If you must know, yes."

"Why didn't you tell me?" Before Sabre could respond, he added, "I told you he wanted you."

"That's exactly why I didn't tell you. I didn't want to hear you gloat."

"Okay, no gloating. Let me use your computer and I'll get out of here."

~~~

Clint arrived on time and carrying two bags of groceries. Sabre led him to the kitchen, where he set them down on the island. He glanced around the kitchen. "Nice set-up," he said.

"It's small, but I don't spend a lot of time in here. The truth is I don't cook unless I have to."

With a slight nod and a wink, he said, "Stick with me and you won't ever have to."

"Would you like something to drink?"

Clint reached inside one of the bags on the counter and pulled out a bottle of wine. It had an ivory label with a triangle cut out at the top containing a raised floral pattern. In gold letters it read: "LINDAFLOR" with a fancy swirl leading off from the "a." Underneath it said "Valle de UCO—Mendoza, Argentina 2005." Sabre knew very little about wines, but the bottle was impressive.

"It's a Malbec wine," Clint said. When Sabre didn't respond right away, he added "Unless you have something better." His voice sounded a little harsh. Sabre couldn't tell if he was hurt because she didn't have a full appreciation for the wine or if he was irritated.

She quickly said, "Maybe." She opened the refrigerator and pulled out a bottle of beer. "Will this do?"

"Shiner Bock! Oh my God, I think I love you."

Sabre laughed and handed him the beer. "If that's all it takes."

"I haven't had one of these since I left Texas. I don't drink much, but if I'm going to have a beer, I prefer this one." He lifted the bottle and held it for a second in front of him. "I didn't know they even carried it in California. I haven't been able to find it anywhere. Where'd you find it?"

"I had to search a bit. I found it at BevMo! In Mira Mesa."

"BevMo!? I don't think we have those in Texas." He stepped closer to her and touched her gently on her cheek. He leaned in and kissed her softly on the lips, lasting for just a second. "Thank you. That was very thoughtful."

"It's the least I could do. After all, you're making the dinner."

Sabre walked over to the cupboard and removed a wine glass. "I'll have a glass of that wine, if you don't mind."

Clint opened the wine and poured it into her glass, opened his bottle, and clinked her glass with his bottle. "To getting what you want out of life."

Sabre found the toast interesting and a little curious, but she didn't want to ruin the mood by questioning him. She assumed it was his way of saying he was glad to be there. They chatted while Clint removed the groceries from the bags. Sabre folded the bags and put them away.

"Cutting board?" he asked.

Sabre removed it from a cupboard and set it on the island counter. Then she carried the block of knives from the counter near the stove to the island.

"Clint picked up a long, sharp knife and examined it. "Nice, sharp Cutco knives. They're the best."

"It was a gift. And they're still sharp because I seldom use them. I'm not allowed to cook without adult supervision."

He chuckled at her comment.

"What can I do to help?"

He moved one of the nearby barstools to one end of the counter. "You just sit here and look beautiful." He positioned himself so he could look at her while he worked.

Sabre sat on the stool. "This is sweet. Let me know if you need anything."

Clint proceeded to slice the tomatoes and the onions. He minced some garlic and chopped the parsley, taking an occasional sip of beer as he worked. "Do you have a grater?"

"Just the old-fashioned kind," Sabre said.

"That'll do. And a small bowl, if you will."

Sabre brought him the grater and bowl. Clint grated the lemon rind until the yellow disappeared. Then he cut the lemon in half and set it aside. After rinsing the grater, he put it in the dishwasher. Sabre was fascinated as she watched. He obviously enjoyed this art form. He moved through the process like a painter creating a masterpiece, yet taking care to clean his tools as he went. When Sabre cooked, she threw some meat or fish along with a vegetable on the George Foreman, sprinkled some seasonings on it, and closed the lid.

"Are you sure I can't help? I could clean up after you. I'm great at that."

"I've got this. You can turn the oven on to 450 degrees for me." He held up his nearly empty bottle of beer. "And you can grab me another one of these."

Sabre did as he asked and then sat back down to watch the artist in action, sipping slowly on her glass of wine. Clint cleaned the salmon and removed the skin. He washed the asparagus, popping off the woody ends. He rubbed extra virgin olive oil around a glass baking pan that Sabre couldn't recall ever having used. Then he poured some dry, white wine in the pan; placed the salmon in it; sprinkled the fish with oregano, garlic, salt, and pepper; and topped it evenly with the sliced tomatoes, onions, and parsley. He finished by pouring the breadcrumb and olive oil mixture he had created earlier over the veggie-topped salmon fillets.

He put the asparagus in another pan and tossed it with olive oil and salt. After setting both pans in the oven Clint proceeded to make a mixture of parsley, garlic, lemon zest, and almonds in another bowl.

"Is that going on the asparagus?" Sabre asked.

"Yes. It's called Gremolata. It's an Italian seasoning."

Sabre had never heard of it, but it looked inviting.

~~~

When they sat down to eat, Clint took a photo of her with his cell phone. "Who knows?" he said. "Someday we may wish we'd captured our first home-cooked meal in a picture."

The dinner tasted superb. Sabre loved fish, but salmon was her least favorite until she tasted the dish Clint had created. She didn't have the heart to tell him earlier that she wasn't a salmon fan. In retrospect, she was glad she hadn't.

About halfway through the meal, Sabre's cell phone rang. She stood up, walked to the coffee table where it sat, and picked it up. JP's picture and name flashed across the screen. She hesitated, then shut the ringer off and returned to the table.

"Answer that if you need to."

"No, it's fine. It's just work."

They continued their conversation over the rest of the meal, each enjoying a glass of wine. Sabre felt a little light headed. She was such a lightweight when it came to alcohol. Clint didn't seem fazed at all from the four beers he'd consumed while cooking as well as the glass of wine he was now enjoying.

They went out on the patio and gazed at the evening sky. Clint put his arm around Sabre, placing his hand gently on her shoulder. It felt good.

"Your weather here is exceptional," he said. "I bet you really enjoy the beach."

"I do, but I don't get there as often as I'd like."

"Okay then, let's go," Clint suggested.

"Now?"

"Sure, I've never seen it at night."

She looked at him. He looked like a little kid asking to go to Disneyland. "Just let me grab a jacket. It might be a little chilly there." As she ran up the stairs she said, "Everyone should see the beach at night."

When Sabre disappeared from view, Tyson Doyle Cooper checked her cell phone and retrieved JP's phone number.

Chapter 48

The Durham Case
* Child: Matt Durham, Defendant*
* Type: Delinquency case*
* Charges: Two counts of First Degree Murder*
* Victims: Hannah Rawlins & Mason Usher*
* Facts: Double homicide. Two teenagers bludgeoned to death*
with a baseball bat.

The Handle Bar smelled of stale beer and cigarette smoke. The odor surprised JP because it had been years since the law in California had passed prohibiting smoking in bars. The small room had eight wooden, square tables, each with three chairs; a bar with twelve stools; a jukebox; and two video game machines. Four patrons sat on the stools and six more were seated at three of the tables.

JP walked up to the bartender just as he yelled, "Tony, put that cigarette out. You know you can't smoke in here."

A man with a scruffy beard and smoke billowing around his face stood up from one of the tables and stumbled out the door.

The bartender, a man in his late thirties, turned to JP. "We go through this every day." He shook his head. "What can I get you?"

JP raised his hand in a gesture that indicated he didn't want anything to drink. "Nothing at the moment." Then he introduced himself and showed the bartender a photo of Ralph. "Have you ever seen this guy?"

"You bet. That's Ralph. He's a regular. He started coming in here about three months ago. Comes in every day about five-thirty and stays until around midnight."

JP showed him a photo of Matt Durham. "Has he ever been in here?"

He sneered. "That's the kid who killed his classmates, isn't it?"

"He's been accused of it. I work for his attorney. We're just trying to verify a few things."

"He tried to come in once with Ralph a month or so ago, but I chased him right out. He had an ID, but it was obviously fake. I chewed Ralph out for bringing him in here."

"I don't suppose that was the same night of the murders?"

"No, it was weeks before that."

"Do you know if Ralph was here the night of the murders?"

The bartender didn't hesitate. "Yes, he was."

JP looked skeptical. "How would you remember that?"

"Because Ralph is a top-notch gamer and that was the first night we played 'Dishonored' with each other. He came in at five-thirty just like always and he was here when word of the murders came on the news. That was a little after nine and they had just found the bodies. I remember they rushed the boy to the hospital, but he died on the way. The girl was already dead."

"Did he come in any days after that?"

"He has been in here every night since then with the exception of the two nights he missed when he was sick."

"When was that?"

"Two weeks ago."

"Do you remember the dates?"

"Just a second; I can tell you exactly." The bartender walked over to a video game and looked at something on the screen.

When he returned he said, "It was Tuesday and Wednesday, the third and fourth."

"You can tell that by the machine?"

"Yes. We play it every night."

"And what about the nights when you aren't working?"

"I'm here at the bar on my nights off. I recently went through a divorce and I have no life. He spread his arms wide. This is my version of Cheers. The truth is I hung out here way too much when I was married. Now I hang out here with the same people I wait on all day long. I drink with them and I play video games with them. Ralph is the only real challenger I've got, though. He's good. I mean really good."

JP spoke to several regular patrons and they verified that the bartender was telling the truth about playing video games with Ralph every night. He left the bar convinced that Ralph was an unlikely suspect or even an accomplice in the murder of Hannah Rawlins and Mason Usher. However, Ralph was not at the bar when the hit-and-run incidents involving Judge Mitchell and Dr. Heller took place. He wished he had better news for Sabre.

Chapter 49

Lan Vong, Mae Chu's emergency contact, lived in the rear unit of a small duplex only a few miles from Mae's condo. A weathered, wooden fence separated the duplex from the house next door. A sidewalk, approximately four feet wide, ran between the building and the fence. JP walked down the sidewalk past the first unit. The L-shaped building had a concrete slab that served as a patio for all the units. He crossed the patio, walking past a concrete table surrounded by benches with an umbrella protruding from the center. There were no plants. In fact, there was nothing but concrete. The area looked cold and uncomfortable to JP, but it was definitely low maintenance.

He knocked on the door. An Asian woman whom JP estimated to be between sixty-five and seventy years old answered it.

"Are you Lan Vong?" JP asked.

"Yes."

"I'm JP Torn. We spoke earlier on the phone."

"Oh, yes," she said. She pointed to the table a few feet away. "We can sit here and talk."

They walked over and sat down. "I appreciate your seeing me, ma'am. As you know, we're a little concerned about Mae Chu. When exactly did you see or talk to her last?"

"A week ago yesterday. She came by and had tea with me."

"Did she say anything about leaving?"

"On the contrary. She was excited about being a Court Appointed Special Advocate."

"So, are you concerned that she hasn't contacted you?"

Lan furrowed her brow and sighed. "It's not that unusual."

"For her to disappear?"

"Mae is a little different than most people her age."

JP shifted on the hard seat, trying to make himself more comfortable. "How's that?"

"She's only twenty-eight years old, but she has been through so much. She came to this country with her parents when she was five years old, but she loved the Vietnamese culture so much that she never really became accustomed to America. I met her parents shortly after they arrived here. Her father had started a dry cleaning business and before Mae graduated from high school he had four different locations. I managed one of the stores, and I was very good friends with Mae's mother."

"Was?" JP asked.

Her brow wrinkled and her eyes closed for just a second. She looked pained. "Yes. She died when Mae was in high school. It's a shame, too. All she ever wanted was to return to her motherland. I think she instilled that same longing in Mae."

"How did her mother die?"

"She was murdered."

"I'm sorry to hear that. Do they know who did it?"

"No, they never found the killer. Her mother was robbed in the parking lot as she left a grocery store. Someone hit her on the head and stole her purse and her car. The police never really had any good suspects. They suspect the car was taken to Mexico because the killer dumped the body close to the border."

"What about her father? What happened to him?"

"He died in a car accident when Mae was in college. The father lived conservatively and had built up a hefty investment portfolio. Mae was an only child so she inherited everything. She has a trust fund that keeps her well cared for so she doesn't have to work. She travels quite a bit and often takes off at the last minute without telling anyone. She really has no one to tell. She has few friends and I'm the closest thing she has to family. Sometimes she tells me if she's leaving; sometimes she doesn't."

"But would she just leave after she had committed to CASA?"

The woman looked pensive. "She might. I had a long talk with her about following through once she agreed to do this and she assured me she would."

"But you apparently felt the need to have the talk."

"I did, but I really thought she was going to stick with it. All she ever really wanted to do was help people, but after college she seldom finished anything she started. This time, though, she sought out the program, signed up, and went through the training. She was quite excited about doing it, so I must say I was a little surprised that she didn't follow through."

"Did she say why she wanted to be an advocate?" JP was hoping he could get some insight into Mae's behavior. Perhaps it would help him determine if she disappeared on her own or with some help.

"She acted a little funny about that. She would talk about what the program did for children and how important it was, but when I tried to get her reasons for volunteering, she would go silent. One time she did say something, but it didn't make a lot of sense."

"What was that?" JP stood up from the hard seat and put his foot up on the bench, leaning forward a little so he wouldn't be looking down too much on the woman.

"These seats are terrible, aren't they? I usually bring out a cushion when I want to sit out here. Would you like me to get you one?"

"No, I'm fine, but thank you. You were saying?"

"Oh, I'm sorry. Mae told me, 'I have to do this to make amends for my father.' I thought she meant 'to her father,' so I said something about what a good girl she had been and she didn't need to make any amends to her father and she corrected me."

"What exactly did she say?"

"She said, 'not to my father, for my father.' I tried to get her to explain but she wouldn't."

~~~

JP drove straight from Lan Vong's house to the Diamond Dry Cleaners on 30th Street. He watched the store from a parking lot across the street. He took photos of three women who either went in with dirty clothes or came out with clean ones. About an hour later, Scott Le pulled up directly in front of the building, jumped out of his car, and ran inside. A few minutes later he exited the store with a broad-shouldered, Asian man in an expensive suit. The "suit" yelled at Scott Le. Although JP couldn't hear what they said, the hand gestures the man made seemed to be telling Scott Le to leave. JP took several photos before Scott Le got in his car and drove away. The other man walked quickly to the side of the store, stepped into a black Lincoln, and left, heading in the same direction.

JP followed them both about a mile down the road when Scott Le turned left and the Lincoln went straight. JP followed the Lincoln. He had no idea where it was going or if the man had anything to do with the Tran case, but there were suddenly too many coincidences. Kim-Ly Tran had a sister, Jade, who was living in a house that was connected to Scott Le. Scott Le was somehow connected to Diamond Dry

Cleaners, and now JP had discovered that Mae Chu's father was also in the dry cleaning business. And Mae Chu was missing. Everyone seemed to be connected, but none of it really meant anything.

JP had two missions now: to find Mae Chu and to find Jade. He was pretty sure if he found one, he would find the other. JP followed the Lincoln to the house in La Jolla owned by David Leland. The double garage door opened. The man in the Lincoln drove his car into the garage and parked next to another black car. JP couldn't see what make it was. The door closed behind him. JP waited a few minutes and then left.

~~~

"Hi, Quang," JP said when the door opened.

Quang greeted him with more enthusiasm than usual. "Did you find her?"

"Not yet," JP said, "but I'm getting closer. I need you to look at another photo." JP pulled out his phone and showed him the photo of the man in the suit at Diamond Dry Cleaners.

"That's him. He's the man who took Jade and that other lady."

Chapter 50

The Tran Case
* Child: Emma, age 18 mos. (F)*
* Parents: Father—unknown, Mother—Kim-Ly Tran*
* Issues: Neglect*
* Facts: Mother left eighteen-month-old girl in locked room and went to work. Apartment complex caught on fire.*

Sabre was deep into the list that Judge Mitchell's clerk had provided her. Since finding the connection to Isaiah Banks, she was pretty well convinced that Banks had killed the judge out of some long-held grudge for the heavy sentence he'd received as a teenager.

She looked up from her office computer just as JP walked in. "Is Klakken investigating Banks?" Sabre asked.

"He's their number one suspect, but they can't find any hard evidence to support it. They'd love to nail him for just about anything. What I don't understand is why he waited so long to seek his revenge. Why now?"

"Who knows? Maybe his anger was aroused when he saw the judge again on his custody case. Or maybe it's just been building and he finally blew up. I don't understand half of what these people do."

JP handed Sabre a report. "The Tran Case," he said. "There is something terribly suspicious on that case. First of all, the CASA worker, Mae Chu, doesn't appear to be off playing somewhere, as everybody thinks. Quang Pham, the teenage boy who rescued Kim-Ly's daughter, identified her. He said she went to the apartment where Kim-Ly lived and then she left, possibly not of her own accord with the mystery Asian man in the black car. But in addition to that, I just found out that Mae Chu's father was in the dry cleaning business."

"Do you think Mae Chu is connected to David Leland and/or the Diamond Dry Cleaners?"

"You can spray perfume on a rotten egg, but it'll still stink."

"So, you don't think it's just a coincidence?"

"Not likely. And I intend to find out."

"If Mae Chu, who just happens to be the appointed CASA worker on this case, is somehow connected to Kim-Ly, that's an even greater coincidence."

"Unless it's not." JP told her about what he had seen at the Diamond Dry Cleaners. "After I followed the man in the suit to David Leland's house, I went to see Quang. He identified Leland as our mystery man who drove away with Jade and Mae Chu. Then Bob went to the cleaners for me and asked for the owner with some story about a suit being damaged. The same man identified himself as David Leland."

Sabre shook her head. "We need to report it to the police."

"I've already done that, but I'm not sure they're convinced there's been any foul play. When I have a little more infor-mation I'll call Greg. Right now they don't really have any evidence that a crime has been committed. They don't think Mae Chu is missing and they don't have anything on Jade. Quang said she referred to someone as her 'boss' but she called him 'Uncle Dave' to his face. I'm guessing she was referring to Leland. And for all we know, he could be her uncle or guardian or someone."

"So what are you going to do?"

JP stood up. "I'm going to follow Leland until he leads me to something. He has shown his face a couple of times already. He'll do it again."

"Be careful, JP. And please check in if you follow him somewhere so I'll know where you are. Giving you something to do will take the boredom off the job."

"If it makes you happy, boss."

Sabre didn't like it when he called her boss, even though he did it jokingly, and JP knew that, which made him do it more often. She gave him a sarcastic smile. "These guys could be dangerous."

"We're talking about guys in the real estate and dry cleaning business. They're not exactly Ninjas." He winked, tipped his hat, and started out the door.

Sabre answered her phone as she watched JP leave. "Wait, it's the hospital," Sabre said. She returned to her call, listened for a minute, said thank you, and hung up. "Dr. Heller is awake and talking. I can see her in about an hour."

Chapter 51

A different policeman was guarding the door at Dr. Heller's hospital room. Sabre produced her ID, he checked his list, and let her pass.

"Hello, Rip Van Winkle," Sabre said.

"Hello," she forced a smile. "They tell me you've been here to see me many times."

"I've always said it's hard to find a good psychologist."

"Thank you." She sounded weak.

"I won't stay long. I just wanted to see for myself how you are doing. Welcome back." She squeezed Dr. Heller's hand lightly. "Have the police questioned you yet?"

"Yes. I couldn't remember much. Since then, a few things have come back to me. I remember it was a black car and the man driving looked Asian. The doctor says I may remember more later, but I don't know. It all happened so fast."

"You just forget about everything else and concentrate on getting well."

Sabre visited a few more minutes and then left the doctor to rest.

As soon as she left the room Sabre tried to call JP. When she reached voice mail she said, "I just left Dr. Heller and she told me it was an Asian man driving a black car who hit her. Be careful. Call me."

Sabre called her realtor friend, Jennifer. "Did you set it up?"

"Yeah," Jennifer said. "I'll meet you at Lawrence Foster's Asset Management Company in ten minutes."

"And you're sure your friend is okay with this?"

"Leave it to me. She's a good friend."

"You know I wouldn't ask if it weren't important. I'm starting to think there's way more to this case than we ever suspected. I haven't heard from JP, either, and that worries me."

Sabre arrived in less than six minutes. She waited in her car until she saw Jennifer pull into the parking lot in her black Mercedes, and then met her at her car.

"Isn't this a little risky for your friend?"

"Jeanne hates Scott Le. She says he's a real creep."

"Well, there's a good chance he won't be working here much longer."

"Jeanne would love that."

They opened the front door and walked into the air-conditioned building. It was a hotter than usual day for San Diego and Jennifer sighed when she walked in.

"You didn't tell her anything, did you?"

"No, I just told her we thought he was doing something illegal. That's all it took. She was concerned about her boss being involved, but I told her I didn't think he was." They walked up to the information desk to find Jeanne on the phone. When she hung up Jennifer said, "Hi, Jeanne. You look fabulous today. Love that color on you."

"Thanks, it's a GW special. I find some of the greatest bargains, as you know."

Jennifer turned to Sabre. "Jeanne is my shopping buddy." Jennifer glanced around to see if anyone else was in the office.

"We're all alone. They're at a big meeting downtown."

Jennifer introduced Sabre and after Jeanne picked up a small bar towel, she led Sabre into Scott Le's office. "I'll be right out in front, just in case." She handed the towel to Sabre. "You may want to wipe the desk down when you're done."

Sabre looked at the orderly office and knew immediately what Jeanne meant. The glass top of the desk glistened. It contained nothing but an Apple computer screen and a keyboard. She knew she would have to be very careful to not leave anything out of place. She didn't want it to come back on Jeanne. She judiciously opened each drawer and thumbed through files. She didn't even know what she was looking for. She tried his computer, but it was password locked and she was no expert at hacking. She gave up on that and turned to the credenza behind her. It contained three drawers. She opened each one, hoping to find something of interest—anything that might tell her something about the Tran case. The top drawer had three pens and a sharpened pencil in the trough, a small box of paper clips, some sticky notes, a pair of scissors, and a box of staples. Nothing personal. The second drawer looked much like the first with just supplies. The bottom drawer on his desk was locked.

The walls had prints of several skylines. One she knew to be Sydney, Australia; the other two she didn't recognize.

Sabre jumped when the phone rang. She took a deep breath and wiped off the glass desk.

When she walked out of the office, she spotted Jennifer who was acting as lookout at the front door. "Did you find anything?" Jennifer called out.

"No, not a thing."

Jeanne was just hanging up the phone. Sabre handed her the bar towel and in turn Jeanne gave Sabre a folder. "It's his personnel file."

Jeanne walked over and relieved Jennifer from her post. Sabre was holding the folder in her hand when Jenn walked up to her. Sabre felt a twinge of guilt. The personnel file seemed like such an intrusion. Sabre spread her lips over clenched teeth. "I don't know. Maybe this is going too far."

"Open the damn thing," Jennifer said. Sabre could hear the excitement in her voice.

"You're really enjoying this, aren't you?"

"Are you kidding me? I haven't had this much fun since we spied on my ex-husband. Come on. Just do it."

Sabre opened the file and read through it. It contained several evaluations. All were positive about dealing with customers, there were excellent remarks for paying attention to detail, and a few concerns were expressed regarding co-workers. One comment caught her eye: *Scott Le's extreme efficiency often leads to extended time frames for executing his deals.*

"What do you suppose that means?" Sabre asked.

"It's just like we thought. He slows down the process so the houses he wants to use aren't released as quickly as they should be."

Sabre continued to read through the file. The last document was an employment form from seven years ago which contained his name, address, marital status, and other personal information from that time period. The last line contained emergency contact information.

"Alex Velasquez just pulled in," Jeanne shouted as she dashed back to her desk. "Sorry," she said, as she tried to snatch the file from Sabre's hand.

"Wait," Sabre said. She held onto the file for about two seconds before she let it go. The last line on the document read: *Emergency Contact: David Leland. Relationship: Brother.*

Jeanne put the file back in her drawer and sat down at her desk. Jennifer took a seat off to the side and pretended to be reading a magazine. Sabre moved in the direction of the restroom, hoping not to be seen. She stepped around the corner just as Alex walked in carrying a tray of cookies.

"Jeanne, I brought you something."

"Thank you, Alex. You're the best." She helped herself to one cookie. "Can you put the rest in the break room so I don't eat them all before lunch?"

When Alex left, Sabre came out. She smiled at Jeanne and mouthed a "Thank You," and left with Jennifer closely behind.

"You have such an exciting job," Jennifer said. Sabre could hear the exhilaration in her voice.

"This is not my job. It's usually not this thrilling and I'm usually not this stupid. That was a dumb thing for me to do."

As soon as Sabre pulled into traffic, she called JP to tell him she had found the real connection between Scott Le and David Leland. She left the message on his voice mail.

Chapter 52

The Tran Case
 Child: Emma, age 18 mos. (F)
 Parents: Father—unknown, Mother—Kim-Ly Tran
 Issues: Neglect
 Facts: Mother left eighteen-month-old girl in locked room and went to work. Apartment complex caught on fire.

JP sat in his car on the street where David Leland lived, but he was parked back far enough where he couldn't be seen. From his vantage point he couldn't see the garage or front doors, but he could see if someone drove out of the driveway. It was nearly nine p.m. when Leland finally pulled out onto the street. JP followed him to Linda Vista but dropped back when he realized Leland was going to the house where JP had seen the sewing machines. JP parked on a cul-de-sac around the corner, grabbed his baseball cap, and walked slowly toward the house. He saw Leland knock, and the same woman he'd seen at that house previously opened the door. JP slowed down, staying back in the shadows as much as he could. He could hear their voices, but they spoke in a language he didn't understand. Leland appeared to be upset about something.

After a minute or two, Leland went inside. JP moved closer to the house and hid behind some bushes that were only a few feet from the front door. He waited. Approximately ten minutes later, Leland came out. JP heard two dead bolt locks click after the woman closed the door behind her visitor. Leland drove away.

JP crept around to the side of the house. The first window he passed had a curtain. He couldn't see in, but he could hear the sewing machines whirring. He passed two more windows that were covered with wooden boards. JP continued around to the back. Three windows across the back were also covered with wood and the back door had two locks. He continued around the other side only to find more boarded-up windows. It looked like only the front two rooms were being used.

When JP returned to his car he discovered he had a message on his phone. Before he had a chance to listen to it, his phone rang again. He didn't recognize the number.

"Hello," JP said.

The soft voice said in almost a whisper, "This is Blossom. You know, from Muffs."

"Hi, Blossom. What's up?"

"Kim-Ly hasn't been to work for two days and I'm worried."

"Is that unusual for her?"

"She never misses work. And the last time she was here she was afraid Jade was in trouble. I think she went looking for her."

"She doesn't know where she is?"

"No. They keep moving around and she....I gotta go."

The line went silent. JP was at a complete loss. He called Sabre and told her what Blossom had told him.

"Can you check on Kim-Ly?" JP asked.

"Let me see what I can find out. I'll call you back."

Sabre called Marla, the social worker, and asked if she knew why Kim-Ly hadn't shown up for work the last two days.

"I knew she missed today, but I wasn't aware she missed yesterday too," Marla said. "She also didn't show up for her visit with Emma today. I've left her several messages but I haven't heard back. When I called her work, they said she called in sick. So I didn't think any more of it. Do you know something I don't?"

"Not really, but if I find out anything I'll let you know."

"And you need to quit working so late," Marla said.

"You should talk. You answered your phone when I called."

Sabre hung up and relayed the information to JP. "What do you think is going on?"

"I don't know, but what we do know is that all three of these missing women have a connection to David Leland. Without watching him every minute of the day, I don't know if we can find out what he's up to. I've followed him several times and he goes to the cleaners, his house, and now to the house in Linda Vista."

"And I can't spare you to do that, nor do we have the resources. Besides, the way these women are disappearing, we need to do something fast."

"Is Kim-Ly officially missing?"

"No. That's the problem. And neither is Jade."

"And Mae Chu is 'iffy' as far as the authorities are concerned."

"So, what do we do?"

"I'm going to see Quang Pham again. I'll see if he remembers anything else that might help us. I don't know what else to do."

"Are you going now?" Sabre asked.

"Yes, I already called Quang and he's expecting me."

~~~

JP entered Quang's apartment and found him visiting with another boy about the same age.

"This is my friend, Kevin," Quang said.

"Hi, Kevin. You're the one who helped Quang save the little girl next door, right?"

He nodded. His face reddened.

"Good, I'm glad you're here. You may be able to help solve this case."

He shrugged. "If I can."

"Tell me what you saw and did that day."

Kevin gave Quang a questioning look. "Just tell him the truth," Quang said. "It might help find Jade."

"We were here studying when we saw the smoke. We knew Kim-Ly was gone because we had seen her leave for work."

"Were there other people in the apartment house?"

"There are only two people who live there and they were both at work," Quang added. "The building only has four apartments and two of them were messed up even before the fire."

"What do you mean 'messed up'?"

"They got trashed by the last people who lived there. The landlord just boarded them up for a while. He said he didn't have the money to fix them right now."

"So, what did you do when you saw the smoke?"

"Quang took the key out of his drawer, and we ran over there and went to her apartment. By then it had started to burn pretty good. I know they called us heroes, but the fire wasn't that close yet. It started in the back in one of those vacant apartments."

"You two *are* heroes. The smoke could have killed that little girl, even if the fire didn't reach her. And no one else seemed to know she was even in there," JP said.

Kevin shrugged again.

"Quang, have you heard anything from Jade?"

"No."

"Did she ever say anything about who she was living with?"

"No, she seemed kind of afraid to even talk about it," Quang said.

"She didn't really know about anything," Kevin added.

"What do you mean?"

Kevin looked at Quang as if he didn't know how to explain it. Quang said, "She didn't know how to use a computer or a smart phone. She was fascinated by what they could do. I'm not sure she'd ever seen a computer. I don't think she ever even saw a television."

"Why do you say that?"

"Because I took my computer over there and she asked what it was. When I showed her, she was amazed. She asked how people could be moving around on there and talking. I tried to explain it was like television, but she just looked at me real funny."

"Do you think she just didn't understand your English?"

"She speaks English very well. She told me she had to learn English as part of her training."

"Training for what?" JP asked.

"She wouldn't tell me."

"Do you know if she was born in the United States?"

"She never said."

"Did she ever talk about being from another country?"

"She was proud to be Vietnamese, but she never said she lived there. She was proud of her culture. That's why she had the jade statue of King-Monk Tran Nhan Tong. She gave it to me for safekeeping."

Kevin spoke up. "I think she must've lived out in the country or something."

"Why?"

"Because she said she liked picking things because she could be outside. At first I thought she meant flowers, but she said sometimes she got to eat the things she picked. When I questioned her, she wouldn't say any more."

JP was totally perplexed and things weren't getting any clearer. Everything he learned just generated more questions. He removed three photos from an envelope and laid them on the table. He pointed to the picture of Scott Le. "Have either of you ever seen this man?"

They both shook their heads.

David Leland's photo came up next. "Quang, you said the last time you saw him was when he left with this woman, correct?" JP pointed to the photo of Mae Chu.

"That's right," Quang said. "He hasn't been back here."

JP pointed again to the picture of David Leland. "Kevin, have you seen this man?"

"No," Kevin said, "but I've seen her." He picked up the photo of Mae Chu and examined it carefully.

"Were you here the night she left with Leland?"

"No. She was here the day of the fire."

JP tipped his head to one side. "Are you sure?"

"Yes. She was standing by the bushes on the other side of the apartment building when we went in. Then when we came out, Quang was carrying Emma. She came up right behind me and asked if the baby was okay. I said, 'I think so,' and she left."

"Did you see where she went?"

"She walked real fast through an opening in the bushes and I didn't see her again. She could've come back, I guess, but I didn't see her after that. There was so much excitement and we just wanted to give Emma to someone and leave. By then, the fire department had arrived. We ran inside here, grabbed Quang's computer, and we went to my house. They were already evacuating this place when we were leaving."

JP picked up the photos with Mae Chu's on top. He held it out, photo side up. "And you're absolutely certain it was this woman?"

"Yes, I'm sure of it."

Chapter 53

Sabre was in her office preparing for the Tran trial that was less that twenty-four hours away. She needed more information. There were still too many unanswered questions. She was debating what stand she would take on the case when her phone rang, bringing her out of her deliberation.

"Mae Chu was at Kim-Ly's apartment when the fire started," JP said. He went on to explain all that he had learned from Quang and his friend.

"That doesn't make any sense," Sabre said. "The case was filed because of the fire. She wouldn't have known about Kim-Ly yet. Do you think it's a coincidence?"

"Highly unlikely, but I can't imagine why she was there," JP said.

"Now I'm more confused than ever." Sabre sighed. "We need more answers before the trial tomorrow. Do you think you can dig up anything else?"

"I have a hunch about Jade's location based on something Kevin, Quang's friend, said about her. He said that she liked to pick things because she could be outside and sometimes she would eat what she picked."

"Sounds like a farm."

"Exactly."

"And David Leland owns one hundred twenty acres of land in Julian."

"That's where I'm headed," JP said.

"That's a long drive."

"I know. It's well over an hour; that's why I haven't been there yet. I haven't had the time, and it didn't seem that important until now."

"I'm finished with court today, so I'll be working in the office all afternoon and evening. What can I do to help?"

"The address of the land is in my report. Can you see what you can find out about it? Is it farmland? Are there any structures on it? Anything that might help me. Also, see if you can find a connection between Kim-Ly and Mae Chu."

Sabre called her friend Jennifer, who was delighted to research the real estate information. Sleuthing had become her latest hobby. While Sabre waited for her to call back, she decided to look for a connection between Kim-Ly and Mae Chu, other than the juvenile dependency case. She also wanted to find a possible connection to David Leland.

She glanced quickly through the information she had received from CASA, through the DSS reports, and JP's reports. She found nothing. She started looking online for any information she could find about any of them. None of them had any social media connections. Sabre googled "Kim-Ly," but found nothing relating to her. She googled "David Leland" and found mostly information pertaining to the dry cleaners that he owned. She had just googled "Mae Chu" when her phone rang.

"What did you find?" Sabre asked Jennifer.

"The land is not really farmland. There are some apple orchards and a lot of brush. It has two structures on the property—a house and a barn—and both were built in 1948. I'm researching a couple of other things, but they'll take a little longer. I'll call you back when I have them."

Sabre called JP and gave him the information. The phone kept cutting out.

"I'm sorry, say that again. I didn't get the last part," JP said.

"It has a house and a barn," Sabre said.

"Got it. The reception is real bad here. I'll call...my way...back...." The line went dead.

~~~

JP drove past a field and then past the dirt road that turned into Leland's property. The sun was beginning to set, but there was enough light to see the two buildings that were situated about a quarter of a mile from the road. Fruit trees lined the edge of the property and circled around behind the buildings. JP pulled off the road and parked his car behind some apple trees. He removed a small flashlight from the trunk and put it in his side pocket. He patted his shoulder holster to reassure himself that his HK P2000 pistol was there.

He moved stealthily through the trees toward the buildings until he was no more than fifty yards from the house. He sat down on a dead tree that had fallen on the ground, creating a bench to sit on. He had decided to just watch a while before he made any attempt to approach the house. He checked his phone. No service. He waited.

~~~

Sabre's Google search turned up very little about Mae Chu. Sabre continued to look for information about her family and her father's business. She eventually came across some articles about her mother's murder. It appeared to be just as Lan Vong, Mae Chu's friend, had reported. She was mugged in a parking lot in Mira Mesa and dumped some thirty miles away in San Ysidro. The case remained unsolved.

Sabre checked the criminal history online for Mae Chu, her mother, and her father. She found nothing for the first two, but her father, Tray Tran, originally spelled Trai, was arrested for a battery in March of 1995. Two months later the case was dismissed at the preliminary hearing. The judge was Lawrence Mitchell. Sabre quickly pulled up the list on her computer of the judge's cases. She highlighted the heading marked "Date" and hit the A to Z button putting them in order from the oldest to the most recent. She scanned the list until she reached *May, 1995*. She looked carefully through the list for Trai Chu. He was not listed. She went back to March, started through the dates again until she reached the end of *June, 1995*. There was no mention of Mr. Chu. Sabre wondered why Mr. Chu wasn't on the list when Mitchell was clearly listed as the judge on the criminal records for several hearings. She knew it was possible that Chu was accidentally left off the list, but coincidences like that didn't set well with Sabre. She knew there had to be another explanation.

She called JP. When it went to voice mail, she said, "Mae Chu's father, Trai Chu, had a case in front of Judge Mitchell in 1995. It was not on the judge's list. I'm worried about you. Call me."

~~~

After about half an hour, JP saw a white van pull onto the dirt road leading toward the house. It stopped in front. JP stood up and moved a little closer, taking care to remain hidden by the trees. Two men, the driver, and a passenger exited the front of the van, walked around to the back of the vehicle, and opened up the back door, which faced him. From his vantage point, JP could see directly into the van as several young girls stepped out. JP counted them as they exited. There were twelve in all.

The night was still and JP could hear the men speaking in a foreign language. The girls said nothing at all. They formed a line and walked into the house, one after another, following one of the men. The other man stayed behind them.

~~~

The more Sabre thought about what she had found, the more she worried about JP. She was concentrating so hard that she jumped when her phone rang. It was Jennifer.

"So, here's what I found," Jennifer said without any small talk. "That property in Julian was owned by a man who owned most of Julian in the fifties. His estate sold that piece of property in 1991 to Trai Chu. David Leland bought it in 2005."

"What date was it sold?"

"June 23, 2005."

"Thanks, Jennifer. I won't forget this one." Sabre hung up before she could say anything else.

She tried to reach JP again. Still no answer. She called Detective Klakken.

"I was just about to call you. They have Isaiah Banks in custody. We have him for ordering the drive-by and then killing the shooter, and we're also pretty certain he killed the judge."

"He didn't do it."

"What?"

"Kill the judge. I'm pretty certain it wasn't him. I saw Dr. Heller and she remembered it was a black car driven by an

Asian man." She proceeded to tell Klakken everything she knew about Mae Chu and David Leland. Then she added, "And I think JP may be in trouble."

"And where is he now?"

"He went to Leland's property in Julian."

"Okay, I'm on my way. I'm already in El Cajon so I'm halfway there."

~~~

JP heard a twig crack behind him, but before he could turn around he felt a hard metal pipe thump him squarely on the back of his head.

Chapter 54

P's head pounded. He tried to remember why. He could hear men's voices and they weren't far away. He stayed very still and listened with his eyes closed. He was glad he did when the fog started to clear and he remembered being hit on the head. He could feel the tape that tied his hands together behind the chair he was sitting on, and it felt like tape across his mouth. His feet were also tied to the chair.

"We need to get another load," one man said in a slight Asian accent.

"It's getting pretty crowded in there," another said.

"Who cares? It's not like they can do anything. Leland will be furious if we don't get them all."

"What about him? Should we get rid of him?" JP figured they were talking about him. He remained still.

"No. We might need him."

"Are we just going to leave him here?"

JP heard them walk toward him. One of them brushed against his knee. He felt a hand touch his chin. JP didn't move. The man pushed his head upright. JP let it flop back down.

"He'll be fine. He probably won't even wake up. And if he does, what's he going to do? He can't see anything and it's not like he's going to hear them." The man chuckled at his own little joke. "Besides, Tim is on watch and we'll be back in a couple of hours."

"If you hadn't taken so long...."

The other man said something in a foreign language and then they both laughed as they walked away. JP remained still. He heard the door open and close. He still remained immobile with his eyes closed until he heard the van drive away. Then he slowly opened his eyes. It was dark outside, but one light remained on in the house. His chair sat next to a sofa with a missing cushion. The other two cushions were dirty and torn. The room appeared to be a combination of the living room and dining room. His hands were tied together behind his back; one foot was taped to the chair; and the other foot ached worse than his head, which hurt just to lift.

Complete silence filled the room. An owl hooted outside. He wondered where the girls were and how many more there were. From the conversation he had heard, the girls were somewhere close, but why couldn't he hear them? He had to figure out a way to break loose and he only had a couple of hours to do it, and that's assuming Tim—whoever he was—didn't come in to check on him.

JP wiggled his hands, but they were tied so tightly that it hurt just to move ever so slightly. He looked around for something sharp to cut himself loose, but he saw nothing. The room was sparsely furnished with just the sofa, a small table, and three dining room chairs, one of which he was tied to. There was a closed door behind him to his right and a doorway straight ahead that led to the kitchen. Through the opening he could see the counter top and a space to its left where a stove likely once sat.

The walls needed paint and the cheap linoleum on the floor was so worn in spots that the wood underneath peeked through. Most of the pattern was worn off except under the table, but the dirt and dust made that almost indiscernible.

JP's left leg and foot were duct-taped to the chair. His knee was bent and his foot was about eight inches above the floor, so he couldn't reach it except with the tip of his boot. His right foot was also taped to the leg of the chair, but his boot rested on the floor. He stepped down on his right foot to lift himself up with the chair. The pain shot through his foot and all the way up his leg. He was certain his big toe was broken. What the hell had they done to him while he was passed out?

He carefully bounced his way around 180 degrees so he could face the closed door. He used his toes to help balance himself as he moved, but the jarring from every bounce felt like someone was pounding him on the head and the foot at the same time.

The door had two deadbolt locks that needed keys to open them. He couldn't tell whether or not they were locked, so he decided to see whether or not he could turn the knob. He bounced his chair until he sat directly in front of it. He leaned over and lodged the doorknob between his head and shoulder and tried to turn the handle. Pain shot through his head, but he didn't stop. It took several tries before he was actually able to turn the knob. He simultaneously pushed against the door, but it wouldn't move.

In spite of the pounding headache, JP bounced his chair across the floor and into the kitchen, nearly tipping over several times. Only three of the cupboards still had the doors on them. There were a refrigerator and a microwave, but there wasn't a stove or any other appliance in the room. There were no dishes or pots and pans anywhere that he could see. All the drawers but the bottom one were missing from their cradles. JP could see inside the empty cradles, but there wasn't anything that might be sharp enough to help him break loose.

Nearly an hour had passed since the scumbags had left, JP thought. And he was running out of ideas. He knew he couldn't sit and do nothing so he made his way toward the front door, wondering if Tim, the lookout guy, could see him if he left. Maybe outside he could find something sharp. At least he wouldn't be a sitting duck. He tried the same technique that he used on the other door, only this time it worked. However, he had to back up so he could open the door. He bounced a couple inches back, then a few more, until he could clear the door. He reached his right foot out, gritted his teeth, and pushed the door open. Then he worked his way to the doorway again and started out.

He looked around but couldn't see where Tim might be positioned. JP would have to cross the porch, go down two steps and another sixty feet to the woods. The first bounce on the porch echoed in the still air as it struck the rickety wooden porch. He stopped for fear Tim might hear it. When he saw no movement anywhere, he continued. It took about eight hops to move across the porch. With each one he expected to break through the creaky boards and end up under the house.

When he reached the steps, JP tried once again to put the weight on his right foot so he could lift himself up and hop down the steps, but he couldn't bear it. With the first pressure he collapsed and tumbled down the steps and to the ground, hitting both his broken toe and sore head on the hard dirt.

"Damn! That hurt," he said softly, hoping that Tim couldn't hear him.

He lay there for a few seconds waiting for the pain to subside, trying to formulate a plan. He scooted himself across the dirt to where the steps formed a right angle with the wall of the porch, leaned against it the best he could for leverage, and stretched his left leg out pulling the tape enough that he could put his foot almost flat to the ground. He tried doing the same with his right foot, but the tape was too tight. Then he pushed against the wall and climbed up into a standing position on his left leg. From there he hopped carefully toward the woods, afraid if he fell he wouldn't be able to get up again. He wanted to stop, lower his body into the chair, and rest but he didn't dare.

By the time he reached the woods, his left leg hurt almost as much as his right. It was difficult to hop between the trees, but at least here he figured he could wiggle his way back up if he fell, so he lowered the chair and sat down, taking the pressure off of his leg.

He took a deep breath, sat very still, and listened to the quiet night...and the footsteps that rustled the leaves behind him.

Chapter 55

"Damn you, Torn," Klakken said exasperatingly. "You just can't stay out of trouble, can you?" He reached down to tear the tape off JP's mouth. "I ought to leave the tape on. At least I wouldn't have to listen to any of your irritating homespun comments."

JP jerked when Klakken ripped off the tape. A pain shot through his head like a lightning bolt. "But that was fun, too," Klakken added.

JP knew he meant everything he said, but he was still thrilled to see him and didn't comment on anything he said. Instead he explained their predicament. "There's only one man here now, as far as I know. I heard them say he was staying behind as a lookout."

"Who's they?" Klakken pulled out his cell phone. "No reception," he said.

"Two men brought twelve young girls here about three hours ago. They went back for more, I think. They'll be coming back pretty soon."

"Where are the girls?" Klakken removed a knife from his pocket and released JP's hands.

"I don't know." JP pulled his arms around in front of himself and wrung his hands together, stretching his fingers and arms. "There's a locked room in the house, but if they're in there they may all be dead. I didn't hear a single sound coming from that room. There's also a barn behind the house, but I haven't heard any noise coming from there, either."

"They may just be too afraid to make any noise." Klakken cut JP's feet loose.

"I hope that's the case." JP stood up, but jerked when he took a step.

"Are you okay?"

"I think my toe is broken, but I'm good. I don't know what they did to me after they knocked me out, but by the looks of my clothes, they may have drug me a ways. Maybe that's how my toe got broken." He shifted his weight away from his toes. "I can walk, just not sure how fast."

"I take it you don't have a weapon."

"No, it's gone." JP tapped his shoulder harness, even though he knew the gun wasn't there.

Klakken pulled his pant leg up and took out a Ruger SP-101 .357 Magnum with a 2-1/4 inch barrel. He hesitated for a second before he handed it to JP. "Here, you might need this to cover my back. Do you think you can do that, Torn?"

"I know we've had our troubles, Shane, but if I tell you a rooster dips snuff, look behind his wing and you'll find a can." He saw Shane's frown. "Let's just do this," JP added quickly.

"Damn it, Torn, only if you promise not to spout any more of those stupid sayings you have stuck up your butt."

"Okay, okay," JP said. "How did you happen to be here, anyway?"

"Sabre called. She told me what was happening and she said Mae Chu's father used to own this property and that he had a case about fifteen years ago with Judge Mitchell."

"So Mae Chu is deep in the middle of all this."

"That's right. She wasn't one of the girls they brought in the van, was she?"

"I don't think so. I think I would have recognized her from her photo," JP said. "So what now?"

"How much time do you think we have?"

"They said a couple of hours and that must be close to running out. I have no idea where the lookout guy is."

"You start to work your way toward the barn, but keep in the orchard. I'm going to run back to the car and try to radio for back-up. It isn't far. Then I'll join you. If those girls are in the barn, maybe we can get them out."

Klakken ran off through the trees and JP started along the tree line toward the barn. He moved as quickly as he could, putting the weight on the heel of his right foot. It still hurt, but not any worse than his head. As JP passed the back of the house he could see it was boarded up just like the house in Linda Vista; he wondered if Jade was there all this time, right under his nose.

JP was almost directly behind the barn when Klakken returned.

"The radio didn't work. We need to try to get the girls out of here. Then we can go for help." He handed JP a set of handcuffs. "Here, in case you need these. I had an extra set in my car."

Klakken pointed toward the barn and drew his Glock 30. "Cover me." He dashed across the weeds. When he reached the barn, he stood behind the back of it. JP followed. Then they both crept around the corner and along the wall to the door. One side of the door was missing; the other hung part way off. They edged their way inside. It was just an open space with junk piled on one side about six feet high. A stove lay on its side, sticking out of the pile, along with broken furniture, books, and other junk. It was covered with dust and cobwebs.

Klakken said quietly, "There's no place to hide in here."

"Then they must be in that locked room in the house, but we'll need something to break down the door."

They looked around for a tool of some kind. A shovel and a rake lay against the wall to the left. Behind the pile of junk were a hammer and an axe hanging on the wall. Both looked pretty rusty and someone would have to climb on the pile or dig their way in to reach them.

Klakken looked at JP's foot. "I'll do it," Klakken said. He holstered his gun, stepped up on the stove, and grabbed a hold of a beam. His fingers sank into the cobwebs. He stepped gingerly on a piece of wood that looked like it was once part of a cheap dresser. Then he put his weight on it and pulled himself up. From there he was able to reach the tools. He tossed them down.

JP let them fall to the ground. They were so old and rusty he wondered if they would fall apart at first swing. Klakken hopped down and picked up the axe. JP took the hammer and they started toward the house. Just as they reached the side of the house, headlights beamed as a vehicle turned onto the road toward them. It was about one hundred yards away.

Chapter 56

"You stay on this side, and I'll circle around the other side of the house. When they step out of the van to unload the girls, we'll strike."

"I'll follow your lead," JP said.

JP stayed back so he couldn't be seen from the approaching vehicle. He watched the lights until the car pulled in front of the house. Then he moved forward, staying close to the wall so he could see what was going on. The car came to a full stop and the engine shut down. Both men emptied out of the front and started toward the back of the van. JP dropped his hammer and placed his gun in position. He waited for Klakken to make his move.

"Stop! Police!" Klakken yelled.

JP stepped forward, pointing his gun at the driver who reached toward his pocket. "Don't even think about it," JP said. "Hands above your head." The man raised his hands slowly. JP moved closer. "Now drop them one at a time behind your back." JP stood about six inches taller than the driver. He had managed to put the first cuff on the right hand just as a bullet sped past his head and into the car window. He saw a man running toward him with a gun in his hand. JP ducked and fired back. The driver flipped around and rammed his head into JP's stomach, slamming him against the car door. JP brought his right knee up into the driver's chin and the man tumbled backward. Another gunshot rang out. This one came from Klakken's gun. JP glanced up, but no longer saw the running man. When the driver tried to stand up, JP booted him in the chest and knocked him back down. Holding him still with his left foot, JP pointed his gun in his face.

"If you even think about getting up again, I'll knock you so far down in your shoes that you'll have to pull your socks down to look out." JP cautiously removed his foot. He flipped the guy over, pulled his hands behind him, and slapped the other handcuff in place. He patted the driver down and removed a gun and switchblade.

"Did you get him?" JP yelled to Klakken.

Klakken came around the corner with the passenger in handcuffs. "The shooter's down. Stay here with these two. I'll check on him."

JP stood behind the van out of the line of fire. From there he could watch both cuffed men on the ground. Neither moved. A few minutes later Klakken returned. "He's dead. Give me a hand."

JP looked inside of the van through the driver's side. He couldn't see in the back because it was sealed off with plywood. He removed the keys from the ignition and placed them in his pocket. Then he and Klakken walked to the back of the van. JP stood with his gun drawn as Klakken slowly opened the back door. Fifty scared eyes looked out at them. About half of the passengers were young girls, the others older women. They were so crammed in the small space that it was a wonder they could breathe. None of them spoke.

"It's okay," Klakken said. "I'm the police. You'll be safe now."

That only made them retreat farther back into the van, cramming them even closer together.

"It's okay, we're not going to hurt you."

One of them murmured, "Immigration pigs."

"I'm not immigration," Klakken said.

"And I'm not a pig," JP said.

Klakken gave JP a stern look. "You're not helping." He spoke again in a soft, comforting voice. "Look, I know you're scared, but we're not here to hurt you or send you home. We're here to help you." It took some convincing, but finally Klakken was able to persuade the scared girls to come out of the van. JP was impressed with this kinder, gentler side of his long-time enemy.

They filed out, one by one, and formed a line, just like they had been trained to do. Still few sounds came from the group. JP started to say something, but Klakken looked at him and said, "It's just as well we have a little order until we can get some help here. I'll get the sleaze balls and lock them inside the van. You take the girls inside the house. Is there room for them?"

"More than in there," he said, nodding his head toward the van.

JP went to the front of the line and led them all into the house. "It's not much, but if you can just find a place to sit, Detective Klakken will be right in." He looked around at the group to see if he could find Kim-Ly, Jade, or Mae Chu but he didn't recognize any of them. "Do any of you know a girl named Jade?"

No one answered. "Or Bich?"

Still nothing.

Klakken came in carrying the rusty axe. Eyes widened throughout the room. Several girls shuffled backward. He looked down at the axe and then set it on the table. "Have any of you ever been here before?" Most of the girls directed their eyes to the floor. "I need to know what's behind that door. We think there may be more girls in there." An older woman nodded her head.

JP pulled the van keys from his pocket and handed them to Klakken. "Try these. There's like eight keys on there."

Shane took the axe outside and then went to the door to try the keys. JP followed him, ready to assist if he needed it.

The second key he tried worked. Klakken opened the door very carefully. JP held his breath, afraid of what he might see, afraid to discover a pile of dead bodies.

The room spanned no more than eight by eight feet. There were no windows and the walls were solid, unlike the rest of the house. A small vent in the ceiling let in a little air, but it was stuffy. JP sighed. They were alive, but some were in bad shape. Three girls were chained to the walls. The others huddled together around a young girl who lay in a fetal position on the lap of another. The one who held her pulled the young girl's torn dress around her to cover her. JP couldn't see the face of the girl in the lap, but he thought he recognized the girl holding her when she looked up.

"Kim-Ly?" JP asked.

She stared at JP with an inquisitive look and then nodded.

Klakken moved the other girls out into the living room. Using the keys they had retrieved from the van, he opened each of the shackles. The girls ran out and Klakken followed, leaving JP with Kim-Ly and the girl in her lap.

"Is that Jade...er...Bich?"

"Yes," Kim-Ly said. Jade looked up when she heard her name, but she didn't say anything.

JP explained who he was and that he knew Sabre would do everything she could to help them. He wasn't getting through to either of them. "Jade, Quang has been worried about you."

Jade sat up. "He has?"

"Yes, he has. Without him, we never would have found you."

Klakken came to the door. "We need to get help and I can do it faster than you can, so you stay here and I'll go to my car and drive until I have reception on either my radio or my cell. I'll be back as soon as I can. I'll check on the guys in the van on my way out."

"Please have someone call Sabre and let her know I'm okay."

"Will do."

JP stayed in the room with Jade and Kim-Ly. After a few minutes, Jade got up and walked into the other room.

"Do you know Mae Chu?" JP asked Kim-Ly.

"No."

"She is the CASA worker appointed on your case. Did she ever contact you?"

"No."

It took a while for Kim-Ly to open up to JP. It appeared to be her concern for her daughter that finally gave her the courage to talk.

"How did you get here?" JP asked.

"David told me if I didn't go with him he would kill Jade and he would steal Emma for his project. Then he threw me in with the young kids."

"You mean these girls?"

"No, the really young ones."

"How young are they?"

"I think the youngest is four. The oldest is around eight or nine. He brings them to the U.S. and then keeps most of them locked up until they are old enough to work. Some of them he sells to families who want a child or to pervert guys. They live at a house in Linda Vista where the women do all the repairs for the dry cleaners. The little ones help with that. Some of them learn to do some handwork. It's mostly easy—boring things, though, like winding thread back on spools. Stuff like that."

"Did you live there when you were little?"

"Yes, I was seven and Bich was four when we came. We lived there together. At first no one knew we were sisters. When David found out, he used the information to make me do things."

"What kind of things?"

She hung her head in shame for a few moments, then said, "Sexual things...and to keep me from acting out or running away. He always threatened to hurt Bich if I did anything wrong."

"Where do the children go when they leave that house in Linda Vista?" JP asked.

"The remaining children who haven't been sold are brought here for a few days to test them. They're about eight or nine years old and get to pick apples during the day. If they don't run off, David has them moved to the 'carnival.' Someone called it that because they move all the time. They live in a house for a few weeks with a couple of older girls; then they move to another house. There are always different houses. It's another test to see if they'll do what he says or if they'll run. Bich was at the 'carnival' when she came to my house, but he found her and made her go back with him."

"What does he do with them after that test?" JP feared the answer.

"A very few of us get to work at Muffs. The ones who do are usually the ones David thinks are the prettiest." She blushed when she said that. "But he always threatens us with something so we won't run or say anything."

"What kind of threats?"

"For me it was easy, he always threatened to hurt Bich. I'm not sure what he held over the other girls, but they were all afraid of him."

"And the others, the ones who don't work at Muffs, what happens to them?"

"They become hookers or seamstresses."

"You seem to know a lot about David."

She dropped her head shamefully. "I was his whore," she whispered. Then a little louder, she said, "It kept Bich safe. He actually seemed to like me. I knew it wouldn't last too long and he would choose another girl, but I was hoping by then I would have figured out a way to get Bich out of it all. She wasn't pretty enough for David's taste to work at Muff's, which meant she would be prostituting. She was already past the age for working and he had a fake ID for her saying she was eighteen. The only reason he hadn't put her out there yet was because I begged him not to."

"How old is she?"

"Thirteen."

"And that makes you sixteen," JP said. His faced reddened with anger and frustration. Had David Leland been there, JP was certain his fist would have found Leland's face in a hurry.

"Yes."

"And the baby....Is that Leland's?"

"Yes." Kim-Ly stood up. "I better check on Bich."

"One more thing," JP said. He showed her a photo on his phone. "Do you know this man?"

"Yes, that's Scott. He's David's brother. I'm not supposed to know that, but I hear things."

"Is he involved in all this?"

She nodded. "Yes, he does whatever David tells him to do."

Kim-Ly walked to where her sister lay curled up in a corner of the living room. She sat beside her and wrapped her arms around her again.

JP went outside to check on the prisoners. They were still handcuffed securely to a bar in the van, which had probably been placed there to use when transporting the girls. JP closed the door back up and riffled through the compartments in the cab, hoping to find something to kill the pain in his head and foot. There was nothing, but in the console he found his cell phone, his car keys, and his gun.

Back inside, the girls started to relax a little and some of them began to talk. JP walked among them, asking a few questions. JP showed Mae Chu's photo to the girls, but no one recognized her. He wondered where she could be and if she were still alive.

Chapter 57

Sabre didn't recognize the phone number for the call on her cell. "Hello."

"This is Detective Keith Franklin. Shane Klakken asked me to call you about your friend, JP Torn."

Sabre's heart stopped for a second. She feared the worst. "Is he okay?"

"He's fine, ma'am. They don't have cell reception where they are, but everyone is just fine. Shane said to tell you it's all over."

"What happened?"

"I can't really say. The truth is I don't know much, but I'm sure your friend will call you when he's back in town."

"Thank you," Sabre said. She took a deep breath. JP was okay.

Before she could set her phone down, it rang again. This time it was Clint Buchanon.

"Is everything okay?" Sabre asked.

"Yes, I'm sorry to be calling so late, but I was driving by your office and saw your light on. I don't want you to think I'm stalking you or anything weird. I was concerned. I hope you don't mind."

"No, it's fine. I had a lot of work to do and it's been a rough day."

"I'm sitting outside. Would it be okay if I came in for a minute?" Sabre wasn't sure if she wanted to see him. When she hesitated, he added, "It's okay. I shouldn't have called. This is rude."

"No. Come to the door. I'll let you in."

When she opened the door, Clint Buchanon looked at her sheepishly. "Are you sure?"

"Absolutely. It's nice to see a friendly face."

He pecked her lightly on the lips. For a second she wished for more. He followed her into her office.

"How is it exactly that you happened to be in the area?"

He smiled, "You think I'm a stalker, don't you?"

"No, but I am a little curious."

"Okay, you caught me. I'm really lousy with directions and I forgot my GPS. Since you couldn't go out with me, I decided to take in a movie at the theater in the Gaslamp. Because I've been here before, I knew how to get to the freeway from here. I was surprised to see your lights on this late."

"I was just finishing up a few things for court the next few days," she said, as she sat down behind her desk.

"You look kind of distressed. I hope that's not because I'm here."

"No, it's been an eventful day."

He walked over behind her and put his hands on her shoulders and began to rub them. "You are tense. What happened today that has you so worried?"

"That feels good." She sighed. "My PI is working on a tough case and we lost contact for several hours. I was concerned."

"And you still haven't heard from him?"

"A Detective Franklin called and said he was okay."

"Why didn't he call himself?"

"JP...that's his name...JP didn't have cell reception."

He kneaded his fingers gently, yet firmly across her shoulders and neck, working the knots out of her muscles. His touch relaxed her.

"I wouldn't think anywhere around here would have problems with reception. We have that problem in the open spaces where I'm from, but this is city."

"He's a good hour or more from here. You lose reception about half way there."

"Would you like me to take you to him so you can see for yourself that he's alright?"

She smiled. "That's very kind, but that's not a good idea. The police are involved now so I'm guessing it's a crime scene. But the detective said everything was okay."

"Good." He stopped massaging her, stepped around, put one hand on each shoulder, and turned her to face him. "I'm going to leave so you can finish your work and get out of here, unless you want me to stay until you're ready to leave."

"No, I'll finish more quickly by myself. I'm almost done. Thanks for stopping by."

"I'll call you tomorrow." He kissed her, lips separated, tongue touching hers for only a second. Then he gave her a light kiss on her still parted lips. "Good night."

Sabre locked the door behind him as he left. She returned to her desk, spent about fifteen more minutes on the case she was working on, closed up the files, and shut down her computer. Then she stacked the files she needed for court the next day. Her phone beeped with a text. The number was local, but unknown to her. It read: *This is JP. Had to borrow phone. Franklin said he called u, but I need to see u. Come to my house right away. Important.*

Chapter 58

As she drove to JP's house, she wondered what happened to his phone. Maybe he lost it somehow. What was so important that she had to meet him at his house? It was all very curious, but she was sure he had a good reason. She started to worry again that something was wrong with him, but if he had been hurt he would be at a hospital. She tried to shake off her concerns.

She parked in the driveway and walked up the sidewalk toward his front door. It was dark along the walkway and there was no porch light on, but there was a light in the house. She thought she heard someone behind her. She turned and saw only a shadow of a man with a cowboy hat.

"JP?"

"No, it's Clint."

"Clint! What are you doing here?" she said irritably.

"Look, I'm sorry. I saw a guy hanging around your office parking lot and it worried me. I waited for you to leave so I could make sure you made it home safely. But then you didn't go home. I just wanted to make sure you were okay."

"I'm okay." She let out a sigh. "But you frightened me."

He put his arm around her. "I'm sorry. I shouldn't have followed you, but that man was pretty creepy. I remembered your telling me you had a stalker once, and I got worried. I know I had no right. Where are we anyway?"

"This is where my PI lives. He texted me and asked me to come over."

"This late at night?"

"It seemed a little strange, but there have been a lot of strange things going on in my cases lately."

"Are you sure the text was from him?"

"It wasn't his phone, but I think he used the phone of the detective who called me earlier." She looked up at Clint. "Now you're scaring me again."

"I didn't mean to do that. Just let me walk you to the door. We'll make sure everything is okay, and then I'll leave."

"Fair enough."

Sabre rang the doorbell. Clint stood back away from the door in the shadows. When no one answered the door right away, Sabre called out, "JP, it's me....Sabre."

Still nothing. She knocked again. No response.

"Do you think there's something wrong?" Clint asked.

"Maybe he's just not home yet."

"Then why would he tell you to come right away?"

Sabre hesitated, then swallowed. She tried not to look him in the eye. "I don't know," she said, trying to keep calm. She knew she hadn't said anything about coming 'right away.' How would he know that? Why was he really here? And why did he show up at her office? Suddenly she felt very uncomfortable.

"Try again," Clint said.

She rang the bell, but now she was pretty certain JP wasn't home. Then she heard a noise from inside.

"Tell him who you are," he said sternly. "I'm sorry. You're here. Let's just do this."

"I think we should go. He obviously doesn't need to see me after all." Sabre moved away from the door just as it cracked open, the chain only allowing a few inches.

"Sabre?" a woman said.

All Sabre could see was the outline of her face and bare legs. "This was a bad idea. I was just leaving," Sabre said, realizing this must be JP's ex-wife or a new girlfriend. Either way she didn't want to be there, especially not with this psycho man.

Before the woman could close the door, Clint grabbed Sabre by the arm and simultaneously slammed his foot against the door. It flew open, knocking the woman down. Clint yanked Sabre through the door and flung her on the floor. She slammed into the other woman, hitting her head against the brown leather sofa. With his foot behind him Clint kicked the door closed. The chain clanged as it hit the closing door. A chunk of wood dangled from it.

Sabre tried to jump up, but Clint kicked her down. This time she fell right on top of the woman who covered her face and cowered. Sabre started up again, but this time the woman grabbed her arm. "Don't. He'll hurt you."

"That's smart advice, Robin," Clint said.

"Who *are* you?" Sabre asked indignantly, looking up at Clint.

"I'm sorry," Clint said. "We haven't been properly introduced, have we? My name is Tyson Doyle Cooper. And this here's my wife, Robin Cooper."

"And you sent me the text so you could follow me here?"

"You're rather smart for such a pretty lady. If I weren't a happily married man, I might just be taken with you."

"Tyson, please," Robin begged. "Just let her go."

"No can do, wifey dear."

"I'll go with you. We'll go home." Robin moved her legs and started to stand up.

Sabre saw the scars on her leg. "Did he do that?" Sabre asked.

"No. No. I was in an accident." She moved slowly, watching to make sure Tyson wasn't going to knock her down again. "Come on, honey. Let's just go home."

He swung at her with the back of his hand, hitting her squarely across the face. She stumbled and fell backwards, hitting the sofa and then the floor. Blood ran down her chin.

"You coward," Sabre spat.

"Just let her go," Robin pleaded again.

"No, I need her in order to teach your boyfriend a lesson."

"He's not my boyfriend. I just needed a place to stay for a little while where I could think, but I missed you so much. I want to go home. Please, Ty, let's just go home."

"Not until I take care of some unfinished business."

Chapter 59

Six police cars were lined up in front of the house on the Leland property. More were filling up the driveway and sirens could be heard even farther down the road. The EMTs were already there and had determined that Tim, the lookout, was dead. The coroner was on her way.

Klakken was inside the house. Two female and three male detectives were taking statements from the girls. JP told Klakken about the other houses and the information Kim-Ly had shared about Scott Le.

"I need to get a warrant for the house where the girls are and pick up Leland and Le before they split. Did she give you any other names?"

"No."

"Can you follow me to the station?"

"Sure, if you'll give me a ride to my car, and a bottle of Ibuprofen wouldn't hurt."

"Let's go. They don't need us here."

JP went over to Kim-Ly and Bich, who were talking to an officer. "I have to leave, but you're in good hands. Everything is going to be okay." JP could still see the fear in their eyes. He wished he could do more for them as he turned and left.

~~~

The station hadn't changed much since JP's day on the force. He sat across the desk from Klakken and his partner Franklin. It didn't take long for JP and Klakken to put together enough information to request search warrants for the houses owned by David Leland and Scott Le and arrest warrants for both of them.

"Thanks for your help," Franklin said. "By the way, I called your friend, Ms. Brown, and let her know you were okay. I told her you would call her when you were back in range."

JP looked at the clock on Klakken's desk. It read 11:58 p.m. He had listened to the three messages Sabre had left him, but they were all much earlier in the evening. "Thanks, it's late. I'll call her first thing in the morning. Now, go get the scumbags, and please let me or Sabre know what happens."

As JP stood to leave he heard someone call his name. He turned. "Bob. What are you doing here?"

"I had to come see a client. She's a crazy lady who can't seem to stay out of trouble. I feel kind of bad for her. Even though she's nuttier than a pecan pie, she doesn't belong in jail. She needs help, but I can't seem to keep her out of jail long enough to get it for her." Bob paused. "Why are you here?"

"Working on a case for Sabre. Long story."

JP limped as they walked outside.

"What happened to you?"

"I think my toe is broken." Bob looked down at JP's foot. "Part of the same long story," JP said.

"There's a bar across the street. Let's grab a drink. I need something after dealing with the crazy lady and it'll be good for your foot. You can tell me your long story over a beer."

"A beer sounds good."

They walked into the bar and took a seat amongst the ten or so other patrons. JP told Bob that they'd broken a sex trafficking ring and he'd probably see it on the news tomorrow. A tired-looking waitress, who clocked in at around sixty, came to take their order.

"I'll have a Corona," JP said.

"Do you have any Shiner Bock?" Bob asked.

"No, sorry. Would you like...?"

"Why did you ask for Shiner Bock?" JP interrupted.

"They're good. Sabre gave me one yesterday."

"Where did she get it?"

"Excuse me, would you like something else?" the waitress asked.

Bob looked back at the waitress. "I'll have...."

"Bob, why did Sabre have Shiner Bock?" JP raised his voice just enough to be intimidating.

Bob raised his hands, fingers up and palms out toward JP. "Whoa there, cowboy. Hold your horses." He turned back to the waitress. "I'll have a Negra Modelo if you have it; if not, bring me a Corona."

The waitress left and Bob said. "She had a date. The guy came by her house to make her dinner. He's all decked out in a cowboy hat and has a Southern drawl that I guess Sabre finds attractive. He likes Shiner Bock, so she bought it for him."

JP stood up before Bob finished his sentence. He threw a twenty-dollar bill on the table for the beer. "I think Sabre's in trouble."

Chapter 60

In the way to Sabre's, JP and Bob tried to call her, but their calls went to voice mail. JP explained about Robin and Tyson Doyle Cooper. Then he tried Robin. When her voice mail came on, he said, "Tyson is in town. Get in your car and drive to the nearest police station. Then call me."

"If he hurt Sabre, that bastard'll be going to meet the devil before the sun rises," JP muttered as he drove.

When they pulled into Sabre's driveway. JP jumped out of the car almost before it came to a full stop. There were no lights on in her condo. He rang the doorbell, but no one answered.

JP pulled his gun from his holster and flipped it around so the barrel was in his hand.

"What are you doing?" Bob asked.

"I'm going to break a window and go inside," JP said. He started toward the window.

"Wait! I have a key."

"Why didn't you say so?"

"You didn't ask." Bob opened the door. "Sabre, are you here?" he called.

No answer. JP stepped inside. "Maybe you should wait out here?" JP whispered. "I don't have another gun for you."

"I'll grab the poker stick from the fireplace."

JP moved slowly across the living room and into the kitchen, then the bathroom. No one was there. Bob took the poker from the fireplace and followed JP.

"Wait down here," JP said quietly. He moved stealthily up the steps, gun in hand. When he reached Sabre's bedroom he whipped around inside, pointing his gun forward. The room was empty. He checked the rest of the house, but it was unoccupied. He flipped on the light switch, came downstairs, and went to the kitchen. There were still a few bottles of Shiner Bock beer in the refrigerator and three empty bottles in the recycle trash.

"Maybe they're out on a date?" Bob suggested.

"But where?"

"Perhaps we should wait here until they come home."

JP opened up the door to the garage but found no car.

"She has her car. What if they don't come back here?"

JP pushed the button for Sabre's cell again. He had already left three messages, so this time he just hung up. Within a few seconds, JP received a text. He didn't recognize the phone number, but he knew it was a Texas area code. The caller sent a photo of Sabre with a note that read, *Missing someone?*

"He has her," JP said.

"He has a *photo* of Sabre, but that doesn't mean he has her," Bob said. "Look, that was taken here at her house."

JP texted back. *What do you want?*

The next text was a photo of both Sabre and Robin. The message read, *Nothing from you, but I have what you want.* The photo was taken in JP's living room.

JP ran out the door with Bob behind him. By the time Bob had locked Sabre's front door, JP had pulled out of the driveway. Bob was barely able to jump into the passenger seat before JP sped down the street. Bob closed the car door and fastened his seat belt. JP broke every speed limit and ran nearly every light between Sabre's house and his.

~~~

"Who did you send the pictures to?" Sabre asked Tyson.

"Robin's boyfriend."

"Please stop calling him that. He's not my boyfriend. We're just friends."

Tyson reached down and yanked Robin up by the arm. "Do you know how this makes me look? You're sleeping with another man. What kind of a man lets his wife sleep around?"

"I haven't been sleeping with him. I swear. Please, Tyson." She sounded like a little girl pleading with her angry father. He pushed down on her arm, knocking her back to the floor.

While Tyson focused on Robin, Sabre glanced around the room looking for something with which she could defend herself. Nothing much had changed since she had stayed here—the same sofa, same forty-two-inch plasma television, the bookcase with the photo of JP's father in his marine uniform, and the two marble cowboy-boot bookends. Memories flooded back of the last time she was here. JP had been trying to protect her, but she'd been forced to defend herself against an intruder with one of those bookends. She wished she could reach one of them now. She wondered where the golf putter was that always leaned against the end of the bookcase. It would've been almost within her reach.

"Why did you send the pictures to JP?" Sabre spoke as calmly as she could. She didn't know if she was more angry or scared.

"Because he deserves to hurt the same way I have been hurting for the last few weeks. He took what was mine. Now I'll take what's his. I'll teach him to mess with my wife."

"But we're not a couple. We just work together."

"I don't know who you're trying to fool, but every time that guy called your eyes lit up. And when you thought he was in trouble, you were so concerned I couldn't keep your attention. You were dating me...." Tyson looked at Robin. "I'm sorry, honey, but it was just a ruse so I could find you. You know I love only you. I thought about banging her just to even the score with you, but she repulsed me. The stupid woman doesn't even appreciate a good bottle of wine when she sees one." His eyes were once again on Sabre. "You were dating me and thinking about him. I'm betting he feels the same way about you, even though he took on my wife for a while."

"It's not like that," Sabre said. "He probably won't even come home." She knew better. He would be here as soon as he received those photos. Everyone in the room knew it, but she tried to sell it anyway. And when JP showed up, he would be ambushed. And what did Tyson mean when he said, "Now, I'll take *his*." Was he going to kill her? She saw a glimpse of silver near the edge of the sofa. The golf club must have fallen. She wasn't going without a fight, she thought.

"He's from Texas. He'll show up." Tyson grinned at his own comment. "Stand up. Both of you."

"Why?"

"Because I said so," Tyson snapped.

Sabre stood up. Her legs felt weak and shaky as she did. She reached out her hand to help Robin, rolling her eyes to her left toward the sofa. Robin accepted her hand and let Sabre help her up. Sabre steadied herself. She thought she saw Robin respond with a subtle nod of the head, but she couldn't be certain.

"Where are we going?" Sabre asked.

"You just don't know when to keep your mouth shut, do you?" Tyson said. He swung his hand out in an attempt to backhand her. Sabre ducked and moved to her left. Robin dodged to her left toward the door. Tyson lunged at

Robin. Sabre grabbed the golf club. Tyson turned toward her, reached out, and grabbed Robin with his left hand. With his right he reached behind his back to grab his gun. His back was toward Sabre. She swung the club like a baseball bat, stepping into it with all the force she could muster. She caught him across the wrist. Sabre heard a crack. Tyson yelled out in pain, his arm falling by his side. His .357 Magnum clanked as it hit the tile. He let go of Robin and when he did, she spun around and kicked him squarely in the face. His head popped back, but the kick didn't deter him. His arm flew up in an attempt to grab her again. Sabre had the golf club cocked high above her head in front of her. She brought it straight down, hitting his shoulder.

Tyson spotted his gun. They all dived to the floor and wrestled to get possession of it. Sabre had her hand on the barrel for a moment, but it slipped away. A shot rang out as the gun went off. The noise resounded in Sabre's ears. Pain shot through her head as her face smashed against the floor. She couldn't move her head. All she could do was watch as the white tile turned red with blood.

Chapter 61

JP pulled up to his house, jumped out of the car, and ran to the front door. He heard the shot just as he reached the entrance. He kicked the door open with his gun in position to shoot Tyson Doyle Cooper.

"Don't move!" Then he called out to Bob. "Call for an ambulance. Someone's been shot."

The mound of bodies on the floor looked like a playground pile-up game gone wrong. Tyson Doyle Cooper had both of the women pinned down with his hips and legs. His upper torso lay on the floor. All JP could see of Sabre was the back of her head. Robin's legs stuck out the other side. The blood pooled around them. JP walked slowly around to where he could see all their faces.

"Sabre, are you okay?"

"I think so."

"Robin?" he asked.

"Yes."

Two policemen rushed through the front door and pointed their guns at JP. He lowered his gun, turned it over slowly, and handed it to the cop, handle first. "I just got here. I haven't touched anything." Sirens bellowed as a half-dozen other cars pulled up.

Bob stuck his head in the door. "I called an ambulance. They're on their way."

"Who are you?" one of the officers asked JP. His name tag read: *Foley*.

"I live here. My name is JP Torn. I'm a private investigator and I'm the one who called this in. The man lying there is Tyson Doyle Cooper. He beat his wife, Robin." JP pointed at her. "When she ran away and came here, he followed her. The other woman is the attorney I work with, Sabre Brown. You can call Detective Greg Nelson at the Sheriff's department to verify it."

"Call and check it out," Foley said to one of the other officers. "And stay with him until you confirm it."

Officer Silva made a call from his cell and then planted himself next to JP.

Four more officers came in the front door. One of them checked Tyson for a pulse. "He's still alive."

"Where's the gun?" JP asked.

"It's underneath him," Robin said.

Two of the officers slowly raised Tyson, watching carefully to keep his hands from reaching for the gun. He didn't try. He must have passed out because he didn't voluntarily move. They raised him up enough so Robin could pull herself out. A gloved hand from another officer reached for the gun and removed it. They lifted Tyson a little higher and Sabre scooted out. They lowered Tyson back to the floor just as the paramedics came in. Blood was hemorrhaging from his side.

Sabre saw a flurry of cops, paramedics, and firemen in the room. Several of them attended to Tyson. A paramedic and JP were crouched down next to her, and a policeman stood over JP. Blood covered the left side of her torso.

"Were you shot?" the paramedic asked.

Sabre looked down and saw the blood. Her hand slid down and she felt her side looking for damage. "No."

"Do you hurt anywhere?"

"Not really." She started to stand up. "Wait, let's make sure you're okay," the paramedic said.

Sabre stretched her arms out. "Really, I'm fine. A few bruises maybe where Clint...er...Tyson threw me down earlier." JP's face colored with anger. As Sabre started to rise, JP slipped his arm around her and helped her up. She saw the paramedics place Tyson on a stretcher. As he rolled past her, Sabre saw that he was bleeding on both sides of his body. The bullet must have gone right through him, she thought.

"Are you sure you're okay?" JP asked.

She turned her face close to his. "I'm good now. How's Robin?"

They both moved to where Robin sat on the floor. Officer Silva followed them. A paramedic was cleaning up her mouth where Tyson had hit her.

"Robin, are you hurt badly?" Sabre asked.

"No," she muttered.

The paramedic said, "I suggested she let us take her in to be examined to make sure there's no concussion, but she refused."

JP was trying to convince Robin to get checked out when Klakken entered the room.

"Geez, Torn, you're like a bad penny everywhere I go," Klakken said sternly. Sabre wondered if he ever laughed because even his attempt at a joke sounded serious. "What are you doing here?"

"I live here," JP said. Then, nodding at Silva, he asked, "Will you tell this officer that I'm not the bad guy here."

"If I believed that, I would. There's trouble everywhere you go. This is the second man shot in your wake tonight."

Robin and Sabre both sighed.

~~~

Sirens blared throughout the city as officers were dispersed to several other San Diego neighborhoods: Linda Vista, Normal Heights, Clairemont, Kearny Mesa, and Mira Mesa. Each and every property, including Leland's dry cleaners, was searched and arrests were made. Scott Le's properties were also searched, and he left in bracelets.

Across town in La Jolla, David Leland was escorted out of his home in handcuffs to join his brother. He was placed under arrest for kidnapping, sexual assault, and murder, which were only a few of the charges he would be facing when the facts were all discovered.

Women and children were taken in droves to the police department for questioning. Among them was Mae Chu.

Chapter 62

Sitting at the table in Department Four attempting to settle their case were Marla Miller, the social worker; Tom Ahlers, the attorney for the Department of Social Services; Richard Wagner, Kim-Ly's attorney, who sat tapping his pencil on his calendar; and Sabre, the attorney for Emma.

Sabre reached across the table to take the report from Marla Miller. A twitch from a nerve caught her in her side. She was sore from the tussling she had taken two nights ago from Tyson Doyle Cooper.

"They arrested David Leland, Scott Le, and several others," Ahlers said. "They're facing so many charges they'll never see the light of day again."

"They found seventy-four women and children; the youngest was two years old," Marla said. "They had a mill in place. They would mostly bring children from Vietnam between four and ten years old because they could get good money for them. Then they'd keep them locked up and train them for either prostitution or the sewing/dry cleaning business. If one of them became pregnant, and had a baby girl, they'd keep the baby in the system. Or, if it was a boy, they'd sell him. So Emma would've been imprisoned if she wasn't Leland's love child. And nobody would've been the wiser if her apartment hadn't caught on fire."

"I don't understand. Leland never acknowledged his daughter. He didn't help Kim-Ly financially or anything," Sabre said. "So, why did he let Kim-Ly keep Emma?"

"Kim-Ly said Leland didn't really want the child, but he would let her keep her as long as it didn't cause any trouble. Maybe he really cared for Kim-Ly. I don't know. Who knows what these fools think?" Richard Wagner, Kim-Ly's attorney, said. "Now, can we settle this case? My client is as much a victim as all the other girls involved with Leland, maybe even more so."

"One more thing," Sabre said. "They've charged Leland with Judge Mitchell's murder. Does anyone know why he killed him?"

Wagner responded, "He was afraid if Mitchell connected him to this dependency case, the judge would figure out that Leland was center stage in a sex-trafficking ring and rat him out to the Feds. Leland didn't relish spending the next thirty years in Adelanto Correctional Facility trying to dodge every 'Bubba' who wanted to play 'drop the soap' with him."

"That's a big jump. How could he make a connection from fatherhood to sex-trafficker?" Sabre asked. Wagner always stopped short of completely answering a question.

"Because the two of them had met before. Years ago Mae Chu's father had a case with Judge Mitchell. It was a simple battery, but it involved a neighbor near his property in Julian where he housed the illegal immigrants. It gets a little foggy here, but I think Mr. Chu paid Mitchell off and Leland knew that. Maybe Leland was even involved. I don't know. I'm just telling you what my client has heard. All she knew for sure is that Mr. Chu's case went away mysteriously."

"So, if the judge was paid off once, why wouldn't Leland just pay him off again?"

Wagner sighed like he didn't have the energy or the inclination to explain it. Then he continued. "Kim-Ly thinks that

Leland planned to pay him off, but maybe Mitchell wouldn't take the bribe. I don't know."

"So, you're suggesting that Leland confronted the judge and he wouldn't take the pay-off, so he had to get rid of him."

"That's right," Wagner said.

Sabre shook her head. "And that's what Judge Mitchell was trying to tell me in chambers," she muttered.

"Probably. Who knows how much he would have told you, or why he chose you."

"So why did Leland go after Dr. Heller?"

"Leland also knew that if anyone ever found out that he was the father of Kim-Ly's baby he would be investigated, especially if they learned her real age. Unbeknownst to me, she had already told Dr. Heller that Leland was the father. The day the judge was killed, this case was on calendar. Just before we started, Kim-Ly asked me if Dr. Heller would tell the judge everything that she had told the doctor. She thought it would remain confidential, just between the two of them. I told her that since her psychological evaluation was court-ordered the doctor would put everything she told her into her report. She got pretty upset. I didn't realize it at the time, but when Kim-Ly saw Dr. Heller talking to the judge before we started the hearing, she thought Dr. Heller was telling the judge who the father was."

"But Dr. Heller wouldn't ex parte the judge like that," Sabre said.

"We know that, but my client didn't know any better. Dr. Heller wasn't even at court about this case; she'd just finished another case and was speaking with the judge about who-knows-what. But when the judge asked Kim-Ly who the father was, she thought he knew, and she panicked."

"What did she do?"

"After the hearing she went straight to Leland and told him that Dr. Heller and the judge both knew that he was the father. That day, Mitchell was killed. The next day, Dr. Heller's office was ransacked by Leland or a couple of his flunkies, but they didn't get the tapes of her conversation with Kim-Ly. We know now that they were in the doctor's briefcase which she had kept with her. When she returned to her office, she was hit and her briefcase stolen."

"So Leland killed Mitchell because he knew about the sex-trafficking and he tried to kill Dr. Heller so she wouldn't tell he was the father of Kim-Ly's baby?" Sabre questioned.

"That's what it looks like," Wagner said flippantly, as if he didn't have time for any more discussion. "Now, can we get started? I don't want to be here all day."

"What's the matter, Wags?" Sabre asked. "Is the surf up?"

He ignored her. "My client is a minor. She's only sixteen."

"We're aware of that," Ahlers said. "We've filed a new petition on Kim-Ly. If you're willing to make her a dependent, we can go forward with this petition today."

"I've spoken with Mrs. Nguyen, the foster mother for Emma. She's willing to take Kim-Ly in and provide a home for both her and her daughter. Kim-Ly would have to go back to school. Mrs. Nguyen is also willing to provide a home for her sister, Jade. Most of these kids will be temporarily housed until INS and all the other government organizations that are involved can sort it out."

"I'll talk to my client." Wagner rose and walked out of the courtroom.

He returned shortly. "Let's do it," he said.

~~~

The Durham Case

Sabre felt beaten up, both physically and emotionally, as she waited for Mike McCormick to bring Matt Durham into the interview room. She hadn't decided exactly what she was going to do at the 707 hearing this morning, but she was glad the case was finally on calendar.

Judge Porter was hearing the case. Sabre didn't really know much about her. The judge had spent many years in felony court downtown and was transferred in to take over Scary Larry's delinquency cases. Someone else would cover his dependency cases until Porter was trained. This judge was no stranger to murder charges and the consensus among the defense bar was that she would likely find Matt unfit to be tried as a juvenile.

Matt was wearing his "innocent child face" when he walked in with McCormick, who acknowledged Sabre, locked Matt's cuff with his right hand to the bench, and walked out. Matt looked around nonchalantly.

"How's it going today?" Sabre asked.

"Okay." Matt tapped his free hand on the counter in front of him as if he were keeping time to music in his head.

"Are you nervous?"

"Not really. Should I be?"

"No. As you know, this is the 707 hearing. The judge will decide which court you'll be tried in," Sabre explained. "There are a couple of other things I want you to know that we discovered in our investigation."

"What's that?" he asked, without looking directly at Sabre.

"First of all, your friend Ralph says he wasn't with you the night Hannah and Mason were murdered. JP checked it out and in fact, he was at a bar and you weren't with him."

"That son of a...."

"Matt, it's only a matter of time before the prosecutor finds that out, too. And then it will look worse for you if they catch you in a lie."

"No one else knows about that alibi. I'll come up with a different one."

Sabre shook her head. "The truth will work better."

Matt looked her in the eyes for the first time since he was brought in. "Will it?" he said sarcastically.

Sabre's stomach felt queasy. This young man committed this horrible crime and had no remorse. "That's not all, Matt. There's a witness who places you in Coach Arviso's office with the 'missing equipment' form the day *after* the murder."

"Who?"

"It doesn't matter who." Sabre didn't ask him if he was there. She didn't really want to know. "The point is the DA is likely to find that out as well."

"I'll just lie when I testify."

"I can't let you do that."

"What do you mean? You've got to let me testify."

"I can't knowingly let you lie on the stand."

"Maybe I'll be telling the truth. You don't know for sure when I'm lying. I've lied to you so many times, how do you know when I'm lying and when I'm telling the truth?"

Sabre felt exasperated. How could she convince this kid that this wasn't a game? This was his life he was playing with. "You're right, I don't know for certain, but it would be a lot easier to build a defense for your case if I knew the truth."

"You don't want to know the truth. Not really. I saw how you looked at me when I saw the photo of Hannah. You don't want me to tell you how it felt to smash someone's head in with a baseball bat." He looked at her as if waiting for a sign of repulsion.

Sabre forced herself to not react.

"That's assuming I killed them, of course, which I deny."

Sabre checked the time. She felt claustrophobic, like Matt was sucking all the air out of the room. "It's almost time for the hearing. I'll see you inside."

~~~

The fitness hearing went forward with all the usual arguments. The ADA Jane Palmer argued that the crime was heinous and that Matt Durham would not benefit from the rehabilitative services of this court because he couldn't be rehabilitated before the jurisdiction of the juvenile court expired. She concentrated on the gravity of the offense and the sophistication of the crime.

Sabre's arguments concentrated on Matt's age and the fact that this was his first offense. She argued that he was an average or better than average student and an athlete and that the juvenile court system had never made an attempt to rehabilitate him. Basically, her argument was that he was quite remarkable in every way and as a result he was neither sophisticated nor treacherous.

Sabre sat down after she presented her case and took a deep breath. She wasn't sure she had the energy to continue on this case, but she still had not made up her mind whether or not she would follow it downtown. If it stayed in juvenile court she wouldn't abandon him. But not following the case downtown also felt like abandonment. How was it any different, really? He was still her client and he needed her services, no matter what he had done. She felt drained, and her body still hurt. In a few days, she would be at full speed again. Then she could handle anything. She had made up her mind.

Both sides rested.

Judge Porter didn't need to take it under submission. She was ready to rule. "I find the defendant, Matt Durham, unfit to stand trial in juvenile court. The case will be heard in the Superior Court, Felony Division, 220 West Broadway, San Diego, California." Sabre wasn't surprised at the ruling, but her time had run out. The judge continued, "Ms. Brown, are you going to request to remain on the case?"

Sabre stood up. "Your Honor...."

"Can I say something?" Matt blurted.

"Please talk to your attorney first," the judge advised.

"But that's it. I want a different attorney."

Sabre was surprised, yet relieved. He was sophisticated, in spite of her shallow argument to convince the court otherwise. He had played her, maybe even practiced on her. The next attorney will not know that he is lying, because she knew Matt wouldn't tell him. His investigation may not uncover all that hers had, either. But it didn't matter. It wasn't her decision or her problem any longer. "No, your Honor. I will not be requesting to remain on the case."

Chapter 63

Failure didn't sit well with JP. He had failed to protect both Robin and Sabre. Robin had to suffer yet another attack after he had promised she would be safe. He should've known better. He was a private investigator; he should have investigated better and been prepared for Cooper to show up. It was quiet at his house without her. Louie missed her, too. He bounced through the house and then ran up to JP and whimpered.

JP reached down and patted him on the head. "I miss her, too, Louie. But she's home now...and finally safe. And that mean husband of hers is facing charges in California and Texas."

But worse than that, JP had brought Tyson Doyle Cooper into Sabre's life and almost got her killed. He knew she didn't blame him, but he blamed himself. He had to make it up to her somehow, but he was too embarrassed and ashamed. She was beautiful and brilliant and educated. He was just a bumbling country boy who wanted to protect her and he couldn't even do that right. He wanted to go to her, hold her in his arms, and keep her safe.

All he could really do is make sure he resolved everything he could on her cases. She had been under so much pressure between the Durham case and the Tran case. At least Durham was over. He was glad of that. He despised that kid and didn't want him on the streets. But there was something that didn't add up with the Tran case. JP opened his file and read through it again. Then he shot up from his chair.

"That's it, Louie," he said. "I'll be back shortly. I'm going for a ride."

~~~

A little over an hour later, JP showed up at Sabre's office. "Does something feel wrong about the Tran case?" he asked.

"Well, hello to you, too."

"Sorry, this is just driving me crazy." JP remained standing in front of her desk.

"Me, too. I've been reading through everything. I have lots of unanswered questions." Sabre tapped the file on the desk.

"I keep wondering what I'm not seeing. I feel about as dumb as a cow lookin' at a new gate. I just keep lookin' but the gate don't open."

"What I don't understand is why they took Mae Chu."

"And why she was at the fire?"

"Let's talk about what we do know," Sabre said. "Mae Chu came to the U.S. with her father, Trai Chu, when she was five years old. He bought that property in Julian and he started a dry cleaning business."

"That eventually became a dry cleaning empire." JP paced back and forth as they talked.

"Right, but what if he also started bringing in illegal workers from Vietnam? Maybe that's why he bought the property in Julian. It was out where no one would see them."

"But why would he bring them here illegally? That was after the immigration laws changed and legal entry was allowed for extended family members."

"True," Sabre said, "but I did a little research and it often took years to get them here legally. For some, it was probably easier to come here and then get legal status later. In fact, when legal immigration rose, so did illegal entry."

"And Chu provided them with jobs that he created through his dry cleaning business."

"Why don't you have a seat?" Sabre said. "Your pacing is driving me crazy."

"Sorry," JP said and took a seat.

"What I can't figure out is how David Leland got in the picture."

"That bothered me, too, so I went to see Lan Vong, Mae Chu's friend. She told me that Leland was Trai's protégé. He was like a son to him, but he had ideas of grandeur that Mr. Chu didn't share. Mr. Chu never wanted his daughter in the business...."

"Because he didn't want her involved in any illegal activity," Sabre finished his sentence.

"That's what I think. And when he died, Mae was left with a nice trust fund, but Leland inherited the dry cleaners."

"Do you think Mr. Chu brought young girls here for prostitution?"

"I'm guessing that didn't start until Leland took over. However, I'm still confused as to why Leland killed the judge. I'm not sure Wagner had it all figured out. And why would Mitchell take a bribe back then and not now."

Sabre reached for a yellow pad on her desk. "I wondered about that too. I was looking at the dates just before you came in." She flipped through a couple of pages and then stopped. She glanced over the page. "When Mr. Chu was arrested, Mitchell was on the bench because he had been appointed to fill a vacancy. However, his election was only months away. I'm guessing the judge needed funding, and Mr. Chu bought his way out of the mess he was in."

"Which would explain why Mr. Chu's case went away and Judge Mitchell was elected," JP added. "So did Mitchell suddenly grow a conscience? I'm sure he still needed money. They always do."

"But not like he did back when Mr. Chu bribed him. He needed money for his campaign then. He was a shoe-in now. Maybe it wasn't worth the risk. Besides, any money he made the last years went to his ex-wives. Maybe he didn't want to give them any more."

JP wrinkled his brow. "But that still doesn't explain why Leland killed Mitchell, tried to kill the doctor, and let Kim-Ly live. Even if he cared for her, he doesn't strike me as the kind to make a choice based on his heart or to leave loose ends. He's smart. He's mean. And he's calculating. He wormed his way into Mr. Chu's life and inherited his entire empire. Then he used all those women and young girls for profit. The guy's a total scumbag."

"That's true," Sabre acknowledged. "He obviously has no regard for other humans, so there's no way he would have let Kim-Ly live. He would have killed her too."

JP stood up and took a couple steps away from the desk. He turned back to Sabre. "Think about this. We know that Leland ransacked Dr. Heller's office and he had her run over in order to get the briefcase with the tapes. There's a witness to that. There are no witnesses to Judge Mitchell's murder. And none of Leland's cars tie him to the killing."

Sabre swooped her hand in the air in an "ah-ha" gesture. "So what if...?"

"Well, butter my butt and call me a biscuit."

Sabre nodded and the look of cognizance matched that of JP's. Sabre smiled. "Let's go see Mae Chu."

"I'll go. You wait here."

Sabre stood up and grabbed her keys. "Am I riding with you or driving behind you?"

JP shook his head. "Dad burn it. You could make a preacher cuss."

"So, I'm riding with you, then?"

~~~

On the ride over to see Mae Chu, JP and Sabre conferred back and forth, dissecting their theory. By the time, they arrived they were convinced they had it figured out. Only Mae Chu could confirm it, but they didn't expect that to be an easy task.

JP pulled up in back of the condo behind the attached garage. He parked his car in front of the garage door, thereby blocking it so Mae Chu couldn't leave. Sabre went around the building to the front door and rang the bell. No one answered the door. She rang again. Still nothing. After several attempts, she walked around back and joined JP. He stood leaning against his car as he waited.

"I think I heard her inside, but she wouldn't come to the door," Sabre said.

"She'll probably leave through the garage. I hope you have time to wait."

"You bet."

It was only about fifteen minutes before the garage door opened and Mae Chu appeared carrying a suitcase.

"Going somewhere?" JP asked.

Mae Chu looked startled at first, but then she walked around her car toward JP and Sabre. "You're the man who's responsible for catching David Leland and his sex-trafficking ring."

"Actually, I'm not the one who forced him out into the open, but then you know that, don't you?"

"I don't know what you're talking about."

"Let me tell you a story. It's about a little girl who was born in Vietnam and came to this country when she was about five years old with her hard-working parents. Her father bought a large piece of property with some apple orchards on it, way out in the country. Then he proceeded to bring more of his family here from Vietnam. But even though the immigration laws had been liberalized, it often took years to bring in extended family, so he found a way to smuggle them into the country. He started a dry-cleaning business and provided them with jobs. Other people needed help, too, so he started more dry cleaning businesses to help more people."

Mae Chu just listened, her face expressionless.

"One day the man got into a physical altercation with a neighbor and the man was arrested. The judge dismissed the case, and suddenly he had enough money for his election campaign."

Again, no response from Mae Chu.

"The young girl's father continued to bring poor people to this country and give them jobs. He opened more dry cleaning businesses. He provided his daughter with the best schools and a nice home. He invested his money and set up a nice trust fund for her so she would never have to work in his business. He didn't want her involved in anything risky or illegal. Meanwhile, a young man had come into his life, the son he never had. Let's call this guy David."

Mae Chu opened the car's trunk and placed the suitcase inside it. Then she turned back toward JP and Sabre without saying a word.

JP continued with his story. "David became the man's protégé. He wanted to take the business in a different direction. The smuggling ring was in place and hadn't been detected in several decades. David believed he could make a lot more money if they brought in young girls for, shall we say, illegal and immoral purposes. The possibilities were endless. But the old man didn't like that idea. He was doing something good for his people. He wasn't interested in the money he could earn by hurting people. This guy David didn't fight him on it. Instead he made sure there was a will or a trust in place leaving the dry cleaning businesses to him. And when that was arranged, and David was in line to inherit it all, the old man sort of accidentally met his maker behind the wheel of his own vehicle."

A look of pain flashed across Mae Chu's face.

"Only it wasn't an accident. David killed him so he could take over everything. The old man's daughter never believed it was an accident, but no one took her seriously. Although she'd never been part of her father's business, she had heard and seen things over the years. She was like a little mouse in a hole and no one knew she was around. So, she watched some more, and she waited. At some point she discovered the sex-trafficking ring and decided to infiltrate it. But David knew her, so she had to come in another way.

"She was very patient and listened to everything very carefully. When she discovered David had a baby by one of his girls, she developed a plan. She maybe even paid the girlfriend to help her. Then she trained to become a CASA worker. Once she had everything in place, she went to David's girlfriend's house and started a fire, knowing full well it would trigger a court case. She wasn't completely heartless, so she stayed around to make sure the baby was rescued. Then she left. She knew she would be appointed on the case because there were so few CASA workers who spoke Vietnamese or who understood the culture.

"What she didn't plan on was finding the same judge that sold out to her father assigned to this case. She knew he could be bribed. Now her biggest fear was that David would go free. She couldn't have that, so she decided to kill the judge and frame David for it. She didn't just kill David because she wanted him to suffer for a long, long time. She could think of no better place for that than prison. It was a perfect plan of revenge."

"Very interesting story; I think I heard it before," Mae Chu said. "But you left out the part about the little girl's mother not trusting the protégé and that she was murdered and her body dumped near the Mexican border." Her voice was calm, but bitter. She took a deep breath and smiled. "It sounds like that girl evened the score. Good for her." She walked to the side of her car and opened up her door. "Now, if you'll excuse me. I have a plane to catch. I've joined the Peace Corps and they're sending me to Vietnam."

Chapter 64

Bob opened Sabre's refrigerator and took out a bottle of Shiner Bock.

"Really?" Sabre said.

"Hey, this is good stuff. No reason to waste it. You know me, I'm a vodka man. There's not that many beers I even like, so when I find one I like, I'm going to drink it. What can I say? Tyson Doyle Cooper, slime bag extraordinaire, has good taste in beer."

"That's about his only redeeming quality."

"By the way, where is he?" Bob opened the bottle of beer and took a swig.

"He's still in the hospital. The bullet put quite a hole in him. Got him right in the abdomen, just below the rib cage. I guess the trauma from the pressure of the gunshot did some damage as well."

"Is he going to live?"

"Looks that way. But then he'll be standing trial for assault and battery, attempted murder, and several other criminal counts here in California. After that he still has charges in Texas to face. He won't be out on the streets for a while."

"It won't be long enough. Too bad the bullet didn't take him out."

"Bob," Sabre scolded.

"Hey, he tried to hurt my snookums. And he beat Robin. That's just not right. That girl's hot."

"And that's the reason it's not right," Sabre said sarcastically.

"No, it's not right on any level. Cooper is a coward, but you have to admit, the woman is hot."

"You're so bad. I don't know how Marilee puts up with you, except we both know you're all talk. But you are correct, Robin is very attractive."

"Are you jealous?"

Sabre wrinkled her brow and tipped her head. "Why would I be jealous?"

"Oh, come on. JP just spent the last couple of weeks with his gorgeous ex-wife and now she's pregnant."

A wave of confusion mixed with anger swept through Sabre's entire body. She felt weak. "She's what?"

"It's not JP's baby, you ninny. I had you worried for a second, though, didn't I?"

"No."

"I did too. You were upset because you like him," Bob said in a mocking tone. "It can't be his because he never slept with her."

"How do you know that?"

"Because I asked him." Sabre took a deep breath. "Look, Sabre, you and JP are both dancing the two-step, or whatever dance it is that cowboys do, but you're both dancing alone. You need to go talk to him. Ask him to dance."

"You're weird."

"I know, but you two are starting to annoy me. You're both lovesick and neither of you will make the first move. You have your stupid trust issues and he thinks he's not good enough for you."

"What are you talking about? He's a way better person than I am."

"Yeah, but he's a cowboy, and you're a top-notch attorney and he has his pride." Bob took another swallow of his beer. Sabre said nothing. "Go talk to him, Sobs. He's at Cahoots."

"The country western bar?"

"Yes, in Mission Valley."

"Is that the reason for your corny dance analogy?"

"Just go. Talk to him." Bob finished his beer, walked into the kitchen, and tossed the bottle in Sabre's recycle basket. He walked toward the front door, opened it, and said, "I'm leaving. Go, or you'll never know. And when you get there, ask him to dance."

~~~

Once inside Cahoots, Sabre waited for her eyes to adjust to the light. It was almost eight o'clock and some of the dance lesson crowd was leaving; the rest of the people were starting to mingle. Nearly all the tables were full, but plenty of standing room remained. In another hour or so, the place would be packed. Alan Jackson's Remember When blared out over the speakers. She walked toward the dance floor and looked around at the tables that surrounded it. She didn't see JP. She wondered if he was on the second level. She looked up, but didn't see him there. If he was on the balcony he wasn't standing or sitting near the edge. He could have been at a table in the back of the room. She decided to make one trip around downstairs and then up, and if she didn't find him, she would leave. She had started to think this wasn't the best idea Bob ever had.

She walked toward the back of the bar behind the dance floor. JP was generally easy to spot in a crowd because his hat always stood out. But this was a room full of cowboy hats. She was nearly three-quarters of the way around when she saw him sitting at a tall table. She took another step forward and realized he wasn't alone. A voluptuous, fluffy-haired blonde with a bright pink flower pinning one side of her hair back from her face sat on a stool next to him. Sabre quickly turned around, hoping she hadn't been spotted.

"Sabre," JP called.

She thought about running, but decided against it. She had already been seen. She took a deep breath and turned back. JP stood up and started toward her. He walked her back to the table.

"Sabre, this is...I'm sorry, I didn't catch your name."

The woman stood up, looked Sabre over from head to toe, turned back to JP and said, "Honey, if this is what you like, I guess I'm not your type. Come find me when you want a real woman."

JP blushed and Sabre laughed as the woman walked off. "I don't mean to interrupt anything here," Sabre said half-jokingly.

"Thanks. She just wouldn't give up." They sat down and JP hailed a waitress as she walked by. "Would you like a margarita? Midori, or something, is what you drink, right?"

Sabre was surprised. He paid more attention to her than she had thought. "No, I think I'll have a decaf coffee with Bailey's and a little milk. Non-fat if you have it. Oh, and whipped cream, please."

JP smiled.

"What?" Sabre said.

"I'm always fascinated by the way you order food or drinks."

Sabre shifted in her seat. "Bob said you were here. I hope you don't mind."

"Hmm...he told me you were going to be here. That's why I came." Sabre shook her head. JP's brow furrowed. "Sometimes our friend, Bob, can be slicker than a greased hog. Anyway, I'm glad you're here," he said.

"Me, too." Sabre didn't know what to say next. For a few seconds, they sat in uncomfortable silence. Then Sabre spoke. "Bob said Robin is pregnant. How's she handling it?"

"She's struggling with it. She always wanted a child but not by that dirt-bag. She won't abort because she doesn't believe in it. I questioned her about adoption, but I don't think she'll do that either. Cooper would fight it anyway. Once he finds out she's having his baby she's afraid he'll become even more controlling, if that's possible. And he has plenty of money to hassle her no matter where he is. If it weren't for her mother, I think she would just disappear. Who knows? Maybe she'll do that anyway."

"I feel for her. She seems like a very special lady. She doesn't deserve any of this."

"She's a good woman," JP said.

The waitress brought Sabre's drink. JP paid for it, along with a generous tip. Sabre didn't even try to fight him on it.

JP said, "I spoke with Klakken earlier today. He said you told him about our theory about Mae Chu."

"I had to report it. Letting it go just didn't feel right. Even though Scary Larry was a little bizarre, he didn't deserve to be murdered."

"You're right. Though I'm more sympathetic to what Mae Chu did than you are, I'd be more so if she had just killed David Leland. After all, he killed both of her parents, raped who-knows-how-many young girls, and pimped dozens or maybe even hundreds of others out to prostitution. Not to mention the little ones he sold to perverts. But her plan all along was to make Leland suffer. I don't think she expected she'd have to kill anybody to get that."

"Do you think she'll ever have to pay for her crime?"

"Klakken said they have nothing substantial to connect her, but he won't stop looking. If it's there, he'll find it."

"So, you think he'll find something?"

"The truth?"

"Yes. Always."

"I bet that she's covered her tracks pretty well. Her car's not damaged. There's no forensic evidence to tie her to the murder. My guess is she'll skate."

They continued to chat for a few minutes about work. Sabre thought how good it felt to be in JP's company. It was comfortable just sitting there with him. But it was time to make a move. Like Bob had said, she had to quit dancing alone. If she was rejected, she would deal with it. Her stomach felt queasy, and she could feel her hands tremble slightly. Her anxiety was getting the best of her. Faith Hill's voice suddenly resonated through the bar telling her to *"Breathe."*

JP took her hand. "Would you like to dance?"

She looked at him curiously. "Did Bob happen to give you his 'quit dancing alone' speech?"

JP laughed. "He sure did."

Sabre could feel her heart flutter. She squeezed his hand and stood up. "In that case, I'd love to dance with you."

From the Author

Dear Reader,

Thank you for reading my book. I hope you enjoyed reading it as much as I did writing it. Would you like a FREE copy of a novella about JP when he was young? If so, scan the QR code below and it will take you where you want to go. Or, if you prefer, please go to www.teresaburrell.com and sign up for my mailing list. You'll automatically receive a code to retrieve the story.

SCAN ME

Teresa

Manufactured by Amazon.ca
Bolton, ON

40452605R00206